So Long, Marianne

Dom Haslam

ISBN: 0992833000
ISBN 13: 9780992833008

For Amelie, Lola and Edward

1

Early Monday mornings were generally quiet in the office, a time of contemplation, characterised by people silently reading their emails, sipping their coffees, and trying to reconcile themselves to the fact there were five whole days until the next weekend. With the horrors of the early morning alarm call and the week's first commute still fresh in their memories, they were determined to delay the onset of work a little longer. Occasionally there might be an outburst of excitement, such as when a girl announced she'd got engaged, but more often than not Monday mornings were a time of inner thoughtfulness and melancholy.

But early Monday mornings were better than late Sunday nights. *Sunday Night Blues*, Adrian called them: those long hours up to and past midnight when the mind remains resolutely resistant to sleep and wanders off of its own accord to dark places of foreboding, doubt and sorrow. Places where work worries, love worries and life worries congregate and have to be faced down. I didn't want to wish my life away, but the Sunday Night Blues made me look forward to retirement, when Monday morning would finally be reclaimed and restful sleep restored to the night before.

That Monday I had an interview to take: someone to cover for our secretary going on maternity leave. I tried to move the cursor on the screen of my laptop to print the CV, but it wouldn't work. I clicked the mouse repeatedly, shifting it this way and that, but nothing. 'This bloody thing…' I said, banging it against the desk.

A snigger: I looked up at Roy, my boss, catching sight of a familiar merry light in his bright blue eyes, the eyes of a naughty schoolboy rather than a man in his early sixties. Through his bushy grey-white beard there were also the beginnings of a smirk.

I turned to my colleague Adrian, who covered his mouth with his hand, his frame juddering as he tried to suppress his laughter.

'You gits,' I said, lifting my mouse and turning it over; on its underside someone had stuck a small post-it note on the laser, on which they'd written the words, *why won't my mouse work?* As I tore it off Carolyn appeared, causing Roy's and Adrian's laughter to choke to a sudden silence.

An austere lady in her fifties with severely brushed forward silver hair, Carolyn was the company boss John's hatchet man, a Minister Without Portfolio who emerged from her lair whenever anything unpleasant or annoying needed administering to. ISO 9001 accreditation? Carolyn will be sending an email about it. Quality Assurance Review? Please refer to Carolyn's memo. Clear Desk Policy? Speak to Carolyn. 'John would like to see you in his office,' she said to Roy, standing tall and straight-backed in a tweed suit.

Roy glanced up at her, his face blanking as he hesitated. 'Can you give me five minutes, please?' he asked.

Carolyn delayed her response, her lips pursed. 'Alright, but be as quick as you can.' She strode off.

I checked my watch; I was late for the interview. I printed the CV and read it while lifting my collar to put on a tie: a twenty-six-year-old New Zealander, with a Masters degree, looking for six months' work before returning home.

In reception, a lady was sitting with her head buried in one of our company brochures. As she rose to greet me our eyes met: hers brown, but a distinct shade lighter than the usual, a flawless, generous, rare brown, with a hint of amber. She looked at me quizzically, waiting for me to say something.

'Oh, hi, I'm Adam.'

'Hello, I'm Nadine.'

I led her through to the interview room. 'Sorry I'm late,' I said, motioning to her to have a seat.

'No problem,' she replied, sitting down.

'Have you come far today?' I asked, pouring her a cup of water.

'From Brixton. It was quite easy, just up the Victoria line and changed at Green Park.'

'I'm in Clapham, so we're not too far from each other!' I said a touch too enthusiastically. I sat down and composed myself. There was something exotic and unusual about her looks which I couldn't quite place: perhaps some Maori ancestry. 'I hope you're not sharing a bedroom with a dozen other Antipodeans?'

Nadine laughed, then looked coy. 'Actually, it is a bit like that. But I'm not here for long, so I just have to rough it a little. Besides, I'm really enjoying Brixton.'

I liked her soft Kiwi accent, the way she changed the sound of vowels, so that Brixton became *Bruxton*. 'Are you looking forward to returning to New Zealand?'

She shrugged her shoulders. 'New Zealand is beautiful, but it's so much more... isolated than the UK. It's going to be difficult to adjust after all the adventures I've had here.'

'Is there no way you can stay longer?'

She chuckled. 'Only if I find a nice English gentleman to marry in the next few weeks.' She smiled, and held the smile.

The heat of a blush flowed to my cheeks but I couldn't resist it, so I sat there grinning and blushing all at once, before shuffling my papers and hurriedly commencing the interview, which didn't take long, as she was clearly overqualified for the role.

Afterwards, I led Nadine back to reception, thanked her for her time and handed her my business card. There was a moment of mutual hesitation; for a second I had a compulsion to kiss her on the cheek, but caught myself, and extended my hand for a formal handshake instead.

We said goodbye and I watched her leave, walking away from the office with a distinctive easy-going stride.

* * *

'Hi, Adrian,' I said, returning to my desk.

'Hi. How was the interview?'

'Yeah, good, she's very bright. I think we'll make her an offer.' I sat down and started checking my emails. 'Which battle were you recreating this weekend?'

'The Battle of Hastings.'

'Pleased to see you didn't get an arrow in the eye.'

'I didn't, but one poor chap dropped a medieval skull mace on his foot.'

'Ouch.'

'Indeed.'

Jason, one of our I.T. guys, appeared, dressed in a black polo shirt tucked into dark jeans, and started unplugging Roy's laptop.

'Is it broken?' inquired Adrian.

Jason mumbled something while continuing his task.

'What was that?' asked Adrian.

Jason lifted his head. 'Sorry, I'm just doing my job.' He picked up Roy's laptop and walked off with it.

Adrian and I glanced at one another; perhaps we had an inkling even then, though neither of us said anything.

A short while later Roy came into view, shuffling slowly back to his desk, only he didn't sit down. Rather, he reached for his briefcase, placed it on his desk, opened its lid and stared into it. He stood very still, before eventually lifting his National Trust calendar off the wall and putting it in the briefcase. He picked up the heavy glass paperweight presented to him after twenty years' service to the company, shook his head and returned it to the desk. His gaze moved about gradually for a while without coming to rest on anything. He pulled open his desk drawer, took out a white plastic tablet bottle and placed it in his briefcase. Finally, he reached up and took down the photograph of his wife Joan that he kept in a silver frame on the shelf above his desk.

Adrian and I glanced at each other again, our earlier inkling crystallising. Blood pumped to my head and limbs, leaving my stomach knotted and cramped.

Roy stood still, head sunk down, staring into his briefcase. I think Adrian and I expected him to say something, but he remained wordless. The more I watched him, the more I realised he was no longer Roy but the ghost of Roy, a shadow of the man he'd been earlier that morning. Suddenly he seemed all his sixty-three years and then some, his bushy beard and brown jumper, once comforting and avuncular, now threadbare and scruffy. 'Are you okay, Roy?' I asked.

He didn't respond. I stood up, as did Adrian, and we walked round to Roy's desk. He didn't turn or make eye contact.

'What's going on?' asked Adrian, reaching out to put his arm around Roy, who backed away, closed the lid of his briefcase and pushed the brass latches at each end in with a click as he'd done thousands of times before. Only this time it was different. This was the last time he would do it.

'I have to go.' His voice was quiet and faltering as he lifted his briefcase off the desk. 'Sorry, boys, my time is up.' He still refused to make eye contact.

'*What?*' I asked. 'What have they done?' Roy pulled on his suit jacket and coat, and moved towards the stairs. I stepped in front of him. 'Roy?'

Roy lifted his head. His once mischievous and penetrating blue eyes were now vague and myopic, seeing only generalities rather than details, and when he blinked, a single tear dribbled unevenly down his cheek into his beard. 'Adam, let an old man leave with his dignity intact.'

I stepped aside.

Roy nodded. 'John assures me the changes won't affect the two of you.' He lowered his voice to a whisper. 'When Carolyn asked me to see John this morning I knew what was coming, so I changed my commission allocation on the system to the two of you.' He breathed out deeply through his nose. 'Now, as someone much braver than I once said, "I'm just going outside and may be some time." I'll be in touch.' He stepped carefully down the stairs and for the first time I noticed how he gripped the banister to ease the effect of the descent on his knees and how the top of his back bowed. Without turning around, he left work for the last time.

Adrian and I stood staring at each other in deafening silence. Eventually, with a quiet word, Adrian suggested we go for a coffee in five minutes' time and I nodded.

Returning to my desk, I sat down and stared at the screen of my laptop without seeing anything. I sensed the conversations in the office but heard nothing. I was conscious only of my own breathing. An era had ended, and the executioner's axe so swift, I knew not what to think or even how to think.

Roy had been my boss since I'd started in recruitment ten years earlier. Adrian had joined us six years ago. Together we found jobs for accountants and finance professionals, mainly permanent jobs, but also some temporary. Our team may have been small compared to the agency's strengths in secretarial and construction recruitment, but we made decent profits. Or so I'd thought.

Carolyn reappeared – the Grim Reaper – standing between Adrian's and my desks. She'd no doubt been in the meeting with Roy when the guillotine fell. She'd probably pulled the release handle.

'John would like to see the two of you at two p.m. to discuss a reorganisation of the Financial Services team,' she said.

My heart went into overdrive. 'What happened to Roy?'

Carolyn turned to face me square on and looked me up and down with slitted sardonic eyes, gauging me for any hint of insubordination. 'He's off the platform.'

I shivered.

'As I said,' she continued, 'John will see the two of you at two p.m. to discuss the changes. Rest assured, you're both part of his future plans.' She looked down at us as if we were something unsavoury she'd just trodden in and left.

2

Wired. That's how I felt most evenings after work. But on the day of Roy's sacking I felt ultra-wired. There should be a dictionary definition for it:

Wired adj: *A feeling of being tense and tired, characterised by weak and shaky limbs, and by an incessant electrical hum coursing throughout your mind and body, particularly concentrated in the area just behind your eyes.*

Once out of Clapham North tube station, I set off at a brisk pace for home, anxious to begin relaxing. My girlfriend and I had purchased a modest two-bedroom conversion flat in a three-storey Edwardian terraced house four years earlier for a quarter of a million pounds. It was like playing monopoly as we increased our offers in increments of £5,000 to secure the purchase, but Louise and I agreed we would be mad not to buy when London property prices kept increasing by fifteen per cent a year.

Inside the communal entrance hall, I stepped over the littering of letters and junk mail scattered on the floor; it was someone else's turn to sieve the bills from the pizza flyers and place them in the wall-mounted mail boxes. Squeezing past the two bicycles that were continually stacked outside the ground-floor flat and forever moulting dried mud all over the place, I climbed the steep stairs, turned the key in the lock, and entered. As the latch clicked closed behind me stillness and silence descended: I was alone.

I sighed deeply. After placing my keys and mobile on the sideboard by the front door, I draped my coat and suit jacket over the arm of the sofa and walked towards the kitchen, stopping as I caught sight of myself in the hallway mirror. I reached for my head; my hairline was definitely receding a little above each temple. Perhaps I was lucky I'd lasted to the age of thirty-four.

Entering the kitchen, I reached for a bottle of Cabernet Sauvignon, the pleasing plop sound of the cork's release signalling the start of the evening's relaxation; I poured myself a healthy measure into a large burgundy glass. Returning to the living room, I turned on the TV: the news headlines were playing, showing hundreds of haggard, stressed people queuing outside branches of the Northern Rock bank, trying to withdraw their money, fearing the bank would collapse due to lack of credit. I couldn't be dealing with news like that after the day I'd had, so switched it off.

I pressed play on the CD player and slouched into the arm-chair without bothering to turn the lights on. Leonard Cohen's rich baritone seeped into the room; I'd been listening to him last night after Louise had gone to bed. I sat back, took a swig of wine and let the liquid double back over my tongue so I got the full flavour. Poor Roy. I tried to picture him breaking the news to his wife Joan. And what would he do tomorrow? He wouldn't find another job in recruitment now.

A muffled sound of jangling keys emanated from behind the front door which then swung open and hit the far wall with a thud: Louise was home. 'Why's it so dark in here? What are you doing?' she asked, turning on the main overhead light.

'Just relaxing,' I said, shielding my eyes from the harsh glare.

'What, in the pitch black?' Louise threw down her keys with a clunk onto the sideboard, started unbuttoning her coat and walked over to the stereo. 'You don't mind if I turn this down, do you?' she asked, turning the volume down to an inaudible level before I'd had a chance to reply. 'I can't tell you how strangely Stephen is acting. It's really winding people up. It's really winding *me* up.' She worked for a PR agency and Stephen was her boss. I'd never met him, but judging from Louise's frequent comments, he seemed a bit of a know-it-all and work zealot.

Louise stood over me, so I shifted my position to block out the overhead light with her silhouette. 'You remember how I told you a couple of weeks ago I had my appraisal and Stephen said I should concentrate more on building client relationships?'

I vaguely remembered. 'Yeah, I remember, more clients.'

'So that's what I've been doing, organising more face time. Anyway, I got back from a client today and Stephen said he'd like a word. Do you know what he said? He said I've been ignoring the bread and butter stuff.'

'The bread and butter stuff?'

'Exactly! My point exactly! What does he mean by the bread and butter stuff? I thought I was doing the right thing by going out more, pressing the flesh and becoming the trusted advisor. It's not easy meeting clients and always having to look your best.' As she spoke, Louise picked up my coat from the sofa, walked through to the kitchen and hung it up behind the door. I heard her ripping open letters, which she must have brought up from the entrance hall downstairs. She kept up the conversation from the kitchen, now projecting her voice. 'I really think it undermines the whole appraisal system when Stephen says one thing and then a week later he's changing the emphasis, telling me to do something else. Don't you think?'

It was bad enough listening passively while she unpacked her work problems in front of me, but did I really now have to offer an opinion and thereby become involved?

'Well, what do you think?' she shouted from the kitchen.

I struggled to remember what the question was. Something about her boss questioning her work? 'Why don't you just ask him to clarify?'

'What's that?' barked Louise. I could hear her loading the dishwasher with the cups and bowls from this morning's breakfast.

'Why don't you just ask him?' I shouted back, determined not to have to leave my chair, particularly as we rarely discussed my work, which Louise routinely dismissed as *men in suits stuff*. I didn't necessarily disagree with her, but still.

Louise strode back into the living room. 'It's not as easy as just asking him. Stephen is extremely busy. As he says, he's money rich but time poor. I'd rather try and work out what he meant and address it myself before meeting him.'

'You make it sound like he's the Prime Minister or something. He isn't so busy he can't spare you five minutes.'

'How could you possibly know how busy he is? We don't sit around all day on the telephone like you. We're more... *creative*.'

I let out an involuntary chuckle. 'How creative do you have to be to sell soft drinks and computer games to impressionable kids?'

Louise glared at me. 'So you think that's all we do, do you? Do you really think that's all my job involves?'

'If my job is just answering the phone, then yours is just brainwashing kids.'

Silence.

We stared at each other as if we were strangers, rather than a couple of seven years. It was my first chance to look properly at Louise since she'd come in. She remained a good-looking woman in that tidy way of hers: pretty, slim, straight chestnut hair cut into a bob. But underneath some vital ingredient was now missing, and I'd begun to doubt whether it could ever be retrieved.

'All I wanted you to do was to listen for a while and be sympathetic,' said Louise. 'Was that too much to ask?' She tutted and walked back through to the kitchen.

The wired tension crept back into my body. I tried to fight it off by taking a large gulp of wine, which emptied the glass, so I walked through to the kitchen to refill it. As I poured, I sensed Louise watching me surreptitiously out of the corner of her eye, like an experienced teacher monitoring an inattentive student. 'Oh, I should let you know,' I said, 'I'm going out with Bill on Saturday.'

'*Wha – T?*' said Louise, the word coming out in two syllables, one on the *Wha* and one on the *T*, as though I'd just announced that Bill and I were gay lovers and had decided to move in together on Saturday and adopt children.

'I just said I'm going out for a few beers with Bill on Saturday.' Judging from Louise's initial reaction, she'd clearly committed us to another engagement, though I couldn't remember what. Generally the ones I forgot were the ones I didn't want to go to. 'He's only in London for a day and I haven't seen him in over a year.'

Louise slowly shook her head. 'I told you last week, it's Jess's birthday party on Saturday.' She tutted again.

'Don't tut.'

'You drive me to it, really you do.'

I tipped back a large measure of wine. Louise gave me another disapproving look.

'What?' I asked.

'You need to moderate your drinking.'

'You drive me to it, really you do.'

Louise closed her eyes and sighed. 'There was a time when we did everything together. If we don't go to something as important as Jess's party as a couple, then what's the point?'

'Oh, come on; and besides, whenever it's my friends we're meant to be going out with, you say you don't like them.'

'It's not me not liking them; it's them not liking me.'

'What? What evidence have you got for saying my friends don't like you?'

'They're just not... my kind of people,' said Louise.

'So people have to be exactly the same as you for you to be friends with them?'

'I didn't say that. It's just that your friends have such a weird sense of humour. It's alienating.'

I knew some of my friends had reservations about Louise. Of course, it was never expressed explicitly; there was just a coolness about the way they inquired about her. If your friends are ambivalent about your partner, doesn't that tell you something?

'So, are you going to cancel Bill and come to Jess's party?' asked Louise.

I recognised that Louise's question wasn't really about our respective Saturday nights, but more a question of commitment, so I paused before responding. I felt exhausted. Exhausted by work, exhausted by Louise and I always arguing, exhausted by always feeling exhausted. 'No, Lou, I'm not. I'm sure we're capable of socialising separately occasionally. Plus Bill is one of my best friends and I hardly know Jess. You'll just have to go without me.'

She looked at me with what was now an expression of resignation rather than anger. 'Fine,' she said and walked off to the bedroom.

3

The days at work following Roy's departure were quiet, sad and empty, like being in the office between Christmas and New Year while everyone else is at home with their families. They say someone who loses a limb continues to feel its sensations after amputation. So Adrian and I would call out to Roy to ask him a question and then realise he wasn't there, or we'd think about asking him to meet a client and then have to think again.

The bleak atmosphere was briefly broken by an email:

Dear Adam,

I am writing to say thank you for taking the time to interview me on Monday and for the job offer. Unfortunately, I've taken a short term contract elsewhere. I may as well come clean – the job I accepted is paying £3 an hour more than yours and as you know, I'm a hard up traveller, so I need every last penny! I do hope you understand.

I did also just want to say how much I enjoyed meeting you and I know I would have enjoyed working for you.

Take care,
Nadine

Did I need to respond? Plus what did that last sentence mean? As I mulled it over I found myself remembering Nadine's charm, her accent and of course the soft radiance of those ochre eyes...

I decided to reply:

Dear Nadine,

Thank you for your email. I'm sorry you won't be joining us, but I fully understand your decision and can only apologise that we can't offer more money.

I agree it would have been good to work together and it's a shame to think that our paths may not cross again, but I hope they do some day.
Kind regards,
Adam

Within an hour she'd replied:

Adam,
My path is leading me into central London this Friday for a couple of hours before I go to a party. You can cross it if you want to.
Nadine

I sat staring at her email for some time, the voices in my head competing for ascendancy:

'It's wrong to go for a drink with another woman,' said sensible voice.

'It's only a drink,' said daring voice.

'You need to talk to Louise to sort out your problems.'

'Sex twice in four months tells you all you need to know.'

'You're not going to meet Nadine.'

'Go on, you *know* you want to…'

…and so I emailed Nadine. It was only a drink. She sent me her mobile number 'just in case'. Each push of my thumb as I entered her number into my mobile was another incremental increase on the guilt scale, but also another notch of excitement.

* * *

Standing outside Charing Cross station, a dense mass of people moved purposefully in all directions. Many were commuters striding for the train or down Villiers Street to the tube, anxious to get home; once I'd rushed back to Louise as quickly. Others were groups of office workers decamping to the bars and restaurants of Covent Garden, their animated expressions and chatter revealing their relief that the week's work was done.

'Hi, Adam!' called Nadine from a few feet away. She looked different, more glamorous and taller than I remembered from the interview, her eyes and lips more emphasised. Her hair hung loose and she wore a short black skirt under a cropped red jacket like a bullfighter's jacket, and black tights and high heels.

I kissed her on the cheek and stepped back. 'You look great. It must be some party you're going to.'

'Who said I dressed up for the party?' said Nadine, grinning. I tried to think of a quick-witted comeback... but failed. Nadine saved me, asking, 'So where are you taking me?'

I had a place in mind, a little underground bar called the Bedford & Strand Bistro just off the Strand. As we descended the steps, I experienced my first pangs of fear that I might bump into someone I knew. The odds were against it in a city the size of London. Besides, I was just going for a drink with a member of the opposite sex; it wasn't a crime, was it?

The bar's stripped wooden floors, chalk white walls and pale marble-topped tables gave the place a calming feel, but this was compromised by a melee of suited blokes at the bar, ties loosened, drinking from tall glasses of lager while shouting at each other and trying to impress the lady serving them. I led Nadine through to a table for two at the rear.

'What would you like to drink?' I asked, thumbing the drinks list. 'It's mainly wine.'

'Something fizzy?'

'I'm game if you are.'

While waiting to get served at the bar, I made a mental note to be careful. I was going to the cinema later with Louise to watch *There Will Be Blood* and didn't want to turn up half cut and start snoring during the film. I'd told Louise I was going for a quick drink with a work colleague; was that a fib or a lie?

'Here's to Anglo-Kiwi relations,' I said, having returned to Nadine and poured two glasses of Prosecco.

She raised her glass. 'How long have you lived in London?'

I counted back the years since university. 'Twelve years,' I said, struggling to comprehend how time had passed so quickly.

'Tell me what you like about London, I love hearing Londoners talk about their city.'

Immediate thoughts weren't positive: stratospheric property prices which meant I'd been cramped all these years, the horror of the daily commute, the traffic jams. I needed to do better than that. 'There's so much to discover in London: the history, the parks, the museums...'

'The only trouble is that it's so expensive,' said Nadine.

'But places like the parks and museums are free.'

'The museums are free?'

'They are; certainly the British and the Natural History are. Thankfully.'

Nadine tilted her head to examine me, or perhaps it was my words she was examining. 'It's strange, isn't it,' she said. 'The City is just about the most hard-edged business district in the world, and yet yours is also the country of the NHS. I can't quite work you lot out. It's as though *you* can't work yourselves out.' She took another sip of Prosccco. 'And of course you invented every sport imaginable and are useless at all of them,' she said, breaking into laughter.

'Steady on!' I refilled Nadine's glass as well as my own, reassured that she'd knocked back the first at the same pace as me. 'So tell me about your future plans?' I asked.

'I have to leave in the spring,' said Nadine, running her finger along the rim of her glass. 'My visa runs out.'

I asked her about the memories she would take with her and she recounted stories about camping in Cornwall, the running of the bulls in Pamplona and Queen's Day in Amsterdam last April. She had the enthusiasm and positivity of the Antipodean or American, which made life seem less complicated, and I was grateful for it. I couldn't help but reflect how Louise and I had fallen into a routine where work dominated our lives, the pay-off being a single meaningful holiday a year: such meagre reward for all our toil.

A while later a waitress arrived, I recognised her as the lady who'd served me earlier. 'Would you like another bottle?' she asked. I looked at Nadine.

'I'm game if you are,' she said.

The waitress picked up the old bottle and gave the two of us a warm smile, as though we restored her faith in romance, having been hit upon all night by the suits at the bar.

The second bottle arrived, and as the alcohol dissolved into my bloodstream and flowed north to be seeped into the spongy fibres of my brain, so Nadine's beauty became more pronounced, more vivid.

'I wonder what it would have been like working for you?' She stared at me with an enigmatic expression. 'Better than my previous experiences, I bet. You probably saw from my CV that I had a couple of jobs in the City. They weren't the greatest experiences, to be honest. I worked for a lot of arrogant dickheads who seemed to think that just because I worked for them I'd be attracted to them.'

'Count yourself lucky the jobs were temporary,' I said. 'Imagine working for those guys permanently, with no end in sight.'

'It doesn't bear thinking about. And you know money was always the bait. They kept asking me if I wanted to go with them to some flash restaurant or other, or else they'd drop into conversation how they'd recently bought a new car or whatever. I suppose they thought a hard-up traveller would be impressed by it all. Do you know what else? The more senior the guy was, and the more money he earned, the greater his sense of... of *entitlement*, as though I couldn't possibly turn him down, as though it was *illogical* for me to turn him down.'

'Money's a strange thing,' I said. 'Those who have lots of it generally fall in love with it, and soon it becomes impossible for them to understand why other people don't share their love. My own view is that there's always going to be someone richer than you are, so if money's your main motivation, you'll always end up disappointed.'

Nadine scrutinised me with bright and searching eyes. 'I knew when I met you you'd be good to work for. One day I'm going to be a boss and when I am, I'm going to behave very differently to how I've been treated here. I'm going to be a demanding boss, but a fair one.'

She told me about her food science degree and spoke passionately of her hopes for a career in the food industry back home in New Zealand, before asking me how my job was going.

'It's going okay,' I said, before the image returned of Roy slowly packing his briefcase in shell-shock. I paused. 'Actually, work is a bit difficult at the moment. My boss was sacked the other day and everything feels very uncertain.'

'Did you like your boss?' asked Nadine.

'Very much, very much...' My voice trailed off. Adrian and I were meeting Roy next week, anxious to hear precisely what had happened; and we wanted to know more about how he'd changed his commission allocation to come to us. But for now, I needed to change the subject to re-inject some energy into the conversation. 'So, if you'd been my boss, would you still have asked me out?'

'Did I ask *you* out?' Nadine asked, smiling.

'You said you were coming into London and I could cross your path if I wanted to.'

'Yes, but it was you who said "it's a shame to think our paths won't cross again", which encouraged me.'

'Did I?' I went back over the email exchange in my mind. How easily I'd convinced myself that it was Nadine who'd done the asking rather than me.

'Yes, you did,' said Nadine. 'So, if I was your boss, I would be tempted to report you to HR for sending inappropriately suggestive emails to interviewees.' She raised her eyebrows.

I laughed, but it came out an octave too high, like a nervous teenager at the school disco after being asked to dance by a girl for the first time. I wasn't practised at flirting; it had been a long time. I brought my glass to my mouth to buy me time to think.

'Now, tell me, how come an attractive chap like you is single?' asked Nadine, keeping up the pressure.

The cogs of my brain whirred at tremendous speed; this was my chance to come clean about Louise. But imagine the embarrassment of it: *Sorry, didn't I mention it before? I'm not actually single, I live with my girlfriend of seven years. Anyway, fancy another drink?* 'I could ask the same thing of you,' I said instead. 'With all these trips and adventures you've had, you must have met lots of guys. You're not going to tell me that your travels haven't unearthed someone special?'

'I think you just answered my question with another question,' said Nadine. 'In answer to *your* question, my travels have allowed me to meet plenty of special people, but not *the* special person.'

What had started out as just a drink, something I could justify in my mind, was rapidly becoming something more, with a commensurate sense of wrongdoing. I certainly hadn't planned to *cross the line*, but then again, if I truly hadn't thought something might happen, would I really have accepted the offer to meet?

Nadine leant forward and touched my forearm. 'As I said, I've only got a few months left before I have to leave the UK, so perhaps you could show me some of your favourite London haunts?' She fixed me with her pale brown eyes.

I nodded and then, having to look away, caught sight of a clock on the wall: 8.30 p.m. An image jumped into my mind of Louise standing alone on a busy street corner in Leicester Square, waiting for me, checking her watch. 'Drink up,' I said, pouring the last dregs from the bottle. 'I've got to go.'

'Aaaah, you spoilsport, we were just getting going,' said Nadine, the drink thickening her accent such that it sounded like *jist gitting go-in.*

'I know, but we've both got places we need to be. If we go for a third bottle, we'll barely be able to climb the stairs out of here.'

'Where have you got to go?' she asked.

'I'm meeting friends at nine o'clock for dinner.' Now I was lying to Nadine, as I'd done earlier to Louise, but I couldn't see a way out of it.

Nadine watched me closely, gauging whether I might be persuaded to change my mind. Or waiting for an invitation to join me and my friends for dinner?

'Ready to go?' I asked.

Nadine leant back in her chair and crossed her arms. 'You're very sensible, Adam. If I was your boss I would order you to stay.'

I knew I'd be playing over in my mind later and for the next few days what would have happened if I'd stayed, but the bottle was empty, so I stood up and pulled my coat on. Nadine did the same, struggling her arms into her coat a touch unsteadily, and as we walked towards the stairs she slipped her arm around mine.

We continued co-joined down the Strand to Charing Cross station, where Nadine was catching a train to her party in Kilburn. At the entrance to the tube I uncoiled my arm from hers and said, 'Nadine, it's been a lovely–'

She kissed me.

Without warning her hands rose up and cradled my head, she pulled me forward, stood on her tiptoes and our lips met flush. We kissed frantically, like hormonal teenagers. I won't say I didn't enjoy it, because I did, but my enjoyment was tempered by the fear of being witnessed by someone I knew.

Eventually I pulled clear of the embrace, our mouths coming apart with a wet sucking sound like that of a large, flat stone being lifted from a moist bed of clay on the edge of a riverbed.

'I must go, I'll be in touch.'

'Promise?'

'Promise.' I walked away towards Leicester Square, and as soon as I rounded the corner, I frantically wiped Nadine's red lipstick from my lips.

4

'For fuck's sake, Adam, I can't take it anymore!'

I awoke with a start: disorientated, confused, scared, the feelings amplified by a finger being jabbed into my ribs. 'What? What is it?!' I cried.

'You're snoring again,' said Louise. 'You always snore when you sleep on your back. Roll onto your front or your side.'

'Sorry,' I said, turning over, my heart racing from the sudden awakening. 'Jesus, Lou, the way you were shouting and poking me, I thought there was an intruder in the flat or something.'

Louise tutted. 'I just want a lie in on Sunday morning like everyone else. I'm tired and your snoring is disgusting.'

'Disgusting? How can breathing be disgusting?'

Louise made a ggrrrr noise in frustration. 'I don't want an argument, I just want more sleep. I'm sooo tired.' She turned away, pulled up the duvet to her chin and sighed.

I closed my eyes, trying to piece together last night... Louise had been at Jess's party while I'd been out with Bill in Covent Garden... what was that meat market nightclub we'd ended up in? The Roadhouse, that was it. God, what a dreadful place. A place like that made you grateful you were in a relationship, rather than having to join the seething mass of hormonal drunks marauding around city centres on Saturday nights desperate to find someone to copulate with. When I'd got home at two a.m., Louise had still been out at Jess's party, and to think I'd been tiptoeing about the flat, anxious not to wake her, until I'd slipped into bed only to discover she wasn't there.

I opened my eyes. Gentle half-beams of dappled light filtered in from around the pulled curtains, giving our bedroom a greyish hue.

Louise now faced me, her head cradled by her pillow, her expression peaceful, the softness of her breathing surprising me. But then her eyelids quivered, she lifted her head and began fluffing her pillow, eventually giving up, tutting and sitting up in bed. 'I can't get back to sleep now,' she said.

'I said I was sorry, and besides, sometimes you keep me awake too.'

'I do not,' said Louise, emphasising each word. 'When have I ever kept you awake?'

'When you whistle.'

'When I what?'

'When you whistle. It happens occasionally when you're in a deep sleep. If your head is at a certain angle, when you breathe in your nose makes a whistling noise. It's very distracting. Disturbing even.'

A look of concern fell across Louise's face. 'I've never heard such rubbish.'

'I'm afraid it's true, your nose makes noises in the night without you even knowing it. It's like in those old Western movies when the tumbleweed blows through the deserted town – that's the noise your nose makes.'

Louise frowned. 'You're just saying this to wind me up... aren't you?'

'Don't worry, I promise not to tell anyone.' I kept a straight face for about three seconds, before breaking into a smile.

'You bastard, I knew you were joking!' She pushed me and I grabbed her and we cuddled. I allowed my hand to travel down the curve of her side until it neared the flare of her hips, letting it rest there, waiting for a reaction or sign of encouragement. Why didn't I just carry on? It had become such a big deal. As I inched my hand lower, Louise moved and the initiation needed morphed in mid-movement into a hug, my hand eventually resting neutrally across her lower back.

'I'm tired,' she said.

'Okay.'

Silence.

In the early part of our relationship there'd been silences, but they'd been comfortable silences, both of us confident in our love for one another such that any lack of words only proved we didn't constantly need to reaffirm our feelings. Over the last few months that had changed. We'd been on some walks together at weekends recently and there'd been long stretches of silence, agonising silence, with barely a word uttered between us, and when something was said, it was so brief it just re-emphasised the sense of isolation. That same excruciating silence prevailed now.

'I'm just going to make myself a cup of tea,' I said, throwing back the duvet on my side of the bed. 'I'll bring you a cup later, when you've had more rest.'

'Thanks,' said Louise, her eyes now closed again.

I pulled on my dressing gown and wandered down the corridor to the kitchen. As I flicked the switch on the kettle I began to reflect: at what point had Louise and I stopped being lovers and become friends instead? Once upon a time Sunday morning meant peeling ourselves off sweat-soaked sheets, flushed cheeks and bathing in a glorious post-coital afterglow. Is it a relationship cooling which undermines the sex; or is it when the sex falters that the relationship wanes?

As I reached for the kettle a wink of blue light caught my eye: my mobile, charging on the counter. I picked it up: '2 unread messages'. Two? Why hadn't I seen them last night? Then I remembered: the battery had gone flat while I'd been out. I clicked on the first message:

> *Saturday 9.22 p.m.: 'Hi Adam, I had a great time last night. Do you want to meet up again? Nadine x'*

Shit, what would have happened had Louise seen that message?! Not that Louise was the type – I didn't think – to check my messages, but still. I clicked on the second message:

> *Saturday 11.38 p.m.: ' andi enjoyed our kiss at charin crors. Your boss Nx'*

The guilt gripped; what was I doing reading text messages from another woman with my girlfriend asleep in the next room? I deleted the texts.

A creak in the corridor: Louise's footsteps. Stuffing my mobile into the pocket of my dressing gown, I started pouring hot water into my mug as she entered the kitchen. 'I'll make you a tea,' I said a little too quickly, pulling another mug from the cupboard.

'Thanks.'

'What time did you get in last night?' I asked.

Louise paced around the kitchen looking for something. 'I really don't know, it must have been about two o'clock. Have you seen my handbag?'

'I haven't seen it. Two o'clock? Are you sure? I wasn't back until after two.'

'Seriously, Adam, I don't know what time it was. Why does it matter?' She walked out.

What was bugging her? I peered around the door into the living room and saw she'd found her handbag. She reached in, her hand fluttering against the insides of the bag liked a trapped bird, getting madder. She grasped something, visibly calmed, and pulled out her mobile. I retreated unseen to the kitchen. She walked in, picked up her tea and walked out again to the bedroom.

I sat down at the small pine kitchen table by the radiator, which gave out a comforting warmth. I sipped my tea and looked out of the window. It wasn't much of a view, just the backs of the houses opposite and a few scruffy gardens below. The gnarled boughs of the laburnum tree in the back garden swayed in a stiff wind and a bare twig at the end of a branch tapped lightly on the window. In the distance the predominant colour was grey, the dark charcoal grey of the slate roofs and the dense sombre battleship grey of the rainclouds, which pushed down on the city with a great weight and strength. I savoured the contrast of the blustery, bitter cold outside and the soothing heat and stillness inside.

I decided to text Nadine:

> *Sunday 8.17 a.m.: 'Hi Nadine. Yes, same time and place next Friday. I enjoyed our kiss too. A x'*

Louise called out from the bedroom, 'Adam, why have you just sent me a text message?'

The fuse was lit and burning down towards the dynamite.

Had you listened carefully enough in the ten seconds of pristine silence immediately after Louise's question, I'm convinced you could have heard the whirring cogs of both our brains rapidly working out the implications of the fact that I'd sent the text message meant for Nadine to Louise. I must have been on autopilot when I sent it and my reflex after seven years of doing so was to click on Louise's name and press send.

A scurrying of footsteps nearing the kitchen, Louise at the doorway, face contorted. 'YOU FUCKER! Who the *FUCK* is Nadine?!'

She grabbed the digital clock off the sideboard and hurled it at me – I ducked – it smashed into the wall behind me, shattering into pieces that fell to the ground with a sound like perverse metallic applause.

I looked back at Louise standing in the doorway, her torso rising and falling in time to her heavy breathing. She walked unnervingly slowly towards me until just a few inches away and stopped. She spoke softly but with a chilling intensity, her eyes ablaze and so wide I could see clear white surrounding the irises. 'Get out of this flat right now, you bastard. Get out and stay out.'

A single inhalation of breath gathered itself gradually in my chest, on and on it went, ongoing and drawn out and of such depth I thought I might float, and standing up slowly – maintaining eye contact throughout – I walked past her, all this happening in the time it took me to draw that one breath.

I walked to the bedroom and put on some jeans and a bottle-green sweater from the cupboard. I pulled out my tattered old sports bag from under the bed and packed only the essentials: a pair of suit trousers, two work shirts and two pairs each of socks and boxer shorts. I put on my suit jacket over my jumper and my black brogues that I could also wear for work tomorrow. I fetched my toothbrush, deodorant, shaving gel and razor from the bathroom and tucked my mobile, wallet and keys into my jacket pocket. I stared into my bag: it wasn't even half full and it amazed me just how few possessions I needed to survive.

Back in the living room, Louise sat head down on the sofa, tapping a message into her mobile with her thumb. As I approached, she placed her mobile to one side and raised her head to reveal a gaunt face and bloodshot eyes.

'All I can say is sorry,' I said. 'I don't expect you to believe this given what's just happened, but I've never been unfaithful to you other than–'

'Just go, Adam, please, just go.'

I walked to the front door, stepped through it and pulled it shut until the latch clicked closed behind me.

Stepping into the street, an icy wind slapped me hard in the face. I set off in the direction of Clapham Common because it was the only place I could think of to go, leaning forward as I walked and turning my head to avoid the wind stinging my cheeks.

Before long, I chanced upon a newsagent and walked in without consciously deciding to. Despite not having smoked for five years, I purchased a pouch of Golden Virginia, a small packet of green Rizla papers, filters and a box of matches. Troubled people smoke, it's a fact.

Reaching the bleak and exposed Common, I found a bench located under a tree that gave a little protection from the wind and rain. As it was early morning there were very few people about, just enough to make the place seem more deserted than it was. Looking out over the Common, I turned over my memories of being here with Louise like pictures in an album: Sunday strolls hand in hand discussing the future; summer days spreading out a rug for a picnic; afternoons with friends playing frisbee and football.

Holding a Rizla paper to my chest and using the breast of my coat as a shield from the wind, I rolled a cigarette. My cold fingers couldn't co-ordinate properly and I rolled it clumsily and lumpy, and when lit it burned crookedly up one side. The first drag made me light-headed and I cursed myself for being tempted by Nadine and wished Louise had sent that blasted text message to me rather than me to her, so she would be the executioner and have to deal with the guilt of hurting another, and hating herself.

The tobacco made me woozy, but still I drew it deep into my lungs. I thought about the things in life that keep you anchored to the floor, steady and able to maintain a sense of control: your relationship, your home, your family, your friends, your job. Cut some or all of those tethers and you could find yourself floating off into a different future, with no certainties. Who knew, it could be a relief to be cut adrift like that.

The dampness from the bench had seeped into the seat of my trousers. I remembered a photograph my mother had on the notice board in the kitchen at home: me, a six-year-old boy in a new school uniform, blond with a cowlick in my fringe and lots of freckles. What dreams had that boy had, what hopes for the future? I was so full of innocence and potential back then, I couldn't help think I'd let that boy down, as well as Louise. I began to choke up.

I made a decision. One of the really big decisions when life changes direction. I was going to split up with Louise and become a single man. Perhaps she would beat me to it and finish with me first. It didn't matter. It was time to start again.

5

I called Roy to agree where to meet. 'But not near work if you don't mind,' he said. 'Too many memories.' So we chose The George, located where the Strand meets Fleet Street, opposite the Royal Courts of Justice and St Clement Danes church.

Adrian and I entered the narrow, timber-framed building with mock Tudor facade, its windows made up of small leaded panes, many with stained glass heraldic shield inlays. Roy was seated inside holding a thick glass jug of bitter. He wore a navy-blue jumper with lighter blue patches on the shoulders and elbows; this, coupled with his Father Christmas beard, gave him something of the image of the old sea cove.

'How are you, Roy?' I asked, once Adrian and I were seated with our pints, also bitter, also in jugs.

Roy took a sip of his beer, which left a little bit of foam in the hair on his upper lip. 'I'm okay,' he said, licking his lips.

There was a short silence.

'How's Joan?' asked Adrian.

'She's well, thank you. A bit shocked, as you can imagine, suddenly having me getting under her feet around the house.'

Another short silence, no one wanting to be the first to raise the subject we all knew had to be addressed.

'You probably want to know what happened last week,' said Roy.

Adrian and I nodded, and breathed out slowly, quietly.

'It's best you know,' said Roy. He took another sip of his beer before recommencing. 'When it was Carolyn who asked me to see John last week, I knew I was a goner. So, before the meeting, I changed my commission allocation on temps to the two of you.'

'Can you do that?' asked Adrian, stroking his goatee beard.

'Not officially,' replied Roy, 'but my predecessor did it for me and John was fine with it. I think all the teams do it. It will mean a decent pay rise for the two of you, and you deserve it. You helped me with many of those placements.'

'Are you sure John will be fine with it this time?' asked Adrian.

Roy shrugged and thought it through a while. 'If you feel uncomfortable with it, perhaps you should speak to him.'

'We're really grateful, Roy,' I said. I paused, struggling to find my next words. 'And speaking of John… couldn't he have let you leave in a more… honourable way?'

Roy shook his head. 'It never works out that way in this industry. John's recruited a new chap to head up the team, from one of the big agencies. Apparently he stated that a condition of him joining was that he wants to lead the whole team – both a new temporary desk and our permanent desk.'

'The bastard,' said Adrian.

'Hang on,' said Roy, raising a hand. 'I've played it over in my mind and maybe John was just using it as an excuse to push me out. In any case, it hardly matters now.'

I took down a full, deep mouthful of beer, after which a tinny metallic taste filmed my mouth. It did matter.

'You think you know a man, but in business I'm not sure you ever do,' said Roy. 'I've known John for over twenty-five years and I thought I knew him, but of course I didn't.' He shook his head, eyes downcast. 'It was like talking to a stranger in that final meeting.'

'Do you mind me asking whether he paid you off properly?' asked Adrian. 'You don't need to answer that of course, it's your private business. But I think Adam and I would take some comfort if we knew John paid you what you deserve.'

Roy's eyes darted up to the ceiling, then towards the door, then back to us. He sucked on his lower lip. 'He paid me, but not a lot. I was in a Catch Twenty-Two. Naturally I wanted a decent payoff, but when I started to fight for it I realised I didn't have the appetite for a grubby squabble. I didn't want twenty-five years to end sourly. I'm probably naive – in fact I know I am – but I wanted to walk away without having stooped to John's level, so I accepted a lot less than maybe I should have. Perhaps I kept some dignity though.'

The front door of the pub was open, showing the toing and froing of commuters beginning their journeys home. Beyond them stood the imposing, gothic stone arched entrance to the Royal Courts of Justice. Some protesters had pinned signs to the black iron railings outside, but from this distance I couldn't make out what they were protesting about. 'That doesn't seem right to me,' I said to Roy.

'There's no point in worrying about it,' said Roy. 'What's done is done. And I don't want you fighting my battles for me. You'll need to work with this new chap John's brought in, so give him a chance. Now then, let's talk about something more positive, shall we?'

Adrian nudged me gently with his elbow. 'Roy,' I said, 'Adrian and I have something we want to say to you. We wanted to say how grateful we are—'

'Oh, nonsense,' said Roy, waving his hand through the air as if swatting away a fly.

'No, no, we insist,' I said. 'This is important. You always said to us that whatever a man achieves in his career and whatever he earns, the true measuring stick is what others thought of him.'

Roy looked down, too shy to meet our eyes. He was from a generation not adept at handling displays of emotion.

'Adrian and I wanted to say thank you for all you've done for us. Not just with our careers, but for helping us become better people. You'll be missed.' I raised my jug, as did Adrian, and finally Roy. We chinked glasses.

There was a long silence, during which Roy's eyes became increasingly swollen and watery with each blink. Eventually, he reached up and wiped each eye in turn with the back of his hand. Adrian pulled two envelopes from his bag. 'Here, this is from everyone in the office,' he said, handing Roy a large white envelope, 'and this is from Adam and me.' He handed Roy a smaller blue one.

'I'll read this later, if I may,' said Roy, holding up the larger envelope and placing it on the table. He took the blue envelope and tugged carefully at its seam until the flap opened. He lifted out the card, opened it and took out the small rectangular documents inside. Before establishing what they were, he took the time to read the comments written by Adrian and myself. He gulped and again wiped each eye in turn.

He turned his attention to the documents. He revolved them and lifted them close to his face, before holding them further away to bring them into the correct focus. His lips moved silently as he read the wording on the face of one of the tickets. 'Two seats for the opening day of the Test Match at Lords,' he said in a hushed voice, and then much louder, 'Pure bloody gold dust!' With his free hand he punched the air. 'Thank you, boys, thank you so much.'

'We remembered how you always said experiences are better than possessions for presents,' said Adrian.

A short while later Roy offered to buy more drinks. He placed a flat hand on the table to lever himself up from his seat, grimacing as he did so. Once standing, there was a noticeable wheezing to his breathing as he asked us what we wanted.

When he was at the bar, Adrian and I exchanged a glance, but didn't say anything. We didn't need to. We'd had suspicions about Roy's health for a while, although nothing had been confirmed. I think we both wondered whether retirement would ease up whatever pressures were bearing in on his body, or accelerate them.

'What do you think about Roy's commission allocation?' asked Adrian in a lowered voice.

'If Roy thinks it's okay for us to have it and everyone does it, that's good enough for me.'

'Mmmm,' mumbled Adrian, staring beyond me.

'What?'

Adrian looked back again. 'I checked company policy on the intranet. It says when someone leaves, their commission reverts to the company.'

'Surely John won't notice. He's rich enough already, isn't he?'

'In my experience it's the rich who notice these things most. And our new boss may pick up on it too.'

Roy reappeared with three more jugs of bitter and eased himself back down into his chair.

'So what are your plans?' asked Adrian of Roy.

'I've got lots to keep me busy, and besides, I need to keep out of Joan's way. She's been running the house for forty years now, the last thing she wants is me getting in the way. I plan to watch a lot of cricket. And the garden could do with more attention. I've let it slip recently.' He paused. 'In a way, I'm glad.' He took an affirming swig of beer. 'It feels like the right time to be retiring. I always said to you both, you were born thirty years too late. If you'd been born at the same time as me, you'd have grown up listening to far better music.'

Adrian and I nodded; we weren't stupid enough to dispute that one.

'And late and boozy business lunches would have been the norm throughout most of your career.'

We nodded again.

'And once you left work or went on holiday, no one could get hold of you. A holiday meant a holiday.'

Adrian and I sighed.

'It seems to me we're living in strange times,' continued Roy. 'Did you see Peter Mandelson saying the other day that he was comfortable with businessmen becoming filthy rich? From a Labour Party minister...' He shook his head. 'The gap between rich and poor is getting ever wider, yet no one seems to want to do anything about it. We're storing up a lot of trouble, I can tell you that.'

When Roy was on a roll, Adrian and I were generally content to listen and to learn.

'All this modern technology just accelerates the process. Far from liberating people to work on their own terms, mobiles and BlackBerrys just allow bosses to put you on call twenty-four hours a day. No one bothers to telephone these days, they just email and consider the task delegated. And another thing, the Prime Minister says he's invented a new type of economy with "no more boom or bust". What a load of tosh.'

'The financial services sector does seem to be doing rather well,' said Adrian.

'Don't be fooled,' said Roy. 'When people start queuing up to take their money out of the bank, you know there's trouble ahead. Greed always leads to recession. I don't know when, but it will. At least I think it will. And that's another thing – I don't pretend to be able to predict the future. Listening to politicians and businessmen these days, you'd think we're guaranteed growth forever. I don't buy it.'

We soon moved on to happier subjects and reminisced about the times we'd spent working together. In many ways that evening was like so many of the evenings Roy, Adrian and I had enjoyed over the years, putting the world to rights and laughing at it at the same time. But the evening was also laced with a trace of sadness and perhaps the happiness and the laughter was just a tiny bit forced. For we all knew, deep down, that we would rarely meet this way again.

* * *

A few days later, Adrian and I had a getting-to-know-you meeting with our new boss, Marcus, and the two consultants he'd brought with him from his last company, Luke and Matt. They were due to start the following Monday. The meeting took place in the company boardroom on the top floor of our offices.

When Adrian and I entered, Marcus, Luke and Matt were talking in quiet voices, seated at one end of the long, rectangular boardroom table, the man at its head clearly Marcus. He stood out in particular because of his glasses, which were the Elvis Costello thick, angular, black-rimmed type. They rose and we all shook hands, the three of them favouring the vigorous, I'm-undoubtedly-a-heterosexual-male bone-crushing variety of handshake.

As we took our seats, a wink of yellow light in the far distance caught my eye through the window. It was an overcast and cloudy day and so I struggled to begin with to determine its source, before realizing it was the apex of the Canary Wharf tower.

We made a nervous, tentative start, discussing the weather and recent football results, with Luke being keen to point out he was a lifelong West Ham supporter. Marcus was perhaps in his early forties, Luke and Matt late twenties.

Marcus began, speaking more in the manner of a presentation rather than an informal discussion, which is how the meeting had been described in advance. 'As I said, I'm Marcus, and I'm looking forward to leading this Financial Services team. John has tasked me with bringing new energy and vision to the FS space.' He paused, comfortable with the silence, before recommencing. 'Did you know that the UK's FS sector employs over a million people and contributes over twelve per cent of UK plc's GDP? And it's all centred on London. And it's set to get bigger, potentially massively so, because financial services is the one sector this country can still be proud of. We're in a new type of economy now, one in which capital investment and new financial products are booming…'

As Marcus spoke, I observed him. The overall impression was one of precision: from the clearly bespoke suit, to his gold letter M cufflinks, to the double Windsor knot of his shiny metallic yellow tie. His face was full of ultra-white teeth, but he never once smiled. As he continued what he referred to as his 'macro-economic outlook', my mind began to wander and I grimaced as I recalled the fatal text message sent to Louise and the fateful moment of pure silence before…

'Now as you know,' said Marcus, looking keenly at me, confident with lots of eye contact and making sure he had my full attention, 'Luke, Matt and I have come from one of the big players. But what we see at this agency is the potential to be more nimble, niche-based and agile, and quicker on our feet. We've noticed how clients are increasingly asking for business partners who are fast and adaptable, and who understand their industries and sectors…'

As he spoke his head was mainly still, his face full of earnest, even pained, expressions. Meanwhile his hands and arms were busy and expansive: a chopping motion here with a flat palm to highlight a point, or a holding out of his arms in a wide circle there to emphasise our shared goals and objectives. He reminded me of Tony Blair justifying his decision to authorise military intervention in Iraq.

'Remember, we're not selling here, we're building client relationships,' he continued. 'Yes, we have to leverage those relationships and yes, we have to monetise those relationships, but we're not second-hand car dealers, we're specialist advisors, advising our clients on the most precious commodity they've got, their people.' He took a deep breath. 'I'm going to be spending the next couple of weeks reviewing the team's clients and finances in detail. I will then meet with you all individually to discuss my plans and agree your objectives. Has anyone got any questions?'

Silence.

My eyes flicked across the table at Luke and Matt, who were staring admiringly at Marcus; they reminded me of expectant little dogs, waiting for the nod from their master. I wanted to glance at Adrian, but thought it might give the wrong impression. As the silence continued I had to fight a compulsion to laugh. This wasn't just because the contrast to Roy's management style was so stark, nor was it because I found it hard to believe that Marcus was entirely serious, as clearly he was. No, I think the compulsion was born of something else: from being ever so slightly afraid.

6

The fatal text message was eventually sent to its correct recipient, and so just five days after leaving Louise, I found myself again descending the steps of the Bedford & Strand Bistro to meet Nadine.

She sat waiting for me at the same table as before, a bottle of champagne immersed in an ice bucket on a stand next to her. She wore a white shirt with large pointy collars, the white contrasting with her tanned skin.

'You'd better enjoy this champagne,' she said as I sat down. 'Each glass is an hour's wages for me.' She gave a fulsome smile, which reminded me that I needed to come clean straight away; I couldn't let myself slide into flirtation and tipsiness which would make it easier to delay or ignore the necessary confession.

'Nadine,' I said, pausing until she realised I had something important to say.

'What?' she replied, her face turning serious.

I took my glass and knocked back half its contents, the bubbles elevating at the back of my mouth. 'I haven't been entirely honest with you about my circumstances.'

The atmosphere chilled to the same temperature as the ice bucket and Nadine's facial muscles slackened. 'How do you mean?'

'When I met you last week I had a girlfriend.'

Silence. Cogs whirring.

'*Had* a girlfriend?' inquired Nadine.

'Yes, the relationship is now over. I'm so sorry for not being honest with you from the outset.'

She didn't say anything for a while and took little sips from her glass without meeting my eyes. 'Did you finish with your girlfriend because of me?' she asked eventually.

The word *because* repeated itself inside my head. 'Kind of... well... not really. You see it was already over, it's just that it wasn't over... officially, if you know what I mean.'

'I'm not sure I do know what you mean, no,' said Nadine, an edge of hostility to her voice.

There was a silence during which I took another swig of champagne; it felt entirely the wrong drink to be sharing at that moment.

'I'm not very comfortable about this,' said Nadine, shifting on her seat. 'It changes everything.'

'It doesn't have to,' I said hurriedly.

'But you *lied* to me.'

The word *lied* felt like a short jab to the stomach. 'But don't you see, I didn't want to jeopardise getting to know you just because of my ex whom I'd fallen out of love with months ago.'

Nadine looked me up and down with an expression rapidly turning to horrified. 'Months? How long were you with your ex for?'

I paused, weighing up whether to underplay the truth, but quickly realising this was the problem that had landed me in this position in the first place. 'Seven years,' I confirmed.

'*What?!*' Nadine leant back in her chair and sighed.

'I'm sorry, it was a difficult situation.' It sounded very feeble.

'You don't say,' she replied, deadpan. She stared at the middle of the table. After what felt like a very long time she swivelled around and lifted her coat off the back of her chair. 'You know, you're all the same,' she said, standing up. 'Even the ones like you who pretend to be different.'

'That isn't true,' I said. 'Please sit down, Nadine. I'm trying to do the right thing here by telling you the truth.'

She leant forward and looked me squarely in the eyes. 'You should have told me the truth last Friday. I'm sorry, I'm going now, I need some time to think this through. It's bad enough that you deceived me, but to deceive your girlfriend of seven years is even more unforgivable.' She pulled on her coat and lifted her handbag. 'And another thing, I don't like being involved in people splitting up. It's hardly as though I'm now going to want to replace your ex of *seven* years, is it?'

She marched out.

I poured myself a glass of champagne to the brim and downed most of it in one glug. Had I thought I could walk straight out of one relationship and into another? I don't think I'd been thinking at all.

A raw emptiness scraped inside the trunk of my body: my punishment for hurting Nadine. My thoughts turned again to Louise and the deep, dense guilt resumed, like someone squeezing my throat, making it difficult to breathe.

7

Six months later, I'd just finished tidying my new flat for the first time when the doorbell rang. I pressed the intercom button. 'Hello?'

'It's Rachel.'

'I'll buzz you in. I'm on the second floor.'

Rachel had emailed me recently, inquiring as to my wellbeing having not seen me for a while. We'd been friends since university – indeed inseparable friends there, so much so that everyone had assumed we were a couple. Yet there'd never been any romance, save one quick kiss opportunistically stolen by me on a particularly drunken New Year's Eve. Ironically, it had been Rachel who'd introduced me to Louise, who was one of her school friends from their hometown in Kent.

She arrived at my door, slightly short of breath. 'The stairs must keep you fit,' she said, kissing me on the cheek.

I showed her in and she embarked on a tour of my modest flat, stepping into the lounge, the bedroom and the kitchen, briefly scrutinising each but noticeably not saying anything. As she did so, I stole a glance of her. I'd not recognised her beauty the first few times I'd met her – I think distracted by the glasses she usually wore - but once recognised, I was trapped. She had a slightly pinched and ever so slightly turned up nose, and a wide mouth you could find yourself staring at before you realised what you were doing. Her demeanour often suggested a certain pride which many mistook as arrogance, though most who alleged it were just intimidated by her cleverness. Eventually she said, 'Remind me how long you've lived here?'

I counted back the months since I'd moved out of my parents' house, where I'd gone after breaking up with Louise. 'About three months.'

'Three months? It's looks like you've been here three minutes. There's nothing here. It's like a bachelor pad minus the black leather sofa and flat screen TV.'

'Okay, so I haven't quite got round to the soft furnishings. Besides... I don't have many visitors these days.' I made a mental note that the flat's condition had spectacularly failed to impress the first woman to enter it. I was pleased with the flat, despite it being tiny. Louise and I had made a decent profit from the sale of our place in Clapham – it would have been more were it not for the Northern Rock crisis spooking the market – and Roy's extra commission had made the mortgage repayments possible.

I switched the kettle on while Rachel sat down at the small kitchen table. 'What made you choose Hammersmith?' she asked.

'I once went for a walk here along the river and liked the atmosphere. It feels like a little island, if that makes sense.' I sat down with a teapot and two mugs, and poured. As I did so, I sensed Rachel's eyes levelled at me. I looked up.

'No one's seen you recently,' she said.

I shrugged my shoulders.

'Are you alright?'

I shrugged my shoulders again.

'Apart from losing the power of speech, that is. I mean, apart from that are you alright?'

I smirked, but it failed to take into a full smile.

'Do you want to talk about it?' asked Rachel.

I hesitated. 'I suppose...'

'Is this about Lou?'

'I don't know... partly... I think. We had to split up. Things weren't right between us for a long time. But I miss her company. Or maybe it's just company full stop I miss. Plus there's the guilt.'

'The guilt?'

'About the ending. And whether I didn't live up to the man she thought I was. For so long we thought it would last forever. The slow unravelling was... heartbreaking.' I stared down into the surface of my tea, which in turn reflected the light from the window. 'How is Louise?'

Rachel paused. 'She's... okay. A little angry.'

'About the ending?'

'Not so much that. More about finding herself single at thirty-four. Women worry about the passing years.'

'You think men don't?'

Rachel nodded. 'Anyway, surely it's time to look forward?'

I leant back in my chair and stared out of the window. 'The thought of starting again with someone else seems so... so daunting. And what's the point when you can get as far along the line as Lou and I and it still goes wrong? Sometimes I wonder whether we should have tried harder–'

'You were right to split up,' said Rachel, an edge of finality to her voice. 'All relationships have a natural lifespan.'

Suddenly it struck me how Rachel might soon speak to Louise. The last thing I wanted was for Louise to hear I was feeling sorry for myself, so I changed the subject. 'How are things going with Richard?'

'They're fine, thank you.' She didn't elaborate.

'So he's–'

'Not left his wife, no. Besides, we're talking about you today, not me. I'm not the one who's disappeared off the face of the earth for the last six months.'

It remained a mystery how a woman of such principle and intelligence as Rachel should have spent the last three years of her life – some of her richest and most fertile – in a weekday relationship with a married man. Shamefully, the fact that her lover Richard still hadn't left his wife made me feel better; it reminded me I wasn't the only one whose love life was a mess.

As we drank our tea, Rachel gave me some tips on how to make my flat more welcoming, after which we headed out for lunch. Although I lived little more than two hundred yards from the concrete and traffic of Hammersmith Broadway, it might as well have been two hundred miles, such was the contrast. The river embankment evoked a different age, like being transported two hundred years back in time, with eighteenth-century public houses bordering the Thames, and old barges and riverboats snuggled together in little waterborne communities in river bends; and just near my flat Hammersmith Bridge in distinctive Harrods green and gold stretching across to Barnes.

After a few minutes we reached a pretty green; on the far side the pavement cut back from the river behind a row of buildings, funnelling us to a secret dark passageway, which brought to mind images of bygone smugglers dragging contraband from their boats for quick and safe storage. Just along the passageway was a tiny, enigmatic little pub, The Dove, and it was open.

Rachel turned and raised her eyebrows.

'Why not?' I said.

We ducked inside into a close, low-ceilinged room with dark oak beams, sectioned off into inner compartments which one could imagine being conducive to clandestine discussions by the smugglers regarding rendezvous and drop-off. It was the sort of place in which you could feel the ghosts of earlier patrons in the fabric of the building and it comforted you. It was the sort of place Roy loved.

We bought drinks and climbed a small set of stairs to an elevated outside terrace with views eastwards along the river. Despite the spring cold, we took seats outside. Near Hammersmith Bridge a lone sculler reached right forward and pulled back on his oars, repeating the practised stroke, over and over, pulling himself further and further away.

'Here's to the first of the day,' I said. We chinked glasses.

'So, what happened to the girl you *didn't* send the infamous text to?' asked Rachel.

I sighed. 'Nothing. I met up with her after splitting up with Lou and came clean about everything. She went nuts.'

'Can you blame her? If there's one thing women can't abide, it's lies. Trust is like a Ming vase, you only get one chance to hold it. If you drop it and smash it, it's never the same again no matter how long you try to piece it back together.'

I didn't respond. I couldn't. Rachel was right; I'd misled Nadine and paid the price. I took a large swig of beer and, having returned the pint to the table, stared at the froth sliding back down the inside of the glass.

'How's single life?' asked Rachel, sensing my introspection.

I drew in a deep breath and slowly let it out again. 'It hasn't been easy. I was living at home for a while and there was no chance of any dates there. It's a sad thing when your parents pity you. They tried to be positive, but I was left with the feeling that their hopes for me hadn't quite worked out as they'd wanted.'

'Have you been on any dates since moving here?'

'None.'

'Have you tried to find any?'

I shook my head.

'Perhaps it's time to get out there and find some,' persisted Rachel.

'Maybe,' I said.

'You don't sound convinced.'

'It's more a case of not knowing where to start.' I folded my arms. 'It's difficult for guys.'

Rachel snorted. 'What's difficult for guys?'

'The whole dating thing. A guy has to put himself out there and risk making an idiot of himself. He has to risk rejection.'

'Ha! Most single guys don't have a problem approaching women; in fact they generally throw themselves at them. It's only you who's locking himself away in a darkened flat for months on end. And besides, you've got it easy; try being a male bee.'

'Why, what's hard about being a male bee?'

'Apparently the queen bee only selects about a dozen drones from thousands to accompany her on her mating flight...'

'Sounds like bad odds. But great if you get selected for the flight.'

'You'd think so, wouldn't you? However, after mating, the drones' genitals explode and snap off inside the queen.'

I lurched forward instinctively, cupping myself like a defender in the wall at a free kick. 'Good god.'

'The drone is actually very lucky... genetically. The snapped off penis acts as a genital plug, thus ensuring the drone's parentage.'

'Bloody hell.'

'Every cloud and all that.'

I smirked again, and it took into a smile.

Rachel reached into her handbag and pulled out a magazine from one of the Sunday papers. She laid it out on the table in front of me and turned to a page toward the back. 'There,' she said, pointing to an advert. In it, a middle-aged couple of... let's say average looks, stared zombie-like into each other's eyes in a staged posture, both wearing demonic fixed grins. The caption underneath read, 'You too can find love!'

'Why don't you sign up to that?' asked Rachel, the edges of her mouth twitching.

'Thanks for that,' I said. 'But I'm thirty-four, for god's sake, I'm too young to join a dating agency, if that's what it is. It looks more like a cult judging from the photograph.'

'What about speed dating then?'

I winced. 'God, no. I can't think of anything less romantic than being herded into a room of nervous singles and made to talk about the weather and what holiday I'm taking this year.'

'Lonely hearts ads?'

I pondered them for a moment. 'Kinda creepy I've always thought. When you read them – not that I do read them, you understand – they often seem to be hinting at some dark forbidden potential, which can only be unlocked together. Or is that just my interpretation of them?'

'No, you're right,' said Rachel. 'A lot of them are strange, but there's also a lot of humour in them too.'

'You seem to know a lot about them.'

'That's because when my mother found out about Richard and me, she started circling lonely hearts ads in the Guardian and posting them to me.'

My mouth fell open. 'She didn't?'

'She did. Typically gentlemen wanting a female companion for long walks in the countryside, cream teas and listening to Radio 4 together.'

I pictured it in my mind's eye. 'Doesn't sound so bad...'

'They were clearly all old enough to be my dad. She was just circling the ones she would have dated herself. Anyway, if not the lonely hearts, how about the internet?'

'I've seen adverts for it. But I'd rather meet someone... you know, normally.'

'But the internet *is* the norm these days. You shouldn't rule it out.'

'I'll think about it. It does have a dark side, of course.'

'A dark side?'

'Yeah, fat, middle-aged men in string vests sitting at their PCs in darkened rooms with family size boxes of Kleenex within easy reach–'

'Oh god please, Adam! Remove that image from my mind or I'll never log on again...'

Rachel and I never did work out a strategy to get me dating that afternoon, but I appreciated her efforts to cheer me up. With the river as our backdrop, we talked and drank and talked some more. Depending on your opinion, or perhaps your mood, Sunday drinking is either complete folly or it's squeezing the most out of the weekend. Rachel swung the argument in favour of the latter while pouring two generous glasses of red wine later in the afternoon, when she reasoned, 'Besides, why have a hangover on your own time?' I knew Marcus would berate me the next day for a lack of energy, but by this time I was beyond caring.

In the early evening we moved inside and sat next to an open fire, which cricked and snapped with heat, warming our faces. We were both a little worse for wear. 'You do realise that meeting women is only half your problem,' said Rachel.

'Is it?'

'Yes.'

'So what's the other half of my problem?' I asked.

'Technique.'

'So you're saying I have no technique with women?'

'I didn't say that. I just think you might want to think about your approach, that's all.'

'You mean scented candles and flowers, that sort of stuff?'

'Maybe, but if you try scented candles and flowers on the first date you'll make her extremely nervous. What I meant was more along the lines of style and charm.'

'So now you're saying I've got no style or charm.'

'Stop it. You've just got to realise that women like a man who puts some effort in. It's hard to define. It comes down to having self-confidence, maybe even a touch of arrogance.'

'*What?!* Am I hearing this correctly? Where did the female eunuch go?'

'Ssshh, Adam, you're drunk. I didn't exactly mean more arrogant.'

'What did you mean then?'

'Well, as I said, a bit of style and charm. But I know what you're like – you probably think being charming and smooth is cheating.'

The drink mist was in my brain and I was at that stage where you have to consciously slow down your speech to try to stop it slurring. 'Do women really fall for a guy just because he's charming? Don't women look beyond all that slick stuff?'

'We don't fall for men *just* because of it. But a little helps. You need to have a bit of... you know... a bit of the old Julio Iglesias.'

'*Julio Iglesias?!*'

'Ssshh! Yes, the more I think about it, the more I think you could do with talking to a man who's successful with women to get some tips. A man who fancies himself a bit but isn't a total cock. I grant you, it won't be easy finding one.'

'But none of my friends are successful with women. Some of them *think* they're successful, but that's not the same thing.'

'There must be someone...' Rachel drained the last of her glass. 'Oh, I forgot to ask, you're coming to Jess and Ben's wedding, aren't you?'

I leant forward, my eyes fixed upon the glow of the fire. I'd received the invite: a thick, embossed cream envelope, out of which tumbled a flurry of cards, gift lists, maps and hotel listings. Just staring at the amount of literature had exhausted me. And that was before I contemplated the event itself: the happy couple, too many other happy couples, and Louise, happily with a new happy bloke probably. 'Maybe I'll come...' I mumbled.

'Maybe sounds like a no.' Rachel reached out and held my forearm until I turned to her. 'Adam, you've got to come. Your friends all want to see you. And weddings are a classic place to meet people.'

'But what about Lou? Is she going?'

She hesitated, her eyes darting this way and that. 'I think she's going. But I'm sure she's going alone. Besides, I'm going, and I'm expecting you to chaperone me.'

The thought of going to the wedding with Rachel made it more bearable. Indeed, it made it appealing.

'Well?' she asked.

'Okay, I'll come.'

'Good, everyone will be pleased to see you. Make sure you reply to the invitation tomorrow and remember to buy something from the gift list. I know what you blokes are like – you always leave these things to the last minute. Now, I'd best be getting back to the tube. Work tomorrow.'

I walked her to Hammersmith tube station, before setting off for home along the river. A cold mist clung to the surface of the Thames, the Victorian streetlamps casting a hazy sodium glow through it, giving the empty embankment a Dickensian feel. I stopped and stared out into the fog, listening to the gentle sloshing of the water below. I thought about what great company Rachel was. And how beautiful she was. And about the injustice of her being wasted on a married man.

8

Although in my inebriated state with Rachel I'd been unable to think of any friends who were successful with women, by the following morning it had become glaringly obvious whom I should talk to...

But I wasn't comfortable with it. For how often do men talk to other people about their problems? More or less never. How often do men talk to *other men* about their problems? Absolutely never. Because seeking help is itself a sign of weakness. And if there's one thing most men can do without, it's a mate who prefers talking about emotional issues rather than sport or politics. Which contrasts with women, of course. Louise had told me towards the end of our relationship, with some relish, 'Oh we girls discuss ev-er-ry-thing.'

'Not everything?' I'd asked, rubbing my chin.

'Yes, ev-er-ry-thing.'

The outstanding choice of who to speak to was Sam. Sam! Sam the man. Sam the man's man. Sam the ladies' man. Sam was a good friend from university who'd spent his life falling on his feet, starting at birth when the right genes bestowed on him exceptional good looks and physical prowess, for he resembled a young Richard Gere, ruggedly handsome in an approachable way. After university he'd set up his own property development business, riding the tide of London's inflating property prices for the best part of ten years. And he did many of the renovations himself, the physical labour doing no harm to his fitness or physique.

Sam had the life force, by which I mean he was a force of nature, a slightly hyperactive guy who made people laugh and spent the rest of the time laughing at himself. He had the decency to use his looks and charisma to enjoy himself, and all his male friends lived a little bit vicariously through him. His motto when chatting up women at university had been, 'No means maybe, maybe means persuade me.' Sam was the man I needed to talk to. So I called him.

'Hello?'

'Sam, it's Adam.'

'Adam! Where the fuck have you been?'

'Well... sort of... recouping, you know, after Louise and I broke up. Listen, do you fancy a beer?'

'Of course. Hey, now that you're single, I bet you're having a whale of a time.'

I hesitated. 'Actually, it's being single I wanted to chat to you about. I need some advice on... well, you know, on re-orientation to being single.'

There was a momentary silence. 'You mean you haven't got laid since splitting up?'

There was no point fighting the truth. 'Er, yes.'

'Shit, we need to talk. Can you meet Friday?'

'Sure.'

'Okay, I'll meet you at that pub near your work, The Cittie of Yorke. Good beer at good prices.'

* * *

By five thirty-one I was out the office. A succession of attractive women passed me from the other direction in business attire: fitted blouses, figure-hugging skirts, high heels, provocative leather boots ending just below the knee, tights – or were they stockings? Goddam it! It was enough to drive a man insane! And surely not all of them could be spoken for? I was beginning to think like Sam already.

Reaching The Cittie of Yorke, I walked along a short passageway and ducked through a low doorway into the dramatic expanse of the back bar, a long room with a vaulted ceiling like a Tudor banqueting hall. Six huge, dark, imposing oak barrels stood above the bar, looking as though they'd once contained a noxious medieval brew such as mead, so strong its fumes alone could render you senseless. Roy had always liked this pub. Opposite the bar were a series of wooden cubicles with ornate lattice carving through which one caught glimpses of people inside, as though stealing a glance inside a confessional. Sam leaned out of one of them. 'Adam! Over here, I've got you a pint.'

I slid in opposite Sam and we shook hands, his vice-like strength causing the bones in my hand to creak. I took a healthy slug of the pint of ale he'd bought me and sighed.

'That first hit of alcohol on a Friday night is truly a blessed moment, isn't it?' said Sam.

'It sure is. It's good to see you, it's been too long.' I raised my pint to chink glasses, but to my astonishment Sam wasn't drinking. 'Where's your drink?' I asked.

'I only drink on two occasions these days.'

'*What?!* When?' This was *not* the Sam I knew.

'When I'm thirsty and when I'm not.' Oh yes it was. Sam lifted his pint from where he'd hidden it, grinned and downed an almighty swig. He wore a fitted black shirt, just tight enough to emphasise his powerful pectorals and broad shoulders. He always looked sharp, but in an understated way. He didn't need passing fads and fashions. If you looked like Richard Gere, would *you* wear a waistcoat, skinny jeans and male jewellery? 'Listen, I'm sorry to hear about you and Louise,' he said. 'She's a great girl.'

'It's fine, seriously. It was time for us to move on and, in a way, I think it was a relief for both of us when it ended.'

A hint of a smirk teased Sam's lips and he brought his hand to his mouth to hide it.

'What?' I asked.

'At least you went out with a bang,' he said, breaking out into a full-blown smile.

'You mean you know how it ended?' I asked.

'The question is more who *doesn't* know. You've gone down in legend! I've got to ask – what did the text say?'

I cringed as it all came back to me. 'I can't remember now,' I said. 'Something about a kiss, I think.'

'Is that all? I'm afraid the Chinese whisperers have been at work; the rumours are that you sent some sort of disgustingly depraved sex text.'

'Great, that's all I need, not only a reputation for being unfaithful, but also a pervert.'

'Ah, don't worry about it,' said Sam, waving his hand dismissively through the air. 'It's history now. And at least it meant you had a quick and clean split. Like any death, it's better over quickly, rather than hanging on grimly through gradual decline.'

'Mmmm, I suppose so,' I said.

'And besides, if Louise thinks you were at fault for sending that text, she's mistaken.'

'What? But I *was* at fault.'

'No you weren't.'

'Why not?'

'Because you were helpless.'

'Was I?'

'Of course you were. And Louise, like every woman, needs to accept it.'

I didn't understand what Sam meant. 'What does every woman need to accept?'

Sam squinted and brought his drink to his mouth, taking down an inordinately long draught of beer, maintaining eye contact throughout, before returning his glass slowly to the table. 'Women need to accept that men are victims.'

There was a silence.

'We're what?' I asked.

'We're victims.'

'Are we?'

'Of course.'

'I don't understand, how are we victims?'

'What women don't realise is this,' said Sam, pausing to take another long dose of his beer and waiting until he was absolutely sure he had my full attention. 'Men are slaves to their male Darwinian genes.' His words hung in the air. 'Rather than being objects of derision and abuse, we should be pitied by women for the unfair burden we carry as men, enslaved by our potent male impulses. You sending that text message to Louise in a trance rather proves my point.'

His comments threw me and various accepted truths rapidly rearranged themselves inside my head. 'So you're saying I'm not entirely in control?' I asked.

'Of course you're not! Do you think the history of mankind would be anything like it is if men could control their uncontrollable desires? Have you not heard of Henry VIII? How can you be in control of something as ferocious and all-consuming as your virulent masculine cravings?'

I took a massive mouthful of beer to steady myself at this revelation.

'Listen,' continued Sam, leaning forward, 'men are taught from a young age that they'll never understand the emotional traumas women experience, be it periods, childbirth, headaches and the rest, right?'

'I guess so.'

'Well, it's time women started to accept the fact that they'll never truly understand the forces inside a man – as I said, our irresistible stallion yearnings. Society doesn't want to hear it, and no one talks about it, but men are victims, don't ever forget that.'

'I'm pretty sure I'll never forget it...' I looked out of the booth across to the bar, now three deep in men queuing to get served. Their universally grey or navy suits and their herd instinct for beer did suggest a certain victimhood.

'Now,' said Sam, 'when we spoke on the phone you mentioned that single life isn't going too well?'

I shook my head and became introspective as I contemplated my long barren spell. 'I don't know, I'm struggling to be honest. I haven't even been on a date yet. And when I do – assuming I do – I'm worried I may have, you know, lost my edge.'

'And it's getting you down, right?'

I shrugged my shoulders. 'I guess.'

'And it seems a bit daunting?'

'It does really.'

'And makes you a little sad?'

'Well, I suppose so.' I didn't remember Sam being this sensitive.

'And you hate it when people are horrible to little furry animals?'

'What?'

'Snap out of it, Adam! You've been conscripted to the army of single men and it sounds to me like you're refusing the call. You should be shot for treason!' With a prolonged colossal glug Sam downed a full half pint and brought the empty glass down onto the table with a thud. He let out a thunderous burp from deep within the pit of his stomach, which resonated around our cubicle and went on so long it changed tone halfway through. 'Right, down the rat hole, that's an order. Get a couple more in and then we're going to have some serious words.'

Stunned, I did as ordered, forcing down most of a pint in one go. When I returned from my fellow victims at the bar with two more beers, Sam was still shaking his head and looking at me disapprovingly. 'You do realise being single is a god-given opportunity?' he said.

'It is?'

'Of course. You're young, you've got prospects and most importantly, you're single. A few years from now you'll be married with kids and look back on this time as the golden age, an era of opportunity.'

'Will I?' I stared down into my full pint contemplating the impossibly distant prospect of a wife and kids.

'Although there may be some bumps on the way,' added Sam.

'What's that?'

'I'm just saying that although being single will generally be great, you may enter some pretty dark places as well.'

'Sounds exciting,' I said.

'I didn't mean it like that,' he said, deadpan.

'What sort of places are you talking about then?'

'Adam, you need to pay attention.' He motioned me closer and I leant in. He spoke quietly and confidentially. 'Being single is like being a boxer. You train, you spar, you go into combat. But no matter how hard you've trained, no matter how ready you think you are, when you enter the dating ring, there're going to be times when you're knocked out flush and sprawled on the canvas. Women have that effect sometimes. You've got to promise me one thing, can you do that?' He transfixed me with a penetrating, mesmerising stare. Clearly a deep, unassailable truth born of hard-earned experience was about to be imparted.

'Okay – okay, I promise, what is it?'

'When you get knocked down, you've got to pick yourself up again. Always, I repeat always, pick yourself up again. Can you promise me that?'

'Okay, I promise,' I replied, but more because his intensity was scaring me rather than because I'd thought through the promise I was making.

'Good. Right, I'm off to the loo. While I'm away I want you to repeat to yourself over and over again, *I WILL pick myself up again, I WILL pick myself up again.*' Sam continued to glare at me even as he rose and started walking away, so that the lesson wouldn't be forgotten.

Clearly I had a lot to learn, but better a crash course like this and a brutally honest tutor. I thought it might be instructive to hear how Sam's dating was going, particularly as an intriguing fact about him was that all his dates and girlfriends over the years invariably had strong physical elements to their jobs and lifestyles: yoga teachers, triathletes, personal trainers, physiotherapists, even a pole dancer. Memories of them came back to me...

'You okay?' Sam had returned.

'What's that?'

'I asked if you were okay, you looked miles away.'

'Oh, I was just... just thinking. Tell me, is there a lady in your life at the moment?'

'Well, I was seeing a girl called Rashmi recently...'

This was not the first of Sam's Asian girlfriends. Since leaving university he'd become increasingly preoccupied with them, until now he seemed to date them exclusively. 'So this Rashmi, was she fit?' I asked, subconsciously knowing the answer already.

'Bullet.'

'Bullet?'

'Bullet fit. Take it from me, that's fit.'

'I don't doubt it. So what happened to her?'

'She had WGP.'

I racked my brain for WGP. Something medical? A rare affliction? I needed to tread carefully. 'I'm really sorry to hear that. Listen, I realise I shouldn't have to ask this, but what's WGP?'

'Weight Gain Potential.'

'Sam! I thought you were talking about a disease or degenerative medical condition.'

'It is a medical condition when you think about it. Look, take Beyoncé – now there's one fat woman–'

'But she's stunning, Sam.'

'Yeah, but it takes five hours in the gym each day and only eating salad to keep her that way. If she led anything resembling a normal life she'd be huge. Inside Beyoncé is one fat mama trying to get out.'

'And did Rashmi look like Beyoncé? Because if she did, you really fucked up splitting up with her, I can tell you that.'

'My point is, once you start dating or get engaged, and especially when you get married, she may take her foot off the gas and then you end up, quite literally, with more than you bargained for.'

It seemed so unfair that Sam could afford to move on from a Beyoncé lookalike. I almost asked him for Rashmi's number. 'It just seems a little... harsh,' I said.

'What, you don't think women think the same way? What about sizeist women?'

'How do you mean, sizeist?' I asked, rubbing my chin.

'You know, women who refuse to date a guy who's shorter than them.'

'Oh I see!'

'A friend of mine – who's admittedly a bit of short arse – his girl-friend dumped him on account of his height, and do you know what she said when she did it? She said, "I don't feel like a woman with a man who is shorter than me." Imagine that! *"I don't feel like a woman."* Jesus. What's the difference between that and me saying I don't want to date someone who will one day weigh more than me?'

'I guess you've got a point.'

'It's more than a point, it's called equality. At least with weight you can do something about it; with your height, you're stuck with it.'

And I thought I had it tough as a single guy. Talking to Sam gave me a glimpse of what an ordeal it must be for a single woman: the pressure to look good, the impossible standards, hell, even looking good at the moment wouldn't suffice, they also had to worry about a future genetic predisposition to run to fat. Then again, perhaps Sam was just being honest. Brutally honest.

I drank a healthy measure of my beer, which finished it. I needed another. 'Shall I get another round in?'

'With chasers,' replied Sam.

I was sure it was Sam's round, but buying his drinks seemed a small price to pay for the tutorial. We drank long into the night, even-tually going for a curry, halfway through which Sam got a text from a water-polo playing Moroccan ex-girlfriend and dashed off to her place. On the night bus home, surrounded by the human detritus of drunks and people falling asleep dribbling, an important realisation struck home: Sam was right. Conscription to the army of single men wasn't optional.

9

In the months following Roy's sacking, we heard little from him. Adrian and I sent him regular emails, but his responses became less and less frequent until one day an email from his wife Joan arrived confirming our fears: Roy had cancer. The news came as no surprise, but the C word still shocked us, heralding an enemy few conquer. We wanted to pay Roy a visit, so emailed Joan to let her know our thoughts were with them, and would she let us know when Roy was able to receive visitors.

Meanwhile Marcus continued to implement change. He'd recently suggested a companywide 'Sales League Table', enthusiastically embraced by John, so that now the company intranet site displayed everyone's monthly results. One had to wonder whether the paltry prizes on offer for those who topped the table were a sincere reward for achievement, or whether in fact the table served as an instrument to embarrass those who, like me, were struggling to make sales and thus humiliate them into working harder.

One positive change was Marcus's recruitment of a new graduate called Carrie, who was proving a valuable addition to the office, being mid-twenties, anxious to impress and one of life's enthusiasts. She had an unconventional but not unattractive face: her ears stuck out a little and she had big eyes which made her look permanently surprised. Then there was her voice, the product of a Home Counties upper-middle-class background which, coupled with her natural sincerity, resulted in a crisp, clear, clipped quality one could never tire of hearing.

'Adam, have you got any work for me to do tomorrow?' she asked, having perched herself on the lip of my desk late one day.

'Your timing is impeccable,' I said. 'I've just had a placement fall through, so if you could search through our recent CVs for a senior manager specialising in indirect tax—'

'Indirect tax?'

'That's VAT to you and me,' I said.

'Bloody hell, people actually specialise in VAT fulltime?' Carrie reached out and jostled my shoulder playfully. 'Hey, imagine being at a dinner party and doing the introductions. "What do you do for a living?" "I'm a VAT specialist." Talk about a conversation killer!'

'It gets worse than that,' said Adrian. 'There's an annual accountancy awards bash and they have a prize for... wait for it... Tax Personality of the Year! Now there's an oxymoron if ever there was one.'

'And there was an email doing the rounds a couple of years ago about an auditor in Norway,' I said. 'Apparently he died at his desk but nobody noticed for a week. When the press asked his colleagues how it had happened, they said he was a quiet type and they'd thought he was just concentrating extra hard.'

Carrie coiled over and let out a squawky laugh. Marcus appeared from nowhere. 'I don't want to interrupt your fun and games,' he said, interrupting our fun and games. 'Adam, how are things going with the VAT vacancy?'

'Funny you should mention that. Carrie is just about to call all the candidates who've recently registered or called us to let us know they're looking for work.'

'Good. Let me know when you think you've found someone.'

As Marcus walked away, Carrie lifted herself up off my desk and whispered, 'Hasn't he got better things to do?'

'No comment,' I replied, with a smirk. Once she'd gone, I sensed Adrian staring at me and turned to find him looking at me with narrowed eyes. 'What?' I asked.

'You know what. Notice how Carrie didn't ask *me* if I had any work for her.'

'She's just enthusiastic, that's all,' I replied, grinning, 'and I'm pretty sure she was asking both of us.'

By now Marcus had returned to his desk. He closed down his laptop and locked it away in his drawer, before ripping open a wet wipe and wiping down his desk. He noticed me watching him. 'What?' he asked.

'Nothing,' I said, shaking my head. 'I was just wondering why you do that every day.'

'Did you know that your desk, keyboard and telephone support more germs than a toilet seat? It's because everyone eats lunch at their desks nowadays and never clean away the crumbs.' He ripped open a second wet wipe, cleaned his palms and each finger in turn, folded the wet wipe and dropped it into the bin. Standing tall, he brought his hands together in a single, loud, muscular clap, rubbed them together vigorously and announced to the office, 'Right, let's all pack up and go. The quiz starts at seven sharp.' He pulled on his Aquascutum raincoat, turned up the collar to ensure the check branding was displayed, and began marching purposefully around the office hoping his enthusiasm would rally everyone.

I stared at Marcus's empty desk. While others slowly built up a sense of identity at their desk over time – a photograph of their spouse or baby, a postcard, a desk calendar – by contrast Marcus expressed himself through a process of reduction. The only thing that identified his desk as his own was the shelf to the side of it, on which he'd neatly stacked various books about the recruitment industry, as well as a number about effective business management such as *Who Moved My Cheese?* by Spencer Johnson and *The 7 Habits of Highly Effective People* by Stephen R. Covey. One could safely conclude that his books did not countenance clutter, either of the personal environment or of the mind, and his philosophy of workplace austerity had found an ally in the company's recently initiated 'Clear Desk Policy', rigorously implemented by the company secretary Carolyn, in order to secure some obscure business process accreditation.

Perhaps Marcus's books also explained his language, which was heavy with corporate phraseology such as 'leveraging off others' (taking credit for others' work), 'empowering you' (getting you to work harder) and 'having confidence in the value of the services we provide our clients' (charging clients more).

'Marcus seems to like a competitive element to his work nights out,' observed Adrian.

'Perhaps he's trying to foster a sense of team spirit to increase sales,' I said. 'Or maybe working so long in sales has turned him into someone who simply now exists in a perpetual state of competitiveness?'

'Perhaps it's both,' said Adrian.

Carrie appeared next to Adrian and me, pulling on her coat. 'Ready to go to the forced fun?'

'I'm good to go,' I said, closing my laptop. 'Are you coming, Adrian?'

'I just need to finish something off,' he said. 'I'll see you there shortly.'

Carrie and I set off down High Holborn. It was dark outside, which reminded me that I'd got up that morning in darkness, commuted to work in darkness and was now returning to the darkness, having not seen natural light at any stage during the day.

'You any good at quizzes?' I asked Carrie as we walked to the pub.

'So so. My family play Trivial Pursuit at Christmas. My dad slouches on the settee semi-drunk and barks out answers irrespective of which team is being asked the question.'

'Sounds awfully familiar...'

'What subjects are you good at?' asked Carrie.

'Sport, the orange cheese, that was my strongest when my family used to play it. The yellows were okay, which were history.'

'That pink pie is the worst,' said Carrie. 'I can never get any of them. I have to pray I get the one entertainment question whose answer involves someone famous after nineteen-eighty. You're probably good at that category.'

'What are you saying?'

'Well, the questions are designed for your generation,' said Carrie, now smirking. 'After all, The Beatles were still going when you were born, so you probably get all the entertainment questions right.'

'The Beatles split up in the sixties! I was born in nineteen seventy-three. Go on, depress me, what year were you born in?'

'Nineteen eighty-four.'

'Bloody hell. So if I was to mention the New Romantics, you'd have no idea what I was talking about?'

'Were they an artistic movement emerging out of Paris in the late nineteenth century?' asked Carrie with a grin. 'If so, you probably knew some of them given your age.'

'Shut it you, and respect your elders.'

We arrived at The Melton Mowbray, its etched glass mirrors and wood panelling giving the place a pleasing Victorian feel. Roy liked this pub. We walked down the stairs near the entrance to a spacious, dark, low-ceilinged room below, which must have once been the beer cellar. Various people from the office were queuing at the bar, while others wandered about self-consciously, trying to find their table.

'Over here, Adam,' said Carrie, tugging my arm after we'd bought drinks. 'We're on the same team, I checked earlier.' When we reached our table everyone was being terribly jolly, but it felt forced, which of course it was. I made sure I sat along the back wall, which at least meant I would be able to watch proceedings, while Carrie sat opposite me and offered to write down our team's answers.

A loud crackle emitted from the PA system, followed by a sharp whine threatening to escalate into ear-splitting feedback. Marcus moved away from the speaker and turned down the volume. 'Right, can I have your attention please?' his amplified voice asked. The conversations reduced to murmuring and then silence. Marcus welcomed everyone and explained the rules: how each round would be ten questions per subject, how for round six a sheet with twenty famous faces would be circulated and round seven would be pictures of twenty well-known album covers for identification. 'Without further ado, let's press on with round one, which is the geography round,' he said.

A few groans came from the audience, particularly from the girl to my left, Kate from Purchase Ledger, who wore a thin gold chain around her neck with a prominent gold K dangling from it. 'I'm rubbish at geography,' she announced. 'Last year me and me other half wanted to go to La Palma in the Canaries and we ended up booking flights to Palma in Mallorca instead!' She giggled manically. A few nervous glances passed between the rest of us.

'Okay, question one,' said Marcus. 'Which US city is known as the city of brotherly love?'

'I know, I know!' shouted Kate. 'It's San Francisco.'

'Well, don't shout,' said Carrie, 'or the other teams will hear. Besides, I'm not sure that's right.'

'Yes it is. I went on holiday there once and we did a bus tour. They have a whole neighbourhood for the gay men.'

Marcus's voice again boomed out of the PA. 'Okay, that's quite a tricky one to begin with, so I'll give you a clue – it's the same city which the film Rocky was set in.'

'It's not Philadelphia, is it?' asked Carrie.

'No, that isn't it,' said Kate. 'Philadelphia's famous for that other film, the one with Tom Hanks looking really ill... what's it called?'

'So what should I write down, what's our answer?' asked Carrie.

'Put Philadelphia down,' I said. The motion was carried and as Carrie leant forward to write my gaze came to rest on the face of a woman sitting on the far side of the next table.

My life changed in the blink of an eye.

Initially struck dumb, a fierce alertness followed, as though the shock of first sight was the penetration of the needle and the subsequent sharpness the plunging of the syringe as a huge shot of adrenalin was pumped into my aorta. She was the most beautiful woman I'd ever seen.

The quiz faded as I stared. She had an unusual haircut: short cropped and light brown, it emphasised her fine facial features and wide set eyes. And then, good god, she smiled, making her eyes squint and large dimples appear in her cheeks and there was something so infectious and mischievous in her smile that I found myself grinning as well. I knew I would need to see her again and again to confirm my eyes weren't deceiving me.

'Do you know, Adam?' asked Carrie, her voice arriving from a distance.

'What's that?' I asked.

'Do you know the answer?'

'To what?'

'To the question! Goodness me, we aren't going to do very well if you don't even listen.'

'Sorry, I was daydreaming. What was the question again?'

'Who wrote the song The Sisters of Mercy.'

'Leonard Cohen.'

'Are you sure?'

'I'm certain,' I said.

'Okay, Leonard Cohen it is,' said Carrie and wrote it down.

As the last question was about music, that meant the rest of the geography round had passed by without me noticing.

Until then I'd thought the idea of love at first sight a nonsense, a fabrication invented by smug couples over-romanticising the moment they met. But ridiculously premature worries as to whether my feelings would be reciprocated had already taken hold, for if not, wouldn't that be infatuation, a love without reason?

Who was she? I hadn't seen her at work, but perhaps she was new? Or maybe she was a friend of a colleague, so that I might never see her again... the thought so terrified me that I resolved not to let the evening pass without introducing myself. Besides, I was now in the army of single men and Sam would shoot me for treason if I bottled an opportunity like this.

I spent the rest of the quiz half listening to the questions, but unable to take my eyes off her, as if my attention was tied to her by a taut string. The shapes and contours of her features, and her expressions and mannerisms, were a wonder. Would someone as beautiful as her ever go for a guy like me? Or is there an empirical scale of beauty and we all have to accept our place on it?

When the quiz ended, I made my way over to Adrian at the bar, all the while keeping tabs on where she was. 'What are you having?' he asked.

'A pint of bitter, thanks. How did you get on?'

'Pretty good. Not sure where my team came, but we got nineteen out of twenty of the album covers right.'

'Which one got away?'

'David Hasselhoff's Night Rocker.'

'Didn't it have a picture of him on the album cover?' I asked.

'Yeah, standing on a car bonnet in distressed denim playing guitar in the rain, but Marcus had blacked his face out. Don't tell me you got that one right?'

'Can't remember, but I doubt it.'

'Good, if you had I'd have disowned you as a friend.' While Adrian placed the order, I looked back to her: she'd gone. No!

I panicked like a parent losing sight of their toddler in a crowd, jerking my head this way and that to find her. Then I saw her – picking up her bag near the stairs, about to leave. In a beat I'd transported myself with a few quick loping strides to the bottom of the stairs where I stood blocking her way out.

'Hi, I'm Adam,' I blurted, holding out my hand and grinning broadly because I felt nervous, excited, stupid and vulnerable all at once.

Her eyes widened in surprise, before softening as she smiled back. 'Hello, Adam, I'm Marianne.' She shook my hand, the feeling of skin on skin releasing another hit of adrenalin. For three long seconds I was speechless as my eyeballs drained my entire body's energy supply devouring the sight of her. Up close she was even more spellbinding, her irises a new definition of green set within a thin black circumference, and framed by long lashes that opened and closed as if in slow motion. Across her nose and cheeks a galaxy of pale freckles made me want to sigh out loud in wonder.

'Nice to meet you, Marianne. Have you just started working for us? I think I'd remember if I'd seen you before.'

'I just started this week, in–'

'Great!' I blurted out, my right hand clasping my chest. Marianne glanced at my hand, then up again, smiling quizzically, her dimples again drawing my attention. 'So how did you do in the quiz?' I asked.

'My team came second, so I guess we did okay. And you?'

'I'm not sure. I think we were denied victory because we didn't know it was David Hasselhoff playing guitar on that car bonnet. You probably got that one right.'

'I did not!' said Marianne, before realising I was teasing. She chuckled. 'I knew that Leonard Cohen wrote The Sisters of Mercy, and that's about as far from David Hasseloff as you can get.'

'You like Leonard Cohen?' I asked.

'I do. Why, are you a fan?'

'Sure, I like him a lot.'

She looked me up and down. 'Nah, I don't believe you, I think you're just saying that to impress me.'

'I am not!' It was my turn to realise she was teasing. 'I'll get you back for that,' I said, smiling. 'Are you seriously going now? These work evenings only get going once the compulsory entertainment ends.'

'I've really got to go, I promised my husband I'd meet him to catch the train together. I'm already late.'

I don't think I visibly reacted; at least, I tried not to, even though the mention of a husband felt like an iron fist reaching into my chest cavity and squeezing every last drop of blood from my heart. 'Fair enough,' I said. 'I won't detain you any longer.' I stepped aside.

'I'll see you around?' asked Marianne.

'You will.'

'Well, it was good to meet you, Adam.'

'And you, Marianne.'

As she walked up the stairs, contrasting emotions churned my insides. When eventually I looked up, Carrie was waving at me from the bar to come over for a drink.

10

At Hammersmith station the commuters huddled together in little conspiratorial groups along the platform where they anticipated the carriage doors would open when the tube arrived. I refused to join them. I had enough competition to deal with that day: competition for clients, competition for candidates, competition for sales and the Sales League Table. I'd be damned if I was also going to compete for a seat on the train.

Once aboard, I stood compressed in horrible intimacy with the commuters, like farm animals being transported to slaughter. As my temperature edged higher, I regretted wearing my heavy winter coat. A tall, bony gentleman squeezed next to me with his elbow in my ribs yawned expansively without covering his mouth and I caught a waft of his coffee-stained breath. A seasickness-like nausea started. My scalp began to itch. A bead of sweat gathered itself between my shoulders and trickled down the centre of my back.

And I was late, something tolerated by Roy, but not by Marcus. At Holborn, I tried to make up time by walking up the giant escalators, each step seeming steeper than the last, my thighs growing heavier and heavier as lactic acid built up in the muscles. I jogged down High Holborn – weaving past a preoccupied businessman emerging absent-mindedly from a coffee shop clutching his morning brew – and once at the office rushed up the stairs to the second floor, entered the open plan, stooped for the last few yards to make my entrance as inconspicuous as possible and slid into my chair.

'Morning, Adrian,' I whispered, pulling my laptop out of my drawer and plugging it in. Hot and clammy from the rush to work, I slipped off my coat and jacket while remaining seated.

'Morning, Adam.' Adrian pulled a face and nodded in the direction of Marcus. No sooner had I logged on and was about to begin work than in my peripheral vision I sensed Marcus standing up and staring at me over the partition which separated our desks, forcing me to look up.

'Were there tube delays this morning?' he asked.

'No, no, I don't think so,' I replied, shaking my head.

Marcus lifted his left arm ostentatiously and with his right hand drew back the sleeve of his shirt to examine his silver Rolex. 'But it's nine forty-six.'

'Sorry, I had lots to do this morning.' I decided against offering any further explanation for my lateness, even though I suspected the lack of a proper excuse would wind him up even more.

'Well, I'm sorry for inconveniencing you,' said Marcus, loudly enough for everyone to hear. 'Core hours are just something that happen to other people, aren't they?'

'I did work late twice last week, so I think it's reasonable to assume a bit of give and take.'

'In case it had escaped your notice, this is a recruitment agency, not the public sector or flipping burgers in McDonald's. You don't get time off in lieu for working a couple of extra hours. We're a service industry. What if a client had rung with an urgent inquiry at nine a.m.?'

'*Did* a client ring with an urgent inquiry at nine a.m.?' I asked.

'No, they did not.' Marcus now slowed his delivery as if explaining something very basic to an errant child. 'But that wasn't my question. My question was: what *if* a client had rung at nine a.m.?'

'Well...' I paused, searching for the right words. 'I guess you would have answered it for me and taken a message.'

Silence.

We stared at each other, both expressionless. Marcus's jaw muscles clenched. 'Let's see if this month's sales statistics put this conversation in perspective, shall we? For now, I want you to make up the time tonight. You need to make the effort to get to work on time – it's called getting out of bed earlier.'

He began preparing for the directors' Monday morning meeting, pulling on his bespoke suit jacket and easing his favourite gold Mont Blanc fountain pen into the inside pocket. He fidgeted with each of his shirt cuffs to ensure exactly the right amount of cuff was visible and straightened the knot on his striped yellow tie. His sartorial preparations complete, he placed some papers in his leather folio, zipped it conclusively and strode off.

I turned to Adrian. 'Hey, thanks for tipping me off about Marcus's mood.'

'No problem. He was ranting and raving again about your time-keeping before you arrived.'

'You'd think with this credit crunch he'd have better things to worry about than me being five minutes late,' I said. 'Anyway, more importantly, how was your weekend?'

'Good, but tiring. The Battle of Bosworth Field was quite a bloody one.'

'My kingdom for a horse!'

'Indeed. We stayed in the Cotswolds. Lovely area. I could see myself living there one day.'

'Tough commute to London though,' I said.

'You sound like Marcus.'

'Shit. Move there immediately.'

'YESSSS!' shouted a male voice. It was Luke, standing and punching the air in triumph. 'We need to get that bell installed in here so we can ring it each time we make a sale,' he said to his colleague Matt, who responded by giving him a high five.

Luke and Matt's temporary staff desk was where the real action was: in other words, the real money. Today, as usual, they wore pin-stripe suits – the thicker the pinstripe the better, for they liked being associated with the City, its glamour and sheen of success. Adrian called them walking barcodes. Wing collars, two tone shirts and 'funny' cufflinks such as a hot and cold tap, or a 'guilty' and 'not guilty' sign, were the other essential parts of their uniform.

Adrian and I exchanged a look. 'Our clients are still recruiting temps then,' I said.

'It makes sense,' said Adrian. 'Temps don't show up on their headcount like perms do. You and I are buggered if the economy keeps sliding.'

* * *

Later that day I had my annual appraisal with Marcus. The meeting started badly when he pointed out that I hadn't finalised my objectives twelve months earlier. This, according to him, sent out 'the wrong message regarding how seriously you take your career'. We'd reviewed my feedback forms and sales statistics for the year, after which Marcus asked me to give him a moment to make notes, the only sound in the room thereafter being the nib of his gold fountain pen gently scratching his notepad.

Appraisals with Roy had always taken place in restaurants. 'After a year's hard labour,' he would say, 'the least we can do is take you for a decent meal.' Here I was now in one of the office meeting rooms: sterile, harshly lit, institutional furniture, coffee-stained carpet tiles.

Eventually Marcus looked up from his papers with a very serious expression. 'So... what do you think your rating should be for the year?'

There were five ratings: Outstanding, Very Good, Good, Areas for Development and You Fail. Just kidding: the last category wasn't really called You Fail, I just can't remember what it was called. I'd received a Very Good rating for the past two years, admittedly coinciding with a roaring economy. 'I'm probably somewhere between a Good and a Very Good,' I replied.

'I think you're a Good,' said Marcus with a swiftness and firmness that suggested he'd already decided.

Although I was paid predominantly by commission, a Very Good rating carried a small additional bonus, which a Good rating did not. 'The thing is,' I said, 'I've worked just as hard this year as last year, and I received a Very Good last year, so I'd be disappointed with just a Good.'

'There's nothing wrong with a Good rating,' said Marcus. 'We award Good to those we consider to be doing just that – a good job.'

'But it suggests my performance is worse than last year.'

Marcus breathed in deeply and just about resisted sighing. 'Let's revisit your SMART objectives, shall we? Now, you remember what SMART stands for, don't you?'

'Sure I do. Specific, Measurable... er...'

Marcus stayed silent.

'... er... Achievable,' I let out a sigh of relief. 'Then the R is... Recorded–'

'No, that's incorrect,' said Marcus, quick as a snake striking. 'The R stands for Realistic. Specific, Measurable, Achievable, *Realistic* and Timed.'

'Oh. But you said earlier my objectives should have been recorded at the start of the year.'

'Of course they have to be recorded; that goes without saying. But that's not the R in SMART. *Realistic* is the R in SMART. In any case, we're getting diverted. One of the *specific* objectives all consultants are given is to increase sales year on year. However, as we've seen from your figures, that hasn't happened, which is why I'm suggesting a Good rating for you this year.'

I tried to think of something to justify a Very Good rating. After all, appraisals are only half about your actual performance, the other half being how well you present yourself, how well you remember all your successes, and how well you *spin* those successes. 'Since you mentioned that the R in SMART stands for Realistic, I'd like to ask whether it's realistic to expect an increase in sales in the current economic conditions?'

The very slightest beginning of a smirk suggested itself on Marcus's lips. 'Luke and Matt are increasing their sales by ten per cent month on month.'

Silence.

I wouldn't haggle. As Roy had said of his final meeting with John, it was too demeaning. I looked past Marcus at the broad featureless wall behind him.

'Okay, so if that's decided, let's think about next year,' he said.

'If we're talking about the future, this is probably the right time to express some worries I have about the state of the economy,' I said. 'Adrian and I have noticed a lot of client nervousness, especially since house prices started falling. If it continues, we're definitely going to see business slow even further.'

Marcus looked up to the ceiling and shook his head. 'All this pessimism annoys me. If too many people talk down the economy, confidence drains away and recession becomes a self-fulfilling prophecy. People should realise things are different now; we're in a new type of economy, led by the financial services sector. The Prime Minister has repeatedly said, "No more boom or bust". Do you really think he'd say that if there was a serious risk of recession?' He blew out a frustrated breath. 'Now, let's focus on what the coming year means for you and let's try and be positive, shall we?' He leant forward, placed his elbows on the desk and brought his hands together interlocking his fingers. He leant his chin on his hands. 'You know, I think this coming year is a really big one for you.'

'Is it?'

'Yes, it is. Now don't get me wrong, you've clearly done a good job here over the years and I gather you are a respected and valued member of the team. But I feel you could up your game and find an extra gear. You're one of our senior consultants and you should be thinking harder about your core competencies, such as finding new clients and emerging markets, and building your team.'

I stared back impassively.

'Let me put it another way,' said Marcus, sensing he was losing me. 'There's a new generation of people coming through, people like Luke and Matt. They're young and hungry and energised. If you're not careful, they're going to overtake you.'

I still didn't react. Good luck to Luke and Matt, but surely he didn't expect me to become like them?

'I think you need to give more thought to the future. You're not going to be single and living in a one-bedroom flat forever, are you? What happens when you have a family and kids? Are you going to have the money to buy a large house? How about a family car? And do you really want to risk sending your kids to the local comprehensive?'

I didn't necessarily resent him for this crude attempt to motivate me; it was his job after all. What concerned me was how he spoke a completely different language to me. All these wants and needs and must haves and minimum requirements made me tense and nervous. Did I really *have to* aspire to all the riches Marcus spoke of? Once you reach a level of comfortable subsistence, isn't all the rest just greed and vanity?

'And there's another thing,' said Marcus, pausing while maintaining eye contact.

'What's that?' I asked.

He paused again. 'I've been studying the team's financials very carefully.' A slight squint began to pinch his eyes. 'I couldn't help but notice how Roy's commission was allocated to you and Adrian shortly before he left.'

Silence. My cogs whirring.

'And?' I said, as nonchalantly as I could.

'It isn't company policy,' said Marcus.

'But everyone does it,' I said, repeating what Roy had said.

'Just because others have done it doesn't make it right.' Marcus raised his eyebrows at me. 'I'll tell you what. If you increase your sales in the next six months by twenty per cent, I'll let you keep Roy's commission.'

'But I just told you how nervous our clients are about taking on new staff. My sales are to a large extent out of my control.'

'I disagree. I think the harder you work, the more sales you make.'

Silence. It was more haggling I couldn't win. 'Tell me,' I said, 'if you do take Roy's commission away, where does it go?'

Marcus hesitated, his eyes flitting from my face to somewhere behind me, to the door, then back to me. 'It goes back to the company.'

Another silence. I now knew for sure I couldn't trust him. I changed tack. 'So let's say I do as you say and try to up my game. How do I go about that?' I genuinely hoped Marcus would be able to impart some commercial insights that I was clearly lacking.

Marcus leant right back in his chair, spreading his legs alarmingly wide and clasping his hands together behind his head. I was grateful for the table between us or my eyes would surely have been assaulted, particularly as he favoured bespoke fitted suits and got so excited when talking about business. As he held his spread-eagled posture, I spotted little sweat patches under his arms, which were at odds with his otherwise immaculate appearance. 'Do you want to know the simple way to make it round here?' he asked.

'Go on,' I said.

'Make me rich.'

I wasn't sure I'd heard him correctly. 'Excuse me?'

'I said make me rich.'

'Can you elaborate please?'

'It's simple. The more you please me by making me richer, the more I'm going to make sure you get your fair slice of the pie. It's such a simple system when you strip it back to basics, it amazes me how few people get it.' Maintaining his expansive pose, he grinned at me, a wide, teeth-baring grin held far too long, as though his facial muscles had frozen. It was the smile a psychopath gives… just before feverishly hacking his victim to death.

I tried to smile back, but inside me a piece of my soul had just died and feelings of nausea began eating me from the inside out. When my consciousness caught up with the nausea, I realised that one of the true horrors of capitalism is working every day in the knowledge that all your hard labour makes someone like Marcus even richer and more objectionable.

Marcus concluded the meeting by asking me to complete my appraisal forms and objectives for the next year 'as soon as possible'. In the brutal sales environment of a recruitment agency there was really only one objective – to make more money – but we always found new and innovative ways to express it each year in our objectives, usually prefixed by the phrase 'Going forward'. 'Going forward, formulate and action bespoke client recruitment solutions'; 'Going forward, develop and diversity client portfolio'; 'Going forward, identify key client stakeholders and monetise those relationships'. When you read them back, you realised you'd articulated your employer's objectives, not your own.

11

'Are you ready?' asked Sam, who had asked to meet me for another drink, this time at Ye Olde Mitre Tavern just off Hatton Garden, a quirky old nooks and crannies pub favoured by real ale drinkers.

'Ready for what?' I replied.

'Stage two.'

'Stage two?'

'Stage two of the tutorial. Of how to deal with being single.'

'Didn't we have the tutorial a couple of weeks ago?' The number of drinks we'd consumed that night had impaired my ability to remember the lessons, though I distinctly recalled that my male Darwinian genes were controlling my destiny and that I should be pitied for it.

'So you're ready to start dating?' asked Sam, a hint of doubt in his voice.

'Well… kinda… I think so.' My only recent romantic interest had been Marianne, but her married status had discouraged me from following it up, despite each glimpse of her around the office prompting the same adrenalin hit as at the quiz night. I slouched in my seat and sipped my beer at the injustice of a man being given such a head start on me that he'd managed to get a ring on her finger.

'You don't sound or look very ready, if you don't mind me saying so,' said Sam.

'I don't?'

'No, you don't. For instance, have you noticed who's at the bar?'

Looking over, two women of about thirty were ordering drinks. I hadn't seen them, or even noticed Sam watching them.

'You didn't pick up on their perfume when they arrived, did you?' asked Sam.

I shook my head.

'Or that neither of them have engagement or wedding rings?'

I shrugged my shoulders.

'Or that they've both put on makeup for the evening and look like they may have changed out of their work clothes? Right age to be looking for dates too, perhaps even to settle down. I bet if we were to approach them, they'd both be happy to talk.'

'We're not going to speak to them, are we?' I asked, rubbing my chin. 'I mean, I thought we were just having a drink and stage two of the tutorial.'

Sam looked at me askance. 'I should be forcing you as a soldier in the army of single men to go and engage with them, but I'm going to let you off. Do you know why?'

I breathed out a sigh of relief. 'Why?'

'Because you're a drain.'

'A drain?'

'An energy drain. Someone who sucks the life out of a conversation or human interaction by doubting himself. There's a time and a place for feeling down, but categorically *not* when you're dating.' He leant forward and beckoned me to do likewise. 'Listen. Women are the hardest fucking creatures on the planet to impress. They're genetically programmed to seek out men of ability, talent, energy and vision. Lethargy is not an option, Adam. You need to bring vitality to each interaction with a woman, so she feels more alive when she's with you than with anyone else in the world.'

I felt drained just listening to him and slumped back into my chair. 'Where do I get this energy from?'

'Okay, we spoke last time about dating being like boxing, do you remember?'

'Sure,' I said, nodding.

'So before he enters the ring, what does a boxer do?'

'I don't know... does he take a dump?'

'*What?!*'

'He might be nervous.'

'No, he trains, you idiot. He trains for the fight. What are you talking about him taking a shit for?'

'Oh, I see. Sorry.'

'Now then, when you were at uni, I remember you played some football and some cricket, right?'

'Yeah, that's right.'

'And now?'

'I've let it slip, to be honest.'

'It's hard to find time, isn't it?'

'It is really.'

'And gym membership costs quite a lot these days.'

'It does, yes.'

'And you prefer to kick back most evenings and listen to that Michael Bolton CD–'

'What?'

'Snap out of it, Adam! Life's not a dress rehearsal. You've got to start exercising. You've got to get match-fit.'

'Well, I do a bit of walking–'

'*Walking?!*' Sam doubled over in laughter and rocked backwards and forwards, pointing a finger at me as he did so. 'That's like saying you *breathe* a bit. Forget walking, that's what my dear old granny does for exercise. You're not getting any younger and your metabolism is slowing. You're looking a bit jowly these days, if you don't mind me saying so.'

'Jeez, Sam, just tell it to me straight, why don't you?' I took a large swig of my beer, then wondered how many calories I'd just taken down.

'Look, you asked for my help. You're big enough to take some constructive criticism, aren't you?'

'I guess so. But is exercise really necessary?'

'Yes, it's really necessary. So start running, every weekend. No excuses, no wimping out. It's the purest form of exercise and it stimulates endorphins, which mean you won't be a drain. When you're out there knackered and everything aches and it's freezing cold, just remember that every mile you run increases your chances of getting laid by five per cent. If you think of that, you'll find the strength to run on, trust me you will.'

'So once I'm fit, what next?'

'Well, when a boxer has trained, he steps into the ring. And what happens when he gets in the ring?'

'He shits himself because he's scared?'

'No, he does not shit himself. Besides, according to your training manual, he's already taken a dump back in the changing room. Come on, what does he do in the ring?'

'He fights?'

'Bingo. So he has to be ready to perform.' Sam took a draught of his pint and peered over the rim of his glass, his eyes travelling up and down my body. He slowly placed his pint down and gave me a look of sympathy. 'You don't look ready to perform.'

'What are you trying to say?' I asked, folding my arms.

'We need to discuss your appearance, but not before I get some beers in.' He downed the rest of his pint and stood over me, forcing me to knock back the rest of mine. 'Oh shit, I forgot to get any money from the cash machine, can you lend me a tenner?'

'Don't worry, I'll get them in,' I said, standing up and walking to the bar. The two ladies had found seats, so Sam couldn't force me to engage. While waiting to get served, I looked myself up and down. It had been a dress-down Friday at work, so I was wearing smart casual: brown brogues, jeans that had perhaps seen better days and a grey shirt that could have been ironed more carefully. I looked pretty normal, so I thought.

'So where did you get those old threads?' said Sam, nodding at my clothes while I placed another pint in front of him.

'These jeans are Next,' I replied, 'and this shirt was a Christmas present from my brother. It's GAP, I think.'

'No, I asked where *you* got your clothes from, not your Dad.'

'That's a bit harsh! It isn't that bad, is it?'

'It's not that bad, but it's all a bit tired. You could do with a refresh.'

'Men don't really care about fashion, do they?' I asked.

'Women like to be flattered, they like men to show they care. Turning up looking like Wurzel Gummidge makes it look like you couldn't give a damn. Get yourself down to King's Road or Covent Garden and splash out some money on clothes – you'll notice the difference in women's reactions to you.'

'Maybe I will,' I mumbled, while fidgeting with a beer mat.

'You're not convinced, are you?'

I let out a deep breath. 'I don't know. The truth is I feel comfortable in places like GAP. The thought of going to some trendy place and having shop assistants fawning all over me and making me try on skinny jeans or something... that's my definition of hell.'

'Who said anything about skinny jeans? I'm just talking about smart, new clothes. Look, clothing alone isn't going to persuade a woman to like you, but the stuff you're currently wearing doesn't sell you. Sorry to be so frank, I'm just trying to help you out here, buddy.'

'And it's appreciated, really it is. I'll look into some new clothes, I promise. So tell me, what do you think about Spurs' results this season?'

Sam sighed and slowly shook his head.

'What?' I asked.

'We haven't finished yet.'

'But I just said, I'll get some more clothes.'

'It's not just your clothes which need addressing, there's also the matter of your hair.'

'What's wrong with my hair?' I said, reaching up and stroking it forward, which had become a recent mannerism. It had only receded slightly, but it was worrying, like the sand in an egg timer slowly draining away. Even more concerning was the fact that I wasn't so much losing my hair, as re-distributing it, each look in the mirror revealing alarming discoveries such as hairs sprouting from my eyebrows and nostrils and ears which I could have sworn had never been there before.

'Where do you get your hair cut?' asked Sam.

'Wherever, just the local barbers, there's one near work.'

'Let me guess, grade three at the sides and back, short on top, £8.50 to you Sir, keep the change.'

'That's it, surely every guy does it that way? Why, where are you suggesting I go?'

'Toni & Guy.'

'You're joking? That's one of those places where they ask you if you want some *product* in your hair once it's cut, isn't it? What is *product* anyway? Makes it sound as though they're going to do something disgusting... in your hair.'

'It's gel, Adam.'

'If it's only gel, why don't they call it gel? I don't like the idea of a strange man rubbing warm sticky liquids on me without being very specific about the composition of it.'

'You can always turn down the product.'

'It's not just that, it's the whole intensity of those places. I'm a bloke, I'm uncomfortable talking about male grooming. And besides, my boss goes there and he's a wanker.'

'Yeah, but does he have a girlfriend?'

'He's married.'

'There you go then. Listen, I know it's expensive, but if I can afford it, so can you. So will you try it?'

I considered it for a while. I suppose if it helped I'd be stupid not to, but surely even Toni & Guy couldn't reverse the ageing process? 'Okay, I'll try it.'

'Good. Now then, have you been on any dates?' asked Sam.

I thought about the last few months of watching perpetual sport on TV and listening to music in my darkened flat, fuelled by a world record breaking supply of pot noodles. 'No, I haven't really got round to any dating,' I confessed.

'Then you need to get out there. You need to step into the ring. And you need to think about the types of women you want to date.'

'That's the thing about you, Sam,' I said, 'you've got a finely tuned idea of what you're looking for. But I'm not sure I want to be ruling out whole races or sizes of women just yet. I guess if you pushed me I'd say I like English girls. I don't know, it must be cultural or something. Maybe familiarity.'

'English girls, you say?' asked Sam. 'Then you've got a problem, I'm afraid.'

'Have I? Why?' I asked.

'Because English girls are the hardest to crack, in my experience.'

'Why is that?'

'It's complicated, but with an English girl you've got to be a chameleon and trapeze artist to pull it off.'

'You mean I can't just be myself?'

'That's a joke, right?' said Sam, with a look of alarm.

'Er... no,' I said.

'Listen, with all women, but especially English women, you can't just be yourself and hope they'll like you. It's much trickier than that. Let me ask you something – are you the type of guy to hold a door open for a woman?'

'Yeah, sure.'

'Good, that's chivalrous and women like that. At least most do, it's only the mad nutter lesbian feminists who have an issue with it and we're not interested in them anyway. How about cooking, do you cook?'

I pictured pouring the boiling water from the kettle into the plastic pot up to the line and struggling to wait the required two minutes until the dehydrated noodles and mysterious powder had synthesised into the nutritious snack. 'A little. I do a good risotto, some pasta dishes, a decent roast.'

'Good, good. Women like a guy who can cook. Now then, would you send flowers to a new girlfriend, perhaps to her office, so all her work colleagues can see how desired she is?'

I cocked my head to one side and looked up to the ceiling. 'Mmmm, that's maybe a bit ostentatious for me. But I would buy her some flowers, you know, for her flat, for the kitchen table, that sort of thing.'

'Okay, so not averse to flowers in the right context. How about poetry, would you write an ode to love for a sweetheart?'

'Steady on, Sam, that's going a step too far.'

'That's my point. Where do you draw the line? Listen, when your old man dated, things were easier. There were accepted expressions of love, like flowers and poetry. These days, you start sending large bouquets of flowers to a woman's office and follow that up with poetry, she'll slap a court order on you banning you from approaching within fifty metres on the grounds that you're a stalker.' He poured a huge measure of beer down his throat, wiped away the froth from his upper lip with the back of his hand and let out an almighty guttural belch. 'As I said, it's complicated. Women these days, and *especially* English women, want you to be all things. They want you to be the traditional alpha male – which means a good job, handsome, sporty, confident, worldly – but they also want you to be in touch with your feminine side – which means being sensitive, caring, emotionally intelligent and good in the kitchen. Men are in crisis, Adam; we don't know what we're meant to be any longer.'

'Crikey,' I said, following his lead and fortifying myself with a voluminous glug of beer, which finished it. I needed another. 'Shall I get the next round in?' I asked.

'With chasers,' replied Sam.

12

About a month had passed since the quiz night when one day I entered the kitchen area at work and *she* was standing in front of the coffee machine. We were alone. A tingling sensation prickled my skin and I gulped down a deep breath silently. Five million years of human male gene evolution then bullied me to glance down at Marianne's waist and appreciate its slimness compared to the swell of her hips, all hugged by a dark brown dress cut to just above the knee. 'Hello, Marianne,' I said, trying to keep my voice calm.

She turned. 'Hi, Adam. How are you?'

'I'm good, thanks,' I said in extreme understatement, for I felt like the bionic man, with telescopic vision and pin-sharp hearing, ready to leap walls or tackle lions. Her perfume reached me: light, fresh, elevating. 'How are you settling in?' I asked.

'Great. Everyone's been really friendly and helpful. I felt like the new kid at school for the first week, but it's getting easier.'

I'd replayed what she looked like in my mind every day since meeting her, yet up close more nuances and subtleties revealed themselves. Was it the light, or was there some hazel in there amongst the green of her eyes? 'I'm glad to hear we've made you feel welcome,' I said.

'Well, most people have made me feel welcome... except you.'

'What?!' The beginnings of a blush moved into my cheeks.

Marianne smirked. 'Just kidding. It's just that you introduced yourself at the quiz and I haven't heard from you since.'

'Sorry about that,' I said. 'I've been working pretty hard.'

The coffee machine bleeped and she picked up her drink, which looked like a cappuccino. 'I don't know why I drink this stuff. It tastes like Marmite from this machine.'

'There's a café just around the corner. Seeing as I've been so rude, perhaps you'll let me buy you a coffee?' My own boldness surprised me.

Marianne's eyes alternated back and forth between my facial features for a few long seconds. 'Okay, let's go for a coffee,' she said eventually. 'I'd like that. Email me.' She smiled and walked out of the kitchen area.

I felt like dropping to my knees with arms held aloft as if I'd just scored the World Cup winning goal. Sam would have been proud of me; I was stepping back into the ring!

Then I remembered her circumstances.

* * *

With considerable difficulty, I left it a day before emailing Marianne. I figured it was only a coffee. She responded saying she could meet me the next day at 10 a.m.

For the rest of that day I tried not to think about her, not wanting to turn it into a big deal. I failed. And the more I thought about her, the clearer it became how much easier it would be if my first proper chance to get to know her tomorrow revealed her as some way flawed and unable to live up to her physical beauty. Then I would be released from the suffocating preoccupation that had already taken hold of me.

As soon as I sat down at my desk the next morning, I checked the time: nine o'clock, just an hour to go. Throughout the next hour I couldn't drag my eyes from the clock, and at five to ten, set off.

I'd forgotten that the coffee place next door had recently been converted into a Starbucks. Previously it had been a café run by an elderly Portuguese couple and I'd been in there most days to buy their delicious pastéis de nata. Starbucks didn't appeal to me, mainly because I was a tea drinker and enjoyed the ritual of making my own. And £1.50 for a tea was a rip-off. I'd never really worked out the appeal of expensive coffee places, but perhaps the morning and afternoon visit to Starbucks was just the modern day equivalent of the fag break of old, a chance to step away from your desk and give yourself a little reward.

On arrival, I joined a short queue and within seconds Marianne came up behind me. 'Hello, Adam,' she said.

'Oh, hi. Cappuccino?'

'How did you know I like cappuccinos?'

'Er... lucky guess, I suppose.' I thought perhaps she had a client meeting that day, as she appeared immaculate in a grey-green pencil skirt, white blouse and high heels. Her damn enchanting perfume again reached me.

We found a table in the corner and sat down opposite each other. 'So...' I said, conscious I had one of those goofy, impossible-to-suppress grins, like someone had just jammed a coat hanger into my mouth sideways.

'So...' said Marianne, carrying the same amused expression as when I'd blocked her exit at the quiz night. 'How long have you worked here?'

I counted back. 'Almost nine years. How about you, what made you change jobs?'

Her expression turned inward to one of seriousness. 'I was doing very well at my last place. I'd built up an incredibly successful desk over four years and had almost a hundred people working on my books. But the owners reneged on the bonuses and commission they promised me.'

'They didn't? Though perhaps that's indicative of the industry we're in?'

'The industry is fine. The problem was the owners of the business, who lied to me.'

'Do you think it will be different here?' I asked.

'I've got it in writing this time.'

I nodded. 'So you really like recruitment?'

'I love it. I get a buzz out of it. How about you?'

I hesitated. 'It's been okay up 'til now, but it's getting tougher.' My mind travelled back to the day of Roy's sacking and the way he'd reached up to Joan's photograph, taken it down and stared at it a while, before placing it carefully inside his briefcase. 'My old boss was sacked a few months ago and there's been lots of changes since.' I thought it best to move the conversation on. 'So how did you end up in recruitment?'

'Well, I did a history degree, which doesn't provide many obvious career paths.'

I shook my head, disbelieving.

'What?' asked Marianne.

'I did history too. At Leeds.'

'Ha! First you copy my love of Leonard Cohen and now you're stealing my degree. Mind you, mine was at Durham, so was clearly harder than yours.'

I laughed, enjoying her feistiness. 'I got a two-one, how about you?'

Marianne's dimples appeared again.

'Don't tell me you got a first, I won't believe you,' I said.

'I did. Don't blame me you didn't study hard enough.'

'What periods of history did you study?' I asked.

'The causes of World War One, the Russian Revolution–'

'Ha! Those sound more like general knowledge to me. I did a proper history degree: the Wars of the Roses, the Tudors–'

'Yeah and you probably spend your weekends dressed up in chain mail pretending to be in battles.'

'No, but my colleague Adrian does and he did a Physics degree. Go figure.'

Marianne sipped her cappuccino and peered at me over the rim of her inordinately large cup, which she held in both hands. As she did so the sparkle of her engagement ring caught my eye.

'Did you go straight into recruitment after university?' I asked.

'No, I did a TEFL course – Teaching English as a Foreign Language?'

I nodded.

'I spent a year in Naples. To be honest, it was pretty terrifying. I was only twenty-one and found myself teaching sixteen-year-old boys. You can imagine their reaction to having a naive, young Englishwoman in front of them...' Marianne shook her head.

Yep, I thought, I can imagine the stupefied reactions of sixteen-year-old Italian boys to seeing a twenty-one-year-old you.

'And some of the kids were from really rough backgrounds,' she continued, looking down and stirring the froth into her coffee. She lifted her eyes, now exhibiting a fierce resolve. 'But I learnt so much about myself that year. I learnt that I had to be brave and back myself. I've been doing that ever since.' She held my stare just a fraction too long, which had the effect of momentarily mesmerising me. Did she do that on purpose? 'Do you like Italy?' she asked eventually.

I did now. I thought on my feet. 'Any country which prioritises food and romance can't be bad,' I said. And in the few seconds since she'd mentioned Italy, I'd mapped out our future together: buying and renovating an old farmhouse in Tuscany for our summer home;

driving the Amalfi Coast in an open top car; wine-tasting tours of the vineyards in Chianti. I'd been hopeless at languages at school, but learning Italian would now be easy, given that my levels of motivation would border on the insane. 'I've been to Naples too,' I added.

'No? Really?' said Marianne.

'I stayed there for a few days when I went interrailing after uni. Caught a ferry from there to Sardinia.'

'I learnt to love Naples,' said Marianne, closing her eyes to picture the city. 'I'm visiting a friend there next month. While she's at work, I'm going to sit in my favourite café all day sipping cappuccinos, reading a novel and watching the world go by. I can't think of anywhere I'd rather be.'

'I did much the same when I was there, in a café with a green striped awning near the train station.'

'No! You're kidding?'

'Why?'

'That's the café I'm talking about.'

'You're doing that thing again, Marianne. First you copy me by pretending to like Leonard Cohen and here you are stealing my favourite café. Where's it going to end?'

She reached out and playfully pushed my forearm, which sent a jolt of energy through me. 'Shut up, you,' she said. 'I bet I discovered them before you. Now, tell me about your time at uni.'

I told her some amusing anecdotes from my time at Leeds: the challenges of living in an all-male house of seven, the three hours a week of lectures, the fact I knew the screenplays of Easy Rider, Taxi Driver and Deer Hunter by heart. I omitted certain details, such as the abject squalor and the monthly pilgrimage my hard-up starving housemates and I made to the local Pizza Hut to gorge ourselves half to death on their eat-as-much-as-you-can deal at £5.99, followed by a skinful of beer and waking up the next morning with the infamously clammy hangover known as the 'cheese sweats'. 'I learnt about life,' I said.

'If you were anything like the men I knew at university, you probably lived in a pigsty on a diet of fast food and beer,' said Marianne.

I laughed nervously, while rubbing my chin.

'You said you went interrailing after uni. How was that?'

'Like you, I learnt a lot about myself. But you know, the best thing to happen on that trip was learning to surf. The school friend I was travelling with taught me. Thinking about it, everyone should teach someone they know about something they love. The world would be a better place for it. I'd spent the early part of that summer temping at a hospital doing cleaning, so the holiday was the payoff. My friend took me to Biarritz and we camped there for two weeks while he taught me to surf. It wasn't easy to begin with, but I remember the feelings at the end of the first day: the salt drying on my skin, the heat of the sun still in my face and all my muscles aching, but aching in a good way. I couldn't wait for the next day to arrive to try it again. After two days I was dreading leaving. After two weeks my body would still feel itself being carried away on waves when I went to sleep at night.'

'It sounds amazing,' said Marianne. She asked me how I'd got into recruitment and I explained how my first couple of years in London had been more an extension of university, financed by a series of mindless and soul-destroying temping jobs. In turn, she told me how after university she'd worked for a recruitment consultancy in her hometown of Bristol, eventually moving to London five years ago.

'Where do you live in London?' she asked.

'In Hammersmith,' I said. 'Next to the river. How about you?'

'Harrow. It's okay.' She shrugged her shoulders. 'Although when I moved to London I hoped to move into London itself. Only reaching Harrow makes me feel like I fell a little bit short. Do you live alone?'

'I do, yes.' A little silence followed. 'I came out of a seven-year relationship last year.'

Another silence, with Marianne keeping very still and concentrated. 'I bet you live in a typical bachelor pad,' she said eventually, 'with a fridge full of beer, and you haven't changed the sheets in months.'

I laughed, while rubbing my chin. I decided against elaborating on my domestic circumstances, figuring that the unnerving accuracy of her description, coupled with a complete lack of home furnishings, heavy solitary drinking and a pot noodle diet were not the best of my qualities to advertise.

Marianne looked at her watch. 'I have to go, I've got to call a client at eleven.' We stood to leave; I'd barely touched my tea. As we walked the short distance back to the office, she said, 'Are you going on this course in a couple of weeks' time?'

'Sure am,' I said.

'It sounds dreadful. Do they have them every year?'

'Yep, every year. Two long and agonising days spent corporate teambuilding. Tends to be free drinks in the evening, which helps you forget what you've just endured.'

We walked up the stairs and entered the open plan office together, said goodbye and I peeled off to return to my desk. One or two people, including Adrian, looked up. The thought of them associating me with Marianne brought back the goofy grin.

I stared at my screen without seeing anything. My heart raced and I was a little short of breath. Damn! Damn damn damn! No personality flaws had been revealed, no psychological defects. On the contrary, she was funny, charismatic, intelligent. And impossibly beautiful. But married to the wrong man.

13

The lawn at the back of the Georgian Palladian house lay flawless, like the baize of a snooker table, and two shades of green from the impeccable straight up and down lines of that morning's mower. It was the year's first day of glorious sunshine, strong enough to leave a bead of sweat on your brow, but without yet having evaporated the scent of moist grass clippings still floating on the air. Near the house some tables had been pushed together and covered with a crisp, white, laundered linen cloth, atop which stood rows of champagne flutes catching the light and refracting it in an amiable way. The guests had congregated in groups on the lawn, the hum of their conversation interspersed with the sound of laughter and the chinking of glasses, whilst a number of children darted about, ducking and weaving between the groups of adults.

'What lovely weather for a wedding,' said Rachel, looking around herself. 'Is there a more beautiful month of the year than May in England?'

'You're right, it's stunning,' I said. 'And they've certainly pushed the boat out.' I lowered my voice. 'Tell me though, how many brides really enjoy their wedding day? There's so much pressure; the pressure to look perfect, the pressure that every last detail has to be spot on. Can you really relax and enjoy it?'

'It does seem rather competitive these days,' said Rachel.

'Competitive? That's one way of putting it.' I lowered my voice further, to a whisper, and turned away from the other guests. 'I don't want to put a downer on today, it's an amazing set-up, but isn't it just a little bit narcissistic? If you were being cruel, you could call it a huge vanity project for the bride. What happens if you haven't got the money for a wedding like this, does it mean you love each other any less?'

'The cost of weddings seems to be going up at the same speed as divorce rates.' Rachel looked past me. 'But you've got to admit, there *is* something magical about a bride on her wedding day.'

'She certainly looks good, if that's what you mean,' I said.

'No, I mean more than that. Look closely.' She put her arm around my shoulder and coaxed me to turn around to look at Jess, the bride, who was moving between the guests with the same teeth-whitened smile she'd worn since the service. 'See how she glides. She's ethereal, somehow embodying all the best qualities of woman-hood.' She nodded towards the groom, Ben. 'He just looks like he's put on a nice suit.'

'She does look amazing,' I said, 'but even I would look good with a diamond that size on my finger.'

'Diamonds don't suit men,' said Rachel. 'Footballers and rappers may disagree, but they're wrong. You see, diamonds are full of mystery and that's why women wear them, as a sign of their mystery. Men have their own qualities, such as strength and courage and determination, but no mystery. That's why men fall in love with women – to try to solve the mystery – but women don't fall in love with men – they just love being loved.'

Rachel's words rendered me silent as I worked through their meaning. 'In case you'd forgotten, Rachel, I'm a single man now, lonely and unloved. When you say things like that about women it scares me.'

She shrugged. 'Actually, it was my mum who used to say that about diamonds. I'm not saying it's true.'

It was Jess and Ben's wedding and Rachel and I were two of the few single people there. Rachel wore a long pale blue dress with yellow floral embroidery and a cropped white cardigan, her look contrasting markedly with the showy dresses and hats of most of the other female guests.

'Is this day ever going to happen for either of us?' I asked. 'You remember our pact: if we're both single at forty we're going to marry each other.'

'I remember. And it looks increasingly likely...'

'How is Richard?' I asked.

She paused and sucked gently on her lower lip. 'He's okay.' She paused again. 'And still with his wife.'

'Is he still making regular trips to London?'

'He works three days a week in London, so yes, he is.'

I turned to face her square on. 'That's not what I meant and you know it. Does he still stay over at yours when he comes to London?'

Rachel looked out unseeingly over the guests on the lawn. When she returned her look to me, her eyes were alive and penetrating. 'Yes, he still stays. And yes, he keeps promising to leave his wife.' Her face now held a fierce concentration, quite mesmerising in its intensity. 'But I still love him. I know you can't understand it, but that doesn't make it any less true.'

'All I've ever said is that he's made you a lot of promises and yet nothing changes. As an outsider looking in, it just seems as though he's... he's getting away with it. He gets to play the family man on the one hand and the dynamic young lover on the other. He's lying to everyone, including himself.'

'Stop being so sanctimonious.'

'If the boot was on the other foot, you would say that friends speak the truth to each other, even when it hurts.'

She opened her mouth to say something, but swallowed her words. Eventually she said, 'I can't just walk away. Not now.'

Marianne popped into my head, as was now often happening. What was she doing today? I attempted to picture her in my mind's eye, but couldn't quite capture her as sharply as I wanted to. I tried to push thoughts of her to the back of my mind to concentrate on the here and now.

A young boy approached, perhaps four years old, dressed in grey check trousers and matching sky blue tie and waistcoat, his hair brushed into a side parting. 'I like your dress,' he said, looking up at Rachel.

'And I like your waistcoat,' she said, squatting down and straightening his tie.

The boy's hand rose to his mouth and his fingers hooked over his lower teeth as he thought through what to say. 'My dad had to do my tie this morning, I'm not old enough to do it.'

Rachel said something about him soon being able to do it, but I wasn't listening, because an electronic pulse of fear shot into my head as a realisation hit me with the force of a lightning strike: I might never become a father.

During my years with Louise, I'd just vaguely assumed it would happen; we would get married and have kids eventually. Now I faced the realisation for the first time that there were no guarantees, no certainties; I could miss out on the most important adventure of my life.

'You okay?' asked Rachel.

'What's that?'

'Are you okay? You look preoccupied.'

'I'm fine. I was just thinking.' I continued to stare at the children dashing about on the lawn.

'What about?' She peered at me closely.

'I was just thinking that by the time my father was my age he had two kids. And not babies either, he had two children, aged what... about six and eight.' Rachel also looked out at the children capering around and seemed on the verge of saying something. For a moment I feared I'd been insensitive to raise the subject, given her circumstances, before suddenly realising I hadn't seen Louise yet. I scanned the guests. 'I haven't seen Lou yet today, have you?'

'She's not coming,' said Rachel, without making eye contact.

'What? But she's one of Jess's best friends.'

'She's... she's a bit under the weather.'

'What's wrong with her?'

'They don't know. I mean, the doctor doesn't know. I'm sure she'll be fine.'

It sounded like a crap excuse, and too coincidental that Louise had suddenly taken ill just before the first major social event since our break-up. 'She hasn't kept away to avoid me, has she?' I asked.

'She's not avoiding you. I can categorically say it's nothing to do with you.'

'Okay... well, that's good.' I saw no point in pushing Rachel further; she shouldn't be forced to take sides. I took a long sip of champagne.

A tall man in black tails with a vivid red waistcoat and bow tie approached the edge of the lawn from the house, rang a clanging bell and announced in a practised, booming voice that the wedding breakfast was about to commence and could the guests please take their seats.

People began drifting towards the house and parents rounded up their children to usher them into a side room, reserved as a crèche. As Rachel and I made our way towards the house my stomach tightened as I thought about the seating plan. What if Jess and Ben had decided to have one of those dreaded 'singles tables'? I joined the scrum at the table plan outside the dining room, each of the tables named after a destination where Jess and Ben had holidayed together. Rachel wasn't on my table. I recognised a few names, but they weren't exactly close friends.

Finding my table, I exchanged hellos with my fellow diners. To one side of me was Laura, a medical student from university, who I remembered as a studious, quiet type. I knew she was married, so I'd been spared a singles table. On the other side was George, another university colleague, a rugger bugger, now a lawyer in the City, who when drunk always recounted a story about the initiation ceremony at the university rugby club involving naked men standing on tables downing pints. I poured myself a glass of red wine and offered some to Laura.

'You've obviously forgotten, I don't drink,' she said.

'Oh, right,' I said, but before properly engaging my brain I'd said one of those lines you immediately regret. 'More drink for me then.'

Laura gave me the thinnest of smiles, the smile of someone who'd heard the line a hundred times before. People who didn't drink made me nervous. I could understand those who'd once drunk and were now abstinent, but to be abstinent from the outset? Some sort of control issue, surely?

Once the goat's cheese, roasted walnut and beetroot starter had arrived, Laura said, 'So, Adam, your wife couldn't make it today?'

'I'm afraid I'm not married,' I said.

'Your girlfriend then – what's she up to?'

'I don't have a girlfriend, either. I'm single. But you may remember I dated Jess's friend Louise for a few years.' Why did I just say that? I sounded so defensive. 'Louise and I broke up recently,' I added.

'Oh,' said Laura, staring at me with a look of bewilderment, as though a single man in his mid-thirties was some kind of mythical, now extinct beast, like a unicorn or a dodo. A long silence endured between us; it seemed my admission of recently coming out of a relationship was a bit of a conversation killer at a wedding breakfast.

I thought a change of subject might ease the atmosphere. 'How about you, how's the family?' I asked.

'Very well, thank you. Oli is almost one now, so as you can imagine, he's keeping Andrew and me busy.'

'And Oli is your second, right?'

'Third, actually. Charlie is our oldest, he's six now and Milly is three.'

'Well, that's great.' The electronic pulse of fear shot into my head again and I gripped the stem of my wine glass so hard I thought it might snap in two. Laura was the same age as me and had three kids already. I was thirty-four... I could be thirty-five or thirty-six before I met someone... then we might not get married for a few years... and of course conception can be difficult...

'Andy was telling me earlier what it's like with three kids,' said George, speaking across me to Laura. 'I don't know how you do it. Amy and I find that two is a madhouse! How about you, Adam, any kids yet?'

'No, not yet,' I said, forcing what I hoped was a cheerful expression. 'At least not that I know of.' I laughed half-heartedly.

George persisted. 'But perhaps in the future?'

'I've got to find a girlfriend first,' I said.

George sat back in his chair and pulled his chin in. 'Jesus, Adam, I didn't realise single men of our age existed any more. Well played, man!' He slapped me on the back, causing me to lurch forward. Perhaps he was jealous of my single status, remembering his days as a single man at the university rugby club playing the biscuit game with the forwards.

Laura diplomatically tried to change the subject. 'Have either of you been on holiday this year?'

'Not yet,' said George, 'but we're going to Tuscany in August. Our oldest, Tilly, was very difficult on the flights last year, especially during take-off and landing.'

'Try getting her to suck on a boiled sweet,' said Laura. 'The sucking helps them equalise their ears.'

'Thanks, we'll try that. And we're a bit worried about Molly, our youngest. She's teething, so we're not sure whether to just take milk powder, or whether she'll be starting solids by then...'

And so the conversation went on: MMR jabs, milk bottle brands, baby seats, nurseries versus nannies, childcare vouchers and a cure-all potion called Calpol. Jesus, give me some. And since when was it obligatory for every child's name to end in an -ee sound? All I could do was sit there, drink, and nod like a puppet while looking like The Joker with a hollow fixed grin and teeth turned purple from the wine.

But Laura and George had just been warming up. 'George,' asked Laura a little later, again across me, 'how did you meet Amy?'

'We met at a party at uni. Do you know, the moment Amy walked into the room I knew, I *just knew*, right then and there I *just knew* that she was the woman I was going to marry.'

'Aaaarrrr,' sighed Laura. 'How sweet. You're so right, it's something you *just know*. When I met Andy, he thought I was a bit boring and I thought he was a bit too much of a lad, but even then, I think deep down we knew there was that connection, that spark.'

'Can I ask how you both *just knew*?' I asked. 'I mean, with all the people in the world, how can you just know they're the one when you've only just met them, or even only just laid eyes on them?'

Laura looked at me, her expression slowly softening to one of pity, as though I were one of her patients at the hospital. 'You'll know, trust me, when you meet her you'll *just know*. And what's more, it'll happen when you least expect it.' She placed her hand on my forearm: another reassuring gesture for the unwell patient. 'I think some single people try a bit too hard.' She patted my forearm lightly. 'If only they just relaxed I think they'd be more likely to meet someone.'

Eventually we reached the speeches, and as soon as the Best Man sat down, I made my excuses and made for the bar, where most of the university rugby team which Ben and George had played in were convening. A drinking game began, the one where you take turns to name famous people using the first letter of the previous surname as the first letter of the next christian name, and no hesitation allowed.

'Client Eastwood.'

'Eddie the Eagle.'

'Switch direction, switch direction, that's a double E.'

'Elle Macpherson.' Large cheer!

'Er...' I said.

'HESITATION!' cried the mob and I had to down a three-finger measure of beer while everyone jeered. I'd got confused by the Mac in Macpherson. I'd also failed to recognise that my drinking companions were generally twice my size and hadn't quaffed as much wine as me at dinner. It wasn't long before the beer mixed with the red wine and the champagne...

Weddings are a classic place to meet people. I'm single. It's time to step back into the ring! But wait! What about Marianne? Shouldn't I be saving myself for her? She's got a husband. And it's Saturday night. She's probably at the cinema, or having a candlelit dinner, but whatever, it's with him. No, forget Marianne, let me have more beer. Yeah, down it!

Yeah, that's Michael Jackson's 'Can you feel it?' Damn right I can feel it! And I bet that bridesmaid Lara can feel it too, standing there in that short dress. She won't mind being interrupted. She wants to be interrupted!

'Hi, you did really well today.' *Shit, that came out a bit too loud.* 'Thanks.'

Why's she turning her back to me? 'Do you want to dance?' *Shit, I think I may have slurred those words a bit, but I think I got away with it, it's loud in here.*

'Not now.'

She doesn't look very happy. This one will make her laugh. 'No means maybe, maybe means persuade me?'

'What? Look, can you let us talk please? We're trying to catch up.'

Fuck this. I WILL pick myself up again. Who cares, she's spent the whole day lapping up male attention, it's gone to her head, who wants to know a woman like that anyway? I want more beer.

Yeah, that's 'Blame It On The Boogie'. I know this one! I learnt the moves to this years ago on that holiday. Let me onto that dance floor!

'Don't blame it on the sunshine' – *Yeah, hands in the air and sway them to the left!*

'Don't blame it on the moonlight' – *Yeah, hands low and to the right!*

'Don't blame it on the good times' – *Pelvic thrust! Pelvic thrusts! You betcha!*

'Blame it on the boogie' - *Moonwalk moonwalk – yeah! What's that? People pointing at me and laughing from the side of the dance floor? They're just jealous, it's called natural rhythm.* 'Don't blame it on the sunshine' – *Here we go again – oh yeah!*

Bloody hell, it's hot, I need another beer. Now that's one pretty waitress, let's block her way. 'Hi.'

'Hello.'

Can't place her accent, but it's foreign. Exotic, innit! 'What's your name?' *Whoops, a little stagger there, how did that happen?*

'I've really got to go, I have work to do.'

I WILL pick myself up again. I'm thirsty, but for a proper drink, none of this warm beer piss. Tequila! That's what I need. Let me get back to the bar. 'Tequilas?!' *Yeah! Where's my credit card?*

Where's Rachel? Fortune favours the brave, right? Women respect a man who's decisive enough to make the first move, right? And what could be more romantic than a kiss at a wedding?

Yeah, 'New York, New York!' This one's brilliant. There's Rachel! It is her, isn't it? Shit, the room's tipping sideways – woah – it's righting itself.

Yeah, great idea, let's all get into a circle. Can-can steps, yeah!

Shit, the song's ending… there she is. 'Hiya!' *She's hugging me back, what have I got to lose? Here goes the lunge...*

'No, Adam, please.'

No means maybe? 'You can't prefer a married man with kids.'

'Fuck off. It would be like kissing my brother.'

14

'Okay – okay, I respect your decision. Thanks for letting me know... goodbye.' I smacked the telephone down with a crack, my hand gripping the receiver so hard it vibrated in its cradle. 'Shit!' I said, too loudly. I'd been working on this guy for months; he'd been to two interviews and both he and the client had been making positive noises about one another, only for him now to turn the job down.

'He said no, didn't he?' asked Marcus.

'Yes, he said no,' I replied.

A flinch of annoyance passed over Marcus's face. 'You really needed that sale, Adam.'

'I told you everyone's nervous and it's getting worse. People are too scared to change jobs. That guy probably thinks if he's the last in he'll be the first out if there's redundancies.'

'Oh come on,' said Marcus, rolling his eyes, 'it's not the economy at fault here. I'm not sure you really prepped that guy hard enough.'

'I've been calling him every other week for six months and every other day for the last fortnight.'

'Yes, but you should have sold him the job harder.'

'What, even if it's not in his best interests?'

'Forget *his* interests, what about *our* interests?'

'But if he takes the job and then quits, the client will–'

'Just *shut up*,' spat out Marcus through clenched teeth, the intensity of his delivery rendering me silent. 'I haven't got time for a debate. If the economy's as bad as you're making out, you'll just have to work harder. Our sales figures for this month are dreadful.'

Adrian had been listening in. 'Surely our figures can't be that bad. And besides, we had a record year last year.'

'Yes, but that was *last* year,' replied Marcus. 'Our success then means that our targets for this year are even more stretching. It's essential we grow.'

Adrian stroked his goatee in contemplation. 'Can't this year's targets be scaled back if there're more problems in the economy? Adam's right, people are nervous.'

Marcus looked at him with just the faintest, barely perceptible, shaking of his head. 'You can't change targets halfway through the year. That would be rewarding failure.' He turned to me. 'Adam, get onto the client to explain what happened, and make sure you blame the candidate, who's clearly a timewaster. I don't want the client thinking we didn't do our homework on that guy. You need to find someone else to fill the vacancy; at least we're the first to know it still needs filling.' He walked off to talk to Luke and Matt, presumably in the hope of more positive news.

* * *

I called Sam. No reply from his home phone. I tried his mobile.

'Hello?'

'Sam, it's Adam.'

'Adam! You in the ring yet? Hold on a second, let me get off this ladder.'

'Why are you up a ladder?'

'I'm working.'

'What, at nine in the evening?'

'Things are a bit tough. How's things with you?'

'That's why I was calling,' I said. 'There's been some developments.'

'Why, what's happened?'

'Well... I think I may have disgraced myself at Jess and Ben's wedding and there's this girl at work–'

'Fuck me, sounds complicated. You free after work tomorrow?'

'Yeah, I am.'

'Good, I'll see you then. But I'll have to be quick, I've got a date later on.'

'Okay.'

'See you then.'

'Bye.'

* * *

We met up near my work, this time in a pub called The Ship, a snug little inn tucked away down a narrow winding alley behind Holborn tube station. It was an aptly named pub too, for inside it was close and musty, with worn wooden floorboards, as if you were being stowed deep in a ship's cramped galley.

'Now, you remember what I said last night?' said Sam, after I'd got the first round in and we'd found seats. 'I haven't got long before this date.'

'Who is she?'

'Her name's Sakina.'

'How did you meet her?' I asked.

'At the gym. I noticed her going into a spin class. I wouldn't normally be seen dead doing a spin class, but needs must and I joined it. Half an hour sitting on the bike behind her persuaded me I needed to ask her out or I'd never forgive myself. I've got a nice restaurant booked, just praying she offers to go halves. Anyway, I've got half an hour.' He checked his wristwatch.

'Okay, I'll be quick, but tell me, how come you weren't at the wedding?'

'I'm afraid I once dallied with Jess's friend Lara and made the mistake of not calling her afterwards. I don't think that group of girls were very impressed. I hear Lara was a bridesmaid. How's she looking these days?'

A far-off feeling of unease crept nearer as vague memories returned of drunkenly approaching Lara by the dance floor. 'Yeah, she looked quite nice,' I said. 'But I can't believe she's still holding an incident at university against you?'

Sam smiled ruefully. 'There's been one or two re-heats over the years...'

'Ah, I see.'

'Anyway, how was the wedding? Weddings are great places to pull. I assume you...?'

'That's what I need to talk to you about. That and this girl from the office.'

'Which do you want to discuss first?'

'The girl from the office.' I took a large swig of beer, at least three fingers worth. 'Her name's Marianne.' I closed my eyes, sighed and shook my head. 'I've got it bad. I've been putting some groundwork in with her. Trouble is, she's married.'

The energy drained from Sam's face. 'Mmmm. I'd avoid that if I were you.'

In the subsequent silence the prospect of any sort of future relationship between Marianne and me appeared to drift away until it was just a tiny dot on the horizon. I stared down into the surface of my pint, at my faceless reflection.

'Tell you what,' said Sam, sensing my introspection. 'How about I tell you what you should normally do with a woman you like.'

'What's that then?'

'ABC.'

'ABC?'

'A – Always, B – Be, C – Closing. Always Be Closing. If you really fancy a girl, you need to be always funnelling her to the conclusion you want, to the close, which means your bed. The great advantage of ABC is that if it works you become lovers and who knows what thereafter, and if it doesn't you move on. It's the never-ending groundwork, the not knowing, the *hope* which kills a guy when he's chasing a woman.' He quaffed off a huge measure of beer. 'There's something else that's worrying me,' he said, wiping his lips with the back of his hand. 'You mentioned *groundwork*, as though this is some sort of long-term project. The trouble with groundwork is that this girl gets the flattery and feel-good factor of you running around after her *and* she gets to return to hubby in the evening. She gets the best of both worlds so's got no incentive to change. Meanwhile you're losing valuable time and effort when you should be out closing other women.'

Talk of closing brought to my mind the tune of *New York, New York* and my inebriated lunge on Rachel. 'That's the other thing I need to talk to you about. I had a disaster with Rachel at the wedding, which, I suppose, was trying to ABC her. You know how she and I have always been good friends? Well, I guess I mistook that for something else...' I looked beyond Sam into the distance.

'Good old Rachel, you always did have a soft spot for her,' said Sam. 'Let me get this straight: Rachel is a girl you've been mates with for years, someone you talk to about relationships and feelings and about what a modern guy you are, am I right?'

'I guess you could say that but–'

'And you made a play for her at the wedding when you were pissed at the end of the night and it was a complete disaster?'

'Well, it was a bit like that but—'

'GBF.'

'GBF?'

'Gay Best Friend.'

'What?'

'Her Gay Best Friend, that's what you've become to Rachel. You're someone she *likes*, someone she can *share her thoughts and feelings with*, and someone who is so unsexual that you may as well be gay as far as she's concerned. It's one of the oldest mistakes in the book, guys showing their feminine side and their emotional intelligence and being *unthreatening* and hoping that's going to win her over in the end. It never works.'

'But can't two people grow to love each other?'

'Nope. Not in the sense of love you want with Rachel and this girl at the office, which is to get into their knickers. You see, after the first few meetings a woman will either have you down as a potential lover or she'll have you consigned to the friend category.'

I rubbed my chin. 'So how do I avoid becoming a gay best friend?'

Sam took a monumental swig to fortify himself before imparting what was clearly going to be a critical piece of information. He smacked his lips, leaned forward and fixed me with that stare. 'You've got to establish yourself in her mind as a sexual prospect from the outset,' he said. 'As I said, all this softly softly stuff and being metrosexual and in tune with your feelings is a bunch of bullshit. By all means be friends, but if you don't ABC her you'll become her GBF. In fact, because you ABC'd Rachel at the wedding and no doubt blew out spectacularly, you're now free to move onto a woman who may actually agree to sleep with you, rather than wasting more energy on Rachel. So in a way she did you a favour by utterly rejecting you and you did yourself a favour by lunging at her or whatever you did. You've been liberated to move on and you should be thankful for it.'

His theory had a powerful logic. There was an important lesson to be learnt from what he was saying, although perhaps not precisely as he had articulated it.

'You know,' he said, 'I think I should open up a new medical practice advising blokes like you who have lost their mojo. A radical new treatment pioneered by Dr Sam entitled *"Stop fucking around and start fucking around"."*

This again seemed to have a powerful logic to it.

'Shall I get the next round in?' I asked.

'Just one more,' replied Sam. 'With a chaser.'

15

Carrie, Adrian and I had travelled up on the train that Thursday morning from Euston to Northampton, before taking a forty-minute taxi ride further and further into the middle of nowhere to the soulless conference centre we now found ourselves in, allegedly near Daventry. Judging from the taxi ride, lack of mobile phone reception and featureless fields that rolled as far as the eye could see, the conference centre was very purposefully located as far from any distraction as possible. Like in a Siberian prison camp or Alcatraz, escape from the compound was the least of your problems.

We'd just had the opening 'plenary' session introducing the two-day teambuilding course, and had now 'broken out' into our respective 'electives'. The tables in the room were configured into a U shape, with Carrie, Adrian and I sitting along one leg of the U, while the facilitator paced up and down at the front. He was a short man, extremely well groomed – indeed, too well groomed: white shirt straight out of the packet, red tie too red, tan too golden, and the hunched and stiff-shouldered posture of a man who spent too much time in the gym.

Marianne walked in – *keep calm, keep calm* – and sat down on the other leg of the U, opposite me. We'd been exchanging daily emails since our coffee at Starbucks, but seeing her in the flesh again still startled my eyes.

'Right, let's do an icebreaker; everyone stand up,' said the facilitator. No one moved. 'Come on!' he shouted, clapping his hands so hard they gave out booming rifle-shot sounds. We dragged ourselves to our feet with all the enthusiasm of people who thought a teambuilding course was a euphemism for doing bugger all for two days. 'Come on, everyone, let's energise. Hold out your arms and shake them, that's it, shake all those cobwebs away and let's get some vitality into this room.' As he shook his arms I saw he had silver shirt armbands just above the elbow, matching his silver tie pin.

Adrian looked at me with a 'What the fuck?!' expression. I glanced across at Marianne, who raised her eyebrows at me.

'That's better,' said the facilitator, 'let's maintain this energy throughout the session. Right, you can all sit down.' He rubbed his hands together. 'Just one or two housekeeping points before we get started. Firstly, can I ask you all to switch off your mobile phones, please? Secondly, can you all use the marker pens in front of you to write down your names on the bits of card provided and place them so that everyone can see?' We all dutifully did as we were told. 'Finally, there's no test of the fire alarm planned today, so if you hear the alarm, run like hell!' A little muted laughter. 'Just kidding. If you do hear the alarm, you can use the door at the front and there's a fire exit to the rear. Right...' Another rifle-shot clap of his hands. 'I'd like us to go around the room and introduce ourselves. Please state your name, department, what you do and lastly tell us an interesting fact about yourself. I'll start off. My name's Brad. I've been working in training and coaching for almost ten years now and before that I was a recruitment consultant running a successful executive search desk–'

'Why's he doing this then?' I whispered to Adrian. Carolyn – John's hatchet man – leant forward from beyond Carrie and gave me a beady glare. My cheeks reddened.

'And an interesting fact about me,' continued the facilitator, 'is that I'm training to do an Iron Man next month. For those of you who don't know, that's a two point four mile swim, a one hundred and twelve mile bike ride and finally running a marathon. Right, now it's your turn. Let's go around the room, starting here.' He motioned towards Carolyn.

'My name is Carolyn. I am the Company Secretary and I have been with the company for over twenty years.' She paused to allow her announcement of her title to settle across the room. 'I have wide-ranging responsibilities across all areas of corporate governance. An interesting fact about me is that I have met two Prime Ministers.'

'Wow!' said the facilitator. 'I don't think I've ever had that one in one of my sessions. Which Prime Ministers?'

'I met Margaret Thatcher in the nineteen eighties at a young businesswomen event and a few years ago I met Tony Blair with my husband at an event promoting small businesses.' Carolyn held her chin up proudly, her status reinforced and reconfirmed for us all to admire and envy.

Next up was Adrian, whose interesting fact was his participation in medieval battle re-enactments; then Carrie – a week spent in the Amazonian jungle on her gap year; then me – surfing. A few colleagues later it was Marianne's turn.

'Hello, everyone, my name is Marianne. I work in the secretarial recruitment team and an interesting fact about me is that I have Leonard Cohen's entire collection of albums, including two signed copies.'

'Great stuff,' said the facilitator with a cheerful enthusiasm slightly at odds with the tone of most Leonard Cohen songs I had heard. My eyes lingered on Marianne, who looked straight at me and winked, the intimacy of the act sending a flutter through me.

'Right,' said the facilitator, extending an outstretched arm expansively to one side. 'I'd like this half of the room to group together for ten minutes and brainstorm what influences a positive working environment.' His other heavily muscled arm then extended over the other half of the room. 'I want this half of the room to brainstorm what makes for a negative working environment. I'll bring round some flipcharts and post-it notes so you can begin designing a presentation...'

'It's like being back at school,' I said to Adrian, provoking a sharp movement from my right. I turned – and Carolyn stared at me, face clenched in anger.

The session ran predictably: chat amongst your friends, rush together a shoddy presentation, pray you don't get asked to present it. At the end of the session, I packed up the file of course papers I knew I would never read and was about to leave, when Carolyn stood in front of me. 'Can I have a word?'

'Okay,' I said, and we waited while everyone else left the room. Surely she wasn't going to admonish me for my comments to Adrian? Or had I not locked away my laptop back at the office? Or failed to comply with Carolyn's beloved Clear Desk Policy?

'Your name is Adam and you're part of Marcus's Financial Services team, is that right?' asked Carolyn, once we were alone.

'Yes.'

'John has committed considerable resource to this event, so it's extremely disappointing to see one of our senior consultants not taking it seriously.'

'But–'

'No buts.' The *ts* of buts came out as a hiss. 'I heard you making snide little remarks throughout the last session. You're meant to be setting an example.'

I said nothing, clamping my teeth to try to quell the anger swelling inside me. The remarks I'd made were harmless and inaudible to all, except to a jobsworth like Carolyn.

'I will be watching you from now on and I want to see you making considerably more effort in the remaining sessions, or else I will be having a word with Marcus. Is that clear?'

Again, I said nothing. This close up, there was a frightening intensity to her sneering, dismissive demeanour; it was a look which said, *Go on, I dare you to so much as show the tiniest hint of insubordination, for if you do, you'll have your P45 within seconds.*

'Well, is it clear?' she asked again.

'Crystal.'

'Good.' She'd gone before the word had completely left her mouth.

* * *

After dinner everyone convened in the bar, encouraged by the chance to have a drink at the company's expense and to be themselves for the first time that day. Carrie, Adrian and I propped up one end of the bar. I moderated my drinking, the Rachel incident at the wedding having made me worried that I was in danger of becoming like Dr David Banner, haunted by the dramatic ending of a past relationship and liable to turn into a crazed creature when pushed too far, in my case by alcohol.

'The girl next to me at dinner had a brilliant story,' said Carrie. 'She had a boyfriend who promised her a romantic mini-break and guess where he took her?' Adrian and I shrugged. 'Here,' said Carrie. 'To this conference centre.'

'No!' said Adrian and I in unison.

'Needless to say, she's no longer with him,' said Carrie.

'I wouldn't mind this place if only it had the decency to be honest about its limitations,' said Adrian. 'I'm not a spa man myself, but surely a hotel needs more than a modest indoor swimming pool with a few sun loungers and branded dressing gowns to make it a spa.'

A raucous cheer went up from the far end of the bar; the secretarial recruitment team were doing shots, Marianne amongst them.

'Right, I'm off to bed,' said Carrie, looking at her watch. 'I've already had two late nights this week, I'm knackered.'

'Same here,' said Adrian. 'And I need to have my wits about me tomorrow to make sure Adam doesn't have any more run-ins with Carolyn.'

'I'll see you tomorrow,' I said, staying to finish my beer. After a few sips I again looked over to the secretarial team, but there was no sight of her. I leant back and forth to establish whether she might be standing behind a colleague.

'Adam,' came a voice from behind me. I swivelled.

It was Marianne.

'Have you had too much to drink? You looked like you were swaying there.' She grinned as she said it, while holding two shot glasses of clear liquid. She stood very close, reminding me how I could never faithfully recapture her distinctive beauty in my mind's eye, because its secrets were only revealed in person.

'Hi, Marianne. This looks dangerous,' I said, taking one of the shots.

'It's Sambuca. We used to drink it in Napoli. My new work colleagues seem to like it too. Down the hatch.'

We knocked back our shots simultaneously; a viscous, aniseed flavoured film coating my throat, while a warming sensation lifted into the rear of my head. After a moment's recovery, I ordered two gin and tonics.

'So is Sambuca your favourite drink?' I asked.

'Nope, my all-time favourite is a French Seventy-Five.'

Everything she favoured was instantly logged in my memory and thereafter took on stratospheric levels of interest because of its association with her. 'What's a French Seventy-Five?'

'Champagne and gin with a dash of lemon.' Her voice was louder and more animated than usual.

'Sounds powerful...'

'So powerful in fact it was named after a French seventy-five millimetre howitzer gun. But I have a better name for it. I call it the G-spot of cocktails–'

I choked on the mouthful of gin and tonic I'd just swallowed and it started frothing back out of my mouth and nose. I brought my hand to my mouth and turned away.

'You okay?' asked Marianne, chuckling.

'Yeah, fine,' I replied, coughing to clear my throat. 'It was just you mentioning... well... you know.'

'I've got something for you,' she said, reaching into her handbag and pulling out a CD. It was *Songs of Leonard Cohen*. 'It's his first album. Do you have it?'

'No, I haven't,' I said in a hushed and reverent voice, taking it and handling it with the same care and precision one would with a priceless relic from the tomb of Christ. I turned it over to review the track listing on the back. One of the titles was *So Long, Marianne*, which I stared at, mesmerised.

'What?' asked Marianne.

'I've just noticed the title of one of the songs.'

Her infectious smile appeared, as did her dimples. 'I love that song. I know that sounds really vain just because it's got my name in it, but it's always meant a lot to me.'

I knew then I would be spending the next few weeks poring over the album, replaying every song, particularly *that* song, and remembering every word of every song, searching for hidden meanings in the lyrics which related to her and me. 'Thanks for this, I really appreciate it.'

'We'll have to meet up once you've listened to it to discuss it.'

'Definitely,' I said, trying to keep the excitement down in my voice. 'Hey, can you put it in your handbag for safekeeping?'

'Sure.' She took a sip of her drink and peered at me. 'So, I would imagine you lead quite a carefree existence, what with being single?'

I liked that she'd asked me a personal question. 'Being single has its advantages,' I said, 'and its disadvantages. It's not a lifestyle choice though; I'm just waiting for the right person to come along.'

There was a short silence. 'Well, it seems you have a few admirers in my team. They we just telling me how you've been off limits for years but are now back on the market. I would be careful if I were you, there's some man-eaters amongst them.'

'I wouldn't want to get into a relationship with a work colleague now would I, Marianne, imagine the complexity.'

We smiled wryly at one another.

'Can I ask what happened with your ex?' she asked.

'Our relationship changed,' I said. 'Over the years we sort of... morphed into friends until finally the romance fizzled out completely.

It was heartbreaking, but towards the end we just argued all the time, so in some ways it was a relief when it ended.'

'I know how you feel.'

'Do you?' I said too quickly, now even more alert.

'I remember falling out of love with my first boyfriend.'

'Oh, right,' I said, deflating. 'What happened?'

'He was a couple of years older than me and the first guy to show me any interest. I'm not saying it was the same as with your ex – I was only seventeen and we only dated two years – but I remember how my feelings changed. Of course, I was somewhat different back then...'

'How do you mean?'

'I was a bit of an ugly duckling in my teens. And painfully shy.'

'Do you really think you've changed that much?' I asked, grinning. Marianne punched my upper arm lightly. 'So why did your feelings for your first boyfriend change?' I asked.

'We grew apart. Or rather I grew apart. Looking back, I'm amazed it lasted two years. He spent most of his time watching football. West Bromwich Albion was his team, he was obsessed with them. He took me to matches and to begin with I loved it: the atmosphere at match days, the big crowds, the chanting and jumping up and down. But after a while the excitement dimmed, or perhaps it was his ability to excite me that dimmed. He accelerated the process by making unreasonable demands of me.'

'*What?!* What sort of demands?'

'He asked me to dress up for him.'

Images raced through my mind: a nurse's uniform? A French maid? A nun? 'Wh...what did he ask you to wear?' I began taking a sip of my drink to steady myself for the revelation of the image that would undoubtedly be indelibly imprinted on my mind forever.

'He asked me to wear a West Bromwich Albion bikini in the bedroom–'

I doubled over and swallowed hard on the mouthful I'd just imbibed to stop it frothing back out of my mouth and nose.

Marianne bent double in laughter. 'Sorry, I shouldn't have done that, but it's true. I wouldn't have minded if it had been something sexy, but a West Brom bikini... I think that was the moment I decided to move on.'

Once recomposed, I rubbed my chin, weighing up whether to ask the question I desperately wanted to ask. Fuck it: 'Did you wear it then?'

'Yes, a few times actually.' The image was thus stamped into my mind forever, like a footprint in wet concrete.

'What about university, any boyfriends there?' I also almost asked *and any more outfits?* but heroically resisted the temptation.

'I'd been so shy at school,' said Marianne, 'so when I went to university I wanted to meet a wider range of people, and men. In fact, it became a bit of a project with the men.'

'How do you mean?'

'I ended up dating various different *types*. I was initially attracted to those who I thought were the most rebellious. So I became a goth.'

'You didn't?'

'I did, and I dated a goth guy. But six months of waking up under a black duvet cover in a room with purple walls started to affect my personality, like Scandinavians who get depressed having not seen sunlight all winter.'

'So what, or rather who, was the next stereotype?'

'Next up was a DJ, who seemed pretty cool initially. But every time I went round his flat I'd spend the whole evening watching him on his decks wearing giant headphones and occasionally pointing a finger in the air and shouting, "Tune!"'

I nodded. 'I used to like clubbing, but hated all that rubbish, like "Are you on the guest list?" and DJs thinking they were the next rock stars. I mean, how difficult is it to put a record on a turntable?'

'I agree, so he got ditched.'

'Who was next?'

She paused. I took a sip of my drink.

'My tutor.'

Coughing and spluttering again. Eventually I said, 'No wonder you got a first! You bad girl.'

'This one wasn't planned though. He invited me to his flat to study. I honestly thought he just wanted to help. But it was exciting. Every young girl has fantasies about older men. What about your relationships at university?'

'It's fair to say I spent the first two years finding myself.'

'You mean getting pissed and stoned with your mates and failing to impress a girl enough to hold down any type of relationship.'

I rubbed my chin. 'Correct. But in my final year I fell for someone and we dated until we left uni.'

'What was she like?'

'She was lovely, very principled, very charismatic. But she was also a vegetarian and a year of eating Linda McCartney sausages eventually put an end to it. No, but seriously, she moved to Edinburgh and I moved to London and we fell out of touch. I've often wondered what became of her.'

'Why don't you look her up on Facebook?'

'I'm not on Facebook.'

'You're kidding me? Why not?'

'Never got round to it. Plus it's a place for stalkers and narcissists, isn't it? Present company excluded, naturally.'

'It's not all weirdos, though I grant you there's some. It's a good way to keep in touch with people. I could be your first friend on there if you like.'

'Maybe I'll look into it,' I said, knowing already that if Facebook meant more access to Marianne, I would be signing up. 'So all the male research you conducted at university must have paid off if you're now married?'

She paused. And paused further. I wasn't going to fill the silence; I wanted to hear what she would say.

'I guess it does,' she said. Another silence followed. 'Anyway, I've done quite enough talking. I think it's your turn to tell me what it's like being single.'

I didn't know how to respond. To say the prospect of dating excited me risked Marianne thinking I had no interest in her. To tell her I had no motivation to date because no one could compare to her would surely scare her off. 'I don't deny there's a sense of potential being single,' I said. 'But it does sometimes seem as though every conversation I hear and every film or TV programme I watch is about being in a relationship. I feel like an outsider. And there's going to things like weddings and everyone looking at you as though you're a freak.'

'Oh, to hell with other people,' said Marianne. 'Just because they're in a relationship doesn't mean there's any romance in their lives. They probably just get a cheap tacky card on Valentine's Day each year. They envy you your freedom and that you can choose to date anyone you want.'

'Not anyone, Marianne.'

She bowed her head and took a sip of her drink. 'I guess not.' She looked at her watch. 'It's past my bedtime, I really should get going.'

'One more for the road?' I asked.

'Best not, I've had far too much tonight already.'

'Then at least let me escort you to your room?'

She hesitated, her eyes flitting left and right. 'I'd like that.'

We left the bar, walked up a set of stairs by reception and along a long carpeted corridor with uplights along its walls. I kept telling myself to play it cool: *for god's sake don't make an idiot of yourself like you did with Rachel at the wedding.* But Sam's voice was also in there, fighting to be heard – *ABC or you'll become her GBF…*

Marianne drew up outside a room. 'This is me.'

'I enjoyed talking to you again tonight,' I said.

'Same here.' She leant forward and kissed me on the cheek.

I almost reached up to touch the spot where she'd kissed me. 'Goodnight, Marianne.'

'Goodnight, Adam.'

A few paces down the corridor I realised I didn't have the Leonard Cohen CD. I returned to her door and knocked.

She opened it, her eyes wide, her expression one I couldn't place: hope, surprise and apprehension all combined.

'Sorry, I forgot the CD.'

'Oh yes, come in.'

My heart jolted as I crossed the threshold of her room and every sight and sound was vivid and amplified. That perfume of hers infused the place; I'd never realised just how… how *moving* a scent could be. She walked over to her handbag on the bed and rummaged in it for the CD, found it, and turned to me, but didn't approach. A short moment of deafening silence followed. 'I don't suppose you'd like a coffee?' she asked.

Oh my god oh my god oh my god. 'Yes, that would be good,' I said slowly, trying not to betray any emotion or excitement. I sat down on the edge of her bed and couldn't help but reflect how she'd be sleeping in this very place tonight, a fact that made it rare and magical.

Marianne walked over to the door of her room and pushed it to until the latch clicked closed behind her.

I was properly alone with her for the first time.

My heart thundered in my chest; I feared it might be audible, each beat pumping out more and more adrenalin. I breathed in and out deeply, but quietly.

Marianne had walked to the sideboard. 'How do you take it?'

'White, one sugar,' I said. Her back was turned as she switched on the kettle. I glanced around her room: her gym kit and trainers were on a chair in the corner and her bag was open on the bed beside me with her hairbrush visible on top of a pale green singlet.

The silence was dense.

The rattle of a cup in its saucer broke the silence as Marianne lifted it and a teaspoon fell off the saucer and tumbled across the floor.

I reached down and picked it up. Be brave, I said to myself, or you'll regret it for the rest of your life. I walked over to Marianne and placed the teaspoon onto the side, now standing alongside her, so close our arms brushed. 'Do you need a hand?' I asked.

'I'm okay, I think,' she said, steadfastly looking down. She placed the cup and saucer back down on the sideboard. 'I'm just... ' Her mouth shaped to say more but no sound came, and she faced me, hope and apprehension again articulated by her features. Our eyes connecting caused her to look back down and begin fidgeting with the cups.

'Marianne?'

'Yes?' she said too quickly. I reached out and put my arm around her waist and coaxed her to turn until she faced me square on. This close up, her green eyes were even fiercer and more inquiring.

I kissed her.

It was a kiss like no other, as though my higher brain functions were disabled, leaving only a deep and profound sub-consciousness controlling my actions, allowing me to express the purest emotion. The kiss went on and on, the universe revolving on its axis with us at its centre.

I took Marianne by the hand and led her to the bed. I undressed her with care and precision, but also with the passion and confidence of instinct, and as her body was revealed an overwhelming desire to kiss and taste every part of her overcame me. That and more is etched into my mind forever, nothing more so than the concentration articulated on her face as we made love.

But even more important than the memories was the message, for in the acts and deeds and touches and tastes of that night spent together, I communicated to Marianne the most important message of them all: that I loved her.

16

I spent Friday in a zombified trance throughout the rest of the course and was no better once I got home to Hammersmith that evening. I kept finding myself perfectly still, staring straight ahead without registering anything, having forgotten what I was doing, as another flashback played out. It was a glimpse of what an addict must feel: thoughts always brought back to the same place, everything interpreted as it relates to your need, the inability to conduct a normal existence.

In desperation on Saturday afternoon I fired up my laptop to find her on Facebook and joined the site. Just seeing her profile was enough to release another squirt of adrenalin, but when I clicked repeatedly on her 'Photos', it gave me a message that 'Marianne only shares some information publicly. If you know Marianne, add her as a friend'. Great, so I can sleep with the girl, but Facebook won't let me see photos of her until we meet its definition of 'Friends'.

By early Saturday evening the oscillations began, between sweeping endorphin rushes from memories of Thursday night, to a deep foreboding because I'd slept with a married woman, then back again. I'd broken the sanctity of a marriage, a union ordained by God, and somewhere deep inside I experienced a hollowness and dread unknown until then. But surely Marianne had broken the rules and promises, not me? Far from offering relief, that thought only increased my anxiety, because I would also be responsible for her guilt, which could only be greater than my own.

It was obvious who I needed to speak to. As soon as I dialled Rachel's number I winced as recollections rushed back of my performance at the wedding.

'Hello.'

'Hi, it's Adam.'

'I know, your number came up.' Her voice was cold and stern.

'Can I meet you? I've got rather a lot to tell you.'

An uncomfortably long pause followed. 'Okay, let's meet for a coffee tomorrow morning, but this time you're coming to me. I'm going for lunch with my parents in town, so I'll meet you on the Southbank at eleven.'

Late Saturday night and with my laptop still open on the coffee table, I clicked on Rachel's Facebook profile. Whatever privacy settings Marianne had used didn't apply and I had unfettered access to her profile. Facebook appeared to be a free for all, snooping positively encouraged, every click opening up new opportunities to pry into others' lives, any genetic predisposition to stalking guaranteed to be triggered and nurtured to cataclysmic proportions. When I scrolled through Rachel's 'Wall' there were links to photographs from Jess and Ben's wedding, including images of a dishevelled drunk guy with cheeks turned beetroot from one tequila shot too many... one of me staggering across the dance floor with vacant eyes, and another of me failing to pull off a John Travolta move with expressions of alarm registered on the faces of onlookers.

After opening a second bottle of red, I decided to look up my first love, Joanna. I'd been thirteen on holiday with my parents in Mallorca when I'd met her – come to think of it, that was the holiday when I'd learnt the moves to *Blame It On The Boogie*. The images I'd faithfully stored of Joanna on my mental hard drive were of the prettiest fifteen-year-old girl imaginable, recently flowered into a woman, radiant and lithe, reclining on a sun lounger, or climbing out of the pool with water cascading down taut, flawless, sunkissed skin.

I found her profile, clicked on her photos, and shattered a dream. A weighty mother in her mid-thirties was revealed, dressed in tracksuit bottoms and baggy shirts, her face haggard and loose fleshed. I took an almighty swig of wine and cursed the site for destroying the idealised perfection I'd previously held so dear.

I moved onto my contemporaries, only for one long orgy of smug self-satisfaction to be revealed. As if the self-imposed pressure to have a lovely spouse who was at once sexy and intelligent and down to earth was not enough, *and* two cute children – one of each sex, one of each sex! – and a big house and car and millions of friends, these things now also needed to be validated by being visible on Facebook, posted on the site for everyone else to enjoy and envy.

Look how happy I am! Look how many friends I have! Envy me my beautiful children! The electric fear of fatherhood denied shot into my brain again. I slammed the lid of my laptop, fell back on the sofa and reached out to the stereo: Marianne's Leonard Cohen album began...

* * *

I waited for Rachel outside the Royal Festival Hall, leaning on an iron railing, the Thames' surface dimpled by the heated river breeze, the sun's rays already strong enough to warm my cheeks. I closed my eyes, listening to the breeze sigh and quieten and sigh again. When I opened them, an elderly couple, perhaps in their seventies, strolled past hand in hand, he bow-legged, she slightly stooped. He wore a tie and she a pale blue straw hat and he said something that made her smile and they swung hands.

Rachel joined me and we found a riverside café. We bought tea – I'd been tempted to buy a cappuccino, but had resisted. At the first natural break in the conversation, Rachel said, 'So?' with an inquisitive raised eyebrow.

'What?' I asked.

'Is there anything you want to say to me?'

I fidgeted with a sachet of sugar, tore its corner, poured it in and stirred it in a clockwise direction. Eventually I had to look up. 'Listen, Rachel, I'm truly sorry about my performance at the wedding, I behaved like an idiot.'

She paused for effect, knowing the long silence would be agonising for me. 'Tell me, how many times have we had the *When Harry Met Sally* conversation, and you agreed that men and women *can* remain just friends?'

'I know, but it was the alcohol. I realise it's a lame excuse and it was me pouring the stuff down my throat and not anyone else, but I just seemed to become a different person that night.'

'You're not wrong. I thought Oliver Reed had risen from the dead. You know they say the truth comes out when you're drunk.'

'I'm not sure that's always true. I can categorically say that doner kebab is not my all-time favourite cuisine, but I often wake up next to a half-eaten one after a night on the sauce.'

'So I'm the female equivalent of a doner kebab?'

'I didn't say that.'

'Whatever. The point is, your behaviour was embarrassing, but more than that, it was an insult to our friendship.'

I grimaced and stared past Rachel down the Embankment; a woman jogged past dressed in Lycra shorts, triggering images of supple tender flesh last Thursday night. I turned back. 'I plead guilty. I should have apologised earlier, but sometimes when you can't remember the details, it's easy to convince yourself they didn't happen.'

'Did you at any stage consider how your behaviour made *me* feel that evening? I'm a woman, for goodness sake; to be just a drunken afterthought at the end of a boozy night after you've already tried it on with the bridesmaids and half the waitresses is categorically *not* the way to impress a woman. And impressing women is a skill you're going to have to master now you're single. *And* you seem to have forgotten that Louise is one of my friends. Can you imagine her reaction if she'd heard we'd been swapping saliva on the dance floor at her best friend's wedding?'

I placed my elbows on the table and cupped my forehead in my hands. All these angles and interpretations hadn't occurred to me. All I'd experienced since the wedding was a displaced feeling of unease that I'd done something slightly shameful, which perhaps I'd be able to put down to drunkenness. I lifted my head from my hands. 'God, I'm so sorry.'

'And you lunged at me to the tune of *New York, New York,* for god's sake.'

I squirmed and shrunk in my seat. 'It would really mean a lot to me if you would accept my apology?' My voice had taken on a whiny, pleading tone.

Rachel paused a final time. 'Okay, I accept your apology. But do *not* let it happen again.' The final line was delivered with a fear-inspiring headmistress-like finality, with me the chastened schoolboy. 'At least not like that.'

'What?'

'I'm just saying, perhaps if you'd asked me out properly rather than lunging at me, I may have accepted.' She lifted her tea to her lips and raised her eyebrows.

At any time in the last fifteen years what she had just said would have represented a seismic event. But a man can have only one number one in his heart at any one time, and that position was now firmly occupied. 'I thought our chances had passed back at university?' I said.

'Maybe, but I've often wondered why you didn't try it on with me more back then. What was it that put you off?'

'I might ask you the same question.'

'The last time we met you told me how men have to risk rejection. It was incumbent on you to make the first move.'

'I may have made a move if you'd given me any confidence in the outcome, but you were always interested in other men: the tall, dark, handsome types you favour. And anyway, by the time we became such close friends it would have been weird to try it on.'

A short silence followed. Both brains' cogs whirring.

'How are things with Richard?' I asked eventually.

'Not that good,' she said, shaking her head and averting her eyes. 'His wife called me last week.'

'What?!' Another seismic event, two in two minutes. 'What happened?'

'I think she must have looked up my number on Richard's mobile. Obviously I didn't know it was her when I took the call.'

'What did she say?'

'God, it was horrific. She asked me if I thought she didn't know. She told me I was about to break up her family and to consider her children.'

'What did you say?'

'I was silent mostly. At the end I just said sorry for all the hurt I'd caused. It was only afterwards I became livid, though whether that was with her, Richard, or myself, I still don't know.'

The cogs of my brain worked overtime, at once computing what Rachel was saying, but also registering again the terrible complexity of Marianne and me, and the fact that the ecstasy I'd experienced on Thursday night was someone else's agony. 'What are you going to do?'

'I don't know. I'm beginning to think it's time I moved on from Richard.' She checked her watch. 'Speaking of time, I must be getting going; I'm meeting my parents soon.'

'Can I walk you there?' I asked hurriedly as she stood.

We walked along the Embankment to Waterloo Bridge. Seagulls squawked and hovered motionless on the breeze before diving for scraps of food dropped the previous night. I knew perhaps Rachel was expecting more questions about Richard and his wife, but I had my own concerns. 'There's actually something else I wanted to talk to you about,' I said as we climbed a set of stairs up onto the bridge.

'What's that then?'

'There's this girl at work...'

'Oh god, sounds familiar.'

'But she's married.'

Rachel stopped dead in her tracks and faced me. 'Jesus, Adam, haven't you learnt *anything* from my situation? Just promise me you won't get involved while she's still married.'

Silence. Her gaze penetrated me to the marrow.

'You're already involved, aren't you,' she said, more as a statement than a question.

I nodded. 'We slept together last week. My feelings for her are... overwhelming.'

'Have you told her that?'

'No.'

'Keep it that way.'

'Why do you say that?'

Rachel leant on the bridge's stone banister. I joined her and we looked eastwards at St Paul's Cathedral and in the background, more angular and taller, and menacing, loomed the City skyscrapers, peeping over each other's shoulders. All the while the dirty green Thames slid slowly downstream with an irresistible weight and power.

'I've often wondered what would have happened if I'd done an Anne Boleyn on Richard and made him choose between me and his wife. But passion got the better of us...' Rachel's words seemed to hang on the air. 'I would advise you to call off this thing you've started.'

I clenched the edge of the banister so hard the veins and tendons on the top of my hand stood proud; a relationship with Marianne suddenly seemed a long way off, and floating further and further into the distance. 'So it's good enough for you and Richard, but not me? Or is your relationship somehow different?'

'Well, it's lasted three years rather than three days, so yes, it's different. I'm sorry, I don't mean to undermine what you've got with this girl, but if I were you I wouldn't get your hopes up. Sleeping with you doesn't mean she's leaving her husband, which sounds like what you want, unless she's mentioned otherwise?'

'No. But surely their relationship must be... flawed if she's prepared to sleep with me?'

'That's self-evident, I would have thought. But that doesn't mean she's leaving him. People think in situations like ours that it's one or both of the couple who get hurt, but the couple are doomed already, and in the meantime you get dragged into it and end up just as hurt as them. In fact, you're the most likely to get hurt, because you've got the least control over the outcome.'

I moved off and we walked on in silence. I looked away from Rachel, westwards along the Thames, to the back of the Savoy and the giant clock on Shell Mex House.

'Do you think this girl feels the same for you as you do for her?' asked Rachel.

'Marianne, that's her name,' I said, but I couldn't answer Rachel's question, so vast was it in its implications, and it took me a while to say anything at all. 'I don't know,' was all I could muster, the feebleness of my words alarming me.

'Then be careful. She may just like your attention. I told you before, women love to be loved.'

'I'll be careful.' But I didn't want to be careful with Marianne, I wanted to be reckless, or rather I wanted her to be reckless, reckless enough to make the leap from her husband to me.

We reached the Lyceum Theatre. 'I'm going up this way,' said Rachel. 'I'm meeting my parents at Rules.'

'Okay, see you soon.' We kissed each other on the cheek and I walked back to the river, head down, preoccupied.

17

I arrived at work early that Monday, my eyes flicking continuously thereafter between my screen, my watch and the door. Earlier I'd skipped breakfast, having not a trace of hunger.

Marianne walked in, but head down, heading straight to her desk, so I couldn't catch her eye. Soon afterwards I sent her an email saying, 'Hi, do you fancy a coffee sometime today?' and moments later received a response, 'Probably a good idea. 10 a.m. Starbucks?'

At Starbucks I joined the queue, different foreign accents emanating from the bustling team of youngsters brewing and serving the drinks. The sight of all the cakes and confectionery on the counter made me nauseous, such was the knot in my stomach. I scanned the room; Marianne was seated in the corner, her hair tied back in a functional style. She saw me and smiled, but the smile was brief as she reached down to her cup of coffee. I bought a tea and sat opposite her.

'Hi, how are you?' I asked.

She stared into her coffee and I sensed immediately that my energy levels were much higher than hers. 'I'm okay,' she said. 'I think...' She kept looking down. 'I've been thinking about what happened last week.'

'So have I,' I said.

'I want to be clear that I have never, ever, done anything like that before.' She still hadn't looked up.

'Nor me.'

She slowly lifted her head and finally met my gaze, her lips drawn down at the corners. 'I'm sorry, Adam, but I think last week was a mistake.'

Silence.

Cogs static.

It was my turn to look away. I experienced a sensation of sliding down a steep slope, further and further away from Marianne, my fall gathering momentum with nothing to hang onto to arrest it. The feeling was the perfect opposite of what I wanted to experience – a feeling of proximity and intimacy with her. 'A mistake?' I said, turning back to her.

Her face briefly contorted, before adopting a pleading expression. 'I didn't mean a mistake. It was... lovely, but it was so... so surreal on that course, like we weren't in the real world. I'm sorry, but I'm married. What we did was wrong.'

'Don't you think what happened proves that your husband isn't the right man for you?'

Marianne breathed out deeply. 'I don't know, but that's a matter for me and him.' She shook her head. 'I can't even look him in the eye anymore.' She said this while not looking me in the eye. 'I don't want you to think I don't have feelings for you, I do. I love our friendship, but we need to move on from last week–'

'You mean pretend it didn't happen?'

'I didn't say that. I think it's important to acknowledge what happened, but it can never happen again.'

The word *never* seemed to be particularly heavily emphasised. My hard wooden seat suddenly became uncomfortable and I shifted my weight from side to side but to no avail. I noticed my surroundings for the first time: the wood-effect laminate furniture, the crumbs in the seams of the green upholstery, the false calming atmosphere the same as every other Starbucks the world over. It was entirely the right place to have your heart broken.

'I adore you, Marianne,' I said.

Marianne's eyes widened. 'How do you know that? You barely know me.'

'Trust me, I know.'

Silence.

Then, gradually, I became conscious of the hideous, oozing, instrumental musak playing in the background, as well as slowly becoming aware of physiological changes setting in: my ribcage feeling as though it was made of matchsticks with a great unseen force pushing in on it, a deep dull aching sensation spreading itself through the very tissues and fibres of my body.

Eventually Marianne said, 'I'm sorry I've hurt you, I never meant to hurt you.'

It was one thing being rejected, but even worse hearing her feeling sorry for me. The adrenalin of excitement I'd previously always experienced in her company was replaced with the adrenalin of anger. Under the table I grabbed my thigh and squeezed it to try to release some of my bitterness. I didn't say anything, for fear of saying something I'd regret.

'You won't tell anyone what happened, will you?' she asked.

I squeezed my thigh again, as hard as I could, so hard the bruise was still visible a week later. 'Of course I won't tell anyone. What sort of person do you think I am?'

'I'm sorry, it's just that it's different for you, you're single. I'm sorry, I shouldn't have asked. I'm just terrified of my world falling apart.'

'But not worried about causing other people's worlds to fall apart?' I wanted to say, but didn't. I didn't know what to say, so I said nothing.

'Your friendship means a lot to me,' said Marianne. 'We can still be friends, can't we? I'm trying to do what's best... for everyone.'

My brain cogs had recovered and now whirred at a great speed and intensity as I tried to work out what to do and what to say. This was exactly what Sam had warned me about, of being consigned to the dreaded friend category, followed by a life sentence of never-ending groundwork, and not knowing, and *hoping* that she would eventually, possibly, just maybe, leave her husband and choose me as his successor. It was intolerable. 'I think we should have a clean break, including friendship,' I said.

Marianne's face dropped and she stared unblinking. 'You don't want my friendship?'

'This isn't about whether I want your friendship,' I said. 'I've already told you how I feel. This is about self-preservation. Staying friends with you would be having my heart broken every day, every time we speak, every time we email, every time we go for a fucking coffee.'

Marianne shook her head. 'But it's as though you don't value me as a person.'

'It's because I value you too much as a person. It's because I love you.'

Silence.

Tears started in her eyes and her bottom lip quivered.

'I'm sorry, Marianne.' I stood up and walked out, thinking, god knows why I'm apologising to her, she's just broken my heart.

18

'What time are you staying until tonight?' asked Marcus who, ironically, was packing up to go home. Luke and Matt had left already, to go to some ghastly business networking event.

'Not sure, why?' I replied.

'That credit control vacancy is still open, isn't it?'

'It is, yes.'

A short silence followed.

'I think an investment of your time tonight trying to find a suitable candidate is critical,' said Marcus. 'We really need to fill that vacancy.' He continued to stare, before nodding at me. 'You really need to fill that vacancy.'

What did Marcus think I'd been doing all day? I'd been on the phone for hours trying to find someone, but it was futile. The recent collapse of Lehman Brothers had left everyone with the sense that the economy was on the brink of a cataclysm that the politicians were powerless to prevent. There was no way anyone would choose to move jobs at a time like this. 'I've called pretty much everyone on the database,' I said. 'It's pointless.'

'Luke and Matt are still making placements and they're always working late,' replied Marcus. 'Seems to me there's a correlation.'

'You can't compare the temporary job market with the permanent, they're completely different.'

Marcus flinched and I thought I heard a tut, but couldn't be sure. 'The common theme is that hard work pays off. You could learn a lot from Luke and Matt's drive and determination. They really earn their commission.'

Another silence followed. I didn't want to say anything which would make it any more likely than it already was that Marcus would take Roy's commission away, particularly as I needed the extra money to make up for my drop off in sales. And to pay the mortgage. So I sat there, tacitly accepting Marcus's seniority and jurisdiction over me.

'Well?' asked Marcus pointedly.

'Okay, I'll make some calls,' I said.

The matter decided in his favour, Marcus zipped his leather folio conclusively and strode off.

The atmosphere in the office slackened appreciably. 'I'd be careful if I were you,' said Adrian. 'The more the economy slides, the less predictable Marcus's behaviour could become. I overheard him telling Luke and Matt the other day that you and I shouldn't be getting Roy's commission. Perhaps he's right.'

'What? You can't want that greedy fucker to get his hands on it. We helped Roy with many of those placements.'

'Of course I don't want him to have it, but he's obviously got an issue with it, and we need him on our side in this recession. He could be saving us our jobs one day.'

Marianne crossed the office toward the exit. I tracked her progress. She didn't look round. She hadn't looked round for three months, since that day in Starbucks. For me, apart from coming to work, it had been three months largely spent in my flat, curtains closed, fitful sleep, a return to the pot noodle and take-away diet and first-name terms with the staff at the local off licence. I left the flat so infrequently, I was no longer responding well to sunlight.

'So,' said Adrian, looking at me, then at the exit, then back at me again. 'How's your friend?'

'Who?'

'You know who. Marianne.'

Except for Rachel, I hadn't mentioned the Marianne incident to a soul. No one was worthy of that precious information. I trusted Adrian completely, but my instinct wasn't to tell him, just in case he made an innocent mistake and let it slip.

'You like her, don't you?' asked Adrian.

'How do you mean?' I replied. A grin played at the edges of my mouth at the thought of being associated with her.

'You know how I mean.'

'What makes you think I like her?' I asked.

'It's the way you look at her,' said Adrian.

'How's that?'

'In the way that every woman wants a man to look at her. I can see why you like her.'

'You can?'

'Sure. She's not my type, but she's undeniably very beautiful and everyone says she's an excellent consultant. They also say she's married.'

'Don't I know it,' I said.

'Then be careful.'

'I'll try,' I said, my voice rather pitiful. Sitting back in my chair, I lifted my feet onto the side of my desk and started thumbing through some CVs. I soon lost interest and stared out across the office at a few colleagues working late. They were mostly single; they had less to go home to after all. Adrian had split up with a long-term girlfriend two years earlier. What had he done to address it? 'So Adrian... no one to rush home to tonight?' I asked.

'Not at home, no.'

'But there is someone?'

'Not so much some*one*, more like two or three.'

My feet dropped to the floor. 'Sorry, did you say two or three?'

'I did. In fact, I've had so many dates recently, I'm thinking of starting a spread sheet to keep up with them. There's two girls I've had first dates with and plan to meet again and tonight I'm meeting someone for the third time. I'm just killing time 'til eight o'clock. As for the amount of women I've been in contact with recently... I've lost count.'

I sat there dumbfounded; at a stroke Adrian had just completely revised my perception of him. One minute ago he'd been my slightly geeky, slightly portly work colleague; now he'd turned himself into... Julio Iglesias.

'So...' I said, rubbing my chin as my brain cogs began to whirr, 'how do you do it?'

'It's easy,' said Adrian. 'Internet dating.'

I'd seen the preponderance of dating site advertisements appearing on the tube and even on TV, but Adrian was the first person I knew to use one. Or perhaps just the first to admit it? Until then, I'd only really used the internet for sports news, booking holidays and occasionally appraising the mysterious dimensions of the female body.

'But if you start dating someone from the internet,' I said, 'wouldn't you forever have people asking you, "How did you meet?"

and you'd be forever replying, "On the internet", which is hardly very romantic.'

'Since when was how you met an accurate predictor of the future relationship? Take Paul McCartney; he met Heather Mills at a charity event. That's romantic, but fuck lot of good it did them. The reason people are unsure about internet dating is that it doesn't sit easily with their sense of destiny.'

'How do you mean?'

'Just think of all the romantic literature and films about two lovers fated to meet and how we're all destined to meet *the one*. Logging on and finding a partner doesn't suggest divine destiny, because logging on is creating your own destiny.'

I rubbed my forehead; Jesus, this was getting deep. I just wanted a piece of the action.

'Or you can look upon the internet on a purely practical level,' continued Adrian, sensing me struggling. 'After all, I've got three dates lined up. How about you, are you dating anyone at the moment?'

'No, not at the moment,' I said, folding my arms and leaning back in my chair.

'Have you dated anyone recently?'

'Not since Louise, no.'

'Got any dates lined up?'

'No.'

'So, if I may summarise, you've been single for a while now, you're meant to be in the prime of your life and you've had no dates, not a single one, you've got no dates coming up and – correct me if I'm wrong here, Adam – you seemingly don't even have the remotest possibility of purposefully, consciously, actively engineering yourself into a position whereby there is any chance whatsoever of you ever again having a date with a member of the opposite sex?'

'Jeez, Adrian, I guess not! But the way you say it makes it sound like I should just shoot myself in the head right now.'

Adrian sniggered. 'Sorry, that was cruel. But think about it; where are you going to meet women these days?'

'I don't know, sometimes I think it would be easier if all single people had a giant S tattooed on their forehead. That way we could easily identify each other. If supporting a good cause or charity warrants wearing a coloured ribbon on your collar, then being single warrants something at least as conspicuous.'

'That's one approach I suppose, but seriously, where are you going to meet someone?'

I shrugged.

'Let me ask you something,' said Adrian. 'What's the most important decision you'll ever have to make in your whole life?'

I pondered the question a while. 'I don't know... what career to follow?'

'But we both fell into recruitment by accident.'

'Oh yeah. Well... it's probably then...' But I couldn't think of what the most important decision I'd ever have to make might be, which surprised me. 'I don't know, what is it?'

'Which woman to spend your life with and start a family with.' A short, loud silence followed. 'And yet there's no lessons on it at school, no university courses. You're on your own with the biggest decision of the lot. And given that, why leave it to chance? Why not use something like the internet to help you?'

'I guess you've got a point,' I said, stroking the back of my neck, mulling over Adrian's words. 'Where do you start with this online stuff, anyway? Do you access some sort of "chatroom" and make new friends that way?'

Adrian shook his head despairingly and motioned for me to come closer. I dragged my seat alongside his and leant forward so I had a clear view of his screen.

'Right, firstly you've got to set up a profile describing yourself. Let me show you.' He clicked on a link on the screen and up came his details. 'Okay, so here's my profile. You post a couple of photographs of yourself, so people can see what you look like. Clearly you want to spend some time choosing the best photos.'

'Clearly,' I replied. Adrian had indeed chosen his carefully, including a few of him travelling. 'Looking good,' I said. 'Particularly that one of you standing outside the pyramids – very Indiana Jones.'

'Stop taking the piss, you've only got one chance to make a good impression. Now look here.' He moved the cursor to scroll the screen down, which brought up a box with some wording in it. 'In this bit you've got to say a bit about yourself. I'd advise you to take your time with this part because how you describe yourself could be the clincher. Women don't just go by the photos, which is what most men do.'

I stared at the screen, like a small child watching a riveting cartoon, absorbing the potential, and the proximity of the potential...
'Adrian?'

'Let me guess, you'd like me to set you up a profile?'

'I'll buy you a pint.'

'No, you'll buy me my pints for a whole evening.'

'Done.' We shook hands on it.

Over the next half hour Adrian helped me set up a profile. It cost £24.99 for the first month, which I considered the deal of the century if it led me to the Promised Land Adrian spoke of and assisted me with the most important decision I'd ever have to make. I couldn't post a photograph yet though, as the only one of me on my work laptop was the dreadful one the company used for business proposals with me looking pallid and nerdy in a suit, and that certainly wouldn't do. A greater worry soon started to nag: 'What exactly is the ratio of men to women on here?' I asked. 'I bet it's impossible odds of like hundreds of guys to each woman.'

'Wrong. There's actually as many women as men on these sites. Women don't have as many doubts as men; they actually think the internet makes sense as a way to meet people because it allows them to pick and choose.'

I rubbed my chin. 'As many women as men, you say?' I paused. 'Adrian?'

'Let me guess, you'd like to look at the women?'

'Can I? Just show me how I start... er... shopping.'

'They're called searches, not shopping. Look, this is what you do.' Adrian brought up a screen that broke down into various compartments, each inviting you to tick a box. 'See here, you have to choose the type of woman you're looking for.'

'Right... kind of like an estate agent website where you choose your location, type of property, number of bedrooms and all that?'

Adrian looked at me askance. 'Yeah, kinda like that... only different. Okay, let's try one. First question: location. Take it from me, just tick London.'

'Agreed, I'll go provincial later, if I have to.'

'Right, age next, what d'ya reckon?'

'Mmmm, I'm thinking someone in their early thirties,' I said.

'Just thirties? What about women in their twenties?'

'Would a woman in her twenties go for a thirty-four-year-old guy?'

'They'd probably love to date an older guy. Maturity can be an asset, you know. If Michael Douglas can bag Catherine Zeta Jones, then the least you can do is consider women in their late twenties. Why restrict yourself? Let's tick from twenty-eight to thirty-five, okay?'

'Done.'

'Right, what about height, any preferences?'

'Nope, I'm open-minded.'

'Okay, we'll just tick four foot ten to six foot four, which should cover all bases. Now then, build?'

'What are the choices?' I asked.

'Okay, starting at the bottom we have slim, then slender, then athletic, average, a few extra pounds, cuddly and fatty.'

'Good god, fatty? Does it really say that?'

'The internet caters for all tastes...'

'Okay, tick slim, slender and athletic for starters. The term average makes me kinda nervous. It sounds rather a broad category, if you know what I mean.'

'But if you don't tick it you may only be left with a bunch of salad-munching gym bunnies.'

'Tick it.'

'Okay, can I tempt you to go any bigger?'

Sam's WGP warning came flooding back. 'Nope, average is as far as I'm prepared to go.'

'Suit yourself. Me, I prefer the larger lady, which at least means we won't be in competition.' Adrian scrolled the screen up and down to ensure all the boxes were ticked. 'Right then, I'm going to begin the search.' He shifted his mouse so that the cursor hovered over the 'Run Search' box and with an affirmative push of his right forefinger he pressed click. A thick, sludgy silence lasting a few long seconds followed as the site processed my preferences and extracted the matched profiles, as my throat dried all the while and I became increasingly light-headed.

The screen flickered, and settled.

'Fuck me...' I uttered. I now knew how Lord Carnarvon felt when opening the lid of Tutankhamun's Tomb... for staring back at me from Adrian's screen were dozens of photographs of beautiful, photogenic, smiling, available, accessible, gorgeous, *single* women. Blondes, brunettes, blue eyes, brown eyes, big smiles, coy smiles, cheekbones, dimples, noses, lips. Oh my god.

'Well?' asked Adrian, smiling broadly at my reaction.

'I can't believe there are so many single women here,' I said, slowly shaking my head, 'and all... all herded together.'

'Herded?'

'Sorry, grouped together. Can we click on a few?'

'Okay, but we've got to be quick, I'm meeting one of them soon, and no, I'm not telling you which one. Who do you want to view first?'

Did it matter? The fact was, I was going to be poring over all their profiles in detail later tonight, and the next day, and the day after that. I picked an outstandingly attractive tall blonde to begin with, the type Rod Stewart would go for. Adrian clicked on her photo and her profile popped up. Once I'd dragged my eyes from her photographs, the profile read as follows:

> *Hi, I'm an attractive, tall (5 foot 9), slender girl, with long blonde silky hair and sparkling eyes :), very good body (used to be a model). I'm very open, kind, outgoing, intelligent and educated, very confident and ambitious. Enjoy fashion, music, sport and travel, like going out to the cinema, concerts, restaurants/clubs and curling up on the sofa with a glass of wine to watch a dvd. I'm looking for a tall (tall is important as I'm tall myself and like to wear high heels), good-looking (also important, I'll be honest I do pay attention to looks) guy, ambitious and successful, intelligent and educated. The rest is chemistry...*

Adrian shook his head. 'Trust me, steer clear.'

'Why, she seems okay... doesn't she?' There was something about her profile that left me vaguely uneasy, but I didn't want to be ruling her out too quickly, not when she was so pleasing on the eye. And single.

'There's lots of warning signs here,' said Adrian, still shaking his head.

'Is there?'

'Did you not read her profile?'

'Yes, briefly.'

'But spent longer looking at her photos? Yes, I used to do that. Don't get me wrong, she's clearly stunning, but do you really think you'd be compatible?'

I pulled my chin in. 'I don't see why not. She may be good-looking, but plenty of guys punch above their weight with women, don't they?'

'This is the real world; you're not Hugh Grant in Notting Hill. And besides, it's not her looks I'm referring to. Just look at her opening line in which she describes herself and how she defines the type of man she's looking for. They're both heavy on looks and appearances. To my mind this girl is a vain, narcissistic bore.'

'Jeez, I guess I need to read the profiles on a deeper level.'

'You need to do more than drool at the photos, yes. The profile always gives away a lot about the person who wrote it.'

'Okay, I'll try harder. Did I miss anything else?'

'Look at her interests, they're so boring.' Adrian leant forward to scan the profile again. 'Everyone likes music and travel. And what about that line about "curling up on the sofa with a glass of wine and a dvd"? That just makes me want to be sick.'

'Okay, I admit it, she's risky. Can we try another, just quickly?'

'As long as you're quick.'

This time I chose someone less conventional, a girl with a nose stud whose photograph showed her standing in a field with lots of tents in the background, presumably at a festival. Surely she'd have something interesting to say:

> *Well am about 5.6, Rarest jewel on venus. I am picky, and yes certain things do matter. I am complex, ticklish, also, BUT mega loving... giving is my biggest fault (I enjoy caring 4some1) You sometimes get exploited. hmmmm... I like alot of stuff, the finer things in life (does that make me a snob?) interior designs, sleeping, shopping, wining and dining, magazines,, all girlie stuff. I am a woman remember. Favorite thing is KISSING, but only the right person, don't kiss 4 fun EITHER. Hopefully I'm hoping to chat to a man who is attractive and deep..((not self obsessed)) passionate, doesn't play mind games, caring, loving...... knows and likes QUALITY! p.s. NO sports freak. Stylish men r very attractive! I am big on eyes. I have NO patience 4GAMES!*

There was a protracted silence after we'd finished reading the profile.

'What language is that written in?' I asked.

'Beats me, but there's lots to fear here. The manic use of capitals and the stream of consciousness style make me very nervous. She's clearly a total nutter.'

'Agreed. Just one more?'

'I've really got to go.'

Adrian reached for his mouse to shut down his PC and in a reflex moment of panic I'd grasped his forearm. 'Please Adrian, just one more, just one, please.' I was still gripping him.

'Alright, alright, choose one,' said Adrian. I released him. He looked down to where I'd seized his arm and rubbed it.

This time I chose someone at random, a girl-next-door type with shoulder length brown hair. Her profile read:

> *I like: My friends, cider, 'Withnail and I', laughing so hard I can't breathe, 'Napoleon Dynamite', waking up still drunk, Janis Joplin, my cat, olives, Eddie Izzard, reading in bed, Jamiroquai, 'The Mighty Boosh', Fridays, the fact that I'm getting braver and more confident as time goes on.*
>
> *I dislike: Music without lyrics, how expensive cigarettes are, falseness, early mornings, Lee Evans, mint chocolate, marzipan, Sunday nights, reality TV. I am a laid-back and positive person (it was tricky coming up with my dislikes). The above is quite trivial, but I think you can tell a lot from the little things. A sense of humour and sincerity are important to me. It'd be good to meet somebody intelligent who doesn't take themselves too seriously.*

'Now that one I like,' I said.

'Agreed, she's got potential.'

'You haven't dated her, have you?'

'No, I haven't. She's all yours.'

'Great.'

Adrian closed down his PC and packed his stuff away. I did likewise; there was no way I was going to hang around making futile phone calls when I could be at home selecting my future wife and mother of my children.

'Right, I'm off,' said Adrian. 'Mustn't be late for a date, women don't like to be kept waiting.'

I was still struggling to digest that here Adrian was, teaching me about the dating game. Still, he'd earned the right. 'Have you got any other tips for me before you go?' I asked.

'The rest is down to you. As with most things in life, the more you put into it, the more you'll get out of it.'

He departed. I vowed to complete my profile as soon as I got home and started to think about which photographs to post on my profile: there was that one of me taken at last year's Christmas party at the centre of lots of revellers – *He looks like a popular guy* – and that one of me in my glasses – *He looks like a cerebral type*.

As I left the office I realised something else: the last hour was the longest I'd gone in months without thinking about Marianne.

19

Saturday. Late afternoon. Internet date imminent.

After undressing, I turned on the shower – waiting until it was piping hot – then switched on the radio to hear the familiar jangle of BBC Radio's Sports Report. Stepping under the powerful jets of water invigorated me and I thought: what could be more life-affirming than this, a single, eligible bachelor, about to spend Saturday night on a date with a beautiful single woman in the world's most exciting city?

My thoughts turned to how my forefathers had prepared for the ancient ritual of dating in times gone by. How about my dad? It must have been great dating in the late sixties, what with The Summer of Love, free love, *All You Need is Love* and all that, but for some reason I soon had the rather unfortunate image of my father standing in baggy chocolate coloured y-fronts with mustard piping, admiring himself in the mirror of an avocado bathroom as he brushed a huge mountain of wiry hair.

As the water hit my face I focussed on the evening ahead. I'd not left anything to chance. I was meeting Emma at 7 p.m. at Embankment tube station and the plan was to go for some drinks, followed by dinner at 8.30 p.m. I'd booked a table at what looked to be a cosy and atmospheric brasserie called PJ's in Wellington Street and I thought a cocktail or two beforehand at Christopher's American Bar next door would set us up nicely.

After the shower, a wet shave, followed by a hefty swig of mouth wash – held in the mouth until it burnt – and three long minutes with the electric toothbrush. Then back to the bedroom for stage two of the preparations, which had to be accompanied by carefully selected uplifting music to get me into a heightened state of emotional readiness. *I'm no energy drain.* I couldn't resist a smile as the opening crash of the symbols of *This Is The One* by the Stone Roses rang out from the speakers.

What to wear to make the right impression? Something simple or she might mark me down as vain, so I plumped for dark jeans, brown brogues and black shirt. As my aftershave gave a pleasurable sting to my freshly shaved cheeks, I tried to imagine what eye-wateringly sweet and pungent cologne my father must have splashed on back in the late sixties: presumably something which came in zebra or lion print packaging, with an intimidating name like Cattleman's Whiskers or Full Choke.

Once dressed, the CD moved on to *I Am the Resurrection* and I reasoned that a quick sharpener might be enjoyable. Enjoyable, or necessary? Who cared? I strode through to the kitchen and found myself a sturdy, thick-glassed tumbler, threw in three ice cubes and poured over a double measure of whisky. Hell, it was Saturday night, I made it a triple, then poured in some ginger ale, the fizz of which cascading over the ice sounding like shingle on a beach as a wave withdraws. Heaven.

I needed to get cracking now as it was after 6 p.m. By the front door, I undertook the final inventory inspection. Oyster card: check. Keys: check. Mobile: check. Wallet: check. iPod: check. Condoms (just in case, just in case): check. Last glance in the mirror squinting with pursed lips: check.

Outside, there was that taste of freshness in the air one gets on autumn days, which signifies the passing of summer, but is also a foretaste of something new, like a new school term, or new football season. On the tube I had my first pang of nerves, for here I was about to meet a virtual stranger and yet romance was a distinct possibility. Internet dating meant going straight to a first date and missing the flirting stage: noticing her across a crowded room, exchanging furtive glances, talking for the first time and asking her out.

Embankment station on a Saturday night is a maelstrom of activity. The ticket hall is a place of convergence and divergence, with people coming and going from Trafalgar Square, Covent Garden and Southbank. So I'd been very specific and asked Emma to meet me by the small steps leading down from the station to the Embankment. I stood there waiting, nervous and self-conscious, much more so than I'd anticipated.

I distracted myself by looking over the concrete wall at the choppy Thames turned silver in the fading sunlight and its hazy reflection of the giant glinting ring of the London Eye, but my thoughts kept returning to Emma. What if she didn't like me, or didn't find me attractive? Would I even recognise her? It was disappointing that she'd only posted one photograph on her profile and that a little distant, grainy and out-of-focus. If only she'd posted a really crystal-clear one.

Suddenly, my personal space was invaded by a tall, looming, bulky presence. An American tourist wanting directions? I leant back, my eyes focussed, and a strange and unwelcome connection was made in my brain between the photograph posted on Emma's profile and this... this *giantess* in front of me. Good god no, it couldn't be... could it?!

My cogs whirred at a million miles an hour. For the briefest nanosecond I weighed up whether to deny I was her date: *'Very sorry, I think you've got the wrong person'*, then turn away – no, run away – into the mass of people in the ticket hall and be gone forever. But I couldn't do that.

'Hi, Adam?' the imposing physical presence said, looking down at me inquiringly and waiting for me to confirm I was her date.

'Hi, how are you?' I replied, putting everything into my smile to make it as genuine as possible.

'I'm very well, thank you,' she said.

'Shall we go? This way.' As we set off up Villiers Street talking about what we'd done that day, I took silent deep breaths to recompose myself. I had a whole hour and a half to kill *before* dinner started. Why hadn't I just asked her out for a quick drink?

We arrived at Christopher's cocktail lounge, all amber soft lighting, glass and mirrors, and highly polished wood, the bar packed with the Saturday evening crowd, making me fear I might bump into someone I knew:

'Hi, Adam, I haven't seen you in ages, who's this you're with?'

'Oh, hi. This is Emma and she's er... she's... my friend.'

'And how do you two know each other?'

'Er... er... we're work colleagues.' Out together on a Saturday night? Unlikely.

'Er... er... she's my cousin.' Too weird.

'Er... er... she's a friend of a friend.' Fuck it, I'd just have to admit she was my date. My internet date.

I ushered Emma to a spot at the back of the bar. 'I'll fetch the drinks. What would you like?'

'Vodka and slimline tonic, please.'

'Sure, on its way.' I turned to go to the bar.

'And Adam?'

'Yes?'

'Make sure it's *slimline* tonic, please?'

'Okay, no problem.'

I hate to admit it, but as I queued, I was glad it was busy and the labour-intensive cocktail mixing took so long, which gave me time to think and ate into the vast expanse of time stretched out in front of me. I snuck a glance back at Emma. She wasn't unattractive, but she bore absolutely no resemblance at all to the picture she had posted on her profile. Mind you, what had Adrian said about photographs: *you've only got one chance to make a good impression.*

Eventually I got served, ordering a Sazerac for myself, a drink which always made me feel a little spaced out, which I figured might help. I returned to Emma and we raised our glasses and both said, 'Cheers!'

'So, you're a lawyer?' I asked, after we'd made small talk for a while.

'Yes, in employment law. It's challenging, but very rewarding. How about you, you're in finance, I believe?'

'I'm a recruitment consultant in the financial services sector.'

'And do you enjoy it?'

I shrugged my shoulders. 'It's alright. I'm not sure I get the same job satisfaction as you, but—'

A woman walking past with short light brown hair and freckles interrupted my train of thought: in reflex my eyes flicked in her direction, then back to Emma, now frowning. Had she noticed me do that?

There was a short silence. 'You're a salesman then,' said Emma.

'Sorry?'

'You said you were a recruitment consultant, which means you're essentially a salesman.'

'Well, sort of, but—'

'Surely that's exactly what you are, a salesman of... people.'

'You make it sound like I'm selling them into slavery! I'm just trying to find them new jobs.'

'Well, every time a recruitment agent calls me, they're invariably trying to sell me a job I don't want. And they always call me at work, which is embarrassing. Perhaps that explains why recruitment consultants have such a poor reputation.'

I fortified myself with another sip of my drink. 'Don't lawyers charge by the hour?'

'Yes.'

'And I presume your charge-out rate is hundreds of pounds an hour?'

The beginnings of a satisfied grin appeared on Emma's mouth. 'I'm quite expensive, yes.'

'Isn't that selling? You're selling units of your very existence.'

She lifted her chin and looked away. In the ensuing silence she didn't seem in any danger of initiating a fresh conversation.

'Tell me, Emma, how many dates have you been on from the site?' I asked, trying to be positive.

'About seven or eight–'

'Seven or eight? Wow, that's a lot. No joy yet then?'

'Clearly...' she said, giving me a smile which was perhaps as insincere as the one I'd given her when we'd first met at the tube station. 'How about you?'

'You're my first. First time lucky and all that!' As soon as the words left my mouth I cringed. In response Emma looked pained, like someone had just told her that a distant relative had died.

I took a huge gulp of the sazerac, which finished it. Emma did likewise to her vodka and tonic.

'Another?' I asked.

'Yes, I think I'm going to need it,' she said.

I returned to the bar and tried to regroup. It was clear this was no longer a date, and if not a date, what was it? It crossed my mind to go back to Emma and say, *'Look, it's clear this is going nowhere, shall we just finish our drinks, shake hands and split?'* Are you allowed to do that on an internet date?

I rejoined Emma with a caipirinha for myself – so bitter from the lime and alcoholic from the cachaça that my jaw muscles clenched after each sip – and another vodka and tonic for her, which I'd made a double.

We chatted more amiably for a while about our respective jobs and the state of the economy, and soon walked next door to the restaurant. Despite being a little early, the waiter was happy to seat us. After a couple of minutes, he returned. 'Would you like to order any wine?' he asked.

'Yes, why not,' said Emma. 'We'll have a bottle of the Pinot Grigio.' At least she enjoyed a drink, I thought.

We perused our menus. The service was efficient, the prompt arrival of the wine soon followed by the waiter stooping with his little notepad ready to take our orders. 'Would you like to order any starters?'

'I'll think we'll go straight to the main course actually,' said Emma. 'As a *main* course, I will have a Caesar's salad.'

'Very good, Madam.'

'And please could you bring the dressing on the side?'

'Of course, Madam.' The waiter bowed towards me. 'And for you, Sir?'

The drinks and nerves had made me ravenous. 'I'll go for the sirloin steak,' I said. 'Rare. With béarnaise sauce and fries, please.'

'Very good. Very, very good.' With a little flourish of his notepad the waiter was gone.

'Are you sure you just want a salad?' I asked Emma.

'I really like Caesar's salad. Plus it's five points.'

'Five points? What, are we scoring the dinner, like on Come Dine with Me?'

'Never mind,' said Emma.

'No, I'm happy to score it, it could be fun.'

'I meant it's only five points on the Weight Watchers scale.'

'Oh, I see! Sorry!' I couldn't believe I didn't see that one coming; perhaps the drinks had blunted my edge. I recomposed myself. 'You really follow the Weight Watchers thing that closely?'

'I don't want to talk about it. All I can say is that it's worked wonders for me.'

Worked? Past tense. Even so, I was grateful we were having a conversation, though hardly the soul-baring, doe-eyed romantic one I'd dreamed of in the days leading up to the 'date'. 'I just wanted to know how they work out the points, that's all,' I said.

'Calories and saturated fat,' said Emma, 'plus how tall you are, how active and your body shape.'

'Ah, but what happens if you have a night of binge drinking followed by a doner kebab?' I chuckled.

'I've *never* eaten a doner kebab,' said Emma.

'Well, alright, but you know what I mean. An evening like that must completely screw the counting.' I poured Emma and myself another glass of wine.

'Needless to say,' said Emma, 'they've thought of that. You can carry forward points.'

I nodded. 'I see. They've got it all figured out, haven't they? Personally, I've always been slightly sceptical about Weight Watchers. Don't they claim you don't need to exercise to lose weight?'

Emma sat back in her seat and folded her arms. 'But I do exercise.'

'I wasn't talking about you. I was just talking about the concept.'

'Well, that was the inference. I'll have you know I walk to the tube each morning and take a longer walk on Saturdays.'

I smirked; the drink was making me mischievous.

'What?' asked Emma, glaring at me.

'Is walking really exercise? My dear old granny might call it exercise, but surely anything you just do in the normal course of events doesn't count as exercise?'

'Yes it bloody well does. You get to subtract points for walking.'

'But exercise is going for a run and getting hot and sweaty, isn't it? Claiming that walking is exercise is like claiming yoga is exercise.'

'Yoga *is* exercise. And I practise... regularly. Some of the fittest and most supple women I know do yoga.'

'Can you introduce me to them?' I almost said, but resisted. Instead, the conversation dried up. It would be fair to say that the following few minutes as we waited for our food to arrive were agonisingly slow. I fidgeted with the stem of my wine glass. Emma scanned the restaurant, occasionally sipping her wine and refilling our glasses.

Eventually our food arrived. The waiter presented Emma with a mountain of greenery, accompanied by a gravy boat of salad dressing, which Emma proceeded to pour onto her salad in its entirety, drowning it. My steak looked delicious: a nicely marbled piece of meat full of flavour, the blood ready to ooze out at the first cut.

After a few mouthfuls Emma waved her fork in the direction of my plate. 'That's bad for you, you know, all that meat,' she said. 'Did you know that a steak can stay in your intestine for up to a week?'

'You mean I'm still extracting goodness from it a week after eating it? Sounds like great value for money to me! Besides, what are those?' I asked rhetorically, pointing at the croutons liberally scattered throughout her salad.

'They're croutons.'

'Aren't croutons a fancy name for fried bread? They must be five points each on the Richter scale or whatever that thing is you follow.' I tried to suppress my laughter, which made my shoulders judder; the drink had really kicked in now and I felt great.

'I won't eat them if you don't want me to. In fact,' she said, placing her knife and fork down either side of her plate, 'I won't eat at all seeing as it so offends you.' Her subsequent stare was quite terrifying: something to do with her eyes burning pure distilled hatred into me.

'What? No, please, Emma, I'm sorry, I didn't mean it like that. Please, eat up.'

An enduring silence followed, Emma continuing to glare.

'Please, Emma, I'm begging you, please eat more.'

Eventually she relented and to my great relief restarted her meal, but another period of wordlessness descended as we both looked down at our plates while we ate.

'Another bottle of wine?' I asked halfway through the meal.

'Why not,' said Emma.

I duly put in the order and the waiter recharged our glasses.

'Can I ask you something?' asked Emma.

'Sure, go ahead.'

'You said I'm your first internet date. Did you recently come out of a relationship?'

Any conversation was better than no conversation, even one about past loves. 'I broke up with my ex last year, so I've been single for a few months now, but I've only just discovered internet dating.'

'How long were you with your ex for?' asked Emma.

'Seven years.'

'That's a long time. May I ask why you split up?'

I decided to omit the coup de grace of sending Louise the text message meant for Nadine. 'I think our relationship had run its course. We both recognised it was time to move on. The ending was a bit... rough, but finishing was a mutual decision.'

Emma flinched at the mention of the rough ending and took a meaningful gulp of wine. She held the stem of her glass between thumb and forefinger and turned it through a series of revolutions. 'I'm sorry, perhaps I shouldn't have asked,' she said. 'I know you're not meant to talk about exes on dates, but we're not young anymore, are we? I mean, neither of us is likely to meet someone who hasn't already been in a long-term relationship. We both have to face the fact that whoever we meet, we won't be their first love. Or even their second or third in some cases.'

'I think you've got to look at the positives as well,' I said. 'At least at our age we know a bit more about what we're looking for in a partner. Presumably we should be able to make a more informed choice next time?'

'Maybe...' said Emma, a dreamy look in her eyes as she tipped back more wine.

'Are you okay?' I asked.

'Yes, I'm fine. Sorry, I was just... reminiscing.'

'Reminiscing?'

'About Greg. My ex. My first love. We dated since we were teenagers. We grew up together, had our first kiss together, lost our virginities to one another' – she pulled an expansive yearning expression – 'took our first overseas holiday together, bought our first house together. We were just so... so good together. Until... well, until it finished.'

'May I ask how it finished?' It seemed fair to ask, given she'd asked me.

She filled her wine glass, took a swig and looked at me intently. 'It was last year when he broke the news.'

'The news?'

'That there was someone else.'

'Oh god, Emma, I'm so sorry to hear that.'

'How can you be sorry? You weren't there, you don't know what happened.'

'I'm sorry – I mean... I sympathise.' God, this was tricky. 'You don't have to talk about it if you don't want to.'

'It was terrible, I'll never forget it.' Her bottom lip closed over her top one.

'What was it? Did he leave you for someone you knew?'

'Worse, much worse than that.' Her voice faltered, its pitch rising and falling unpredictably.

'Did you catch him in bed with someone?'

She looked at me with a great intensity and wailed in a high pitch, 'Worse!'

I wanted this to end now; it was becoming weird. 'I don't know, did he sleep with your mum or something?'

'*What?!* That's just sick, what's wrong with you?'

'I'm sorry, you kept prompting me to guess and–'

'He's bisexual.'

Silence.

Fuck me, and I thought my break-up was bad. Internet dating may not have found me my dream date, but it was proving good therapy. Topping up our glasses, I held mine up, inviting her to chink it with hers, which she did. 'To new beginnings,' I said.

'I'll drink to that,' she said, knocking back half a glass.

'So, have any of your internet dates led to a second date?' I asked.

'Only one, and it was a massive misjudgement.'

'Why, what happened?'

A faint look of disgust settled on her face, a slight dilution of the nostrils, as if she'd caught a waft of something unsavoury. 'I wasn't really sure about him after the first date, to be honest, but sometimes you try to convince yourself that it may work out. Stupidly, I agreed to a second date.'

'And?'

'We both had one drink too many...'

'No crime there.'

'Yes, but it's what the drinks led to.' She took another swig of wine. Her eyes were very glazed.

'Which was?' I asked.

'Once we'd left the pub, we started kissing in a shop doorway...'

'Nothing wrong with that, it was a date.'

'It only encouraged him. He became... over enthusiastic.'

'Our passion can overcome us.' I recalled Nadine and I kissing manically outside Charing Cross station.

'You don't understand. He started... grinding.'

'Grinding?'

'His body against mine. Then he went rigid.'

'Rigid?'

'Then completely lifeless, like he'd turned to jelly.'

'Jelly? Was he drunk? Perhaps he felt ill.'

'No, it wasn't that. He kept apologising while looking down... at which point I noticed a wet patch.'

'A wet patch?'

'In his groin area.'

'He'd peed himself?'

'No, you idiot, he'd become... over excited. From all the grinding.'

'Oh right! Jesus.' To think when I'd first spoken to Adrian about internet dating I'd been frightened about all the competition; if Mr Trigger Happy was who I was up against I should have no problems! The internet dating therapy continued to work wonders.

'Then he just walked off...' Emma was slurring her speech now. 'You wouldn't behave like that on a second date, would you?'

Why was she asking me about a second date? I took a large swig of wine to buy time to think. Did she really want a second date with me, after tonight? Did she actually see a *future* for the two of us? The alcohol had made my mind foggy; I needed to tread carefully. 'I'd like to think I'd be a little bit more... reserved on a second date,' I replied.

'Good. It would be nice to have my faith in men restored by a gentleman–'

'But I'm not sure yet about this whole internet dating thing. As I said, you're my first date and I'm just getting my confidence back after Louise. You know how it is.'

'I do know how it is, unfortunately...' Emma's voice faded and she stared into the straw-coloured liquid in her glass, her eyes vacant and expressionless. 'It just seems so... so *hard*.' The word 'hard' came out as a warbling lament, followed by her shoulders trembling.

I realised to my horror that she'd started sobbing. 'Please, Emma, please don't cry,' I said, but she continued. I didn't know what to do. I sensed sly stares from neighbouring tables. Perhaps they thought we were a couple and I'd just admitted to an affair, or confirmed our relationship was over. Perhaps, though, the truth was even more disturbing: that I was sitting opposite a woman I'd met just two hours earlier and had already reduced her to tears.

Emma's wine glass started shaking; she was still gripping its stem. Fearing she would cause a spill, I reached out and took hold of her hand, removed it from the glass and held it in a bid to comfort her. 'Emma, I'm not that nice, really. Seriously, if you got to know me you wouldn't be upset like this. I'm not worth a second date.'

She looked up at me with watery eyes wide with confusion. 'What did you say?'

'I said I'm really not worth getting upset about. I'm not that special. I'm–'

'I'm not crying about you, you arrogant pig, I'm crying about Greg, my ex.' She threw my hand off hers, her eyes shimmering like chips of broken glass. 'My god, what's wrong with you men?'

'I'm sorry.'

Silence.

I asked for the bill. When it arrived, guilt moved me to offer to settle the lot, but to be fair to Emma, she insisted on paying half.

We headed outside. 'I'm going to Covent Garden tube,' said Emma. 'It's easier for me to get home from there.'

'Listen, Emma, I'm really sorry about tonight.'

'You say sorry a lot, do you know that?'

'Sorry – shit, I did it again. Best of luck finding that special someone. I'm sure he's out there, it's just a matter of finding him.'

'Good luck to you too, Adam.' She pecked me on the cheek and was gone.

I walked down to the Strand, but wanted to get away from the mass of people there, so cut down a back street to the river, where it was much quieter and stiller. I stopped and leant against the Embankment balustrade, the concrete rough and cold on my forearms, the air cool and fresh on my warm, alcohol-infused cheeks. I stared out across the oily black Thames. The gentle waves of the night river made lapping and plopping sounds against the Embankment wall far below. I felt as sad and lonely and empty as the old disused barge chained to the riverbed beneath me, rocking in the pull and swell of the tide.

20

Another melancholic Monday morning, silently sipping my tea and contemplating the futility of making calls to clients implementing redundancy programmes. And the previous night's Sunday Night Blues had been particularly acute, Marcus looming large and Marianne also making repeated appearances, prompting me at one stage to get up out of bed to watch an hour of late-night poker on TV.

Things would have been more bearable if I'd managed to do something positive on the weekend. Perhaps visited some friends, or a place of historic interest or natural beauty. That way I could have said I'd made the most of my free time. But what had I done? Vegetated in my flat, that's what I'd done. I'd slept in late both mornings, ordered takeaways both nights, eaten pot noodles for both lunches and polished off three bottles of red wine and a four-pack of Red Stripe. But that wasn't all I'd achieved. I'd also watched two Premiership football matches, three hours of live darts coverage on Saturday night and the film *2001: A Space Odyssey* on Sunday night. I'd spoken to no one at all, which rather left me with an empty feeling that perhaps I hadn't existed, or somehow the weekend hadn't happened.

My personal mood was mirrored by the collective mood in the office, for a deep sense of foreboding had taken root as we all became increasingly aware that the dreaded impacts of the recession couldn't remain external phenomena for much longer. The government had recently been forced to nationalise three of the major banks and was now coming under pressure to guarantee personal bank deposits. Economists were predicting that the next generation would be the first in centuries to be poorer than their parents. The economy wasn't so much in recession as in meltdown.

Still, it wasn't all bad news that day, because Marcus wasn't in yet, which made me happy for two reasons: firstly because his absence under any circumstances had become something to be celebrated and secondly, it meant he was late, which was one of his great dislikes and contrary to every management book he'd ever read.

It was 10.42 a.m. when he arrived (I checked my watch, just as he always did with me) and started chuntering to himself throughout the process of logging on, tapping his keyboard aggressively as he did so.

'You okay, Marcus?' Adrian asked.

'Not really, no. Our boiler broke over the weekend and the guy fixing it this morning said I've got to pay the first two hundred quid. What's the fucking point in taking out a policy if you end up paying half the cost? It's bloody theft, that's what it is.'

'It's always in the small print,' said Adrian. 'They lure you in with some deal, but don't tell you the catches.'

'Damn right,' said Marcus.

'Thatcher's Britain, that's what my dad calls it,' I said. 'Commercial exploitation and opportunism at every turn. It's not what something's worth any more, it's what the market will bear.'

'Spare us your politics,' said Marcus. 'This is about the small print, as Adrian said.'

As you can imagine, Marcus's miserable mood did wonders for the already sorrowful Monday morning atmosphere. And from a personal perspective, work was bad enough already. I'd had a rough time of it recently, culminating in one of my placements quitting his job within six months of starting, meaning we'd had to refund the client half the fee we'd charged them. The company's Sales League Table, automatically and prominently displayed on the intranet home page, continued to hammer home my failings.

BANG! Luke smashed his telephone receiver down. 'YESSSSSSSSS!' he shrieked, standing and running hyperactively on the spot, pumping his arms up and down. 'Result!' he shouted. 'Twenty pound an hour margin. We need to get that bell set up in here like we said and ring it each time we make a sale. I'm moving on up that league table, just like the Hammers!'

Marcus had erupted out of his seat the moment he heard Luke's wail, and now reached him and shook his hand. 'Well done, well done,' he said, 'a few more of those and our figures won't be so bad.'

Matt had also risen to join the congratulatory orgy and he slapped Luke on the back. 'Another one of those and we'll definitely win that mini-break to Riga!'

'What's the deal?' asked Marcus.

'Some guy who lost his job when the economy dived,' said Luke. 'He's desperate and totally ignorant of hourly rates. The client's paying us forty-five quid an hour and he's just taken the job for twenty. After National Insurance that's a clear twenty-pound margin. That's what I call a reee-sult!' He repeatedly flicked his forefinger in the air, like cracking a whip, so that it made a clicking sound.

My immediate thought was how Roy would have reacted to such an obscene margin. Mind you, he wanted for so much less than Marcus, Luke or Matt. You had to crave things to be so dishonest.

Marcus returned to his desk. 'You know,' he said, addressing me while pointing his thumb back over his shoulder in the direction of Luke and Matt, 'you could learn a lot from those guys.'

'Such as?' I asked.

'You could learn from their energy and determination.'

I waited while I worked out how to respond. 'Are you saying I don't have any energy or determination?'

'No, I'm just saying that they're prepared to work long hours and make the calls, and it shows in their results, as you've just seen.' Marcus sat down and started typing, clearly thinking the conversation over.

I ground my teeth as a red mist of rage descended. I bent the bic biro I was holding so hard it eventually snapped in two with a crack. 'And dirtier,' I said.

'What was that?' asked Marcus, looking up.

'You pointed out that Luke and Matt have more energy than me and work harder. I just added that they're also dirtier.'

Marcus cocked his head toward me as if he hadn't quite heard me correctly. 'What did you just say?'

I projected my voice. 'I said they're dirtier than me.' I kept looking at Marcus, but out of the corner of my eye I could see that both Luke and Matt had turned round.

'What the *fuck* is that supposed to mean?' asked Marcus, now standing up. Silence settled across the office, so complete that I could hear the gentle continual hum of the air-conditioning system. Colleagues stared at their PCs, pretending to be working, but their complete absence of movement or sound confirmed they were listening.

'I mean they make their money dishonestly and you encourage it,' I said.

'You what? What's dishonest about making money? It's called good business.'

'It's more a question of how you make it. If the client doesn't know what the candidate is earning and the candidate doesn't know how much you're charging the client, then that's dishonest.'

'That's a bit rich coming from you, who seems to be actually *costing* us money at the moment. You know, I'm sick and tired of your backchat. Carolyn told me all about your disruptive behaviour at the teambuilding course. It's about time you started respecting your seniors. Maybe then one day you'll understand how business actually works.'

I leant back in my chair and balled my hands together into a fist in my lap. 'You know, you're right, business confuses me. For instance, when your insurer asks you to pay the two hundred pound excess on the policy you've signed up to it's – how did you describe it again? – bloody theft, but when you find a desperate out-of-work guy who's just lost his job and screw him for twenty pounds an hour, that's called good business.'

Marcus squinted at me, as though he'd underestimated an enemy he previously thought he'd mastered. My telephone rang; I looked at it, then at Marcus, then answered it.

As soon as the call ended, I left the office before Marcus could resume the argument. I walked down High Holborn until I came to a large roundabout with a white stone church on its far side. In the church's small secluded garden, I sat down on a bench, alone, thankful it was so still and quiet, the trees and hedges insulating the garden from the traffic and commotion of the street outside. My heart was still racing.

I leant forward with my elbows on my thighs and rubbed my cheeks and eyes. I remembered again the photograph my mother had on the notice board in the kitchen at home of me as a six-year-old boy, conscientious and hopeful, starting out at school. Hadn't that boy done as he was told? Hadn't he studied hard for his GCSEs and A-levels, gone to a decent university, obtained a degree? Yet somehow I'd ended up in this... this mess of a career in sales.

My work gave me no connection to anything in the outside world that meant anything to me. I thought about what it would be like to have a job making something with my hands which I could use or see, or a job which gave me some connection with society at large. I wish I'd known all this earlier. When I'd started looking for work in the mid-nineties, it was all about making money. Anything less was weakness.

I'd been sold a dud, for to survive and prosper in a City job required the personality traits of a psychopath: skill in manipulating and flattering others, a strong sense of self-entitlement, a readiness to exploit others and a lack of empathy or conscience.

I was thirty-five years old. Could I really see myself as a recruitment consultant in, say, ten years' time, still making the endless phone calls to clients and candidates, still being managed by the likes of Marcus, still looking at where I was towards the bottom of a Sales League fucking Table? A dull ache of dread formed in my stomach at the thought of it.

But the system had trapped me. I had a large mortgage. Worse still, my own sense of self-worth seemed tied to my income. Why?

I knew I had to change career, but I needed time and money to work it all out – the two commodities least in supply.

I'd let the boy in the photograph down. I no longer felt angry with Marcus, I felt overwhelmingly sad for myself.

21

I decided to give internet dating another shot. But with a refined selection criteria. No more women with only one photograph on their profile, or whose photographs were hazy, indistinct, or taken at a distance. I sent messages only to women with at least three clear photographs that proved *beyond reasonable doubt* that I would find them attractive in person. It was a *dating* site, for Christ's sake: physical attraction was a must.

By god, the new search unearthed some stunners. I spent a number of evenings one week appraising them at length and in depth. With some there was admittedly a tension between my head and my heart, particularly those who advertised their charms in short dresses, low-cut tops, or even, in the case of two of them, in bikinis. Or was it a tension between my head and another vital organ? Either way, Adrian would have advised me to steer well clear and my head agreed, but my heart/vital organ said *go for it*, for as Sam had said, being single was a golden age, a time of opportunity, you've never had it so good. And if I was up against a load of Mr Trigger Happies like the chap who'd been on a second date with Emma, well, I had every reason to be confident about my chances.

I sent out about ten messages to the winners of the beauty parade and waited expectantly. And waited. And waited some more. A week or so later I was forced to accept the fundamental flaw in my methodology: it needed someone to reply. I was hurt by this, but not particularly surprised, for while I'd carefully chosen the best possible photographs for my profile, ultimately I'm pretty average when it comes to looks. Mid-table. And my morning ablutions were now a time of worrying revelation, for the man in the mirror was beginning to recede slightly and thin out, and there were an increasing number of grey hairs around my temples, all of which served to remind me that time wasn't on my side.

But you never know when your luck is about to change on the internet, and it did for me two weeks later when I got a reply. The lady who responded was quite simply frighteningly beautiful. Actually, the word beautiful doesn't do her justice. Judging from her profile – three clear pictures, no room for doubt – she was Audrey bloody Hepburn, a woman of staggering loveliness. Her name was Sophie and the only annoyance was that her profile was disappointingly short on detail, which meant I couldn't get a proper feel for her personality. Mind you, with looks like hers, I guessed she didn't need to sell herself. Sophie's reply had been very succinct and made clear that she preferred to meet in person rather than exchange lots of emails. Which suited me! We agreed to meet the next Saturday night...

* * *

Saturday night, 7.30 p.m., outside the Marks & Spencer opposite Covent Garden tube station. I looked expectantly across the road in the direction of the station exit. Why was I so nervous? Sophie might be exquisite, but that didn't mean she was out of my league, did it? Surely a bit of personality, charisma and charm can make up for a little discrepancy on the empirical scale of beauty? Besides, women are less interested in looks, right?

I decided to people-watch to try to take my mind off my nerves. A mesmerising mass of humans streamed in and out of the station and walked up and down the pedestrian road leading to the piazza. Every age and race converged on that corner. It was a place of animation and emotion: faces blooming as they greeted old friends or family; people weighed down with shopping bags getting stuck in the ticket barriers; occasionally a youngster staggering from the tube station red in the face, having ignored the lifts and bravely taken on the 193-step ascent from the platforms far below.

I chewed my thumbnail. I checked my watch: 7.38 p.m. I could understand Sophie being a little late; she wouldn't want to arrive early and be standing alone on a street corner, she'd likely be chatted up and harassed. I'd emailed her my mobile number, but she hadn't sent hers back, so I had no way of getting in touch.

I fidgeted with my mobile and clicked on the internet to scan the sports pages, scrolling through the football results without really taking them in. I clicked back to check the time: 7.51 p.m. Shit! This was now extremely worrying. Does anyone ever turn up twenty minutes late for a date? What if she'd had second thoughts? I decided to give it until 8 p.m.

I saw her.

There was absolutely no mistaking it was her, a flurry of beiges and browns, with softly tanned skin and blonde hair cascading over her shoulders. She walked tall with a straight back and her head held high, giving her an air of confidence and diffidence to the world around her.

She approached, spotted me and smiled, her flawless white teeth gleaming; I stared at them transfixed, as if waiting for her to run the tip of her tongue across their front like in a toothpaste advert. Her high, plucked, widely arched eyebrows emphasised eyes of a vivid dark blue. Her skin was so taut across her face and neck that I could see – or perhaps just sense – her muscles moving underneath, such was her leanness.

She kissed me on the cheek. 'Hi, Adam, so where are you taking me?' she asked, but I couldn't immediately respond as I was momentarily rendered speechless by her radiance, vitality and sheer... healthiness.

'Er... I've booked a French restaurant, not too far from here.'

'French? Good choice, let's go.'

As we walked, I caught glimpses of Sophie's tight white jeans and knee-length brown boots, which together gave her legs the impression of being even longer than they already were. Under a light brown raincoat she wore a beige cowl neck jumper, which afforded views of her neck and collarbones. She carried a particularly large version of that brown Louis Vuitton handbag that every woman seems to own, or want.

Walking down the street soon became unsettling, as every man coming from the opposite direction stared at her with laser-like focus. I could have forgiven them this, but not the ridiculous faces they pulled. Some squinted like Clint Eastwood, or at least as they thought Clint Eastwood squinted, while some did a disturbing thing with their lips, like a pout. Others glowered with a quiet intensity, trying to look like some guy out of a Gillette advert. Do women really have to put up with this behaviour on a daily basis?

I'd booked quite a posh French restaurant for dinner. I know, I know. Had I not learnt my lesson from the date with Emma? Why had I committed myself to a date lasting hours when I could just as easily organised a quick drink? Need I say more than remind you what this girl looked like? Was she really the sort of woman to be impressed by a gingerbread latte in Starbucks surrounded by crowds of animated tourists with Harrods and Hamleys bags? Of a half of Bishop's Finger in an old man's spit and sawdust pub?

After a short walk, we entered the atrium of the restaurant and an army of waiters and waitresses converged on us and whisked away our coats. A tall, bone-thin and immaculately attired waiter led us briskly to our table and stood behind Sophie's chair, easing it under her as she sat down. Once seated, he picked up each of our napkins in turn, flourished them and draped them over our laps with a flick of his dexterous wrist while looking the other way. He conjured up two menus, handing one to Sophie with a smile and a bow and one to me in more businesslike fashion.

'Shall I get the sommelier?' he asked me in a tone of voice which suggested he didn't quite consider me capable of choosing my own wine, or else he doubted I knew what a sommelier was.

'Yes, thank you,' I replied affirmatively, trying to give the impression that I dined out in places like this every week. As he backed away his gaze lingered just a fraction too long on Sophie for my liking.

When I turned back to Sophie, she sat poised and upright in her chair, looking over and beyond me around the restaurant with restless eyes, almost as though she expected to see someone she knew. 'Have you had a busy week?' I asked.

She let out a half laugh. '*Every* week is busy for me, but I wouldn't have it any other way. It's just how it is in the City. If you want the rewards, you have to put the effort in, don't you think?'

'Er... yeah, I guess.'

'Tell me, what do you do for a living?' she asked.

'I'm in recruitment.'

She stared at me impassively, compelling me to elaborate to make it sound more commercially impressive.

'In financial services, mainly accountants and finance professionals.'

'Ah, so that's why you said you were in finance on your profile?'

'Well, they didn't have a box for recruitment, so I thought finance was closest.' Sophie looked... underwhelmed. I decided to turn the conversation back to her; it seemed safest. 'Sophie, tell me what you do... in the City?'

'I'm a commodities trader,' she said.

'Oh right, so you buy and sell commodities?' I winced at the lameness of my question.

'Sort of, but not quite. We don't actually buy and sell them, we more try to anticipate the market and buy and sell contracts accordingly.'

'If you don't me saying so, it sounds a bit like gambling,' I said.

'You've been reading too many newspapers,' replied Sophie.

'So all these problems in the banking sector are made up, then?'

'No, I didn't say that, but it's also not true that all bankers are bad people, as seems to be all the rage in the papers. We're no worse than any other profession.'

'Perhaps a little worse than nurses or charity workers?' I asked. Sophie didn't respond. Or smile. I needed to move the conversation on, and quick. 'To be honest, I'm a work-to-live sort of guy rather than live-to-work, if you know what I mean.'

'But the ability to live depends on the amount that you earn.'

There was a certain logic to Sophie's statement, but also something intrinsically flawed, but before I could work it out the sommelier arrived and handed me the wine list. I turned the pages, but was more preoccupied with the extortionate prices than with the names or grapes of the wines. Maybe Sophie was right about the importance of money. The sommelier asked us what we were thinking of eating and started talking me through a selection of the reds. I nodded sagely at his words, but his first two recommendations were over £50 a bottle, which rather left his third suggestion as the favoured option, priced at £34.

'That last one sounds delicious, we'll take a bottle of that,' I said.

'A fine choice, Sir,' he replied.

Heartened that the sommelier had been safely negotiated, I hoped for an upturn in the conversation.

'Where did you go to university?' asked Sophie.

'Leeds. I studied history. I have to confess, it only involved about three hours of lectures a week, but I needed the spare time to recover from all the late nights.' Happy memories came flooding back of the all-male house of seven I'd lived in during my second and third years and the week-long stand-offs to see who would break first and do the washing up. And of course the cheese sweats, though I thought perhaps Sophie may not find them so amusing. Finally the conversation was turning.

'I studied finance,' said Sophie. Perhaps not.

'Finance? Is that a degree? I know Maths is a degree and I've heard of accountancy, but finance? Who pushed you into that?'

'It may sound unusual to a history student, but I wouldn't be working for an investment bank today if I'd wasted three years studying the names of kings and the dates of battles.'

'Those who fail to learn from history are doomed to repeat it. Do you know who said that?'

'No, but I feel sure you're going to tell me.'

'Winston Churchill.'

'Very impressive, but even he would admit that it's unfair for the taxpayer to pay for the likes of you to attend university for three years spending only three hours a week working and the rest of the time getting pissed.'

'Winston Churchill drunk a pint of Pol Roger champagne while lying in bed every morning dictating *A History of the English-Speaking Peoples*, so I think perhaps he would have applauded me.'

Judging from Sophie's silent thin-lipped expression, she wasn't used to not having the last word. Thankfully, the sommelier returned and during the time it took for me to taste the wine and for him to pour it, I tried to work out how to get the conversation back on track. Before I'd decided, Sophie leant back in her chair and smiled broadly, which restated her stupefying beauty. 'Let's not argue,' she said. 'Now tell me, how have you found internet dating?' She kept smiling, which was a little unsettling, but I was grateful she'd moved the conversation on positively.

'I'm a novice,' I replied. 'I've only had one date before you and that was a bit of a disaster. How about you?'

'I find it infuriating. All that stuff about adding people to your "favourites" and "winking" at each other, it's all so bloody facile. And you wouldn't believe the amount of freaks that send me dodgy messages.'

'Dodgy messages?'

'I'll leave it to your imagination,' she said with a resigned look.

'Have you been on many dates?'

'I've been on more dates than I care to remember from a number of different sites. One or two were... interesting, but that's about all.'

'But you've persevered with it?'

'I don't know why. I figure it must be a numbers game; if you go on enough dates, you'll meet someone eventually. But take it from me, you can't tell what someone's like from their profile, so I wouldn't bother spending too long analysing them. You need to meet in person to tell what someone's like.'

This directly contradicted what Adrian had said about reading the profiles carefully. 'Right, so you're saying I should just go on lots of dates?' I asked, for clarification.

'It's all about chemistry,' said Sophie. 'Personal chemistry. It's that feeling when you click with someone. You know that feeling, when you *just know* you belong together? The internet can't tell you that.' She took a small sip of her wine and dabbed her lips lightly with her napkin. 'You must excuse me, I'm just off to the loo.' As she strode to the toilet a number of pairs of men's eyes followed her. They just couldn't help themselves.

To be frank, I was exhausted. From the initial long wait outside Marks & Spencer not knowing whether Sophie would turn up, to her intimidating good looks and dress sense, to every man staring at her and now her unnerving certainty about everything. And let's face it, the conversation hadn't exactly got off to the best start, although perhaps just at the end there it was improving?

The haughty waiter hovered close by. 'Is Sir ready to order?' he inquired with a tilt of his head and a raised eyebrow.

'Er, not yet, can you give us a while?' I said.

'Certainly, Sir,' he replied, and retreated. For all his snotty attitude he seemed a bit amateurish to me, trying to take an order when only one of the diners was seated. I took a large slurp of wine to fortify myself for Sophie's return. How to play it when she got back? She was a stunning woman, that much was undeniable, but there was something about the prospect of dating her which was like standing at base camp looking up at Mount Everest; before me stood a challenge which would require Herculean effort and application, but one that if attained would see me fêted and lauded. It tired me just thinking about it. And there was this troublesome concern that I just wasn't – what was the word? – as *aspirational* as her.

The waiter floated back into my personal space. I shot him an angry look, but it didn't deter him. 'Sir, are you ready to order now?' he asked.

'No, actually, I'm not. I'd like to wait for my date to re-join me and then we'll order together, if you don't mind.' I completed the sentence with a false smile.

'Are you quite sure, Sir?'

'Yes, I'm quite sure. I'd like to wait if it's not too much trouble.' My frustration resulted in a slight raising of my voice and the couple on the next table glanced over.

'I'm sorry, Sir, I thought perhaps your companion had left you her order.'

'Left me her order?' I asked incredulously. What was this guy on? Had he been quaffing the brandy stock? 'No, she did not leave me her order, but she'll be back in a moment from the toilet and then we'll order together.'

'But your companion isn't in the toilet, Sir, she asked for her coat a while back and left the restaurant.'

Silence.

Insanely fast cog whirring.

Sophie had walked out of the date.

Oh my god.

A hot flush rose up through my body and enveloped my neck, cheeks and forehead. 'Oh yes,' I said, thinking as fast as I could. 'Sorry, where was I? Oh yes, my companion had to leave to... to... to see a friend in distress. Terrible matter, quite terrible.'

A friend in distress? Jesus.

The waiter smiled, clearly enjoying my discomfort. 'I see, Sir.'

'If you don't mind, can you just bring me the bill, I'd like to settle up?'

'Whatever you say, Sir,' he replied and left.

I bowed my head and stared at the table, the white tablecloth taking on a new brightness as if a spotlight shone on it from directly overhead, my eyes travelling along the length of a little peak of ironed fold pressed into the cloth. I took a gulp of wine without tasting it, my eyes becoming hypnotised by the curious viscous film of alcohol sliding back down the inside of the glass. What had just occurred? The internet had produced a 'virtual' date, an apparition who had appeared and disappeared without trace. Sophie's and my 'relationship' had been like going from the quayside to the lifeboats and missing the whole Titanic part in the middle.

This was far worse than being stood up. Just a few minutes in my company had persuaded Sophie to write me off as a person. To vaporise me. She'd behaved like a Roman Emperor clenching his fist and extending his thumb horizontally before gauging the mood of the masses and plunging his thumb downwards to the delirious cheering of the bloodthirsty throng.

After paying the bill – no fucking tip – I grabbed the bottle of wine to swig from on the journey home, beyond caring about the questioning looks of others. Once home, I poured myself an obscene measure of Laphroig whisky to counteract the adrenalin still flowing through me, gulping down the first mouthful as one would a cold beer. I rolled a cigarette, kicked off my shoes, fell back on the sofa and reached for the stereo: Marianne's Leonard Cohen album began...

As the whisky and nicotine took hold, so the adrenalin subsided, to be replaced with anger. What sort of person walks out on a date? Come to think of it, Sophie hadn't even apologised for being so late in the first place. She deserved to suffer for the pain she inflicted. An eye for an eye. I hoped her next internet date would treat her as she'd treated me, and worse. Perhaps he'd break her heart, or better still, he'd be a nutter, maybe even a stalker. Yeah, that's what she needed, a stalker, one of those real nutcase jobs, double lock your doors and file a restraining order–

Hang on! What the hell was happening here? Was I really going to let a woman I hardly knew and whom I'd met for a grand total of thirty minutes get under my skin like this? Was I so pathetically fragile that one (admittedly drop dead gorgeous) woman could shatter my self-confidence?

I took a huge slurp of the peaty amber medicine. That burning sensation felt so right so soon after being rejected. Leonard Cohen's soulful crooning also helped; that guy had to have experienced some serious women problems in his time to be able to sing like that. In a moment of alcohol-induced clarity I decided on the problem with Sophie: she knew she was beautiful, exceptionally beautiful, and somehow that made her ugly.

My mind fell back into the alcoholic fog, my eyes drooping as the last of my consciousness drained away. Leonard Cohen's soulful dirge *Bird on a Wire* was the last thing I remembered before passing out fully clothed on the sofa.

22

An email from Joan arrived one Wednesday afternoon in early October:

> *Dear Adam and Adrian,*
>
> *I trust you are both well?*
>
> *I know that you emailed recently to ask Roy out for dinner and I'm sorry it's taken us a while to reply.*
>
> *There's no easy way to tell you this, but Roy is gravely ill. Indeed, the last time he left the house other than to go to the local shops and hospital was back in the summer when he and I went to Lords with the two tickets you kindly presented to Roy on his retirement. We had a wonderful day, thank you.*
>
> *As you know, Roy has been in poor health for some time, but until now it has been manageable. However, just recently there has been a significant deterioration and the doctor has advised that it could be a matter of weeks, even days.*
>
> *Roy still speaks often and fondly of the two of you. It would mean the world to him to see you again and I'm hoping you might be able to pay us a visit this coming Saturday? Say 11 a.m.?*
>
> *Please let me know if you are able to make it. I know you are both busy, so please don't put yourself out. If you cannot make this Saturday, then perhaps another time?*
>
> *I look forward to hearing from you,*
>
> *Kind regards,*
>
> *Joan*

Adrian and I both had prior engagements that weekend. All were cancelled within minutes and a response sent to Joan confirming we would be there.

* * *

Adrian and I met under the large four-faced clock suspended from the ceiling in the middle of the concourse at Waterloo. We picked up a bouquet of white lilies in Marks & Spencer for Joan and contemplated what to buy Roy. 'Do you think the doctors still allow him to drink?' asked Adrian.

'I've no idea, but it's what he'd want,' I replied. 'Experiences not possessions for presents.'

'Let's get him a bottle of his favourite Pouilly-Fuissé. Do you want anything for the journey?'

'No, I'm not hungry,' I said.

'Nor me.'

We boarded a more or less empty four-carriage train to Twickenham and sat facing each other in seats by the window. As the train eased out of the station, its wheels passing over the tracks made dampened, muffled clickety-click sounds and the sun's soporific heat passed through the high and broad carriage window to warm our faces.

We sat in silence. A great weight pressed down on the top of my lungs and my throat felt pinched as if fighting against a tightly buttoned shirt collar.

There was familiarity to be found in the scenes playing outside of the window as the train snaked out of Waterloo. Glimpses of the Thames behind the MI6 tan and green Lego building, before a broadening of the tracks into the endless platforms of Clapham Junction. Soon the concrete grey of the city centre became diluted by occasional and then more frequent patches of grass or field. The autumn trees blended earthy coloured leaves of burnt oranges, pale browns and saffron yellows, with a little green still in there fighting off the inevitable.

'Let's not mention my troubles with Marcus to Roy,' I said to Adrian.

He nodded.

We fell back into silence. Adrian periodically tapped his forefinger against his mobile phone. I chewed at the edge of a fingernail, inspected it, and chewed it again.

We reached Twickenham and alighted. Roy and Joan's house was a short walk away: a 1930s mock Jacobean with herringbone red brickwork, located down a broad, tree-lined street. A wisteria out of bloom crawled over the white-paned bay window.

I rang the doorbell. The door opened and I had to look down from where I expected to see Joan to actually see her, she being more stooped than before. She looked up at me from under a fringe of fine flyaway white hair, her deeper facial wrinkles articulating the pressure of providing full-time care.

'Come in, come in, how lovely to see you,' she said. 'Good journey?'

'Yes thanks, it's not far from Waterloo. These are for you,' I said, handing her the flowers.

'Oh, you shouldn't have. They're lovely though. I'll put them in some water in a minute.' She laid the bouquet on the sideboard and led us along the hallway. Just before entering the living room she stopped and turned. 'As I said,' she whispered, 'Roy's not too well-'

'We understand,' said Adrian, putting his arm around her.

She looked down, then up again. 'Thank you.'

We entered the living room.

What was left of Roy sat closed-eyed in a soft armchair with feet up on a footstool, a rasping edge audible to each intake of breath through his parted mouth. It took a conscious effort to override a natural urge to express shock at his deteriorated condition. The disease wracking his body was on the verge of victory, his once rotund frame now shrunken and inward, his once broad, moon face now pinched and beady. He had a green tartan blanket over his legs and the Guardian newspaper folded on his lap with his reading glasses on top. There was a strong odour of lavender in the room and I spotted a plug-in air freshener in an extension cord by the TV.

Adrian and I sat down on the sofa, both leaning forward, forearms on knees, hands held together. Joan laid her palm on Roy's shoulder and he stirred, breathing rapidly in and out a few times and blinking. His sight wandered around the room for a while before landing on us, and he summoned some energy from deep within himself and a little of the old sparkle returned to his eyes. 'Hello, boys,' he said. He eased himself into a more upright position, resulting in him wheezing through his nose.

'Hi, Roy,' Adrian and I said in unison. I handed Roy the bottle of wine.

Roy lifted his reading glasses to his eyes and examined the bottle. He nodded. 'Only the best. Thank you so much.' He placed the bottle down by the side of his chair and sighed from the effort.

I was about to ask, 'How are you, Roy?' but caught myself just in time.

There was a pause. Joan asked whether we would like tea or coffee and left the room.

'Did you boys see that Tendulkar's become the highest Test Match run scorer?' asked Roy. 'Good to see the Indians beating the Aussies too.' His voice was very quiet, so Adrian and I stayed leaning forward and listened intently.

'Adam and I have been following it on the internet in the office,' Adrian said.

I was about to say how much Marcus hated Adrian and I logging on to check scores and talking about cricket, but thought better of it. 'Of course, we're keenly anticipating the Ashes next year,' I said instead.

A brief silence followed, during which we all absorbed the realisation that Roy was unlikely to see another Ashes series. We struck up conversation again about the forthcoming rugby internationals, sporting discussion being a powerful distraction from thinking about, and dealing with, real life.

Joan returned with the tea and poured us all cups from a Dalton teapot into delicate white cups imprinted with British wild flowers. When she handed a cup and saucer to Roy, his shaking hand caused tremors to reverberate through the china until he placed the saucer by his side. Joan left the room again.

'How's work?' asked Roy, and then coughed sharply.

'So so,' said Adrian. 'You've seen the news. Things are very quiet as you can imagine.'

'No more boom and bust,' said Roy quietly, with a chuckle. 'And this new boss of yours, how is he?'

Another silence. Adrian looked down and stirred his sugar into his tea. I stared ahead and pretended to take a sip of my tea, despite it being too hot to drink.

'Is he that bad?' asked Roy, glancing back and forth between Adrian and me.

I shrugged my shoulders, but soon I felt Adrian's eyes on me. 'He's okay,' I said. 'He's just got a very different approach to you.'

'How different?' asked Roy, leaning forward and coughing again, harsh and croaky, bringing his hand to his mouth to stifle it.

'He's a stickler for timekeeping and workplace tidiness,' I said. 'He dresses in sharp suits and uses lots of corporate speak. You would have loved him.'

Roy grinned, as did Adrian.

'And it was his idea to bring in a Sales League Table,' Adrian said. 'They're offering mini-breaks and spa days for those who make the most sales.'

Roy shook his head and his eyes focussed on a faraway place. With an effort, he gathered his concentration and looked at us squarely. 'Is he pushing you hard?'

I glanced down at the patterned carpet, which was threadbare in places.

'Well, is he?' asked Roy.

'Yes,' I said.

'Then stand your ground. Being at my stage of life gives you an interesting perspective. I can tell you one thing for certain; I don't look back on my life and regret not working harder. We all have to face the question eventually: do you want to reach the top of your profession and miss out on family, friends and interests, or do you value those things more than money and status? I don't doubt that you two know the answer to that question already, which is why you're here.' He coughed again and his head fell back onto the armchair. I dreaded the next cough and when it came I fought a compulsion to wince. Roy closed his eyes, momentarily drained of vitality.

Joan re-entered the room with a plate of biscuits and saw Roy at rest. 'Just give him a few minutes,' she said, almost as if he wasn't there. 'He just needs a moment to get his energy back.' She offered us the biscuits and out of politeness we both took one, but I was utterly drained of appetite and ate the biscuit mechanically without tasting it or enjoying it.

Joan told us about the new gardener she'd hired to come in once a fortnight and how she'd taken up bridge. She'd been married to Roy for forty years and I wondered how she'd cope after he'd gone. She was a strong and resourceful woman, that much was obvious, but who knew what a blow it is to have to survive without the person with whom you've shared your whole adult life.

Roy stirred, like a man slowly coming to after a long sleep. When his eyes found us again it was as if for the first time that day. 'Sorry about that, boys,' he said. 'My energy levels aren't what they were. Now tell me, what's going on with your love lives?'

'I've been internet dating,' said Adrian.

Roy's brow furrowed as he worked through the meaning of Adrian's words. 'Well, I never,' he said.

'It's very mainstream these days,' said Adrian. 'It's helped me find a nice girl called Sarah.' I looked sharply at Adrian: this was news to me. Adrian displayed the coat hanger jammed sideways in his mouth grin.

'How's Louise?' Roy asked me.

'Actually, we split up a while ago. Just after you left work in fact.'

'Nice girl,' said Roy, before pausing in a way which made a *but* inevitable, 'but I was never convinced she was right for you. I hope that doesn't sound rude.'

'No no,' I said, 'it makes perfect sense.'

'It seemed to me you had different perspectives on life. You'll find someone,' said Roy. 'It's a matter of finding your best friend. Of course, you've got to find her damn sexy too. Let me tell you, the best decision I ever made was marrying Joan.' Adrian and I turned to Joan, who smiled infectiously. 'Be fussy, Adam,' said Roy. 'Ignore what anyone else tells you and go with your instincts. It's not easy trusting your own judgement – it's easy to let others divert you – so stay focussed on what's important to you, not what others tell you is important.'

Adrian spoke for a while about Sarah, even of how he'd managed to get her to start attending battle re-enactments and how it wouldn't be long before he would have her in a suit of armour. Adrian deserved such happiness and it lifted all our spirits to hear the tone of certainty and contentment in his voice.

At the next natural break in the conversation Roy raised his arm to signify his intention to speak. Adrian and I waited for his words. 'I know this will sound like I'm trying to be your dad, but there's something I'd like to say.' He coughed again, his throat sounding like dry paper. 'If someone was to ask me what the achievement of my life is, I would tell them being father to my two daughters. The day my eldest was born was the beginning of my real life. The time before that was just preparation. You won't know what I'm talking about until you're fathers yourselves, but you will. Fatherhood is the making of a man. If you're lucky enough to become fathers, remember it's the hardest thing you'll ever do but also the most satisfying, if you do it well. I think what I'm trying to say is, it's time you boys settled down and became men.' Roy's head again fell back on the sofa and his eyes closed.

Shortly Joan stood up and walked over to him. 'I think he's tired,' she said. There was a short silence as Adrian and I decided what to do. We weren't sure how long he would need to recover. Joan sensed our unease. 'I'm afraid he's likely to sleep for some time now,' she said.

Adrian and I stood up and thanked Joan for her hospitality. We edged towards Roy, who stirred, and with a great effort lifted his head a little before it fell back again onto the armchair. Adrian and I leant forward over him, as did Joan.

'Adam and Adrian are going now,' said Joan to Roy, who again made an effort to muster himself and opened his eyes.

'Don't get up, Roy,' said Adrian, reaching down and taking hold of Roy's hand and squeezing it. I did likewise with his other hand.

Roy looked up at us, his eyes wide and blue and alive and searching. It was as though he was focussing all his bodily energy into his eyes, so that he might memorise the sight of us for all eternity. 'Goodbye, my boys,' he said. 'Take care.'

23

'She did *what?!*' asked Sam, leaning forward, face contorted, eyes scrunched.

'She walked out on me.'

'The bitch! So she just said, "I've had enough" and left the table?'

'It was worse than that.'

'*Worse?* How could it possibly be worse?'

'She didn't say anything. She just left. She pretended to go to the toilet and never came back.'

Sam's facial muscles slackened and drooped, and very, very slowly he said, 'Oh... my... god,' before leaning against the bar, eyes vacant, lost in contemplation at the horror of it.

It was another Friday night and I'd just recounted the story of my date with Sophie. Earlier I'd divulged a little bit about Marianne. Sam had reasserted his ABC theory: I now knew where I stood with Marianne and was free to move on. I thought his ABC theory had failed: yes, I'd enjoyed a night with Marianne, but now I was neither in a relationship with her nor able to move on.

Unusually, Sam had asked to meet in a wine bar in Soho, where we were sitting on barstools at one end of a long chrome bar. It was the sort of place where you got little change out of a fiver for a beer, of which they sold only the bottled lager variety, and where the bottles of spirits behind the bar stood on mirrored shelves backlit in electric blue.

'Tell me,' said Sam, 'these dates you've been on, where did you meet the women?'

I hesitated. I still hadn't entirely got over the stigma of internet dating, but why was there a stigma at all? And besides, Sam was one of my best mates, if I couldn't tell him, who could I tell? 'I've been internet dating,' I confessed.

'Internet dating?! Ha – I was just about to suggest it as I've recently discovered it myself. Talk about a kid in a sweetshop. Shaadi is my favourite.'

'You're online dating too?' I asked, a wave of relief sweeping through me. 'And what's Shaadi?'

'Shaadi's the number one online matrimonial services provider to the Asian community,' said Sam.

'But you're not looking to get married. Or Asian.'

'Mere trifles, Adam, mere trifles. So, how many brides have you met up with?'

'Brides?'

'Internet brides. That's what I call dates from online sites.'

'Oh, right. I've met two, both complete disasters. The first was a big bolshie lawyer and the second was the walk-out date.'

'Mmmm...' said Sam, sucking on his teeth. 'I think we need another beer to analyse this.' While he ordered the next round, I took in the bar. The male patrons favoured sculptured haircuts and tightly fitted suits, while the women dressed like they wanted to be noticed. Soft, crisp, jazz-funk music played from slim silver speakers fixed to the exposed brick walls.

'I presume you've listed your non-negotiables?' asked Sam, handing me another beer.

'My non-negotiables?'

'You mean you haven't heard about the non-negotiables?'

I probably had a worried look on my face by now. 'Should I have done?'

'Of course!' Sam shook his head. 'Christ, if you've got no criteria when it comes to women, you're going to send yourself crazy. You'll be stamping and snorting like a randy billygoat at every skirt that passes you by!'

'I'm already as randy as a billygoat at every skirt that passes me by.'

'Fair enough, but I still think you need to list your non-negotiables.'

'But I *am* negotiable when it comes to women; I'm desperate.'

'Good god, man, pull yourself together! You're not desperate, you're just in a lean patch; and part of your problem is that you've got to be clearer on the type of woman you want.'

'But I kinda just thought I'll know the type when I see her, you know... instinctively.'

'You worry me, really you do,' said Sam, shaking his head. He beckoned me forward for another intimate revelation and I dragged my bar stool closer. 'Look, these non-negotiables reduce the risk of choosing the wrong woman. Think about it, how many people end up in a relationship and start persuading themselves that they can overlook a problem or fault in their partner? We've all done it, thinking that compromise is normal, foolishly trying to convince ourselves that the issue doesn't really matter. This just delays the inevitable and before you know it you've wasted three, four, five years of your life, and that's not an option at your age if you want to settle down. You've got to choose carefully. No matter how bizarre your non-negotiables, I can guarantee you there's a woman for you out there.'

'Really?' I asked, rubbing my chin.

'Think about it. You've heard of women sending love letters to serial killers serving life sentences and they end up marrying them?' I nodded. 'And how about those feeder guys who shove ten tons of ice cream into their partners until they're beached whales and then spend their lives immersing themselves in every nook and cranny and the folds of–'

'Okay – okay, I get the picture. If the only women I can get are serial killer groupies and weight gain junkies, well, I may as well reach for the bottle of brandy and pearl-handled revolver right now.'

'My point is, there's a woman out there for every man, but you need to lay down some criteria.'

'So what are *your* criteria?' I asked a little pointedly.

'Okay, I like that; the student challenging the teacher. Why don't you guess?'

'That they're Asian?'

'Actually, I do relax that rule. Middle Eastern women also do it for me, but I think you've got the point. Come on, what else?'

'Well, I couldn't help but notice how most of your girlfriends have been gym instructors and triathletes, things like that; and how could I forget your comments on WGP?'

'That's right, I like healthy women,' said Sam. 'But hey, this isn't about me, it's about you, so let's discuss *your* non-negotiables and narrow *you* down. Let's start with her looks.'

Marianne leapt into my mind: her short hair, her freckles, her dimples. But she was history now and I couldn't let her define my future. I needed to stay open-minded. 'I'm not as fussy as you when it comes to looks,' I said. 'Clearly I've got to find her attractive, but I've got no... preconceptions about what she might look like.'

'You want her to be attractive, you say?'

'Of course.'

'Ah, but pretty attractive or filthy attractive?'

'Filthy attractive?'

'Yeah, what filth factor they score. Come on, you remember us playing the top five fittest girls game at uni? You must still play it?'

'Sure, the guys in the office play it all the time. After a few beers it's a must.'

'So, an important and often overlooked variation is the top five filthy girls game, the ones who would be best in bed. Try it sometime, it reveals some interesting results. Now, returning to the non-negotiables, we need to work out what type of women you're attracted to. So, on the one hand, it might be the pretty girls, the girl-next-door types, think Meg Ryan, maybe Sandra Bullock. Then you've got your elegant ladies, think Julia Roberts, maybe Nicole Kidman. And finally you've got those who rate high on the filth factor, like Scarlett Johansson and Angelina Jolie. You need to come off the fence on the type of woman you like.'

'Mmmm,' I said, Marianne in a narrow lead, but Scarlett Johansson jockeying with her for pole position. 'I think I can take or leave the girl-next-door types because it's difficult to see them... well... you know–'

'Being filthy in the bedroom?'

'Well, I'm not sure–'

'Come on, that's exactly what you mean! Be honest with yourself. Now, describe this woman to me.'

'So... I think what I'm saying is, I want a woman who's elegant, with a distinct and discernible touch of... of...'

'Sluttishness. Just in the bedroom, I mean.'

It seemed futile to fight the truth. 'Yes, I guess so.'

'Give me some examples.'

I gave it some thought. 'Cate Blanchett, for one.'

'Mmmm, interesting selection, I can see that.'

'A young Catherine Deneuve.'

'Like it! You're warming up. Now then, what about her personality traits?'

'Someone who can laugh along with me, and at me where appropriate.'

'Good sense of humour, as they say in the lonely hearts ads.'

'You know what I mean,' I said. 'And intelligence. Intelligence is a must. And I don't mean necessarily in an academic sense – I mean more someone who knows stuff.'

'Such as?' asked Sam.

'Oh, I don't know. Who knows interesting things, like why you're meant to salute magpies, why swans mate for life, where the shipping forecast places are located, that sort of thing.'

'Each to their own, Adam, each to their own, but it'll certainly help narrow down the candidates, which is a good thing.'

As I continued thinking about the qualities of my ideal woman, I remembered just how uncomfortable I'd been in Sophie's company, and thought perhaps I should also define what I wanted to avoid in a woman. 'And another thing,' I said, 'and it's a really important thing. She absolutely mustn't be too... aspirational.'

'How do you mean?' asked Sam.

I paused for thought. 'She mustn't think someone's worth is directly linked to their wealth or status.'

'I like that, you're on a roll.'

'And someone to the left of the political spectrum.'

'Okay.'

'And who doesn't have to wear short skirts and high heels in order to look sexy.'

Sam looked alarmed. 'But who may choose to wear them, right?'

'Of course, at the right times,' I said.

Sam smiled and tipped the top of his beer bottle at me. 'You know how you said earlier that you didn't know what you were looking for in a woman, but would know her when you saw her?'

'Yeah...'

'Well, you just listed a dozen or so non-negotiables. I suggest you use them when searching for those internet brides.'

He had a point. Taking an affirming swig of beer, I vowed to write down my non-negotiables tomorrow. 'Another beer?' I asked.

'Of course,' said Sam.

I caught the eye of the barman, who after serving us left the miserly one pound of change from a tenner on a little silver plate, placing it on the bar nearer to himself than to us, clearly expecting me to leave it as a tip. Sam reached out, picked up the coin and gave it to me. 'They're already overcharging, don't give them any more.'

'Listen, Sam, thanks for all the advice, I appreciate it,' I said. 'What did you make of the Spurs match last night?'

'*What?!* You think we've finished the tutorial?' Sam laughed vigorously, rocking backwards and forwards on his stool. 'Okay, so let's say you find an internet bride who meets your non-negotiables. What then? Are you absolutely sure you're not going to screw up the date? Think about it, the more you like her, the more nervous you'll be on the date.'

'You mean I can't just see what happens?'

'See what happens? You mean like you did with Rachel for years on end and got absolutely nowhere? Like you did with your last internet bride and she disappeared into thin air? No, you categorically cannot just see what happens. You have a role to play in determining the outcome.'

'What sort of role?'

'Sorry, I meant roles, plural,' said Sam.

'Roles?'

'Yes, different situations call for different roles.' He pulled his stool closer and motioned for me to lean in. 'On a date, you need to master certain character types and be able to switch and transition.'

I genuinely had no idea what he was talking about. 'Switch and transition? Sounds like A-level electronics.'

'No dummy, switch and transition between characters, in order to make an impact on the date.'

'Can't I just be myself?'

Sam shook his head. 'If just being yourself was enough, there'd be no single people in the world. Take it from me, you need at least three personalities to hand for a date.'

'Three?'

'Yes, three. Bare minimum. Number one is all about trying to make a positive initial impression.'

'Okay, that makes sense. How do I do that?'

He took a long swig of his beer, before pausing and looking me square in the eye. 'By being Mr Effervescent.'

'Mr *who?!*'

'Mr Effervescent. He's the first impressions count guy.' Sam now spoke with speed and intensity, with lots of hand gestures and facial expressions. 'He's the charismatic, cheeky, sparky guy with a quick quip and ready smile. He's outgoing and popular, and his mates cheer when he enters the pub late. And crucially, he's the guy who gets a girl's attention.'

'So I start off as Mr Effervescent?'

'Yes, to get you an in. Of course, if you're internet dating, you'll have the intro already, but first impressions are still extremely important because you've got to establish yourself straight away as confident and assured. If you don't, you may lose her from the outset. She may even have you down as a gay best friend if you make a weak first impression.'

'Right then, a confident and assured opening, I think I can do that...'

'Good, let's see you do it.'

'*What?*'

'Why do you think I brought you to a wine bar? We're here because there's lots of women. If I was just meeting you, we'd be in a grotty old man's pub.'

'Thanks.'

'You're welcome. Right, so which woman are you going to approach?'

Sam's eyes wandered to one side and lit up as they latched onto something. Or someone. Coming from behind me a striking woman approached; an olive-skinned, jet-black-haired Cleopatra, she swivelled her hips with a gentle circular undulation to squeeze past us which drew Sam's eyes downward. He then held his head high and closed his eyes in contemplation, allowing the air displaced by her movement to return and wash over him. 'Persian,' he said.

'What?'

'She's Persian. Hailing from modern day Iran.'

'I know where Persia is – but how the hell do you know she's from there?'

'Trust me.'

I would have put my flat on him being right. The way Sam had just smelled the air and assessed the bouquet reminded me of a wine connoisseur who can tell you not only the grape, maker and year, but also the precise corner of the exact field the grapes had grown in. Sam took the appreciation of women to a level I never knew existed. Indeed, it was more than an appreciation, it was an addiction, and like any addiction, he wasn't fully in control of it. His obsession was at once a genius and a madness, a gift and a curse. He truly was enslaved by his male Darwinian genes.

'Look, she's talking to a girlfriend,' said Sam, still staring at the Persian. 'Go and talk to them.'

'Are you serious? Why would I do that?'

'Because you need practice and so I can observe you, that's why. Go on, I want you to effervesce. I'm serious, this is really important.'

I started fidgeting with my mobile to buy me some time. 'But what will I do?' I asked in a whiny voice.

'That's my point, you've got to be fun and energetic and make a strong impression.' Sam got up from his stool and started cajoling me to get up. 'Go on, get over there,' he said. 'And don't look back at me like a chump while you're doing it.'

I stood up and walked towards the two women as slowly as I could to delay the inevitable. As I got within a few feet I froze to the spot. Heat rushed to my cheeks. I looked back at Sam, who held a stern face and waved me on.

I stepped forward between them. 'Hello,' I said.

They turned to me, both expressionless. They said nothing, the silence stodgy and uncomfortable. The Persian's friend had light brown eyes, like Nadine's, and was as pleasing on the eye as the Persian.

The silence lingered.

'Have you got any Iranian blood in you?' I asked the Persian.

They both looked at each other, eyes widening. 'How the hell did you know that?' asked the Persian.

'Er... lucky guess, I suppose,' I said.

'It's a bit freaky if you ask me,' said the friend.

'Listen, I'm sorry for interrupting you like this; I just wondered if I could buy you both a drink? I'm with my friend over there.' I nodded back toward Sam, figuring if they saw him it might increase my chances.

'It's really nice of you to offer,' said the Persian, 'but I'm engaged.' She lifted her left hand to show me an outrageously large diamond, so big it was difficult to believe it really was a diamond.

'Size matters,' I mumbled.

'Sorry?' said the Persian.

'Nothing.'

'We're here tonight to discuss my wedding.' She nodded at her friend. 'She's my head bridesmaid, so thanks for the offer, but we've got lots to discuss.'

'No problem. And good luck with the wedding.' I sloped off back to Sam, who looked past me, his eyes locked on the Persian's friend. I glanced back over; her eyes were also dwelling on him in critical appraisal. 'The Persian is getting married,' I said. 'And her friend – who I see you've noticed – is the head bridesmaid. They said they were busy. Anyway, I did pretty well, I thought.'

Sam dragged his focus away from the Persian's friend and looked at me pityingly. He shook his head.

'What? What did I do wrong?' I asked.

'You looked shifty.'

'Shifty?'

'Yes, like someone about to commit a crime. Eight-five per cent of communication is non-verbal. You can try and be Mr Effervescent all you like, but if she's picking up from your body language that you're nervous or unsure, it's going to confuse her and put her off.'

'So what did I do wrong?'

'You fidgeted and squirmed. The stiller you are the better, it conveys confidence. And another thing... you pouted.'

'I did not!'

'Oh yes, you did. You did a weird thing with your lips like you were about to suck through a straw. It wasn't a good look.'

'Jesus...' I said, remembering the dimwits pulling faces at Sophie as we walked to the restaurant. I needed another beer; this stuff was harder than I thought. I ordered two more, despite it being Sam's round. He was too busy eyeing up the Persian's friend to notice. Hang on, was that a pout playing on his lips?

'Hello, Sam?' I said, passing him a fresh beer.

'Oh, sorry,' said Sam, noticing me again.

'You said I had three new personalities to master. So who comes next after Mr Effervescent?'

'Then Mr Comfy Sofa comes along.'

'Mr Comfy Sofa?! Who the hell is Mr Comfy Sofa?' I asked.

'He's the guy who listens more than he speaks, who shows he cares. He's a bit like your old sofa at home, familiar and comforting and reassuring. The role of Mr Comfy Sofa is to show her that you're a modern man, in touch with your feminine side and your emotions and all that stuff.'

'So I listen a lot and empathise, that sort of thing.'

'That's it, but be careful, because Mr Comfy Sofa is dangerously close to being a gay best friend, so he's just a transition phase. The crucial point about Mr Comfy Sofa is that he persuades her that you find her infinitely interesting. Now, the mistake you've made in the past is staying as Mr Comfy Sofa for too long. In fact, with someone like Rachel, for about ten years too long, so it's imperative you move on to the next role.'

'Okay – okay, I need to transition. Who's next after Mr Comfy Sofa?'

'Finally there's...' Sam paused to take a colossal gulp of beer, before bringing down his bottle with a thud onto the bar. 'Alpha Male Man.'

'*Who?!*'

'Alpha Male Man.'

'He doesn't wear a full-length body stocking like Spiderman with a giant A embroidered on his chest, does he?'

'You could try wearing that, but I wouldn't advise it. At least not on the first date. But seriously, this is the guy who knows what he wants and who crucially now establishes himself as a seducer. He's very much an ABC kinda guy and makes clear to the woman that he sees her as sexual rather than just a friend.'

'How does he do that?'

'He's got to be confident talking about women as more than friends. So he may mention other women in his life, maybe even some ex-girlfriends – but not too much, you're not trying to rub her nose in it – just mention other women enough for her to realise there's some competition out there. Also, Alpha Male Man may disagree with his date from time to time, which shows he knows his own mind and isn't a pushover. Believe me, it isn't easy to disagree with a woman you want to sleep with, but if you just keep nodding like a puppy at everything she says with your tongue hanging out, you'll never get laid.'

'What next?' I asked, turning my head a little to make sure I heard clearly.

'Now we're getting to the really important part–'

'I know, I know, what does he do now?'

'Alright, alright, I'm just getting there. At this point Alpha Male Man may add some light physical contact – say touching her arm as he speaks to emphasise a point. The natural next move, at the right time, is to hold her hand, and if she doesn't resist and seems comfortable with it, you're onto something.'

It all sounded good in theory, but doubts persisted. 'But won't she find it a little unsettling?' I asked.

'Why?'

'Well, according to what you're saying, I enter the conversation like a whirlwind, suddenly fall silent and bore into her soul with my eyes, and finally transition through the gears like James Hunt, grab her by the hand and drag her to bed.' I couldn't help a chuckle at the absurdity of how it all sounded.

'It's meant to take place over the course of an evening, dumbo, not in the first five minutes. And besides... if you don't like my technique, tell me about yours.' There was a short silence. 'Adam, you're not fourteen any more. These are successful, demanding, got it all, want it all, modern day women we're talking about, not your teenage sweetheart Mary-Jane Rottencrotch behind the bike sheds. I'm not saying these tips are foolproof, but they're a start.'

He was right; some self-awareness during the dating process couldn't do any harm. 'Okay, I'll try them,' I said.

Sam's eyes lit up, just as they'd done earlier at the entrance of the Persian.

'Hello,' said the Persian, standing next to us with her friend. 'We finished our discussions about my wedding and decided to reward your earlier bravery by letting you buy us a drink.'

'I'll get them in,' I said, taking the orders and offering the Persian's friend my stool next to Sam. The Persian joined me at the bar.

'My name's Tala, by the way,' she said.

'Adam,' I said and we shook hands.

'Our two friends seem to have hit it off,' said Tala. 'Your friend's not a ladies' man, is he? He looks a bit too pleased with himself for my liking.'

'He was, but he's looking to settle down,' I said. 'As long as your friend meets his non-negotiables, she'll be fine.'

'His non-negotiables?'

'You mean you haven't heard about the non-negotiables?'

Tala had a worried look on her face. 'Should I have done?'

'Of course!' And so a long conversation commenced about Tala's non-negotiables and whether her fiancé met any of them. Each time I caught a glimpse of Sam, he was in full Mr Comfy Sofa mode, empathising and agreeing a lot and perhaps on the verge of reaching out to hold her hand...

Much later that night, in the early hours, Sam and I were still sat at the bar, now slouched, the Iranians long since gone, but not before Sam had got Tala's friend's number. 'Last time we met,' I said, 'you were going on a date with a girl from a spinning class. What happened?'

'She was what you said earlier, too... *aspirational.*' Sam stared across the bar, eyes glazed from the alcohol. 'Everything I did she scrutinised to make sure it lived up to some ideal, or cost...'

'Best shot of her then,' I said. 'One more for the road?'

'Go on then,' said Sam.

'Your round, I believe,' I said.

Sam's eyes travelled in slow motion from where they'd settled on the far side of the room, across the full spectrum of the bar, before eventually landing on my face. His eyelids rose and fell like blinds being hoisted and dropped. 'I can't,' he slurred.

'Can't what?'

There was a short silence, the cogs of Sam's brain almost audible as they clanked slowly round. 'I've lost it all.'

'Lost what?'

'My company. I've liquidated it.'

'*What?!* What happened?'

Sam's face set in sadness. 'I overstretched. Bought a place at the top of the market... now got to sell it at a huge loss to keep up the mortgage on the flat I'm renovating. I may lose my own flat, which I put up as security. I'm bankrupt. I'm bankrupt because I was too fucking greedy.'

'Jesus, Sam.' His problems put my own work issues into clear perspective. 'Why didn't you say anything earlier?'

'Don't you see? Don't you see I need nights like tonight so I can forget all the shit in my life and be myself? Tonight's the first time in weeks I've felt alive again. That's why I didn't say anything.'

I called the barman over and ordered two more doubles.

'So what are you going to do?' I asked, another hit of the peaty whisky hitting the base of my nose and diffusing into my head.

'Not much I can do unless the bank gives me more money,' mumbled Sam. He knocked back the whisky and peered into the bottom of his empty glass as though some fateful message might be found written there. 'But the bank keeps saying no.'

We both remained wordless for a while. 'No means maybe, maybe means persuade me?' I said eventually.

Sam smiled, the rubbery, gurning smile of one who's had one too many. 'I'll drink to that,' he said, signalling with a heavy arm to the barman.

24

Friday night, 5.30 p.m.: payback time. I've given you five days of hard graft, now you give me five hours of power drinking. That's the deal. And speed is of the essence: *Log off, the weekend's started; Let's get there quick before the rush begins; You don't need dinner – eating is cheating; Finish up, I'll get the next round in; Drinking games? I've got a good one; Was that last orders? Better get some shots in; Curry, anyone?*

Tonight's venue was Ye Olde Cheshire Cheese off Fleet Street. Carrie, Adrian and I entered and shuffled along a narrow corridor so busy with patrons they had to lean back and clutch their drinks to their chests to let us past. We turned left down steeply descending steps to a room deep underground, its walls sweating from the amount of people squeezed in there. It was easy to imagine yourself standing in the precise spot where your medieval ancestor had stood imbibing some strangely brewed Benedictine beer, fiercely fermented and frothing, and so strong it could strip paint. Roy had always liked this pub.

While Carrie and Adrian queued at the bar, I scanned the room. In one corner some colleagues stood by a long table, in amongst them Luke and Matt. At the adjacent table sat some of the secretarial recruitment team, which meant –

I stood transfixed, memories of our night together returning...

'Here you go!' shouted Adrian, holding a pint towards me. 'Jesus, anyone would think you don't want a drink.'

'Oh, sorry, thanks,' I said, taking the pint and sipping the head off. 'I was just seeing who was here.'

We stood near our colleagues and started the obligatory moan about how hard our weeks had been. 'Still, it could be worse,' said Adrian. 'You must have played World's Worst Jobs?'

'Can't say I have,' I said, while Carrie also shook her head.

'It's simple,' said Adrian. 'You have to describe the most terrible job you've ever done. Points are awarded for the general awfulness of what you had to do and for the eloquence with which you describe the horror of it. Right, Adam, you go first.'

I gulped back some beer and cast back my mind. 'Mmmm, well, I would have to say the summer I spent cleaning the local hospital when I was sixteen. The job was hard and physical, especially when it was hot, but you also had to endure the frequent groans of pain coming from the wards and the sorrowful expressions of the patients. What you definitely didn't want was a job in a clinical area, which often meant wiping up some form of bodily fluid. But the worst was the night shift. I had to team up with a guy who'd worked for years on the night shift; in fact he refused to do any shifts *other* than nights. Weird fucker he was, morosely wandering the corridors in the dead of night, half-stooped and shifty-eyed, ferrying *refuse* in thick black bin liners from the theatres to the incinerators.'

'Refuse?' asked Carrie, anxious-faced.

'Leftovers... from operations,' I confirmed.

She gasped and brought her hand to her mouth.

'It's fair to say my colleague was a... solitary and nocturnal type. I remember he got reprimanded one night for storing dead bodies in the hospital chapel when the mortuary was full. Apparently a relative of a dying patient went to the chapel to pray for their recovery and stumbled over the dead bodies in the dark.'

'Jesus...' mumbled Carrie under her breath. Adrian, on the other hand, was trying to stifle his laughter.

'I was grateful to get back to university at the end of those holidays, I can tell you.'

'So you stuck it out for the whole summer?' asked Adrian.

'I had to, I needed the money.'

'Can't have been that bad if you lasted the whole summer. We'll have to dock you points for the job being survivable, but still, good effort. Carrie, your turn.'

Carrie took a deep breath. 'For me, it's definitely one summer I spent working in the kitchen of an old people's home. Now don't get me wrong, it had some good points, especially some of the residents, who were charming and full of great stories—'

'There's no points awarded for describing pleasant aspects of the work,' said Adrian. 'In fact, any consolatory aspects mean docked points. Now, carry on, and concentrate on the dreadfulness.'

'Well, the mealtimes were pretty challenging–'

'*Pretty* challenging,' interjected Adrian.

'Okay – okay,' said Carrie, 'mealtimes were terrible and I still have nightmares about them. You see some of the residents couldn't eat solid food, so the kitchen manager – who was also a solitary and nocturnal type – made me cut open cheap sausages, remove the innards and liquidise them with warm water and a powder thickener, then pour it into bowls. He said it was necessary so the residents got enough protein, but the cheap sausages were mainly cartilage and sinew. Then there was the time they were short-staffed and I was made to work in the dining room feeding the gruesome gruel to the residents through a straw.'

Adrian and I recoiled and turned our heads away in unison as we pictured the watered-down offal being sucked up through the straws and digested.

'I don't think I've used a straw since,' said Carrie.

'Your go, Adrian,' I said. 'You'll do well to beat that.'

'My worst job was a week spent on a battery hen farm in the summer of 1994…'

Carrie and I both pursed our lips in an ooooh shape at the mention of a battery hen farm. Adrian continued. 'I was made to enter a spooky, rickety wooden structure and in close to darkness crawl around in sawdust and chicken shit carrying a plastic bucket which I had to fill with eggs picked out of the tiny coops. I half choked to death from the feathers and bits of straw and dirt floating about in the air and, oh god, the heat. Then there was the din of clucking noises the hens made – never-ending it was – interspersed with gut-wrenching CLUCKAAAAWWWK sounds whenever they laid an egg. There was an awful fluttering of wings each time you reached into a coop and the hens would peck your hands as you stole their eggs. I haven't eaten chicken since. Or eggs.'

'Oh my god, it sounds revolting,' said Carrie, scrunching her nose in disgust.

By contrast I was trying not to laugh. 'Sounds like a bad gig. Remind me not to go to KFC later.'

After two more rounds I felt the call of nature and headed upstairs to the gents, which was empty, the only noise in there being the distant bottled sound of voices from back in the bar and the gentle hiss of the pipes, allowing me a moment of reflection.

It was useless; I couldn't stop thinking about her, especially when she was in such close proximity. I'd spent the last six months trying to put her out of my mind, and failing spectacularly. Was it possible that my feelings could be this strong without reciprocation?

Returning downstairs, I moved through the doorway into the bar and an arm shot across me. 'Here, I got you a pint,' a female said and with an outstretched arm she ushered me towards a table in the corner away from the others.

It was Marianne.

The adrenalin hit.

Emeralds.

Freckles.

That perfume.

I looked at the pint she was holding, then at her, and took the pint. 'Thank you,' I said. I sipped the top off the beer and waited for Marianne to say something.

'So...' she said.

'So...' I replied.

'Are we allowed to talk?' Her face was neutral.

My cogs whirred. I'd rehearsed over and over in my mind what I would say when I spoke to her again, but now couldn't remember any of it. I knew I didn't want to sound bitter, which risked only poisoning myself. I waited until Marianne took a sip of her drink before saying, 'You're not trying to seduce me again, are you?'

Marianne bent double, choking and coughing on her drink. Once recovered, she smiled, dimples pronounced, and by god it made me feel alive to see her face light up like that.

'I've missed you,' she said.

I paused, weighing up whether to employ equally emotive language. 'Not nearly so much as I've missed you,' I said, caving in.

'How's single life treating you?'

Memories of Emma and Sophie came back. 'It's been... interesting,' I said. 'And how's... how are things with you?'

'They're okay,' she said, her expression again neutral.

I pondered whether to ask more, but decided against it. 'Hey, I must give you back that album you lent me,' I said.

'No, I want you to keep it. Have you listened to it?'

Only every goddam night for six months. 'Occasionally, yes,' I said.

'Well? Do you like it?'

No, it makes me feel suicidal because it reminds me of not being with you.
'Yes, I like it very much,' I said. We spoke for a while about the songs on the album.

'I heard you and Marcus had a blazing row the other day,' said Marianne at the next break in the conversation.

I nodded. 'Yeah, we don't get on I'm afraid.'

'You're not thinking of resigning are you?'

It seemed an odd question. 'I'm thinking about it, but it isn't the best time to be looking for a new job. In fact, I'm not even sure my future lies in recruitment. I've got some big decisions.'

Marianne nodded but said nothing, her face becoming long and pensive and her gaze averted.

'What?' I asked.

'We've all got big decisions.' She looked back at me, the green of her eyes iridescent in the half-light of the underground room.

'Why, what's yours?' I asked, my heart beating faster.

'It doesn't matter.'

'It does matter. I want to know.' I reached out and touched her upper arm.

She paused. 'My husband wants to start a family.'

I don't think I reacted visibly. I tried not to, even though the mention of her starting a family with another man felt like a herd of elephants stampeding on my ribcage. I lifted my glass and downed half my pint in one slug and didn't give a damn if she noticed. 'I'm not sure I can comment on that,' I said. 'It's hardly as though I'm objective.'

'Sorry, I shouldn't have mentioned it-'

'Are you going to start a family?' I asked hurriedly.

Marianne hesitated. 'I don't know. I feel too young to be a mother, but my husband is older than me and it seems wrong to deny him.'

I took another slug of beer while looking away.

'I shouldn't have brought it up, I'm sorry.' She knocked back the rest of her glass.

'I think we both need another drink,' I said. 'But not here.' I led her upstairs to a bar on the ground floor where we were less likely to be interrupted by colleagues. 'Don't worry,' I said, while ordering two gin and tonics, 'I won't make you down a Sambuca.'

We stood against the bar, leaning in on one another, to ensure we could hear each other. It crossed my mind how anyone seeing us together would think we were a couple and foolishly I dared to imagine it. It was dangerous to want something that much; it risked being presumptuous with god.

We made small talk for a while, but as always with us, it felt like a prelude to a more intimate discussion – and so it proved.

'Do you want children one day?' asked Marianne later, as though the question had just come to mind.

'Yes,' I replied, nodding.

'I wish I had your certainty. Perhaps it's because my upbringing wasn't so great.' A look of helplessness drew down upon her face and I had to fight an instinct to step forward and hold her.

'May I ask what wasn't so great?' I asked.

'Family stuff... by which I mean my mother.' The vulnerability in her face dissolved and was replaced by something else: resolve, or determination. 'But she means nothing to me now.' She took a large gulp of her drink.

'Are you still in contact with her?'

'Barely. Just Christmas cards and very infrequent telephone calls.' She hunched her shoulders in a slow shrug. 'Anyway, enough of my dysfunctional family, it's boring–'

'No, I want to hear it,' I said too quickly, reaching out and touching her hand. 'Only if you're comfortable discussing it, of course?'

'It's not something I've spoken about to many people.' My heart leapt that she felt able to take me into her confidence. 'My mother's not a good person,' continued Marianne. 'She thinks only of herself, and her own happiness.' She shook her head very slowly, looking down, her bottom lip protruding. 'My parents broke up when I was sixteen when my mother left my father for another man. I don't think children should have to go through all that in their teenage years when they're finding it hard enough working out their own lives.'

I nodded. 'Do you get on with your dad?'

Marianne stood up straight at the mention of her father. 'Very much so. He's the kindest and most honourable man I've ever known. But he's never recovered from my mother leaving him. He's never had the confidence to date another woman…' Her voice trailed off. 'No one ever understands it, that's what gets me. Had my father left my mother that would have been explicable, the husband trading in the wife for the younger version, or whatever. But my mum leaving my dad was so unexpected, so shameful. I don't think either my father or I saw it coming…' Again, she was lost in her own thoughts. 'How did we get onto this anyway?' She glanced at her watch. 'I've got to go soon.'

I didn't ask her why she had to go and she didn't offer a reason; it was obvious why. Or rather for whom. But in her demeanour I sensed reluctance.

'Can we talk to each other next week, or is our friendship still banned?' she asked.

I hesitated before responding. 'You hurt me, Marianne.'

'I know,' she replied without hesitation. 'And I hate myself for it.' In the succeeding silence it was possible to believe that Marianne and I could have been together, had it not been for an accident of timing.

I walked her to the door, where we both stopped, neither of us moving to open it. Once again she looked into my eyes for just a split second too long, which rooted me to the spot. That was a moment I should have been brave. Despite everything, I should have kissed her. How life's course may be different if we'd been braver at certain times, times which may never come again.

'I'm going to hail a taxi on Fleet Street,' said Marianne. 'You should go back and have some more drinks.' I nodded and she turned to leave.

'Marianne?'

'Yes?'

I didn't know what I'd meant to say. 'Nothing.'

She stepped toward me and kissed me on the cheek, before leaving. My cheek tingled where she'd kissed me.

You'd be forgiven for thinking that Marianne and I talking so intimately was the only noteworthy event of that evening, but if you did you'd be wrong, because a few hours later I was having sex with Carrie.

* * *

I woke up the next morning in an unfamiliar bed, in an unfamiliar room, head throbbing, throat dry. Carrie stood over me, wrapped in a beige towel pulled up over her breasts, her hair wet and dark and curly from the shower. 'Hey sleepy head, how are you feeling?' she asked.

'A little hazy...' I replied.

She leant forward and kissed me, but didn't stop, her tongue prising my lips apart and wriggling into my mouth, energising my entire being from being asleep to alert in seconds. She reached up and pulled off her towel while straddling me, before leaning forward and reaching out to her bedside table – the size of her swinging breasts just above my face making me realise why the women in the office euphemistically referred to her 'good figure'. She picked a condom out of the drawer, ripped open the wrapper with her teeth and rolled it on. She closed her eyes, shifted her hips, and sighed as I entered.

The sober repeat of last night's activities was so much more satisfying and memorable.

Almost as soon as the act was done, Carrie got up and started dressing. 'I'm sorry, I've got to go. I'm meeting my Mum in Selfridges and I'm already late.' Once dressed, she reached up to her still wet hair. 'Fuck it, it'll just have to dry on the way.' She buffed her hair with her towel, swept through it a few times with a broad hairbrush and then kissed me on the cheek, smelling clean and fresh – unlike me, I imagined. 'Don't worry,' she said, 'my flatmate's away, so you've got the place to yourself. The bathroom's next door if you need it and there are towels in the airing cupboard. I'll text you later.'

I heard the latch to the door of the flat click closed and Carrie's footsteps hurry down the stairs, followed by the thud of the front door shutting after her.

Total silence. I sighed and closed my eyes. A short while later I got out of bed, the soiled prophylactic dangling from my diminishing manhood. I reached down and tugged it off, a globule of sperm dribbling down my leg. Where to dispose of a used condom in the house of a woman you barely know, or have only just achieved intimacy with? Down the toilet? No, think of all the marine life and sea birds eating it; what a dreadful way to go, choked to death on a mouthful of rubber and semen. How about wrapping it in a tissue and hiding it at the bottom of her wastepaper basket? How often does she empty it? It could be there for weeks, festering, congealing, eventually emitting strange gaseous odours. Fuck that. I wrapped it in a tissue and put it in my trouser pocket to dispose of later.

I fell back onto the bed. Fuck, my head hurt. What exactly happened last night? I tried to reconstruct the evening's events in my mind, but the concentration unleashed powerful waves of throbbing pain throughout my cranium. Snapshots flashed up but were gone again before I had a chance to piece them together: Mr Effervescent buying tequila shots at the bar, Mr Comfy Sofa holding Carrie's hand on the way out, a stop in the taxi to go to the cash machine... or was that a different time?

Then it struck me like a bullet: FUCK! What would Marianne think?! My sleeping with Carrie was major office gossip. Could I blame the drink? What a feeble excuse for choosing to obtain a biblical knowledge of a woman. If I blamed the booze, what would that tell Marianne about the type of man I was: the type of man who sleeps with a woman and laughs it off as a drink too many.

But why was I worrying about Marianne? I'd just had a great night with a beautiful young woman and we'd enjoyed fantastic sex. Twice. And besides, presumably Marianne slept with her husband, didn't she? My stomach lurched at the thought of it.

Needing the loo, I wandered through to the bathroom. It was a female bathroom: every inch of the bath rim littered with shampoo and conditioner bottles of varying shapes and sizes, two candles sitting in little glass cups, potpourri in a bowl in the corner. And there in the corner two of those funny razors with flattened ends with which I understood they shaved their legs, and items I had to guess at – was that a pumice stone and that a hair net hanging from the shower? Best not look in the mirrored cabinet; god knows what feminine hygiene products I might discover in there.

After strolling back to Carrie's bedroom, I sat on the bed and cast my eyes around the room, struck by the sense of colour and clutter – but clutter in a comforting way. A small glass chandelier hung from the ceiling and the walls were adorned with various posters: an art nouveau print, that blue and white Matisse, and the promotional billboard for the film Casablanca.

I looked across to the dressing table, backed by a large oval mirror, cloudy in places with age, with ornate gold gilding and a Venetian mask perched on top. I pictured Carrie looking in that mirror, evoking the spirit of a long-lost Victorian age of glamour, an artist's model in Montmartre, maybe sipping an absinthe.

I glanced to my other side, at her bedside table, from whence the condom had come. What else did she keep in there? Best not to look. Yet it was so still in that room, so silent, just me and no one else in the house, and in that perfect tranquillity it was possible to believe that if you did something and yet no one saw you do it, perhaps it didn't happen at all. I leant over and pulled on the drawer, which slid open with a guilty creak. Reaching in, I touched some cardboard – no, it was photographs. I pulled the top one out, fell back onto the bed and lifted it to my face.

It was a picture of me.

What the?!

I reached into the drawer and picked out some more photos: there was another of me and also a few of work colleagues, which must have been taken on a recent work night out. I replaced them and closed the drawer, the fright serving me right for poking about in someone else's belongings.

I dressed hurriedly, anxious for some fresh air.

* * *

Outside Carrie's flat the concrete paving stones carried puddles as though they'd just been washed, and it was as though the sky had been washed too, so pale and fresh was its blue, drained of the heavy humidity of the previous day. I tried to get my bearings, having no memory of where I was. It looked like any other street where a young person might live in London, the tired houses all converted into flats, their shallow front gardens cracked with weeds and filled with plastic recycling boxes and old bikes.

I wandered to the end of the road, to a newsagent, and bought the Guardian, a bottle of Lucozade and chewing gum. Back outside, I necked half the Lucozade in one hit, giving me a jolt of invigoration – which reminded me – and I reached into my pocket for the soiled condom, now leaking into its absorbent tissue wrapper, and tossed it into a dustbin.

A few streets later I found Kennington tube station. Once home, I opened my laptop to continue researching a new career. It wasn't easy. How many thirty-five-year-olds suddenly launch into a new career and make a success of it? I'd heard the proverbial 'city trader turned plumber' stories, but had anyone actually met someone who'd made such a leap? Teaching had always appealed – *surely* some job satisfaction? – but my research confirmed a year of retraining, an oversupply of humanities teachers, a modest starting salary. Perhaps Human Resources – poacher turned gamekeeper?

It was all too draining, so a bit like with exam revision, I found a way to avoid it, by logging onto Facebook. A little gentle stalk-ing of Carrie brought back pleasant memories of last night and this morning, after which I reviewed the recent comments posted by my 'friends', but soon enough I was leering at photographs again – Look how happy I am! Look how many friends I have! Look at my children – One of each sex! One of each sex! Facebook isn't a social networking site, it's an antisocial networking site, involving little or no meaningful interaction with anyone, just gawping at photos and inane comments. How I fondly remembered the days before Facebook, when people and life's events carried so much more mystique and glamour.

I slammed the lid of my laptop, fell back on the sofa and reached for the stereo: Marianne's Leonard Cohen album began...

25

One day shortly after my relationship with Carrie began, I wandered into the kitchen area at work, which was only sectioned off from the main office by a wall to shoulder height, so conversations in there were liable to be heard by those outside.

'Hi, Adam,' said the now familiar female voice behind me as I strained my teabag. I turned. It was weird seeing Carrie fully dressed, as most of my recent images of her, and certainly those stored on my mental hard drive, were of her naked.

'Oh, hi,' I replied.

'How are you today?'

'I'm good, thanks, just grabbling myself a tea to try to get my brain going this morning.' It felt strange having such a banal conversation with her, yet we daren't talk more openly with colleagues lurking about nearby.

'Have you got a busy day?' asked Carrie, tilting her head to one side. She had this Mona Lisa thing going on, with just the very edges of her mouth threatening to break into a smile. It made me nervous. And excited.

'Yeah, I've got a few things to do,' I said.

'What are you doing later?'

'Later?'

'After work.' She smiled and winked.

'Er… I don't know.'

'I'd like you to help me with something.'

'Really?'

'Yes.' She winked at me and raised her voice. 'I'm thinking I'd like you to become my appraiser. That way you can appraise me regularly. Performance management is so important, don't you agree? I'd like you to assess my personal development later on and provide feedback.' She reached forward, squeezed my hand and left. She hadn't ordered a drink.

After an increasingly frank email exchange that afternoon regarding our respective favoured bedroom proclivities, we agreed to meet back at my flat, only we happened to meet outside the lifts. When we entered and the doors closed, we found ourselves alone, and without a word started kissing hungrily, only breaking off at the last second as the doors opened again.

We rushed back to my flat and once inside clawed at each other's clothes, which were rapidly strewn on the lounge floor, some less a few buttons, some ripped. Carrie wrestled me into the black leather armchair under the window, straddled me, grasped me, lowered herself with a sigh and began a rhythmical rising and falling. The lights were on and the curtains open.

My hands slid along the backs of Carrie's taut thighs and held her buttocks, and I started to lift her to carry her to the bedroom, only for her to forcibly push me back into the chair. 'No,' she said, panting. 'I like it like this and to hell if someone sees us.'

Afterwards, as she lay flopped across my chest, breathing deep in the nape of my neck, she said, 'I like having sex before going out, it takes the pressure off the rest of the evening.' I stroked her back, contemplating her words. She had that leanness which comes naturally to a twenty-four-year-old, a litheness and suppleness of muscle and flesh. 'You know,' she said, 'I've always had this fantasy about sleeping with an older man. I like it when you tell me what to do in the office, knowing that later on I'm going to be sleeping with you.'

I rubbed my chin: I now knew how a woman must feel if a man says her prodigious bosom is an important factor in attracting him to her.

'I like it that you have the confidence to tell me what you like in the bedroom,' she continued, craning her neck to look up at me. 'I'm sure you've got lots more things you want me to do.' She traced a fingernail down the side of my stomach, making me judder. I wondered whether the bedroom inhibition and exhibition was because my relationship with Carrie had found me rather than being sought, which meant I wasn't sure how much it mattered to me. That hint of indifference seemed to work wonders; I made fearless requests, and the more provocative those requests, the more enthusiastic her responses.

Occasionally I worried about the implications of sleeping with a work colleague, particularly a relatively new graduate, but because no one mentioned anything to my face, it was easy to kid myself that people weren't gossiping. I was shaken out of that misapprehension one morning at work, when I was again in the kitchen area, this time Luke entering and tapping a number into the drinks machine. He wore a grey pinstriped suit and bright metallic red tie – the suit too tight, I think chosen because he thought it made him look thinner, whereas in fact it had the opposite effect.

'Hi, Luke, good weekend?' I asked.

'Yes, Sir – the Hammers won! How about you?'

'So so. I caught up on some rest.'

Luke sniggered. 'You probably need it.'

'Sorry?'

'The rumours are rife about you. As they say, you're only as young as the woman you feel, eh eh?!' He leant toward me and lightly punched my upper arm.

I feigned ignorance. 'What?'

'Don't be shy.' He lowered his voice and whispered, 'You've done well there, great pair on her. Mind you, you know what they say, don't shit on your own doorstep.' With that pearl of wisdom he slapped me on the back and waddled off, clutching his extra-sugared hot chocolate and chuckling to himself as he went.

A hot flush rose up my neck and flamed out across my cheeks; what gave Luke the right to come out with comments like that about my love life? And another thing: I'd always hated the expression *don't shit on your own doorstep*. Quite apart from being a vulgar way of expressing the sensitive act of lovemaking with a work colleague and the dangers thereof, why was it always the guy least likely ever to get laid who said it?

Of course if bloody Luke knew about Carrie and me, everyone knew. Shit. I hated the thought of being office gossip, even if those who gossiped tended to be those with the most uneventful lives. I pondered again on what Marianne would think. She and I were emailing again on a daily basis; she'd never mentioned anything about Carrie.

One Saturday a few weeks into our relationship I took Carrie to Borough Market as she'd never been. We arrived early to avoid the crowds. It was one of those icy cold days with a sky as clean and polished as a lens, when everything is seen with an unusual focus. Steam billowed from our mouths as we walked and talked. Carrie uttered a simple 'Wow' when she first saw the stalls spread out under the Gothic majesty of Southwark Cathedral and the railway viaducts traversing overhead. We entered the market and caught wafts of onions frying from a hamburger stall, and then melting cheese from a Swiss raclette stall. For brunch I bought Carrie one of the legendary chorizo and red pepper baps stuffed with rocket from the Spanish foods shop. We roamed the stalls, Carrie buying a tub of tapernade and me a bottle of Malbec from the Cartwright Brothers, where you were guaranteed some free tastings to set you up for the day.

We reached a stall selling just a single variety of cheese – Comté – it being so good the proprietors didn't feel the need to expand their selection. We used toothpicks to spear samples from a bowl on the counter.

I stopped chewing.

Every muscle in my body set still, in direct inverse proportion to the extent my mind was racing.

There, fifteen feet away, stood Marianne.

She wore a pastel green scarf that caught the light and lit up her face. Images and emotions splintered through my mind as the adrenalin hit again: our first kiss, the concentration in her face as we'd made love, my overwhelming yearning to be with her and close to her.

I glanced at the man next to her, her husband. The image I'd formed of him until then was that of a tall, handsome, chisel-jawed, Alpha Male. He wasn't. It was difficult to see him clearly because he was looking down, but he appeared to be of average height, with short brown hair, of medium build, and older than I'd expected. He was average, just like me.

I stared again at Marianne, who looked up. Our eyes locked. She smiled and I returned the smile: a moment stolen back to ourselves independently of our respective partners, and I cursed fate for its mistake of landing us with the wrong people.

'Are you alright?' asked Carrie, nudging me.

'Yeah, sure,' I replied, turning to face her. She'd bought a slice of the cheese and was tucking it into her oversized handbag. When I turned back Marianne and her husband were walking away.

A man in his mid-thirties stood between Carrie and me at the Comté stall with his young daughter perched on his right forearm, her arms around his neck. She was wrapped up in a pink bobble hat and scarf, her cheeks turning red from the cold. She must have been two or three years old.

'Dadda?' she said.

'Yes, darling?' replied the father.

She pointed at the samples on the counter. 'Cheese!' she said. The father gave her a piece, which she ate. 'Mmmm… more Dadda, more cheese!'

I stared at the father. His face captured pure happiness as he gazed adoringly at his daughter, oblivious to everyone around him. I'd never seen a man so contented. The electric pulse of fear shot through my head again, the same sensation as at the wedding.

'Come on,' said Carrie, tugging my arm.

The market was crowded now and our progress was slow as we squeezed past the mass of people. My mind raced: here I was along-side a woman to whom I'd made love last night and again this morn-ing, and all I could think about was another woman.

We reached a sweets stall and Carrie said something I didn't catch. 'What's that?' I asked.

'I said I love these.' Carrie pointed to some chocolate brownies.

'Well, why don't you get one?' I said with no energy in my voice, so that it sounded like an accusation, despite that not being what I'd meant. Carrie shot me a glare. 'Sorry, Carrie, let me buy you one,' I said, reaching for my wallet.

'No, it's okay,' she said, turning her shoulder and reaching into her purse.

We moved along from stall to stall in silence. After a while Carrie stood in front of me. 'Adam?'

'Yes?'

'Are you okay?'

'Yeah, I'm fine.'

'You seem preoccupied.'

'I'm just a little tired.'

Carrie tilted her head; she wasn't convinced. 'Do you want to go to the pub for a drink?'

'Sounds good,' I said, figuring that a drink might help take my mind off everything swirling around inside it.

We found a pub on the edge of the market, The Market Porter. The heat inside made my cheeks prickle such was the contrast with the bite of the cold outside. A sweet smell of cloves from mulled wine filled the air. I fetched drinks while Carrie found us a table in the corner.

'Thanks for bringing me here today,' said Carrie, taking a sip of her wine.

'No problem.'

'I really liked that chorizo sandwich you got me. And you were definitely right to bring us early, the queues are so long now.'

I nodded, but I was thinking about Marianne and her husband. I hated him for being average. Had he been a young George Clooney, it would have been easier to reconcile his capture of Marianne. As it was, it felt like an intruder had stolen my life, playing the part preordained as mine.

'What's wrong, Adam?' asked Carrie.

'What's that?'

'I asked what's wrong.'

'There's nothing wrong.'

'I can tell something's up. You leapt out of bed this morning to get to the market and now you're here you've gone all quiet and sullen.'

'I'm not sullen.'

'Yes you are. You may have been born in the nineteen seventies, but I don't think that's an excuse for suddenly becoming a grumpy old git.'

'Sorry,' I said, holding my pint glass so tight I thought it might crack; Carrie's frequent references to my age were starting to annoy me. I took a long draught of my beer and tried to think of something positive to say. 'So, you bought some of the Comté cheese?'

'I did. We should have it later in with that bottle of wine you bought and the tapernade. Maybe we could also get some bread and some salad?'

'Sounds good.'

Carrie peered at me over the rim of her wine glass, judging my mood. I summoned some energy from somewhere. 'Hey, did you see that chap standing next to us by the cheese stall?'

'No, I didn't notice.'

'You must have seen him; he stood between us, the guy holding his cute daughter in the pink hat and scarf.'

'Sorry, I didn't see them. Why do you mention it?'

'He just had a really cute kid, that's all. I kinda felt a little jealous of him.' Carrie stared blankly. 'My brother's got two kids,' I continued. 'To start with I felt a bit sorry for him, he always looked so washed out whenever I saw him, but now I'm starting to see what's it all about.'

'Anyway,' said Carrie, 'what other stalls should we visit?'

I shrugged my shoulders. 'I don't mind.'

She tutted. 'God, Adam, why can't you show some enthusiasm?'

I shook my head. 'A second ago I'm talking about my nieces and you couldn't give a damn, but I'm supposed to care about which cheese stall we go to next?'

'I don't want to talk about kids,' said Carrie in an intense hushed voice, not wanting other patrons to overhear. 'It's not something that's in any way relevant to me at this stage of my life.'

'Yeah, but when you're a bit older–'

'I hate it when people assume I'll want children one day. It's as though they think women are just baby-making machines, with no independent worth outside of motherhood. As if we're freaks if we don't want kids.'

'Hang on,' I said. 'I didn't say that. I was just asking, that's all.'

'I don't want kids. The thought of being pregnant horrifies me.'

Silence.

I chose not to press the point. After all, it's meant to be women trying to pin men down about such things, rather than the other way around. But something wasn't now right between Carrie and me: something insurmountable.

'You seem upset with me,' she said eventually, eyeing me suspiciously.

'No, not at all. I just didn't realise how strongly you felt about it.'

'I thought I'd told you before I don't want kids. Perhaps I didn't. It's just something you're going to have to accept, I'm afraid. It's not as though it's something I can compromise on.' The tone of her voice exactly matched the content: firm, decided, final.

I stared down into my pint, a dark mood gathering itself inside me. Our age gap was suddenly a yawning chasm and our intense physical relationship seemed... purposeless. 'I'm not sure it's working,' I said.

'*What?*' said Carrie, leaning forward.

'It's not working. This thing. Us. It's not working.'

The energy drained from her face. 'What are you talking about? You're not telling me this is about me not wanting babies?'

'It's not about babies, it's about us. It's about us being different ages, different *generations*. We want different things.'

'So what are you saying?'

I looked directly into Carrie's eyes and slowed my speech, wanting to hurt her for being so dismissive of my dreams. 'I'm saying we may as well go our separate ways.'

Her face fell further. 'But I thought we were getting on so well. I can't believe you can just change like this.'

'I haven't changed at all. I've just come to the realisation we're incompatible.'

She breathed in and out so fully that her head rocked a little back and forth. Her agitated eyes wandered all over me with barely disguised contempt. She reached out and picked up her purse from the table, placed it in her handbag and stood up, reaching for her coat. 'If that's how you feel I may as well go. It would have been nice if you'd spoken to me earlier about these things, before I got so... so involved.'

I stared at her as though she was a stranger.

She walked out.

I reached again for my pint, knowing Carrie's feelings should have been uppermost in my mind, but thinking only of Marianne.

* * *

Later that evening I was slouched at home, towards the end of the bottle of Malbec I'd bought earlier at the market. Leonard Cohen played on the stereo. I smoked a roll-up. Back to the old pre-Carrie bachelorhood routine.

I needed someone to talk to. Rachel. She only spent certain weekdays with Richard, as at weekends he went home to play Family Man. So I called her, and she was in, but sounded distant. 'You okay?' I asked.

'Yes, fine,' she said, sniffing.

'Are you sure?'

Silence.

'Is it Richard?'

'Yes.'

'Do you want to talk about it?'

'There's nothing to discuss. What were you were calling about?'

I explained the day's events. Rachel was silent for some time. Eventually she said, 'I'm worried that had you not seen Marianne today, you'd still be with Carrie.'

'Why's that worrying?'

'Because you're still not over Marianne. She's affecting your decisions even now.'

I drew deeply on my roll-up, contemplating whether to deny it, but realising it would be pointless.

'I think your problem is that you're not living in the present,' said Rachel.

'How do you mean?'

'You spend half your time worrying about the past, by which I mean Marianne, and the other half about the future, such as whether you and Carrie are ultimately compatible. Worrying about the past and future means you can't function in the present.'

I reached for the wine. Sometimes Rachel's braininess could be downright annoying. 'I thought I was doing the right thing today,' I said. 'If Carrie and I want such different things, what's the point?'

'You may well have done the right thing, but perhaps for the wrong reason. It's this Marianne girl who concerns me most.'

'Is seeing Richard the right thing? I'm not allowed to love a married woman, but you're allowed to date a married man. Explain that to me, will you?' I instantly regretted my words. 'I'm sorry, I didn't mean to say that, I–'

'We've split up.'

'*What?!*'

'Richard and I have split up. I ended it yesterday. Are you happy now?'

'Listen, Rachel, I'm sorry–'

'It's okay, I should have ended it earlier, as you've always said.'

'Let's meet for a drink. We've both got lots to discuss.'

'I'm taking a holiday for three weeks over Christmas. I need a complete break from everything. And everyone. We can meet up when I return.'

'Okay. Are you sure you don't want to discuss it now?'

'No, let's talk when I get back. I've got to go now, I'll speak to you soon.'

'Okay, bye Rachel, and take care.'

'Bye.'

26

Very little work was done that day in the office for it was one of those times – like when the IT system goes down or there's heavy snow and few have made it into work – which legitimise taking your foot off the gas and blaming it on somebody or something else. Everyone was noticeably more jolly than usual and the feeling of excitement intensified throughout the afternoon as the anticipation grew. In the late afternoon Carrie and two colleagues returned from the hairdressers sporting spectacular hairdos, which drew appreciative oohs and aahs from colleagues, thus sparking the rest of the ladies into action and the convoluted ritual of female preparation began. A procession made for the toilets, re-emerging sometime later utterly transformed in elegant ball gowns or figure-hugging cocktail dresses, accompanied by a diffusion of that evening's carefully selected perfume. You had to hand it to the girls; they had a proper sense of occasion. Tonight was our annual Christmas party – other halves not invited – which had been delayed until January to save costs in this time of austerity.

Easy for guys of course: black tie, done. When I entered the gents to get ready there were already half a dozen guys crowded in there, all steadfastly refusing to make eye contact lest they appear remotely comfortable in the company of other men in a state of undress. The toilets were in desperate need of refurbishment, particularly ghastly being the three cubicles separated only by the thinnest plywood partitioning which ended three feet from the ceiling and a foot from the floor, which meant each groan, splash and sigh from the next cubicle was clearly audible. What sort of sicko designs toilets like that?

I walked over to the final bit of free space in the corner, squeezed next to a urinal that periodically made loud gurgling noises like satisfied burps. My unfortunate position was compounded by being hemmed in by John, the owner of the business, and Stephen, our Finance Director. Stephen was the archetypal accountant: tall, lean, sharp-featured, a keen long-distance runner, a stickler for detail and a consummate professional. Nice chap too. I caught sight of his waistcoat in the mirror: good grief. Although a conventional black on the front, it had a 'novelty' cartoon pattern on the back, depicting various Disney characters in garish colours.

To my other side John, a prodigiously sized man grown fat on the profits of others' hard labour. Up close, his eyes looked even more tired than usual, resting in puffy little hammocks of flesh. A sprinkling of black hairs and liver spots covered his loose-fleshed upper arms and shoulders, which jiggled as he pulled on his tent-like white dress shirt. The blubbery bulk of his stomach hung low over his saggy white y-fronts, his frame supported by short, thin, ghostly white pigeon legs that seemed barely capable of supporting his weight.

Suddenly I wanted to engage John in conversation. Why? After all, this was a man who'd barely spoken to me for the last nine years because I wasn't one of his big fee earners. This was the man who'd treated Roy so disgracefully. Yet I felt compelled to converse, I think because I feared silence would betray my real feelings towards him – that he was a greedy old fool whose only interest in others was the extent to which they made him richer.

'Hi John, looking forward to the do?' I asked.

'Yes,' said John, noticing me for the first time, 'and at the Charing Cross Hotel too, who would have thought it? In 1979 I posted my first advert in the Evening Standard asking for construction workers to turn up to the hotel if they wanted work. That was before I had my first offices. How things have changed...'

'Indeed,' I said, not knowing what else to say. I needn't have worried though, for successful businessmen always have an inexhaustible capacity for talking about their own success and an equally infinite capacity for deluding themselves that you want to hear their whimsical reminiscences.

'Do you know,' he said, 'I recruited a chap that day who worked through the agency for twenty years. All because we shared a drink that afternoon and he trusted me to find him work from that day onward. You see, business is all about people and that's why events like tonight are so important. Most good business is done in the bars and restaurants of London; you'll do well never to forget that.'

'I'll try not to,' I replied, though I was more concerned about the poor sucker who'd worked through the agency for twenty years with John trousering the commission all that time. I tried to imagine John's reaction if I'd started to reminisce about my early career, when after graduation I'd temped in various London offices doing data input and other soul-destroying administrative tasks for £5 an hour. Or perhaps I should have challenged him to a game of World's Worst Jobs?

After changing, I fetched Adrian and we agreed a quick sharpener was needed before the main event, so we popped along to the Sherlock Holmes pub behind Charing Cross station. Two pints later, we entered the upstairs bar in the Charing Cross Hotel where pre-dinner drinks were being served, with most of the office already there, standing in groups of those they worked closest with. Adrian and I grabbed a glass of bubbly each from a table by the bar – clearly cava, not champagne – and joined Marcus, Luke and Matt, who were enjoying a lively debate about the respective appearances of our female colleagues.

'And at the bottom of the list,' said Luke, 'has to be Kate. I mean, talk about mutton dressed as lamb.'

Matt giggled. 'What is she, a seven or eight pinter?'

'You really think she drinks that much?' asked Adrian.

'No, you idiot,' said Marcus. 'Matt's saying it would take seven or eight pints before you'd consider shagging her. Take a look for yourself.' He nodded towards where Kate stood wearing a burgundy strapless ball gown, which although extravagantly billowing from the waist down, was unforgivingly tight up top, squeezing her pillowy bosom upwards and outwards like a toothpaste tube squeezed too hard.

'Look at Carrie, great pair on her,' said Luke, before looking worried as he remembered I was present and hurriedly adding, 'and that girl Marianne is gagging for it. Just look at that dress. I bet she goes like a train.' I kept composed, concentrating hard not to betray any emotion, before following his line of sight...

A noise emanated from my lips: a stifled gasp, or was it a sigh? She was standing in a short, dark green dress cut to mid-thigh, which with her four-inch stiletto heels made her legs appear immeasurable and inexhaustible, with a slight but noticeable muscular definition. I entered a trance-like state, time standing still and my facial muscles relaxed to the point of turning to liquid.

Adrian nudged me discreetly in the ribs.

'What?'

He whispered, 'Your mouth is hanging open and you're about to start dribbling.'

'Oh, sorry,' I replied, standing up straight and recomposing myself.

The floor to ceiling wooden partitioning at the far end of the room rumbled open and concertinaed, allowing access to the dining room. Adrian and I were on the same table, along with billowing ball gown Kate, Stephen of comedy waistcoat fame (please god, don't let the waistcoat be the main conversation throughout dinner) and one or two others. It could have been worse – I could have been landed with Luke and Matt, which would have meant two hours of conversation about Porsches and Roman Abramovich's new yacht.

The food was the usual dire mass catering: a tiny strip of anaemic salmon dressed with one or two lonely capers and a drying slice of lemon, followed by rubbery turkey with *all the trimmings*, comprising reclaimed meat chipolatas wrapped in fatty white bacon, roast potatoes soft on the outside and hard in the middle, and boiled to death bitter Brussels sprouts. The wine was equally bad, but there was lots of it.

'But he did love me, Penny, you've got to give him that,' said Kate towards the end of the dessert, by which time we'd been through most of the wine.

'That wasn't love, it was something... something different,' said Penny, our Credit Controller, who worked alongside Kate in the Accounts Department. Her cheeks had blossomed to a deep rouge, betraying the fact she didn't usually drink and tonight she'd had one too many.

'It was unconventional yes, but it was love,' said Kate. 'He was just very... very traditional.'

Penny was not to be deterred. 'Traditional is one way of putting it, but he didn't just make you wash the dishes and do his ironing, now did he?'

The conversation was nearing some jagged rocks, for the rumours in the office were that Kate's ex-husband was a bit of a nutter, and Penny was particularly sensitive about men since her ex-boyfriend ditched her in favour of an Estonian girl he'd met on a stag do in Tallinn.

'No, I grant you, it was more than that with Ryan,' said Kate, 'but you've got to understand he was a man's man, very old-fashioned and liked things done proper. But I won't deny that when his obsession began, things became very... difficult for me.'

Adrian leaned towards Kate. 'You don't have to talk about it if you don't want to.' He might have added that a problem shared with a table full of colleagues is a problem shared with the whole company.

'It's alright, I like to get it off my chest from time to time,' said Kate, clutching her wine glass, tilting her head back and throwing back its contents before replenishing it. 'It all started to go wrong when Ryan started turning his body into a temple...'

'You mean he began working out or something, like a mid-life crisis?' I asked.

'No,' said Kate with a glazed eyed look of confusion. 'I mean he actually turned his body into a living temple... in my honour.'

'Oh... I see,' I replied, though I couldn't see what she meant at all and judging from similar confusion registered on the faces of others, I wasn't alone, only no one wanted to ask what we all craved to know, which was how did this temple manifest itself.

'Ryan was always into his tattoos, you see, just like his dad,' continued Kate, with everyone listening intently. 'For many years he had the words LOVE and HATE tattooed across the knuckles of his hand. I think his love for me started turning to obsession when he went to the parlour and got that tattoo changed.'

'What to?' asked Adrian.

'He had the word HATE changed to KATE.' There was a sharp collective intake of breath from the table. 'I didn't know whether to be flattered or afraid when he did that. I suppose I was quite touched, but it wasn't a feeling that lasted long – positive feelings rarely did with Ryan. You see, he always took things to the extreme.'

'Such as?' asked Penny, somewhat provocatively.

'Everything. He drove like a maniac, constantly cussing and swearing and trying to run people off the road, and god, the curries he ate! King prawn phaal, always a king prawn phaal and make it extra hot he'd say, as hot as you can make it. The kitchen staff used to come into the restaurant to see if he could eat it. The sweat used to pour from him! He was almost down to his underpants by the time he finished!'

'Most guys like a hot curry, you certainly can't hold that against him,' said Adrian, trying to steer the conversation away from the dark alley it was in danger of finding itself.

'I could have coped with the curries, it was the tattoos which upset me. I think he was scared of losing me. He kept telling me my job in the City was giving me ideas above my station. It started with my name tattooed all over his body, but it soon progressed to pictures of me. Eventually they were everywhere... including...' Kate's voice fell away and with half-closed eyes, looking upwards such that only the whites were visible, she concentrated intently to conjure up the image of that specific tattoo which had clearly had such impact on her. In the ensuing silence all eyes were upon her. 'I really don't know how he... sustained himself when he got that one done,' she said, shaking her head. That was the end. I haven't seen him since. The last time anyone saw him was my sister in Bluewater shopping centre.'

'Was he okay?' Adrian inquired.

'Not really. My sister said his latest tattoo was a thin dotted line around his neck with a picture of a small pair of scissors at one end next to the words *cut here.*'

Penny, who'd been listening intently and absorbing Kate's stories, appeared fortified by the revelations, as though they proved beyond doubt that all men were intrinsically guilty because they were capable of such things. 'This is what I mean about men,' she said. 'Take that Tiger Woods. Have you seen his wife? But she wasn't enough for him, was she? Oh no. Despite being the most stunning woman in the world and bearing him two beautiful children, he still had to go out and sleep with those... those *sluts.*'

Surreptitious glances were exchanged: we'd never heard Penny speak like this before.

'All those women he slept with have to take some of the blame, surely?' I said. 'I mean, they must have known he was married.'

'He probably threw thousands of dollars at them! He had dozens of them on the go!' Penny's voice was now shrill and tinny, as though she wasn't quite in control of it.

'Perhaps he's a sex addict or something,' I said. 'He probably needs help to deal with it–'

'Oh *pleeeeassse!*' shrieked Penny. 'You men, any excuse. No one had ever heard of sex addiction until recently; it's the most ridiculous excuse I've ever heard. You're not really telling me that there's a medical condition which causes rich men to sleep with as many women as possible, are you?'

'The male Darwinian gene may explain it,' I almost said, but resisted. Instead I replied, 'But if so many pleasurable things can lead to addiction, why not sex? We all accept drink and drug addiction, and what about gambling and food addiction? Why not sex addiction?'

'You can't win this conversation, Adam, I have too much ammunition,' said Penny, her voice carrying well beyond our table. 'Men are always thinking with what's in their trousers. Take that Formula One guy – what's his name? Mosley? What he got up to was disgraceful. Imagine the effect on his poor wife.'

'I'm just saying, it's difficult to judge,' I said. 'We don't know all the facts.'

'Difficult to judge?' shouted Penny, her eyes penetratingly, petrifyingly wide apart. 'Difficult to judge? He fucked Nazi call girls!'

Stunned silence.

Continued stunned silence.

Silence that felt like it might continue forever more silence. I stared straight ahead, shell-shocked.

'Can we talk about something a bit more festive?' said Stephen. 'This is meant to be our Christmas party. Now, I got this new waistcoat last Christmas from my boys...'

A short while later, as coffee was served, John rose and banged a spoon against a wine glass to bring everyone to order. The congregation fell silent.

'I want to begin by thanking everyone for all the hard work you've put in throughout the last year. Thirty years ago I was sitting in a suite in this very hotel, recruiting construction workers, and I would never have imagined then that today, all these years later, I would be standing here addressing what is the pre-eminent, mid-tier recruitment business in London. I know it's not been the easiest year for any of us, indeed it's been the hardest I can remember, but let me assure you, if we can maintain our unrelenting focus on our clients, a zeal to serve them and...'

I zoned out. This was a re-hash of the garbage he'd been spouting in the toilets earlier. It was as if he was stuck on autopilot, with a series of set piece speeches to be employed in any circumstances, to any audience. How the hell had he reached the top? More importantly, how the hell had I found myself spending ten hours a day working for him?

I glanced about, gauging my colleagues' reactions to John's speech. Almost to a man they were staring at him with soft, droopy, puppy eyes and warm half-smiles, like scientologists watching a Tom Cruise movie. It was frontal lobotomy stuff and worse still their minds were apparently given willingly... happily... even joyously to this drivel. I took a huge gulp of wine and thanked god that although I might not be at the top of the Sales League Table, I still had self-determination and sanity.

To wrap things up John announced various award winners, including 'Recruiter of the Year' and 'Best Newcomer', and handed each winner a bottle of champagne. A single, cheap bottle of champagne their reward for coming top after a whole year's hard labour, and they actually looked happy about it!

As soon as the applause subsided for the last prize, a stampede began for the bar. I sat still, still dazed from Penny's earlier verbal assault.

'You look like you could do with a drink,' Adrian said.

'And a sex change,' I replied. 'Jesus, remind me never to defend the male of the species in front of Penny ever again.'

We joined the queue at the bar as the disco started up, and a few of our more inebriated colleagues stumbled onto the dance floor. A moment later, a distinctive green to one side caught my eye.

Marianne, also queuing.

'Go and speak to her,' said Adrian, catching me staring. 'And Adam?'

'Yes?'

'It's time you told her how you feel.'

I nodded and asked Adrian to get me two Sambucas. With that, he patted me on the back and left me to it. I drew a deep breath into my lungs and took confidence from the thought that while I'd often doubted her feelings for me when we were apart, I'd always had complete confidence in her when we were together.

As I approached, my heart sped up and my senses sharpened. 'Here,' I said, holding out the shot glass. 'I got you a drink.'

She turned. Her lips flickered briefly into a smile before returning to a neutral setting. She took the drink. 'Thanks,' she said, sipping it. 'You remembered my drink.'

'You think I would have forgotten?'

'I don't know.'

I'd pictured Marianne's face in my mind's eye a million times and yet here before me it had dared to change. I had to blink two or three times to take in and interpret the changes, the slight darkening of the eyes and fuller lips from the makeup.

I lifted my glass and in unison we knocked them back.

'I needed that,' I said. 'I think I fell into a coma when John was giving his state of the union speech.'

'Well, I was sitting next to your colleague Luke. He spoke about cars a lot and had his mobile phone next to his plate the whole way through dinner, which I thought was very rude.'

'Believe me, whatever you experienced couldn't have been as harrowing as what I've just endured.'

'It can't have been that bad.'

'Penny starting talking about Nazi call girls.'

'No! Penny? You mean the quiet, sensible lady from accounts?'

'The very same.'

'Goodness, I would never have thought it.' There was a brief silence during which Marianne looked into both my eyes in turn, back and forth, as though searching for something. 'How's Carrie?' she asked. There was an edge to her tone of voice, a hint of accusation. 'I'm happy for you that you've met someone.' She didn't look happy.

'Why, what have you heard about me and Carrie?' I asked.

'I heard Carrie talking about you by the coffee machine recently and it wasn't the first time. She seems to take pleasure in me being within earshot.'

It was one of the dangers of dating a young woman in the office: you couldn't trust her to keep shtum. 'I'm not seeing Carrie anymore,' I said.

Marianne paused. 'Really?'

'Yes, really, although I'm not sure why I have to explain myself.'

'I didn't ask you to,' she said, lifting her chin and looking away.

'Marianne?' I said, waiting for her to turn back to me. 'If the subject of my love life is fair game, may I ask you how your husband is?'

Again, she faced the bar. To my other side, I sensed a presence. They say if someone stares at the back of your head long enough, eventually you look round. I looked round. Carrie, with colleagues, but glaring at me. I swivelled back round to Marianne; the last thing I needed was to have to deal with Carrie.

'Marianne?' I said, moving closer so we were tight next to each other. 'I only have feelings for one person, but she's spoken for.'

'How do I know you mean that? You could have said the same thing to Carrie, for all I know. And there could be more women besides. You're single, remember, you can do as you please.'

'I could say the same to you. How do I know this isn't just flattery for you? This way you get a husband at home and a boyfriend at work too: the best of both worlds, so you're never short of attention.'

'If you think this is about flattery, you don't know me at all,' said Marianne, her voice faltering.

I didn't know what to say because words were so inadequate, just vocal sounds inscribed in space that disappear. It's only the sincerity behind them that counts, and how can one ever hope to validate that? I wished at that moment, more than anything I'd wished for in my life, that Marianne could have been granted unfettered access to my heart, so she could understand my true feelings. Then, finally, she would know, for once glimpsed, the purity of my love for her could never have been doubted again and my martyrdom assured.

'I just didn't know how to react when I heard Carrie talking about you,' said Marianne. 'I didn't realise I would care so much. And then when I saw you together at Borough Market... I... I just don't know.' She shook her head and there was just the faintest bloodshot tint to her eyes, which reframed their green, making them more nocturnal and feline. 'I argued constantly with Simon that day after seeing you and Carrie together. Seeing the two of you together undermined something very important to me.'

'I don't know what I'm meant to do,' I said. 'Stay single indefinitely while hoping and praying you split up with your husband?'

'I never asked you to do that.'

'But you resent me if I get involved with another woman.'

'I don't resent you, I just don't know if I trust your feelings for me.'

'I've never felt this way about anyone in my life.'

'But how can I be certain of that?'

I paused. 'Certainty like this comes once in a lifetime, Marianne.'

Silence.

Continued silence.

'If I was single, I would be with you,' said Marianne eventually. Her words at once elated me and crushed me, because they seemed to offer me the thing I most wanted in the world and at the same time snatch it away. It was like god was playing a game with me, placing what I so wanted within reach, but denying me the chance to take it.

'I don't know what to say, I can't wait forever,' I said.

'I know, I know.' She reached out for her empty shot glass and held it.

A tap on my shoulder.

Carrie. 'In case you hadn't noticed, she's married,' she said, her top lip curled into a snarl. A flash of her right arm and her drink splashed into my face as I bent double and swirled around.

'Are you okay?' asked Marianne, putting her arm around my waist.

'I'm fine,' I said, wiping the wine from my face with my sleeve. When my eyes cleared I saw Carrie walking away, but the stares of all my colleagues at the bar were crawling all over me. 'I'd best go,' I said quietly, wanting to spare Marianne the guilt of association. 'The whole office is looking.'

Walking off, I passed Marcus, his expression odd but vaguely familiar. As I approached the door, I realised what his expression was: the look he gave Luke and Matt whenever they made a sale, a look of admiration and respect.

I reached the exit, only to feel another tap on my shoulder.

What?! I snapped back, expecting it to be Carrie, only to register Luke standing before me, his face flushed from alcohol. He had a serious expression and beckoned me forward with a hand gesture to whisper something in my ear.

'Remember,' he said, 'don't shit on your own doorstep.' He laughed and walked back to Marcus and Matt.

27

Adrian and I had been expecting the news for some time, but that made it no easier when it finally arrived by email.

> *Dear Adam and Adrian,*
>
> *It is with much sorrow that I write to inform you that Roy lost his long fight with cancer late last night. His two daughters and I were with him at the end and he died very peacefully.*
>
> *Roy had particularly fond memories of working with the two of you and would often speak of you both. And of course he was delighted to see you when you were kind enough to pay us a visit a few months ago and enjoyed your regular emails.*
>
> *It would mean so much to me and the family if you could come to the funeral, which is being held at Saint Mary the Virgin in Twickenham at 11 a.m. on 20 March. We will be having drinks and some food afterwards at Roy's local, The Hare and Hounds.*
>
> *Kind regards,*
> *Joan*

After I read the email, an overwhelming loneliness descended. It wasn't as though I'd had much contact with Roy in his last months – it wasn't possible, given his deterioration – but nevertheless he'd been there, with Joan in Twickenham, a presence, still felt and still somehow guiding. No longer. The realisation brought on a constriction in my throat and around my heart, but also a determination to draw the positives from a life so well lived.

* * *

Arriving at the church from the train station, I joined the others standing stiffly by the entrance, nodding to some, saying polite hellos to others, despite not really knowing who any of them were. A light drizzle like a mist fell, leaving the graveyard grass and tombstones beaded with raindrops. From inside the church came the tender melancholy swell of the church organ, rising, falling, and rising again.

Adrian's old Golf drew up outside the wall of the churchyard, cleaned and polished for the journey, in the same way that I'd shined my shoes to a high buff for the occasion. I watched his approach with Sarah up the flagstone pathway, Sarah tall and poised, her legs and feet invisible under a long black dress, giving the impression that she was floating.

We were introduced. Up close there was something of the earth mother about her, something to do with her height and long dark red hair and strong chin. She had a natural ability to put you at ease and make you feel you were the centre of her attention.

I followed Adrian and Sarah inside. They moved together as one, holding hands, his arm around her waist as they sat down, and her head momentarily resting on his shoulder. I tapped Adrian on the leg and when he leant towards me I nodded subtly at Sarah and whispered, 'She's miles out of your league.' He smiled and raised his eyebrows.

I spotted the deep red-brown mahogany coffin with simple silver handles on a stand at the front, just beyond the front pew. There was something quite shocking about thinking of Roy's recently deceased mortal coil residing in that box.

A white-haired vicar in a long black cassock walked gently forward and at the precise moment he came to a standstill, just in front of the coffin, the last bar of the organ's dirge completed.

'Thank you to you all for coming here today. We are here to remember and celebrate the life of Roy Hamilton...'

Mention of his name was all it took to throw the switch. I began to tear up, and as much as I tried to compose myself, I couldn't stop the tears running down my cheeks. I tried to resist bringing my hand to my face, which would give away I was already losing it. I'd forgotten to bring a handkerchief, eventually wiping away the tears with my fingers, prompting Sarah to reach across Adrian and hand me a tissue.

I'd been to three previous funerals, all grandparents, and the thing that stuck in my memory was just how upset my parents had been. They'd wept as the realisation struck home that no one would ever love them as much again as their mother or father, for no one else is capable of the purity and depth of the love of a parent. In the front pew the shoulders of one of Roy's daughters gently juddered, and Joan's consoling arm moved around her back. The sight set me off again.

I struggled on through two hymns and a reading, before Roy's friend Colin stood up to give the eulogy. He peppered his summary of Roy's life with amusing anecdotes which made us all laugh, but finally he had to bring his tribute to a conclusion. After a prolonged pause, which made it clear he was about to reach the ending, he spoke slowly and evenly.

'It seems to me there are many ways to measure a man's life. It would be easy, I think, to take an inventory of his material wealth, and his works and monuments, but I'm not sure we would necessarily be any the wiser as to what sort of man he truly was or how he was viewed by others. Or perhaps we could try to measure his power and influence, but again, I'm not sure that would get to the essence of the man. All those things really tell you is the extent to which the man aroused envy, for as Roy always said, we live in times where great importance is mistakenly attached to material wealth.' Colin took in a deep breath. 'Roy had all the material wealth he wanted, indeed he was very grateful for it, but that wasn't the measure of the man. No. The true yardstick is always this: was the man's life good, or was it bad; or to ask it another way, was he loved, or was he loathed? Because at death all envies are gone, as is all power, all wealth too. But love remains and endures.' His voice broke and he paused, gulping deeply, before bringing a handkerchief from his pocket and dabbing his eyes. 'All those here today were lucky enough to have their lives touched by Roy and all will agree with me, I'm sure, that he was loved dearly, as much as any man has been loved, and his death is felt as a loss beyond what my words are capable of describing.' He waited and summoned whatever composure was left in him in order to continue. 'A beacon of light has been extinguished, but only extinguished on earth, for Roy will always remain a guiding light to those who knew him, like a singular star in the night sky. Roy – goodbye from us all, we'll never forget you.'

Colin stepped down from the lectern in some distress, but by god I loved him for it. I loved him for loving Roy the way I did and for saying so.

The opening bars to the final hymn, *Abide with Me*, piped gently from the organ. It was as if all the emotion of the day was distilled into that last hymn, which in a way was fitting, for it would surely be the last time so many people would stand together in collective recognition of Roy's impact and importance on their lives.

As the final verse began, the pallbearers crept around the coffin and lifted it with silent strain onto their shoulders. They turned, slowly and purposefully, and shuffled their feet in unison to bear Roy outside. The congregation followed and there was something very ancient and elemental about the process of lowering the body enclosed in the coffin to its final resting place in the damp earth. The vicar's voice was diminished somewhat in the open air and by the rustling of the wind through the branches of the trees, but still clear: 'We bring nothing into the world, and it is certain we carry nothing out. The Lord giveth, and the Lord taketh away; blessed be the name of the Lord.'

Standing back from the congregation, I gathered myself. After a few final words from the vicar the service was over and details were passed around of the pub where we were to meet. I told Adrian and Sarah I would see them there.

Once everyone had dispersed, I stood alone in the drizzle and looked down at Roy's small tombstone. It was located under an apple tree in the corner of the graveyard. In black lettering on light grey stone, it read:

Roy Hamilton

Born 27 February 1944, Died 16 March 2009

Devoted husband, father and friend to many

To live in hearts we leave behind is not to die

28

In the weeks following the 'Christmas' 'party' a number of female colleagues – led by Penny – kept silent whenever near me, maintaining steely straight-ahead stares, thus ensuring they wouldn't be forced to engage with the cad, the bounder, the rake, the lock-up-your-daughter male scumbag. Which contrasted to the reactions of many of my male colleagues, of course. The likes of Luke and Matt were only too happy to talk to me, liberally sprinkling every conversation with innuendo and suggestion, as though they needed to share in something or prove something to me. At least Marianne was consistent. Our emails and meets for coffee continued, but I sensed that the dramatic conclusion to the Christmas party had reinforced to her just how complicated things had become.

Women problems weren't my only concern at work. Each day I went through the motions of putting in calls to clients, only to be told they had a recruitment freeze on, or that they were going through a redundancy programme. Some even accused me of insensitivity for calling at such a difficult time. As helplessness and hopelessness gripped the office, so we awaited our fates and a gallows humour developed:

'Hey, Adrian, you know that job you're trying to fill? Can you put me forward for it?'

'Call yourself a recruitment consultant? You can't even find yourself another job!'

'Have you tried interviewing yourself for that vacancy you're trying to fill, Adam?'

The tension heightened one week when the directors disappeared into meeting rooms. Rumours began doing the rounds: we were all going to have to re-apply and be re-interviewed for our jobs, we were going to be forced to move to cheaper business premises outside London, and of course the big R – redundancy. Such a horrible word. It loomed so large and was spoken about so often, I decided to look up its meaning:

Redundancy /noun (pl **redundancies**): **1** being redundant. **2** *chiefly Brit* no longer required for a job.

I decided to look up *redundant*.

Redundant /adj: no longer useful or necessary; superfluous.

Good god. *No longer useful? Superfluous?* No wonder redundancy carried such a stigma. Like cancer, things could never be the same once you'd experienced it, and life ever after lived in fear of it happening again.

Given the hovering axe, I'd sent off a number of applications for jobs in Human Resources over the last few weeks, but was getting used to certain standard responses:

'Due to the prevailing economic conditions, we have cancelled all recruitment.'

'Unfortunately, due to the large number of applicants...'

One particularly insensitive response read:

'If you do not hear from us within 6 weeks, consider yourself unsuccessful.'

And of course the usual baffling business-speak:

'We are unable to take a favourable action in respect of your application.'

Then one bleak Tuesday morning, one of those days when it remains so overcast and grey it's as though the night never quite ended and the new day never quite began, the email which we'd all been dreading arrived. At the time I'd been printing off screen shots of charge-out rates and pay details relating to the contract staff placed by Marcus, Luke and Matt, knowing that neither the clients nor the candidates knew what the other were being charged or paid respectively. I figured such information was a tidy little insurance policy should Marcus try to sack me following our recent argument. When I returned to my desk, Adrian said, 'It's arrived.'

'What has?' I asked.

'Our fate. Check your emails.'

There it was, the email to which Adrian referred, with Outlook Calendar invite attached, and a red exclamation mark denoting it as an email of 'High Importance'. A meeting was to be held, attendance compulsory, that Friday afternoon at 4 p.m., to discuss *the future strategy of the company*, a suitably vague way of luring everyone to learn their fates.

'Always deliver bad news late on a Friday,' said Adrian. 'It's a business strategy. It'll be in one of Marcus's books, I promise you.

If you get bad news on a Friday, you start off angry that day, go for some drinks that night, calm down throughout Saturday when you're at home with your family and friends, and by Sunday you *begin to accept*. It means that by Monday, you're focussing on how to deal with the bad news, rather than questioning it.'

'The fuckers,' I replied.

Friday arrived. It was a long, slow, drawn-out day, there being little incentive to work when you could be out of the job by the end of the day. From a quarter to four we all made our way to the company boardroom on the top floor of the building in a solemn procession of near silence.

When we arrived the room was about half full, everyone choosing to take their seats from the back, for already seated at the front in a line behind the long rectangular table normally used for board meetings were the company's six directors, including John, Marcus and Carolyn, their demeanours unnaturally stern. It felt like being back at school assembly with the teachers about to announce the expulsions of certain as yet unnamed miscreants.

Soon the seats had absorbed as many of us as they could but people kept streaming in, standing in whatever space was available. It reminded me of watching a key Prime Ministerial announcement in the Commons, when MPs are forced to sit on the stairs and stand in the aisles; you would have thought they'd have designed a room big enough for such important occasions.

John stood up from behind the long table, dressed in a charcoal grey suit, white shirt and pastel yellow tie, holding a small piece of paper. He hauled his hulking frame round to a lectern placed to one side. Without being asked, the room fell silent in anticipation of his imminent words and the purity of the silence was frightening, so many hopes and fears articulated by it. A wink of yellow light in the far distance caught my eye through the window behind John and because it was a crisp, clear day its source was easily visible: the apex of Canary Wharf tower.

'Good afternoon, everyone, and thank you for taking the time to attend this meeting. We all know that the last few months have seen the most challenging economic conditions since the Great Depression, and not even I was around when that occurred...'

A few muffled laughs, only they weren't really laughs, more just sharp, bitter exhalations of breath to break the tension.

'Now what this means is that everyone has to tighten their belts, and I wanted to call everyone together today so that you could all hear first-hand the plans the company has put in place to cope with the recession. This is the first time in thirty years that we've had to announce measures such as we're announcing today, but I can assure you that they are absolutely necessary in order for us to cut costs and so survive and eventually prosper in the future. I'm now going to hand you over to Carolyn, who will give you details of the plans. Can I ask you to save your questions until the end, please, when I and the other directors will take questions from the floor.'

While John shifted his great bulk back to his chair, Carolyn stood up and approached the lectern; once there she stood tall and erect, her demeanour cold and efficient. 'Thank you, John,' she said crisply and clearly. 'All businesses have to make hard decisions in times of recession. As you all know, this is the most severe recession of our lifetime and regrettably we have been adversely affected. You will all be aware that our financial performance is dramatically down on last year and well off budget. This means the business has been forced to cut costs and while we have made as many savings as possible in areas such as overheads and procurement, we have now been forced to address our human resources.'

If you'd ever been in any doubt as to whether the organisation valued you as a person or simply treated you as a resource for profit, you weren't any longer. Mind you, the clue was in the name of the department: Human *Resources*.

Resource (usu in pl): a source of wealth or revenue.

'The reduced profits of the company cannot sustain the current employee headcount. Therefore, the business regrets that it has been forced, due to the unprecedented economic conditions, to make twenty-five per cent of the workforce redundant.'

A smattering of gasps from the audience, and murmuring at mention of the R word. For me, it was almost a relief that the enemy, which until now had prowled about menacingly in the undergrowth, was now out in the open.

Carolyn raised her voice. 'And an email will be sent to those affected after this meeting, informing them that their job is redundant and inviting them to meetings on Monday at which the redundancy terms will be confirmed. These terms are *more* than generous and we would encourage all those affected to accept them. I must warn everyone...' she paused for effect, '... that those who do not accept the terms of the redundancy will not be re-offered the original, generous terms at a later date.'

Confused looks amongst the audience: could they withdraw the redundancy terms if you dared to question them?

'We have been as objective as possible regarding this process,' continued Carolyn. 'The criteria used to select those made redundant included an assessment of their performance rating at their last two annual appraisals, length of service for the company, and sickness record...'

Sickness record? I tried to think of the last time I'd pulled a sickie...

'...and in this way we have fairly chosen those selected for redundancy. However, I am afraid the redundancy programme alone will not be enough to address the severe financial difficulties we are experiencing. We are *all* going to have to make sacrifices. Therefore, for those who are *not* being made redundant, we will be asking you to accept a ten per cent reduction to your basic pay and a thirty per cent reduction to your commission.'

Restlessness in the audience, people turning to one other and talking openly, swear words audible amongst the chatter.

'This will initially be for a year-long period,' said Carolyn, again raising and projecting her voice to bring the audience to attention. 'After a year the position will be reviewed. May I just reinforce that this pay restraint is absolutely necessary, and if we had not taken this step, we would have been forced to make more redundancies. Full details of the measures announced today are available on the intranet site immediately after this meeting and we will be asking those subject to the pay restraint to sign revised terms and conditions of employment on Monday. If any of you have any questions regarding today's announcement, I will be available next week to answer them. I will now hand you back to John.'

Did I notice just a flicker of that almost imperceptible smile as Carolyn walked briskly back to her seat? Another dose of workplace medicine successfully administered.

In the same way that Adrian had identified that businesses give bad news on Fridays for good reason, so the structure of this presentation had the stench of the consultant's influence all over it, what with John providing the perspective and market conditions to begin with, Carolyn delivering the bad news in the middle and John now ending it, presumably with an upbeat message, to reinforce the leader's positive personal impact.

John had waddled back to the lectern. 'I realise this news is difficult and I'm very sorry that we will be losing so many good people, some of whom have been with the business for many years. In terms of the pay restraint, as Carolyn said, we're all in this together and we all need to make sacrifices, but I can give you my personal assurance I will review pay in a year's time, at which point we will do everything we can to revert to the original position. Finally, can I just say that I'm certain we have the foundations here not only to survive this recession, but also prosper in the future, and that we will continue to be the pre-eminent, mid-tier recruitment business in London. Now, to finish, has anyone got any questions?'

Asking a question at a meeting like this was unquestionably a career-limiting move. It was a private company, John's little fiefdom, and dissenters were not tolerated. Those who dared to stand up to the regime suffered fates like Roy's – a Stalinesque termination of employment: ordered to leave the office with immediate effect, your laptop removed from your desk, your personal effects collected together in a cardboard box by Carolyn and forwarded to your home address with a compliments slip and a P45. Thereafter you were airbrushed from the company's history, your name never so much as mentioned by the directors and your contribution not acknowledged. *Vaporised*.

And so, inevitably, John's call for questions was met by complete silence. And the silence lingered.

'Yes, that lady over there – Harriett,' said John.

Someone wanted to ask a question! This was going to be interesting...

'What if someone is applying for a mortgage?' said Harriett. 'Won't a reduced salary affect their application?'

John looked down at the lectern and paused before replying. 'No, during the period of restraint we'll maintain what's called your *reference pay*, which is a figure equivalent to your pre-restraint salary and which should be taken into account by the bank or building society.'

Adrian whispered, 'Planted question, had to be, John read the answer.'

I was still trying to work out what *reference pay* was when John said, 'Right, any last questions?'

Silence.

John and the directors could never have imagined in their wildest dreams that this meeting would be so painless for them.

Something clicked, and my brain cogs whirred at a million miles an hour: what if *I* spoke up? What did I have to lose? Except my job, but my job wasn't going anywhere in any case.

'Since there are no more questions,' said John, 'I'd like to thank everyone for–'

'I've got a question,' I shouted, standing up. Every person in the room turned to me and stared. 'Carolyn said that everyone has to take a ten per cent pay cut; does that include you and the directors?'

John gave me an ambiguous look, a furrowing of the brow because I'd dared to inconvenience him, yet he remained calm to show the audience he wasn't in any way ruffled. 'Yes, of course,' he said, 'I've asked all the directors to accept the ten per cent restraint and they have all agreed to it, as have I.'

'Carolyn also mentioned a thirty per cent cut to our commission,' I said. 'As I understand it, the directors have a separate bonus scheme, so may I ask if that scheme is also subject to the same cut?'

John's face hardened as he considered his response. While he did so, I thought, *I may have been completely anonymous to you for the last nine years, but I'm not quite so anonymous now, am I?*

'I haven't divulged details of the directors' bonus scheme for thirty years and I have no intention of starting now,' said John.

Strong murmuring from the audience and one or two boos.

'I'll take that as a no then,' I said, 'which if you don't mind me saying so is unjust.' With my senses heightened, I gauged a certain solidarity from my colleagues, contrasting with the irritation on the faces of the directors. I noticed Marcus, his face turned tight with fury. Before standing up, I hadn't factored in just how excruciatingly embarrassing this would be for him. His discomfort was a bonus; and not one subject to a thirty per cent cut.

John's lips had tightened to a thin line and he shook his head. 'The directors take on far more risk than the rank and file,' he said, his words harsh and clipped, 'and that's why their bonus structure is different.'

Rank and file? Not a turn of phrase that would have pleased the management consultant who'd advised the directors on this meeting, I felt sure.

'What, more risk than not being able to pay the mortgage?' I replied.

'This is an economic situation, you idiot,' said John. 'It's a recession. Have you not been watching the news or reading the papers? Stop trying to politicise it.'

'I'm sorry, but when we achieved record profits last year, I don't remember our commission being *increased*, yet you're now asking us to accept it being cut when your bonuses remain untouched.'

'How dare you stand there and question me, you impertinent little...' John caught himself just before delivering the insult he craved to spit at me.

'But you just asked for our questions, surely you remember?' I stared at him, awaiting his response, the silence so pure I thought those around me would be able to hear my heart, which thumped like a drum. My throat had dried and I was light-headed, almost floating. It was as if someone else was playing the role of me, while I hovered somewhere up in the corner of the ceiling looking down on the character who was in fact me.

The silence kept on going.

'This meeting is over,' said John, and to everyone's astonishment he walked out of the room, head down, mumbling to himself as he went. The audience started looking at each other in confusion, everyone talking amongst themselves. Carolyn quickly strode to the front and shouted, 'Right, that's the end of the meeting, if anyone has any questions next week, please refer them to me.' But no one was listening.

The meeting broke up. Adrian shook my hand and that encouraged others to do likewise. Many also patted me on the back and offered words of support.

As I walked out of the boardroom my emotions were scattered; I felt vindicated for speaking up, but scared shitless about my job and what the future held.

Adrian and I returned to our desks and closed down our computers. The redundancy emails hadn't been sent yet.

'Drink?' said Adrian

'Damn right,' I replied.

29

Suspended in space, floating through the boundless eternity of stars. This was not sleep, but something vaster and more comforting, cushioned in an endless amniotic fluid, a return to the safest sanctuary of all. At an immeasurable distance, in a galaxy far, far away, a voice called:

'Water... water... water...'

A primordial force began lifting me upwards, an inverse gravitational pull, silent but powerful and I rose, like a diver without enough weights, pulled inexorably to the surface. A deep-rooted instinct told me to resist, but it was useless, and I floated upwards... and all the while that voice:

'Water... water... water...'

Half in sleep and half awakening, the yearning for water screamed silently within me. My throat was so dry it felt like it might rip with each intake of breath and my vital organs strained in desperation to suck up every last atom of fluid from my being.

'Cool, refreshing, revitalising water, the true essence of life...'

Consciousness began filtering into my mind; as it did so a nauseating throbbing thundered throughout my skull in time to my heartbeat and the faintest head movement caused fierce shooting pains in my forehead. At the same time, my brain stem was being sucked back down my spinal column in search of any remaining moisture in my parched body.

'Pure, ice-cold water, trickling, tickling and teasing down a mountain stream, its meandering flow over and amongst smooth stones resembling marbles and lozenges...'

Now awake, the craving for water overwhelmed me. I opened my eyes to the minimum possible aperture–

'*ARGH!*' A stinging sensation rushed into my eyes and they snapped shut. '*What the?!*' Then I remembered: contact lenses. '*Shit!*' I squinted and made out the blurred outline of the glass by my bed, reached for it and pulled it to my lips.

The glass was empty.

'*Fuck!*' I threw off the duvet, hauled myself up off the bed and staggered through to the bathroom, using an outstretched hand to locate the walls to balance and direct myself. I leant forward to the mirror, close enough to sense my breath causing a blush of steam on the glass, and opened my eyes to reveal lifeless, bloodshot eyeballs staring back at me. Raising my hands in a swift practised movement, I rolled the dried lenses away from my irises, immediately feeling a surge of release in my eyes. I blinked a few times and vindictively washed those little fucker lenses down the sink, cackling to myself in victory as they were flushed away, never to torment me again.

Keeping the tap running – I wanted that water ice cold – I filled my glass, lifted it to my dried, gummy mouth, and necked half a pint. The relief! My internal organs shuddered back to life as if my body was some complicated electrical appliance just plugged into a socket and all the lights suddenly flash and wink.

It didn't last. As soon as my body absorbed the water, I started shaking and had to sit down on the toilet, leaning forward, head in hands, cold but sweating.

Sometime later I stood up and inched my way through to the lounge, scene of the final stage of last night's brutal drinking session with Adrian. It wasn't a pretty sight. Or smell. The coffee table was littered with damning evidence: Rizla papers and scatterings of tobacco, a greying slice of doner spilling from a greasy paper wrapper, two empty shot glasses nestling around an empty whisky bottle. Clearing up could wait.

I shuffled through to the kitchen and stood in my boxer shorts, staring at the sink full of soiled crockery and utensils. I opened the refrigerator door; the entirety of its contents comprised a tub of margarine, a half-empty tube of tomato puree, and a cucumber on the bottom shelf which had decomposed into a fetid, watery, translucent green ooze. I slammed the fridge door closed in disgust and sighed; this meant getting dressed and braving the shops outside in the real world. It meant interacting with people. The thought of it started to overwhelm me and I slumped against the counter to support my weight, breathing heavily. I needed to lie down.

Lurching back to the lounge, I slumped horizontally onto the sofa, using the armrest as a pillow. I switched on the TV. What I needed now was televisual entertainment of the most undemanding kind. I flicked through the channels: some civilian protestors were clashing with an army in a square – I didn't know where and I didn't care; an energetic lady in Lycra doing sit-ups (my droopy eyes lingered awhile on her abdomen until a bead of spittle formed on my bottom lip); then I struck gold – Trans World Sport, that tasty hors d'œuvre on a Saturday morning for the sporting gourmand. Sport sport sport. Can a man ever really get enough, particularly when hungover? Sport acts like a heavy dose of tranquilliser to a troubled mind, my particular favourite being Test Match cricket – the ketamine of sport – which could zone me out in a trancelike state for eight straight hours at a time.

What might I have been doing now if I'd still been with Louise? Perhaps struggling to put up a shelf? Or on one of those hideous shopping excursions, traipsing behind her like a dog on a leash, forced to give an occasional opinion on an item of female fashion? But nothing, I repeat nothing, was as excruciatingly awful as a trip to IKEA. 'It's good value,' Louise would say before we set off, 'and besides, you like those meatballs they do, it'll be fun.' But when you got there, good god. All those animated first home couples buzzing around filling their baskets and trolleys with cut-price clutter, while men like me followed behind their wives and girlfriends with that vacant, faraway look in their eyes, which said, 'Is this it? Is this what I'm condemned to? Is this my reward for a week's hard work?' My brow started beading with sweat.

The slice of doner again caught my eye. I couldn't, could I? Everything about its dried wax ghoulish appearance said I shouldn't, but I needed sustenance to tackle this hangover… I reached for the putrid flesh–

Knock knock.

Someone at the door. Go away. Since living alone I generally ignored the door and telephone calls. When with Louise, answering them had been part of everyday life, but I'd learnt they were invariably salesmen, or worse still someone with something important to say, which meant another thing to do, another responsibility, another bullet point on the to-do list.

Knock knock knock.

This one was persistent. Could it be a parcel? I dragged myself upright from the sofa – my sweaty body coming away from the leather with an unsavoury slurp sound – and still just in my threadbare boxer shorts walked to the front door, readying myself to politely but firmly tell the intruder to go away. I opened the door, poking my head around it so the invader couldn't see my state of undress.

'Rachel?!'

Her eyes widened. The cogs of both our brains were almost audible.

'You've clearly forgotten you invited me round,' said Rachel.

'How did you get up here?' I asked, confused as to how she'd got into the building. I remained hiding behind my front door.

'Someone was coming out as I arrived, so they let me in,' said Rachel. 'Why are you leaning around the door like that? It's making me nervous. If you've pulled I'm more than happy to meet another day, I won't take offence.'

'No no, come in,' I said, opening the door to let her in while continuing to hide behind it. 'Please, go through to the lounge.'

I'd forgotten that my lounge currently resembled Helmand Province.

'Oh my god,' said Rachel, sharply turning her head away and burying her face in the collar of her jacket to shield her nose from the onslaught of odour left over from last night's drinking, smoking, belching, farting and sweating, which had left the lounge with a dense, heavy, masculine musk, the pungent bouquet exhibiting slightly sweet, sticky notes at its top end. 'God, if ever proof were needed that men need the civilising effect of women.'

My cheeks began to redden. 'How about we go through to the kitchen? I can explain everything. I don't normally live like this... honest.'

She shot me a doubting look and walked through to the kitchen. I scurried into my bedroom to grab my dressing gown. On the one hand I was pleased Rachel was here; after yesterday's public showdown with John I was grateful for a friend to talk to. On the other hand, the remnants of the drink were still beating sluggishly in my head and I'd just been getting used to the idea of lying on the sofa all day watching sport. Sport sport sport.

In the kitchen, Rachel took off her coat and immediately rolled up her sleeves and started doing the washing up.

'Thanks, Rachel, but you don't have to do that, really.'

'I do if I want a cup of tea,' she said, placing two mugs on the window sill, there being no room on the draining board. 'Where's your drying up cloth?'

I shrugged.

'No matter. Please tell me you have teabags?'

'In the cupboard,' I replied, pointing.

She opened the fridge door for some milk. 'Jesus,' she said, backing away from the ooze that was once a cucumber.

I sat down at the tiny kitchen table and cupped my head in my hands. It wasn't until a woman came into my home that I realised how desperate it had become. How desperate *I* had become.

Rachel sat next to me. 'What are these?' she asked, picking up the top piece of paper from a pile of documents on the table.

I lifted my head. 'Nothing,' I said, reaching for the paper, but she snatched it away.

'Application for residence in New Zealand?' she said, reading from the paper. 'You're not really thinking of emigrating, are you?'

I shrugged my shoulders and dropped my head back down into my hands.

'Adam, you can't leave, there's too much for you here.'

'Such as?'

'Your family and friends for starters. And your job, your–'

'I'm about to lose my job,' I said.

'What? Are you sure?'

'I told the board of directors they were a bunch of bastards in front of the rest of the company yesterday.'

'You didn't...' Rachel must have weighed up the evidence of my degraded physical condition and the degenerating domestic environment I inhabited and decided I was telling the truth. 'I'm so sorry. Is that definitely it then?'

'Yes.'

She took her time before responding. 'Well... you hate that boss of yours and you haven't been happy there for a while. Maybe it's for the best. And let's face it, you've never been a salesman and you can take that as a compliment.' She put her arm around me; for the first time in longer than I could remember, I didn't feel utterly alone. I started to well up. 'Promise me you won't make a rash decision about leaving England. Please, Adam?'

I sighed. 'I don't know how serious I am about leaving. I just know I'm fed up here.'

'But there's so much opportunity here.'

'I don't have the energy for opportunities. Everyone else seems to have the motivation to deal with their lives, but I don't any more. I used to love London, but it's become the loneliest place in the world.' I blew out my breath in frustration. 'I'm just so bloody angry with how everything turned out.' I remembered again the photograph of me my mother had in the kitchen at home. What dreams had that boy had back then, what hopes for the future? I began to choke up.

'Not everything can be that bad,' said Rachel.

'That's just it, everything *is* bad. Everything is broken. I'm about to lose my job, I've no idea what to do with my life and I'm unable to find anyone to love me. And without love, nothing else seems to matter very much.'

'Lots of people love you, Adam.'

'Not the one I want to love me.'

'You mean Marianne?' asked Rachel.

I nodded.

'Is she still with her husband?'

I nodded again.

'Do you want to talk about it?'

I'd never tried to articulate to anyone before just how much I adored Marianne. No one was worthy of that disclosure, until now. 'The whole world and everything in it reminds me of her,' I said. 'I'm trapped. If I watch TV or a film and there's a couple in it, then they're her and me. Every song I hear is about her. If I'm out on a date, I spend the whole time sitting there looking at the poor girl opposite me wishing she were Marianne. Anything and everything reminds me of her, everywhere I look, every taste and sound, even smells remind me of her. My whole world is defined by her and it scares me. I'm not even sure love is the right word for what I feel. It's more a madness, or a sickness. I don't sleep properly because I keep waking up to thoughts of her and the injustice that we're not together. I hate this world for denying me the only person I've ever truly needed.'

Rachel smiled sympathetically and nodded. 'Have you told her how you feel?'

'Yes, at our Christmas party.'

'How did she respond?'

'She couldn't, we were interrupted by Carrie.'

'What?'

I recounted the story. Rachel's lips slowly parted when I got to the part about Carrie throwing her drink in my face. 'So where does all this leave you and Marianne?' she asked. 'Do you think she will ever leave her husband?'

I shook my head. 'For so long now I've hoped and prayed she'll leave him. But now... now I'm scared that if she did she'd want to be single for a while, and then... then I can only imagine the competition I would have. I think I'd be crushed by the hope that she'd choose me, but she'd have all the men in the world to choose from and I doubt whether an ex work colleague who reminds her of the fag end of her last relationship is going to win that particular battle… Rachel, I'm sorry, here I am droning on about Marianne and we haven't discussed you yet. How was your holiday? And how are things with Richard?'

Rachel stood up and filled the two mugs she'd washed up with water. She handed one to me and sipped the other while remaining standing and looking out of the window. 'Let's not talk about me just yet. I think I owe it to you first to give you my honest advice about Marianne.' She sat down again, but even before she spoke her expression betrayed the fact that her prognosis wasn't positive. It was the look a doctor gives a patient just before giving the news that yes, it's cancer, and yes, it's at an advanced stage. 'Move on,' she said, leaning in on me. 'Just find a way, any way, to move on. Both Richard and Marianne are married, they've made their choices, and life is so often about choices which have already been made.'

Her words felt as if she'd placed my heart in an orange squeezer and slowly pulled the long lever down, draining it of all blood and vitality, leaving only a worthless pith. 'So that's what love does for you, especially unconditional and unreciprocated love,' I said, looking down and scratching at a thin crack on the top of the kitchen table with my forefinger.

'What's that then?' asked Rachel.

I looked up. 'Gives you an infinite capacity for self-delusion.'

'You aren't deluded; you're a victim of circumstance and timing. And besides, there must be someone else out there, you've just got to keep looking for her.'

I slumped further in my chair at the thought of continuing the search. 'Do you know,' I said, 'now that I think about it, I wonder whether the internet dates, and Carrie too, were all a way of distracting me from the pain of not being with Marianne. Perhaps Marianne was part of the reason Carrie liked me too.'

'How do you mean?'

'Because my obsession with Marianne meant I was indifferent to Carrie, and indifference to a woman seems to be a powerful attraction. Unconditional love on the other hand is more likely to scare them off.'

Rachel played with her bottom lip, pinching it in the centre between thumb and forefinger. 'I think that business with Carrie was most unfortunate,' she said eventually.

'Why?'

'You hurt Carrie, can't you see that?' There was sharpness to the way she spoke. 'What's the difference between the way Marianne has treated you and the way you treated Carrie?'

'It's different.'

'Is it? It's obvious how much Carrie liked you, you must see that? I'm sorry, but whenever you talk about Carrie I feel sorry for her. Women are apt to be just as involved as men, and generally more so. When we're unhappy, we hurt more than you know.'

I made a hard and conscious effort to empathise with Carrie, to really empathise. I imagined Marianne standing at the bar at the Christmas party talking intimately to one of my male colleagues and how I would have felt about it. I thought about the little boy in the photograph who'd not only screwed up his own life, but was now taking it out on others.

Something snapped inside me, and I broke.

I began to sob, head bowed, shoulders jolting. It was a hopeless weeping, prompted by Carrie, but fuelled by something deeper: a profound unhappiness, a purposelessness, an absence of love.

Rachel put her arm around me again. I was grateful we'd always remained friends and not become lovers, so now could talk freely without the complexity of romantic interest or history. 'I'm sorry, Rachel, you shouldn't have to see me like this,' I said.

'I'm sorry for having a pop at you about Carrie.' She pulled gently on my shoulder, urging me to sit up straight. 'Now listen to me. You've got to break out of this cycle of choosing the wrong women. Starting with Marianne. You're playing with fire chasing a married woman. And this whole internet thing, it's caused you to lose all perspective. You either place women on a pedestal, or else you reject them completely. Where's the balance?'

I wiped my eyes with the sleeve of my dressing gown. 'If I'm getting it wrong all the time, what do you suggest I do?'

'Pick the woman *you* want, not the woman you *think* you should want, which is something different.'

A bit like with much of Sam's advice, there was some sort of logic here, yet I felt none the wiser. 'Sorry, now I'm really confused,' I said.

'What I'm saying is, you'll know you've met the right woman when you don't have to persuade yourself she's the right person and when you don't have to justify her to anyone else and especially not to yourself. Perhaps the yardstick of love is how compatible you are, not just how infatuated you are.'

I rubbed my head, my thumb on my temple and three fingers making little circles in the very centre of my forehead. There was too much to take in here, especially with a pickled brain.

'Maybe I should have stayed with Lou,' I said. 'Perhaps we should have worked through our problems.'

'Trust me, you *had* to split up with Lou,' said Rachel, putting her hand on my forearm. 'There's something you need to know about Louise.'

The way she said it made it sound extremely grave. My heart sped up. 'She's alright, isn't she?'

'Jess and Ben have split up.'

'What? But they've only been married a year. And what's that got to do with Lou?'

'Lou is with Ben.'

Cogs whirring. Super fast.

'What do you mean she's *with* Ben?'

'I mean they're an item. Ben left Jess last week to move in with Louise.'

It took a moment for my understanding to catch up with my hearing. 'Well, I'll be damned...' I said, unsure of my feelings. 'How long's it been going on between Ben and Lou?'

'For quite a while. Since...' Rachel's eyes lifted skyward as she counted back in time. 'Since before Ben's wedding to Jess.'

'Before?'

'That's why Louise didn't go to their wedding; she was too upset about Ben getting married.'

I shook my head. 'Fuck me, and there was I thinking she didn't turn up because of me.'

'I guess you believed what you wanted to believe. You're not too upset, are you?'

'Wait a minute,' I said, a niggling concern crystallising into a question. 'When did this thing between Lou and Ben start *exactly*?'

'I don't know, although I remember at her thirtieth birthday party Jess went to bed early after drinking too much. Ben and Louise were chatting all night, Lou even stayed after everyone else left. I think it started then. I'm sorry to be the one to break it to you, it's just that everyone's going to be gossiping about it and I thought you should know.'

'No, I really appreciate it. And how's Jess?'

'In pieces, as you can imagine.'

There's always someone in an even shittier place than you are. Then something twigged: Jess's thirtieth birthday party had taken place the night before Louise and I split up. Which meant Lou was involved with another man *before* I sent her that dreadful text message.

'Rachel?'

'Yes?'

'Will you give me five minutes to have a shower? I'm going to buy you lunch and you're going to tell me all about your holiday, and about Richard.'

'Okay, but can you afford to buy lunch? I thought you were about to lose your job?'

'I'm definitely going to lose my job, but not without a fight. And a payoff.'

30

I was neither angry or upset with Louise, nor experienced a sense of betrayal. In comparison to Roy's death, and to Marianne, she and Ben seemed an irrelevance, which confirmed that any romantic feelings for her had long since been extinguished.

The work situation was more pressing. I kept checking my emails over the weekend, but no redundancy email. I didn't know whether to be relieved or confused. Or perhaps they'd taken me off the redundancy list after my performance last Friday, thinking I'd now resign and they'd save themselves a payoff?

I called Adrian on Sunday afternoon to try to make sense of it all.

'It's because we've been there too long,' he said, 'which means making us redundant is too expensive...' His words hung in the air a while, before he added, 'That's not the only reason, you understand. Clearly we don't deserve redundancy full stop.'

'Clearly,' I replied. 'So who *has* gone then?'

'Carrie for one, poor thing. And Kate.' He updated me on the rest of our colleagues deemed *no longer useful;* it was like a battlefield roll call, with attendant guilt for those fortunate enough to have survived. Poor Carrie. My throat tightened as memories of our break-up returned. Now this.

Although I'd dodged the redundancy bullet, my performance last Friday was another matter. Colleagues had perished for far less, their exits quick and clean, just like Roy's. The tap on the shoulder was coming on Monday.

Sunday night therefore became a frantic exercise of online research, trying to get to grips with the varied fields of employment law, negotiation strategy and payments at the end of employment, which were grouped together under the alarming heading of *termination payments* in most articles. It was a lot to cover in a short space of time, but if three years at university had taught me anything, it was how to cram a vast amount of work in at the eleventh hour before a deadline. Then a flash of inspiration: Emma! She'd been an employment lawyer, right? I checked my mobile and I still had her number, so I called her. She was, to put it mildly, surprised to hear from me, and was quick to confirm she'd met someone from the internet, but the twenty minutes of her time that night were an invaluable crash course in knowing my rights. By Monday morning, I was ready for battle.

The atmosphere in the office that morning was funereal, no one making any more noise than was absolutely necessary, lest they disrespect the dead. And the living dead were indeed amongst us: the occasional person emerging from behind closed doors stooped and tearful, their fate confirmed; others in a trance slowly packing away their pitifully small belongings, thus ensuring that by tomorrow there would be no trace of them and no memory either, the corporate machine marching on mechanically without them. Gone *and* forgotten.

Marcus was in redundancy meetings when I arrived for work, but it wasn't long before he sent me an email, notifying me that he would like a meeting, its purpose described rather apocalyptically as *a discussion regarding your future*. Or lack of it, I thought.

At 11 a.m. I knocked on the door to John's office and Marcus's booming voice called out, 'Come in.' I turned the handle and pushed. Marcus was not alone; Carolyn sat to his left, poised and erect in her seat, a vulture on its perch ready to swoop down for carrion. Both were seated behind John's imposing mahogany desk, Marcus in John's intimidating, burgundy studded leather upholstered chair – although perhaps throne was a better term for it.

Marcus and Carolyn both wore deadly serious expressions. Mind you, what with this morning's series of meetings and last Friday's announcement, they were practised. 'Take a seat,' said Marcus.

In contrast to their comfortable seats at the desk, my designated chair was one of those old ones for use at a pc: no arm rests and it swivelled around its axis and shifted about on its wheels at the slightest touch unless you could steady yourself at your desk, which I couldn't, as they'd placed me in the middle of the room, in isolation. It was a Mastermind chair. Had Marcus been able, he would have turned on a spotlight to shine directly into my eyes, and as I took my seat I recalled that the man behind the concept of Mastermind had been interrogated by the Nazis.

There was no offer of a glass of water, although two full glasses and half a bottle sat on the desk in front of Marcus and Carolyn. Marcus turned slightly in the direction of Carolyn. 'I presume you know Carolyn, our Company Secretary?'

'Yes, I know *of* Carolyn,' I replied. Carolyn gave me the weakest sliver of a smile, while looking at me over her half-rim glasses.

Marcus leant forward, rested his elbows on the desk and slowly brought his hands together into a ball. 'Presumably you know why we've called you to this meeting?'

I wet my lips. 'Not precisely, no, but I'm sure you're going to tell me.' I sat as still as possible with my hands resting comfortably in my lap. What had Sam said about body language? Staying still conveys strength and masks nerves.

'We're here because of the incident last week, when you embarrassed yourself, and me,' said Marcus.

'Well, had I known it would have embarrassed you, I wouldn't have said anything. I wouldn't have wanted to inconvenience you in any way.'

Marcus flinched. 'And last week's incident was the culmination of a series of incidents recently,' he said.

The word *incident* seemed to me to be purposeful, evoking the feel of a police inquiry. I stayed silent, not wishing to commit myself further until I'd heard the entirety of the charges laid out against me.

'You've continually challenged all my recent decisions and tried to undermine me,' alleged Marcus. 'Last Friday proved you're now openly defying *all* the directors, who've been forced to take tough decisions in unprecedented times of economic turmoil. Your sales are non-existent and then there's the matter of you accepting Roy's commission allocation for the last eighteen months, despite it being expressly against company policy. Therefore, after consultation with our Human Resources department, I've decided to give you a written warning, I'm revoking Roy's commission and I'm putting you on a month-long probation period during which you will be set clear performance objectives.'

I'd seen this process before; called *managing someone out*, it involved ratcheting up the pressure on the employee through close scrutiny of their work, to such an extent that their lives in the office became intolerable and so they chose to hand in their resignation, thus bringing the employment to a conclusion and avoiding a costly pay-out for the company. 'I'm sorry, but I'm still unclear what you're warning me for,' I said. 'I seem to recall John asked the audience for questions last week and I took up his offer. I don't see how that constitutes defiance.'

'It's not just about last week,' said Marcus. 'It's also because of your poor performance in the office and taking commission not owed to you. The sales statistics confirm you're underperforming. Aren't you?' He was getting a little short with me, just as John had last week, which encouraged me.

'Last week you lot were blaming the economy for the results. You yourself just said that the directors have had to make tough decisions in *unprecedented times of economic turmoil*. How come the same reason doesn't justify my drop-off in sales? Or do you think a few hours of me working late will hold off the global recession?'

A twitch fluttered through Marcus's face. 'Don't get clever with us. This goes beyond the recession. There are plenty of consultants still making sales – Luke and Matt, for instance. It seems to me a case of you not having the aptitude for this type of business. Maybe it's a little bit too fast-paced for you.'

Perhaps Marcus had a point. Perhaps I wasn't cut out for a hard-edged commercial environment, but I hardly thought that a weakness or a failure. On the contrary. 'Isn't it strange,' I said, 'how the things we detest in people, such as sharpness, greed, egotism and self-interest, are the characteristics of those who succeed in our economy? And the characteristics we admire, such as kindness, generosity, honesty and understanding, are the traits of failure. I must say, Marcus, you are a resounding success in today's economy and that says everything about you.'

Marcus's face clenched. He slowly shook his head. 'Spare us your naïve morals,' he said. 'At least I actually do some work when I'm in the office. All your effort these days seems to be spent seducing young girls rather than making money.'

Keep calm, keep calm, he'll only win if you lose it and tell him what you really think of him. 'At least it proves some people in the office like me,' I said. 'I can assure you no one likes you.'

'It's not about being liked in business, it's about being respected.'

'What makes you think anyone respects you?'

Silence.

Continued silence.

Carolyn leant forward and cleared her throat with an affected little cough. 'Seeing as you have such strongly held opinions about this company, which you so forcefully articulated last Friday, I wonder whether it may be in everyone's interests that you consider your position.'

'Define *consider my position.*'

'I mean why don't you resign? After all, you've already upset John, so one might surmise that your career prospects here are already limited.'

'That would suit you very well now, wouldn't it, getting rid of someone who had the guts to stand up to you? If you're so keen to be rid of me, I suggest you compensate me for breaching my contract.'

'AH-HA!!!' exclaimed Carolyn, as though she'd made a telling discovery. 'And now we get to the nub of the issue, don't we? You're all the same, aren't you? Always after something for nothing. I've seen it all before, you know, the likes of you strolling in here as though we owe you something, when in fact you should be grateful we let you work here so long, seeing as you're completely out of your depth. As for the ingratitude and disrespect you showed John last week, as Marcus says, you are a disgrace.'

Her aggression unnerved me; I wasn't used to dealing with open confrontation, whereas she lived for it. I dug my nails into my palms to counter my nerves and anger, making a conscious effort to stay perfectly still and think clearly, remembering what I'd learnt last night.

'Tell me,' I said, addressing Carolyn, 'what exactly gives *you* the authority to think you can speak to me like that?'

'Don't adopt that tone with me, young man, or I'll have you thrown out of here. I don't have to justify myself to the likes of you. I've been an office holder of this company for over twenty years, since you were barely out of your nappies. My expertise lies in areas of which you have no comprehension.'

'Such as?'

'Quality. Risk. Process. Governance. Human Resources.'

'Human Resources?'

'Yes, Human Resources.'

'Are you sure?'

'Yes, I am sure. What's your point?'

'Well, perhaps you could enlighten me on something, seeing as you're such an expert in the field of Human Resources. Please tell me why I wasn't asked whether I wanted any representation at this meeting? And when Marcus told me I was to be given a written warning, why wasn't I notified that I had a right of appeal? It seems to me there's lots that's highly irregular about this meeting, what from there being two of you and only one of me, to your threatening and bullying behaviour towards me, to your assertion that John has already decided my career here is over, and finally to you denying me my rights of representation and appeal.'

Silence.

Her cogs whirring.

Sunday night's research and phone call to Emma were paying off.

Carolyn and Marcus stared at me, pondering their next move. I stared back, alternating my line of sight back and forth between them.

'You seem awfully quiet, Carolyn,' I said. 'Or am I to *surmise* that you've denied representation and the right of appeal to every poor sucker who's been in here this morning? I must say, an oversight like that really would be an embarrassment, especially to such a renowned authority on Human Resources.'

Carolyn brought her hand to her glasses and fidgeted with the rim. 'This isn't just about you leaving here, you know, it's also about your future. We may, for instance, choose not to give you a reference. Or if we do, we may give one that is – how can I put this? – slightly ambiguous.' She gave me a strange and unsettling smile, lips retracted, teeth exposed.

Emma had said most references these days were simply short statements of fact, as employers were too scared to put anything too detailed in writing. I needed to hold my nerve. 'If I was to find out you'd provided a compromising reference, I would retaliate,' I said.

'HA!' said Carolyn. 'How would you do that?'

'I have plenty of information regarding this company's – how can I put this? – irregular pricing practices.'

Marcus's face tightened further and his chin jutted out. 'Everything my department has done has been completely legal and above board and agreed between all parties.'

'Yes, and MPs expenses were all signed off too, but I'm not sure many people would agree that made them right.'

'It's called business.'

'Pimping, money laundering and the arms trade are all businesses.'

'Why, you little shit,' said Marcus, the *sh* in shit coming out in a long hissing sound. Carolyn raised an arm and beckoned him closer, and they began a whispered conversation. After a while, they turned back to face me.

'All that information you've stolen is confidential,' said Marcus, 'that, and the commission you've taken, is theft.'

'It's your theft that's in point here, Marcus, not mine.'

'You'll return whatever information you've stolen, or we'll prosecute you,' said Carolyn.

'Don't make me laugh,' I said. 'In the long history of government and business leaks, tell me, how many prosecutions have there been? I'll tell you how many – absolutely fuck all, that's how many. And besides, I can't see what your problem is. Surely it must be fair for everyone to know where they stand on pricing and pay? After all, this is your beloved free market we're talking about here, the thing which you two have got such an *aptitude* for, remember? Surely information should be free and available to all in a free market? Or does a free market mean a market free from regulation, scrutiny and morals so that the likes of you can make filthy amounts of money while everyone else lives in ignorance of what you're up to?'

'Shut up!' shouted Marcus.

'No, I will not shut up. If I don't get my way here today I'm going to send the information I've gathered to all the candidates you've screwed so they know how much you charged the client, and to all your clients so they know how little you passed onto the workers, you greedy, bloodsucking parasite.'

Marcus was halfway out of his chair before a short, sharp cry of, *'Marcus!'* from Carolyn reminded him where he was, causing him to sit back down.

'Let's cut to the chase, shall we?' said Carolyn. 'We are prepared to offer you £5,000 if you sign a compromise agreement renouncing any claims and leave this company today.'

'£5,000?'

'Yes, £5,000.'

'That's a fucking joke, right?'

Carolyn pulled in her chin in surprise. I'd read last night that in negotiations where there is no future relationship at stake, you should *completely dismiss* the other side's first offer, preferably with as much sense of injustice as possible.

'It's most certainly not a joke,' she said. 'Personally I think we've got grounds to dismiss you for cause and you can damn well try and sue us and see how far you get.' Perhaps she had read the same negotiation advice as me.

Now was my time to put them under pressure. *Always open extreme* was the advice, and come down in small increments. 'I would suggest that £50,000 is a much more reasonable figure,' I said.

'*What?!*' said Marcus. 'That's preposterous. How did you work that out?'

Always be able to justify your proposals, the article had said. 'I'll tell you exactly how. I'm on a three-month notice period, which is £7,000. And I want £30,000 compensation, which is the tax free limit, to cover the multitude of complaints I have against you. And finally, I want the same amount of redundancy pay that you're giving to everyone else, which I've estimated at six months' pay, which is good value for nine years' loyal service. That all comes to £51,000, but I'm prepared to round it down to £50,000.'

'But we're not making you redundant,' said Carolyn. 'If we agree to make you redundant, you'll be subject to the same formula as everyone else, which in your case comes out at...' She looked down at her notepad. '£17,500, and that's including your notice period.'

'You seem to have forgotten about the events of last Friday, which surprises me given that you called my performance a disgrace. As I wasn't on the original redundancy list I think there could be one or two questions asked as to why I now appear to be leaving the organisation. People might infer that my legitimate questions to John last Friday and my leaving are somehow linked, and I'm not sure a tribunal would look too kindly on that. The figure is £50,000.'

'£50,000 is *far* too much,' said Carolyn.

'Not relative to the cost to this business's reputation if I carry out my threats.'

'£30,000 is our final offer,' said Carolyn.

What had the advice been? Never use the words *final offer* in negotiation unless you mean it, because if you move thereafter, it undermines your credibility. 'No,' I replied. 'But I'm prepared to move to £47,500 on the condition that I have a power of veto over any reference you give me.' *Move down in small increments and always justify them.*

Carolyn and Marcus resumed a whispered conversation. The creases in Carolyn's forehead were deeper than I remembered and the bags under her eyes heavy and darkened like bruises. She faced me again. 'We can agree to that condition but only if you come down to £35,000. I suggest you accept our offer now, before we withdraw it.'

'I've got all day for this and won't be rushed into anything. As I said, £47,500 is my offer.'

'£35,000 is what *we're* offering,' said Carolyn. Marcus leant over and whispered something in her ear. 'And Marcus reminds me that you won't be able to work for anyone else during your notice period.'

Always get something for anything you concede. 'I'm sorry, but I thought we were talking about a complete severing of the ties here. If you're going to deny me the right to work for three months, it's going to cost you—'

'Don't try that!' spat out Marcus through clenched teeth. 'If we're agreeing to pay you for those three months, you'll bloody well do what we tell you.' He shook his head and tutted loudly.

'I'm sorry, it's definitely £47,500, because I doubt you're stating that condition to the others leaving here today.'

'NO!' shrieked Carolyn. 'This has gone on long enough. We can go to £40,000 but that is our *final offer.*'

'You said £30,000 was your final offer a minute ago,' I said.

Her eyes shifted from side to side as she backtracked in her mind.

'I'll tell you what,' I said. 'Seeing as I'm a reasonable man, I will accept £46,500, with £30,000 tax free and with an agreed reference. That is as low as I am prepared to go, and trust me, I *do* mean it.'

Carolyn stared at me throughout the ensuing silence. It was an ambivalent look: certainly some enmity, but also some grudging respect. And it was a long way from the dismissive look she'd given me when I'd first entered the room.

'£46,500 it is then,' she said.

'That's agreed then,' I replied.

Carolyn reached over the desk, picked up the telephone and tapped in three digits. 'Jason, Adam is leaving us. He won't be working his notice period in the office, so please close down his laptop.' She gave me a snide and caustic little smile, as if a final point had been scored, before standing and walking to the door, stopping once alongside me. 'I'm going to get the terms drawn up into an agreement,' she said. 'I'll be back in a minute with it for you to sign.' She walked out.

Marcus and I were alone, both still seated, both staring. His eyes lay deep in his head behind his thick-rimmed glasses, and they glittered with hatred. There was no sound whatsoever: the calm after the storm.

'You think you got yourself a nice little deal there, don't you?' he asked after a while.

'Your opening offer was £5,000, we ended up at £46,500.'

'Yes, you're very clever, aren't you? Only I can't help but think you've made a mistake.'

'I have?'

'Well, the gardening leave will stop you working for three months and let's face it, the market will then be awash with out of work recruitment consultants looking for jobs.'

'Perhaps my future lies outside the industry?'

'I don't think so. You won't just walk into another job and get paid the same amount.'

'Why do you care what I do? Did my performance last Friday wind you up that badly?'

Marcus's eyebrows drew down into a scowl. 'I've got a lot of contacts in the world of recruitment. You may think your veto over the reference was a cute move, but there's also word of mouth, and if anyone asks me about you, I'll tell them the truth.'

'You mean you'll tell them what a first-class recruitment consultant I've been, how much money I've made for this business over the years, and that it was only the worst recession in a century which slowed me up a little there towards the end?'

The door opened with a whoosh and Carolyn strode in with two pieces of paper, which she laid side by side on John's desk. 'Please review this,' she stated as an order rather than a request. 'The full compromise agreement will be sent to you in due course, but you have to see a lawyer first.'

I feigned surprise. 'Thank you, Carolyn, and well done for finally following a procedural point correctly.' I shifted my chair up to John's desk and checked the terms of the 'Agreement in Principle'. I signed both copies, as did Carolyn. She handed me a copy and promptly left the office without so much as looking at me or saying a word.

I rose and prepared to leave.

'Wait,' said Marcus, getting up and walking to the front of John's desk. He stood in front of me, very close. He lifted his right hand and levelled his forefinger like a pistol between my eyes. 'As I said, this industry works by word of mouth. If anyone asks me about you

I'm going to tell them what a rude little lazy shit you are. And I'll tell them not to recruit you.'

I remained motionless, staring at Marcus without blinking. 'You know, you're right, I've got many faults, but at least I can look myself in the mirror each morning with a clear conscience. Every time you see your reflection, what do you see, Marcus? I'll tell you what you see. You see a wretched bastard who's never thought about anyone other than himself his whole miserable life, you loathsome, grasping, greedy capitalist *cunt.*'

It's a horrible word, the c word. But effective. The final t twanged resoundingly around the room as I walked out.

Returning to my desk, I picked up my bag, which I'd already packed with my remaining few belongings. My laptop had been removed from my desk, just as with Roy. I said goodbye to Adrian and a few others and we agreed to meet for a drink later in the week. Without turning around I walked down the stairs, out of the front door and into the street.

I was free.

I would never set foot in a sales office again. But that great relief was tinged with sadness. Sadness because the good book says 'love your enemies'. Sadness because I could have behaved like Roy and not demeaned myself by haggling for John's gold.

But on Sunday night, as I'd thought through the strategy I would have to adopt to get the payoff I deserved from the company, and which would buy me time to find a new career, I'd worked out that I couldn't afford to act like Roy and would rather have to behave like Matthew, Marcus, Luke and John in the final showdown. I had to act like a cunt.

And it had worked.

* * *

Later that day I called Sam. 'Hi, Sam, it's Adam.'

'Adam!'

'Listen. Do you fancy a drink? We can compare notes about being out of work.'

'You *what?!*'

'Don't worry, they had to pay me off, so it's not all bad,' I said.

'Let's meet up tonight. I managed to sell one of the flats – got a horrible price for it, but better than losing it to the bank. I owe you lots of drinks, not just for all those you bought me last time, but also for in introducing me to Farza.'

'Farza? Who's Farza?' I asked.

'The Persian's friend. She and I are an item. In fact, we're in love.'

31

Freed from Marcus's micromanagement and with a healthy bank balance for the first time in my life, I decided now was the time to be positive; I returned to online dating.

But while I still had faith in the dating site, I'd lost it with Facebook, hating myself for logging on to stare aimlessly at other peoples' lives: Look how happy I am! Look how many friends I have! Look at my adorable children – One of each sex! One of each sex! It made me hope Facebook would still be with us in fifty years' time and these people's last posting a photograph of their grave's headstone. Look how big my headstone is! Goodnight.

So I decided to close my Facebook account. They don't make it easy though, do they? Signing up is such a simple process: a few clearly designated boxes inviting you to enter basic personal details and BANG! you're in and getting dozens of emails every hour telling you if anyone has so much as breathed in the direction of your profile. But try and exit the system and the system doesn't like that. Oh no, the system doesn't like that at all. The system is designed specifically not to like that and therefore the system will only let you leave with the greatest reluctance.

I clicked on any and every page I could find but there was absolutely no indication of an option to close the account. A wired tension crept into my body. Surely something so fundamental should be simple? I kept clicking on the pages that logically should have given me the option, such as 'Account Settings' and 'Edit Profile', but nothing. The tension began to tighten and turn to anger. I went to the Help pages but still couldn't find anything, only invitations to 'Learn More About Facebook' and 'Use Mobile Facebook', every page and every prompt another attempt by the site to extend its tentacles into and around every aspect of my life. When I eventually found the 'Deactivate your account' option illogically stored on a security setting page, I clicked it resoundingly, thinking the game was won, but oh no, the site had one last trick up its sleeve: it responded to my escape attempt by throwing up pictures of the most photogenic women I'd ever encountered on the site, accompanied by the rhetorical question, 'Are you sure you want to leave?' and then by the somewhat speculative statement, 'Rachel and Marianne are going to miss you!' The programmers of those sites are sick people. They need help.

Turning my attention to the dating site, as soon as I logged on something caught my eye: in the top right hand corner of the screen it said Message (1), which was a surprise, because I hadn't used the site recently. I clicked on the message, which was succinct: 'Sorry it's taken me so long to reply. Are you still on the site? Catherine'.

The message was from one of the women I'd found applying Sam's non-negotiables technique a few weeks earlier. Her message was very welcome, but what had taken her so long to reply? I clicked on her profile and remembered it instantly, for hers had been one of the few to engender real optimism. She was singularly attractive, but in a welcoming rather than intimidating way. She dressed with character: just smart enough to be considered stylish, yet with a discernible hippy edge. Her written profile also had plenty to recommend it, expressing a passion for literature, camping, scuba diving and... gardening. Yes, it surprised me too that I suddenly found gardening appealing, but references to her wellington boots and green fingers gave the hobby an earthy appeal I hadn't until then appreciated.

After an exchange of emails over the next few days, Catherine suggested a lunchtime date, which I assumed meant she'd learnt, as had I, that first dates were best squeezed into a short space of time, which reduced pressure and limited the disappointment when there was no mutual attraction. She told me to be at Baker Street tube station at 1 p.m., which was near her work.

* * *

I was a few minutes late to Baker Street, not good form for a date, but it reminded me how I would never again have to endure Marcus berating me for my timekeeping, the thought of which had me leaping up the stairs from the tube station platform, bursting through the ticket barriers and striding through the lobby until there, with her back to me, looking out onto the street basking in spring sunshine, was the girl I assumed was Catherine.

'Catherine?' I asked, as I came alongside her.

You need to see certain people's faces just once to know their essential character and Catherine was one such person. Hers was a face of kindness and generosity, characterised by a natural predisposition to smile. She had shoulder-length black hair with a wave in it, and haunting pale blue eyes. She had a fine, strong nose and wonderfully full lips, which for some reason provoked the immediate thought, *now there's a bonus*. The lips broke into a wide smile when she recognised me: a smile that evaporated all my customary nerves about being on a first date. She was a little taller than I'd expected and even more beautiful in the flesh than in her photographs, which hadn't captured a distinctive ethereal quality.

She looked me up and down, noting my jeans and casual shirt. 'Have you taken today off as a holiday, just to meet me?'

'Er... no actually, I'm between jobs.' She didn't react to this and that reassured me and said something important about her. I mirrored her by looking her up and down. She was dressed in dark blue jeans and a white collarless shirt with a subtle blue flower motif embroidered around the neckline. 'So what's your excuse,' I said. 'It's unusual to have a dress-down day mid-week.'

'Ha! Very funny,' she shot back, grinning. 'It's a perk of working in the charity sector. I don't have to dress to impress every day.'

'So where are we going?' I asked.

'The sun's out, so we're eating out; we're going for a picnic in Regent's Park.' She led me up the road to a deli she knew and we chose a lunch of parma ham, a fresh baguette, a salad box and a big ball of mozzarella scooped out of a white porcelain tray with a large wooden ladle. I tried to pay half, but she waved away my ten pound note, saying, 'No, this one is on me. But the next one is on you...' As she turned to leave the deli she looked back at me smiling and said, '... and I've always wanted to go to the Savoy.'

We walked up the road and into Regent's Park. I hadn't realised quite how elegant it is, its manicured lawns broken up by carefully attended flowerbeds of pale pink azaleas and han purple crocuses. There were seas of vivid bluebells, delicate little lanterns drooping in the wind, as though bashful. We sat and Catherine unpacked the lunch, placing the items between us on the grass.

'You'd better get stuck in,' she said, ripping apart the baguette and attacking the ball of mozzarella, 'or else I'm going to take all the parma ham and mozzarella and leave you the bread and salad.'

I did as I was told and tucked in.

Catherine asked about my internet dating. I recounted my encounters with Emma and Sophie, and she laughed a deep belly laugh when I reached the point in the Sophie story when the waiter confirmed that my date had left without telling me. 'I'm sorry, I shouldn't laugh,' she said, still laughing. 'At least with a picnic you'll be able to spot me when I make a dash for the exit. You sound quite experienced with internet dating?'

'I'm not sure about that. I don't think you need to have been on many dates to experience some pretty weird stuff. A date implies intimacy, but with internet dates you've never met the person before. It's little wonder many turn out as strange experiences. What about you, have you any good stories?'

'Mmmm, I'm not sure I should tell you this one, but anyway... I went for a date one Saturday afternoon in Soho once and the guy bought me a drink. When I offered to buy him one in return he said he couldn't because he had a hairdresser appointment.'

It was my turn to laugh out loud. 'You almost have to admire a guy who uses such a brazen excuse,' I said. 'Unless of course he did actually have a hairdresser appointment.' If so, he must have been a Toni & Guy kinda guy like Marcus, I thought to myself, momentarily forgetting that's where I'd been for my last two haircuts following Sam's advice. My hair looked the same as it had previously, only it took twice as long to cut and cost four times as much.

'The worst part was that I was standing up and pulling a tenner out of my purse and asking him what he wanted to drink when he told me,' said Catherine. 'It was humiliating, having to sit back down, collect my belongings in silence and saying an awkward goodbye. It's a wonder I went back online after that.'

'But you did?'

'I did. It draws you back, don't you find?'

'I guess so,' I replied. 'Can I ask why it took you so long to reply to my message?'

Catherine smiled regretfully. 'I really wanted to reply, but I was seeing someone at the time you sent me your message.'

'Oh,' I said, sounding terse, but I just couldn't think of anything else to say. It was a perfectly valid reason for her late reply, but the thought of her with another man already brought on a sense of unease.

'Don't worry,' she said, lying back on the grass and propping herself up on an elbow to face me. 'He wasn't right for me at all. It only lasted a couple of months, but you'll appreciate I couldn't reply while I was seeing him?'

'Of course not.' A couple of months? Had it got quite serious between Catherine and this chap? 'So... what wasn't right about this guy you were seeing?' I asked as nonchalantly as I could pretend to.

'He couldn't bear my cat, for one. He kept claiming he was allergic to it and shooing it away. It wasn't long before I began to wish I could shoo *him* away, so the cat and I could be left alone in peace.'

I like cats, I thought to myself, so no problem there.

'And another thing,' continued Catherine, 'he was incredibly fussy about his food and kept asking for it to be changed in restaurants. "I asked for this to be well done, can you take it back to the chef and ask him to cook it a bit longer?" he'd say, or, "The menu said green beans and you've given me broccoli instead, please replace it."'

'It's a risky business treating waiting staff like that,' I said. 'You never know what the chef will do to your food.'

'I told him that once!' Catherine shook her head. 'Each trip to a restaurant was so exhausting, my nerves shredded while I watched him hunched over his plate carefully examining every last item of food in minute detail and waiting for the inevitable call to the waiter to register his next complaint.'

I made a point of ostentatiously tucking into some more bread and ham, even nodding and murmuring approval as I chewed on it, like a gourmet.

'And another thing...' started Catherine.

This is great! I thought to myself. I should ask more women to list their ex's faults; it's a wonderful ego boost.

'...when we got – you know – got passionate...'

Wait a second! I wasn't ready for this much detail.

'...he insisted on neatly folding his trousers *and* his boxer shorts and carefully placing them on a chair before getting into bed. Each slow, diligent, methodical fold was a killer blow to the moment of passion.'

I made a point of lying back languidly and writhing about a little in the grass and soil, carefree to the effect it would have on my clothing, all the while my mouth still stuffed full of bread. 'So what took you two months to get rid of him?' I joked in a muffled voice. 'Mind you,' I added quickly, 'I guess you wouldn't have known about the trouser folding habit until what, the second month, so perhaps that explains it.'

Catherine smiled, her full lips parting and widening slowly. I couldn't keep my eyes off them. 'Good recovery,' she said. 'But you know, the main reason I didn't finish it earlier is because I made the mistake – and not for the first time – of trying to persuade myself that everything was okay and that I could ignore his flaws. Maybe flaws is the wrong word. There's nothing intrinsically wrong with not liking cats and being a fussy eater and OCD about your clothes, it's just that they *are* flaws when it comes to compatibility with me. Sometimes I've made the mistake of thinking it's easier to carry on with what I've got, rather than trying to start all over with someone else, which can seem so... so daunting.'

'Trust me, I know what you mean. It can be a very brave decision to choose to be single.'

'I keep telling myself I've made the right decision because the right person may come along.'

'Ah, but how do you know they're the right person?'

Catherine tilted her head skyward and pondered the question a while. I liked the way she took her time to give a thoughtful response. 'I suppose if I knew the answer to that I'd have met the right person by now.' She paused. 'But I think I'll know I've met him when I stop persuading myself that he's the right person, because he just *is* the right person.'

Wait a minute; wasn't that more or less what Rachel had said? I closed my eyes, the sun warming my face, its heat causing slow swirling clouds of glowing orange to drift on the underside of my eyelids. Lost in a reverie, I thought about how much I hoped no one else from the internet would email Catherine and that we could be given time to see if our connection might last and deepen. I wanted to say something along those lines to Catherine, but realised it wouldn't sound right, so I stayed silent and the silence endured and I don't know how long we stayed that way but it was a comfortable silence. In the far distance I could hear the gentle hum of a lawnmower and the odd tweet of birdsong closer by.

Eventually, I opened my eyes to find Catherine's pale blue eyes locked onto me. It was a look I initially took to be inquisitiveness, before realising it was too intense to be that. It was a look that signalled something important. I got the distinct impression that the cogs of her brain were revolving and that perhaps she was making a decision. Does the man ever really choose when it comes to relationships, or are men only really capable of thrusting themselves crudely forward for selection? We are told that it is women who have the pressure to look beautiful, to lose weight, to wear the right clothes, but why? For surely women are the choosers, not men, and if anything it should be men trying to maximise their hopes of selection, like peacocks displaying their iridescent plumage.

As Catherine watched me I had an overwhelming feeling that she liked me. In fact it was more than a feeling, it was a certainty. I don't know how I knew it, but I did, and it was a certainty overwhelming in its power, a power with the potential to change a world.

Catherine and I learnt a lot about each other that afternoon, as if we were making up for lost time. She'd also come out of a long-term relationship a couple of years previously, so I told her about Louise and she told me about her ex. She spoke of her interests, and as important as the interests themselves was her passion for them. In response I told her about me, just plainly about the things I enjoyed and why I was who I was. I didn't need to sell myself.

Sometime later she asked me what I'd been worried about her asking. 'How come you're between jobs?'

'It's a long story. Put simply, I was unhappy in my old job and needed a change.'

'It's brave choosing to change jobs at a time like this... but perhaps, in a way, it's a good time to do it.'

'It was as much a necessity as a choice. My old job was very competitive and I grew tired of it all. The trouble with working in an environment like that is that there's only two possible gears, fifth and reverse, so if your motivation dims it's obvious which direction you'll soon be travelling in.'

'Do you know what you'll do next?'

'I'm trying for jobs in Human Resources. I'd like to get some qualifications to help ensure I never have to return to a sales job again. I don't suppose I'll ever be rich, but at least I won't be miserable.'

Catherine nodded. 'I've always thought there's two ways to be rich. One is to earn more, the other is to want less.'

Unlike some of the advice I'd received over the last few months, this made perfect sense.

'Because wealth is relative,' she continued. 'If you're grateful for what you've got, you're rich whatever your means, but if you always aspire to more, you're poor whatever your riches.'

It was my turn to stare at her. What a woman.

'SHIT!' she shouted, checking her watch. 'It's almost three o'clock. My work colleagues are going to think I've been abducted by a nutter from the internet.'

'Thanks.'

'You're welcome, come on, I've got to dash.'

We packed up the remains of the lunch and walked briskly back to the tube station. Once there, we stood opposite each other, self-conscious and unsure. I leant forward and kissed Catherine on the cheek. She looked at me very seriously, perhaps inviting me to say something?

'I'll email you,' was all I could think of, which clearly wasn't good enough. 'I'd like to see you again Catherine, if that isn't too bold?' I added.

'It certainly isn't too bold. Actually, someone once told me you can take a walk along the canals which cut under Regent's Park up to Camden Lock. I'd like to do that walk, so perhaps you might like to chaperone me?'

'I would like that very much.'

She kissed me on the cheek and left.

I stood still, numbed but elated. Slowly, I began experiencing my body: the air filtering into and out of my lungs with a great depth, my blood flowing invisibly through my veins and arteries, right through to my fingertips, which throbbed delicately. And I experienced where I stood: the magazines and confectionery and drinks in the newsagent stand were all vivid and colourful; and the sounds of conversations, and of the ticket machines, and of the stations announcements, were all louder and clearer than before. And I felt a kinship with the people passing me and around me. And I was not afraid any more.

As I walked into the lobby of the tube station something made me stop and turn around, like the giant invisible hand of a god reaching down and swivelling me. Catherine had crossed the road and was about to turn the corner and move out of sight when she also stopped and turned around, just as I had, and looked back at me. She smiled and waved, then rounded the corner and was gone. We'd both looked back, and for some reason that seemed very important.

I had too much energy to go home and it was only 3 p.m., so I did something I'd always wanted to do, one of those London tourist things that Londoners never seem to find the time for, and visited the Sherlock Holmes Museum at 221b Baker Street. Afterwards, I walked back into town through Hyde Park and along Sloane Street to Sloane Square where I got the tube back to Hammersmith. In many ways it had been the perfect day, because for once, everything had been straightforward and simple.

But life isn't straightforward or simple. And so it proved later that evening as I was lying on my sofa at home listening to Marvin Gaye's What's Going On album, when I received a text.

From Marianne:

> *Wednesday 10.47 p.m.: 'I feel the same for you as you for me. Meet me in the Chancery Court Hotel tomorrow at 6 p.m. M x'*

32

The next morning I called Rachel to beg her to leave work early to advise me on a matter which couldn't wait. She said she had a lot going on, but perhaps sensing some desperation in my voice, agreed to it.

I spent the day doing anything and everything to keep my mind off my later meeting with Marianne. I had a sudden compulsion to clean the fridge and then the bathroom. In the afternoon I went for a run along the river to clear my head.

I met Rachel at her Covent Garden offices at 5 p.m. and we walked down to The Coal Hole pub on the Strand, its high, dark-beamed roof and flagstone flooring giving it a reassuringly medieval feel. Roy would have liked it. 'What are you drinking?' I asked.

'Just an orange juice, please.'

'Are you sure?'

'I'm certain,' said Rachel. 'I'll go and wait for you upstairs, this place will be busy soon.'

I ordered a beer and the juice and joined her. She didn't seem herself somehow: her posture poor, and a lack of vitality. Her hands were curled together into a nest in her lap and the crow's feet at the corners of her eyes were more pronounced than I remembered.

'So what have you got to tell me?' she asked.

'I've got lots to tell you.'

'That makes two of us.'

'Is it Richard?' I asked. 'I thought it was over between you two?'

'It's Richard-related. But I want to hear your news first.'

A goofy grin broke out across my face as I recalled yesterday's date with Catherine. 'I've met someone,' I said.

Rachel raised her eyebrows. 'I thought this was about Marianne?'

'It is, partially, but I met someone from the internet yesterday – Catherine – and I'm feeling really positive about her. Only trouble is, late last night Marianne texted me to say she feels the same for me as I do for her and could I meet her tonight.'

Rachel pulled her seat flush up to the table. 'She said she feels the same for you as you do for her?'

'That's it,' I said.

Rachel paused and took a sip of her orange juice. Her restless eyes told me her cogs were working overtime. 'It's still ambiguous,' she said eventually.

'Is it?'

'Yes, it is. It's a continuation of this thing you've had with Marianne rather than a solution to it.'

'But surely it's different; surely her statement goes so much further than ever before?'

'It's not her text which is different, it's your circumstances,' said Rachel. 'Particularly if you like this Catherine as much as you seem to. That's the point about Marianne, you've never had anything to lose. Now you have. In fact, now you stand to lose everything. You're in the same position as Marianne's always been in.'

Silence.

'Only you can make this decision,' said Rachel. 'I know you asked to meet me to hear my advice, but you have to make this decision on your own.'

I looked at her evenly and nodded. 'So what's your news?'

Rachel looked down, appearing to shrink into her seat.

'Are you okay?' I asked.

She took some time to look up again, and when she did she blinked, and a single tear trickled down her cheek. 'I'm pregnant.'

Silence.

Lightning speed whirring.

Should I express elation or commiseration? I chose the former. 'That's brilliant news.' Rachel's head fell forward again and she sniffed. I stood up, picked up my chair and placed it next to Rachel's. I sat down and put my arm around her. 'Well? It's good news, isn't it?'

She leant her head on my shoulder. 'It is good. But also so terribly complicated.'

'When did you find out?'

'Yesterday.'

'What does Richard think?'

'He doesn't know yet. I'm telling him tonight. I wanted to tell him in person.'

For some time we stayed locked together in silence. The fact my arm was around her seemed a more articulate expression than any words were capable of.

'I'm keeping it,' said Rachel, turning to face me square on. 'In case you were wondering, I'm determined to keep it.'

'Irrespective of what Richard thinks?'

'Yes.' She had that look of resolve I'd always so admired, a beautiful, almost terrible strength. 'I know some may disapprove, but I've given four years of my life to him and I'm not getting any younger. I have to do this.' She breathed out deeply and leant her head back on my shoulder.

After a while I beckoned her to sit up straight, held both her shoulders and looked at her closely. 'Whatever you need me to do, I'll do it,' I said. 'I'll drive you to the scans, come round and cook you strange meals when you get cravings. Whatever you need, I'll be there.'

She smiled and cried all at once, the corners of her lips alternating between up and down. She leant forward and hugged me. 'Thank you, Adam. That means more to me than you'll ever know. Now, I think it's time you got going to meet Marianne.'

I arrived at the Chancery Court Hotel. An archway in the middle of its long, imposing, neoclassical facade allowed entry to the central courtyard, manned by a hotel representative in ash-grey tails and top hat. He watched my approach with keen eyes. Did I need permission to enter or have to tell him where I was going? I settled for a simple 'Hello,' to which he tilted his hat to me and said, 'Sir'.

Within the archway a doorway to the right led to the bar, which had the feel of a study or library: quiet, dark, soothing, with high ceilings, textured bottle-green wallpaper and a luxuriant claret and green shag carpet soft under foot.

A waiter in a pressed white shirt and night-black waistcoat intercepted me as I entered. I asked him for a table for two and no sooner had I been seated then another waiter descended, bringing exotic nuts and nibbles along with a drinks menu dominated by champagnes, cocktails, brandies, whiskies and fine wines. It was a drinks menu designed to make you feel guilty if you only ordered a beer. I ordered a beer.

My stomach was knotted and my breathing shortened, like a mild asthma. I recalled the evening all those months ago when I'd first laid eyes on Marianne at the quiz night, since when not an hour of conscious time had passed without me thinking about her and experiencing various shades of this same nausea, be it longing, jealousy, unease, confusion, hope, or desperation. Or had it abated since meeting Catherine the day before?

The waiter arrived with my drink, continuing to hover after placing it on the table. 'Would Sir like to start a tab?' he asked. I think what he was really trying to say was, 'We can't trust anyone these days, Sir, and the drinks here are ruinously expensive, so can we please take temporary ownership of your credit card as security?' I paid him in cash.

I sipped my beer and checked my watch: it was time. For eighteen months my love for Marianne had defined me. It had been put on trial by the fiercest test of all, that of being unreciprocated, and yet it had survived and, perversely, flourished. I was a martyr for my love for Marianne.

I reached for my glass, but before I'd touched it the atmosphere in the room shifted and I looked up to see why. The eyes of various patrons flicked to a spot behind me. I turned. Marianne, just inside the door, talking to a waiter. She scanned the room, spotted me and walked over, and I rose to greet her.

We kissed each other on the cheek, the brief feel of her lips on my skin triggering my adrenalin and that scent of hers again, so damn enchanting. She unbuttoned her beige, double-breasted raincoat and removed it to reveal a mint green dress, or was it turquoise? It was difficult to tell in the soft lighting, but it was a statement, conventional enough to be considered businesslike, but fitted to give a clear appreciation of her shapely body. As she sat down it hit me again, hard, just how frighteningly powerful her beauty and sex appeal was and it was everywhere: there in the way the millimetre precision length of her dress allowed a tantalising glimpse of a small freckle on the top of her right thigh; there in the subtle movement of the muscles in her exposed upper arms as she pulled her seat up to the table; and there in the way she held my stare just a fraction of a second too long with her emerald eyes. But there was also something in her demeanour which was more shy than usual and also more vulnerable, something to do with the way she held her head and a slight pinching of her features.

It was difficult to find any words. 'So...' I said, delegating responsibility to Marianne to say something.

'So...' she said, smiling equivocally.

'You asked to meet me?'

Her front teeth bit down on her lower lip. 'I've missed you. It's been difficult getting used to you not being around the office.'

A waiter arrived and placed a gin and tonic on the table in front of her; she must have placed an order with the waiter by the door. She picked it up and tipped back a large measure. We made some small talk, but it soon cut to silence.

'Did you mean what you said in your text?' I asked.

She paused, maintaining eye contact throughout. I sensed her torso rising and falling in time to her breathing. 'I've felt something for you since the very first time we met at the quiz. It's the connection we have... and then the night we spent together...' She slowly shook her head. 'The intensity of it all frightened me, don't you see that?' She reached up and drew her fingers across her forehead. 'You've made me think again about the choices I've made and whether I got them right. It's the agony of having only one life; you can't compare it to a previous one or get it right in the next. You only get one chance.' She bowed her head and a single tear, pigmented black from her eyeliner, dribbled down her cheek.

Now was my chance to state the case for Marianne and myself, yet when I searched within myself for the words which I knew were within me, an image of Catherine kept coming to me instead: her turning to look back at me from the opposite side of the road at Baker Street and waving. Marianne, love of my life, or Catherine, whom I barely knew? I thought of the little boy in the photograph in my parents' kitchen, the boy with the blond hair and the cowlick in his fringe and his endless sense of wonder at the world. What decision would be most faithful to him?

'Marianne, there's something I've got to tell you,' I said, searching for the right words to describe what I'd started with Catherine. But my thoughts were diverted by the pain in Marianne's darkened eyes and anguished face, which communicated to me something I'd never until then been able to accept. 'You're not going to leave Simon, are you?'

There was what felt like a very long silence.

She shook her head. 'I can't leave him. If I left him for you I'd drag all my history with me, including Simon's broken heart and all the guilt I'd feel for ruining his life…' With each blink her eyes filled with more tears. 'Two years ago I had a miscarriage…' She looked past me, her eyes veiled with pain.

'I thought you said Simon was recently pushing to start a family?'

'I'm sorry, I didn't want to go into the details. He's been asking me to try again for a family. It's taken me this long to get over what happened last time. After all we've been through… it would kill him if I left him. I'm not the same person I was when I met him, but we are the choices we've made.'

I nodded.

'If I tried to make a fresh start with you,' she said, 'I'd blame loving you for all the hurt and pain I would feel. I can't make my history disappear, however much I love you.'

I reached out and Marianne did likewise and we held hands, and I experienced again the sensation of the universe revolving on its axis, with us at its centre.

Soon the waiter was standing by our table, but neither of us looked up, hoping he would soon realise he wasn't wanted. He didn't take the hint, forcing me to glare at him to go away, only I sensed that perhaps I'd seen him somewhere before…

A sharp gasp from Marianne, like she'd seen a ghost. 'Oh my god! Simon, what are you doing here?' Before she'd completed her sentence she was out of her seat and standing between Simon and me, raising her hands to his chest and backing him away from the table.

'Doesn't this look cosy?' said Simon, looking at me over Marianne's shoulder. She continued to push him backwards but he pushed her arms away forcefully. He snarled at Marianne, 'I read your text message to lover boy here last night and thought I would come along to join the party. Like mother like daughter, isn't it, Marianne?'

'No!' she screamed, her face contorting. Again she raised her hands to Simon's chest to push him away. 'Let's just speak at the bar, this isn't what you think it is. Please, Simon, let's talk.'

The real waiter arrived and asked Simon to calm down, which in turn allowed Marianne to drag him by the arm to the bar.

I bowed my head, experiencing again the sensation of the lighting picking out my table in isolation, while the rest of the bar faded into a dark, anonymous background. The sounds around me retreated, becoming muffled and indistinct. A tiny crack in the rim of my pint glass caught my attention and I turned it round to drink from the other side.

At the bar Marianne and Simon were in conversation, she making animated gestures with her hands, he with his arms folded. Marianne's face was long and sad and desperate. Seeing in her such distress broke my heart and triggered a guilt that perhaps I'd caused all this anguish. Or had I been just a symptom of their problems?

I stared at Simon. Even since seeing him at Borough Market I'd never consciously thought about him; rather he'd existed in my sub-conscious as a vague and partially formed concept standing between me and happiness. No longer. He'd become a real person, with real hopes and fears. My conscience bridged me to him and I felt sorry for him, not envious of him, for weren't he and I as much alike as any two men could be: didn't he and I share a love for the same woman?

Marianne broke off from the conversation, returned to me and sat down. Her pale skin had become lightly translucent with a tracery of veins under her skin, like rivers on an atlas. Her eyes had lost their ferocity, the irises now blending into the bloodshot whites. 'Simon wants to speak to you,' she said with a plaintive, high-eyebrowed expression. 'He wants to sort it out once and for all. I'm so sorry. My relationship is in your hands.'

All I could think about was how much I wanted to reach out for her and hold her, which might have shown her what words were inca-pable of expressing. 'Don't worry, Marianne, I'll do the right thing.' I stood up, squeezed her arm and set off to the bar, those few yards becoming a thin lit alley at night, to the sides all darkness and shad-ows and peoples' voices sounding groggy, like they were underwater.

I arrived at Simon, who stood square on to me, feet planted, hands by his sides. This close up, I could see he was greying a little at the temples and I wondered whether it was living with someone as singularly desirable as Marianne that had sped that up, all that looking over your shoulder.

He edged forward and fixed me with a stare. His irises were dark blue with black radial lines leading into the black holes of his pupils. Deep down in each pupil I saw my own face reflected, as though two of me were looking back at me.

'Marianne is my wife. I want to know what's going on between you and her.'

'Nothing is going on,' I said deadpan. 'We're friends and we used to work together and that's it.'

'*Used* to work together?'

'Yes, used to. I got fired last week.'

Simon's intensity diminished a touch at the realisation that Marianne and I wouldn't be working together, or perhaps he experienced a little moment of satisfaction at news of my sacking. But he soon gathered himself and his intensity returned. 'And I'm supposed to believe it's all innocent, am I, after catching the two of you holding hands in a hotel?' A thick vein on his temple throbbed annoyingly.

'Let me be clear,' I said, 'There's nothing going on between Marianne and me, at least not in the way you think.'

'So you're not sleeping with her?'

'No.'

'Have you ever slept with her?'

'I'm not here to be interrogated, I'm here to explain. The reason we were holding hands was because Marianne just told me about the two of you trying for a family.'

Simon scrutinised my face, gauging me for truthfulness. I held his stare. 'Now you listen to me and listen carefully,' he said pointing a finger in my face, which made it two fingers in my face in the space of two weeks. 'I want you to stay away from Marianne and that includes any grubby little text messages, is that clear?'

His tone of voice annoyed me, but was understandable. 'With respect,' I said. 'I think what I'm about to say to you is a lot more important than anything you've got to say to me. Marianne and I don't work together any more so you don't need to worry about us meeting every day. But let me be clear, if she ever wants to meet up with me – as a friend – then that's down to her and me. What *you* had better realise is that your relationship with Marianne is down to you and her; it has nothing to do with me. So if you'll excuse me, I've had enough of this conversation and I think you and Marianne need to talk, not you and I.'

I walked away toward the door. Simon made no attempt to stop me. I looked over at Marianne, still sitting with a resigned look, but watching me closely. I gave her the briefest nod but then turned away as I now had to, pulled open the door and stepped out into High Holborn, still busy with commuters making for the tube. I stood for a moment, before heading up High Holborn and left down Kingsway, walking with steps as light as a bird, not now in an untethered and rootless way, but rather in a way that a great burden had been lifted and a new freedom found.

Arriving at the river, I spotted a red post box - which reminded me – and I reached into my pocket and deposited three letters through its slot. Each letter contained photocopies of pay rates and client charge out rates, and were sent to three contractors victim to twenty pound an hour margins.

I leant against the Embankment balustrade. The late spring evening sun, low in the sky and ebbing, threw out the last of its warming orange light across the clear city sky. The Thames moved with a quiet purpose upstream, its surface glassy and even.

I thought of Rachel. She would be with Richard now, breaking the news that she was carrying his child. I prayed they would reach some understanding.

I thought of Catherine and of how much Roy would have liked her. Should I text her? No, not now. Tonight was a time for reflection, about work and about love and about moving on. And I didn't need to rush anything with Catherine because I felt entirely sure about her and me. I don't know how I felt so sure, but I did, and it was a certainty overwhelming in its power, a power with the potential to change a world.

Printed in Great
Britain
by Amazon